AFTERLIVES

AFTERLIVES

An Anthology of Stories About Life After Death

Edited by

Pamela Sargent
&
Ian Watson

VINTAGE BOOKS
A DIVISION OF RANDOM HOUSE
NEW YORK

A VINTAGE ORIGINAL, August 1986
FIRST EDITION

Library of Congress Cataloging-in-Publication Data

Afterlives : an anthology of stories about life
  after death.

  1. Future life—Fiction. 2. Science fiction,
American. 3. Science fiction, English. I. Sargent,
Pamela. II. Watson, Ian, 1943–
PS648.F87A38   1986   813'.0876'0838   85-40687
ISBN 0-394-72986-2 (pbk.)

Manufactured in the United States of America

Text design: Helen Granger/Levavi & Levavi

Contents

INTRODUCTION
BY PAMELA SARGENT AND IAN WATSON   xi

THE AMERICAN BOOK
OF THE DEAD
BY JODY SCOTT   1

TIME OF PASSAGE
BY J. G. BALLARD   29

OF SPACE-TIME
AND THE RIVER
BY GREGORY BENFORD   47

OUT OF MY HEAD
BY JAMES GUNN   89

A WORK OF ART
BY JAMES BLISH   113

THE RAPTURE (poem)
BY TOM DISCH   137

WOOD
BY MICHAEL N. LANGFORD   139

A WOMAN'S LIFE
BY W. WARREN WAGAR   161

INTO THAT GOOD NIGHT
BY JAMES STEVENS   179

PROMETHEUS'S GHOST
BY CHET WILLIAMSON   217

SMALL CHANGE
BY URSULA K. LE GUIN   247

A DRAFT OF CANTO CI
BY CARTER SCHOLZ   257

DUST
BY MONA A. CLEE   269

DIARY OF A DEAD MAN
BY MICHAEL BISHOP   297

FAIR GAME
BY HOWARD WALDROP   313

IN FROZEN TIME
BY RUDY RUCKER   335

TROPISM
BY LEIGH KENNEDY   345

IF EVER I SHOULD LEAVE YOU
BY PAMELA SARGENT   353

TIME'S HITCH (poem)
BY ROBERT FRAZIER   373

THE ROOMS OF PARADISE
BY IAN WATSON   375

CHECKING OUT
BY GENE WOLFE   399

THE REGION BETWEEN
BY HARLAN ELLISON   405

ACKNOWLEDGMENTS   492

But man dies, and is laid low;
man breathes his last,
and where is he?

Job 14

Introduction

PAMELA SARGENT
AND IAN WATSON

What happens after we die?

As far as we know, among Earth's many creatures only human beings live with the awareness that they will one day die. Only people react to that ultimate fact of life by believing in an afterlife.

Originally, this may have been the result of viewing the world in a magical, animistic light. If every object in sight—beast, tree, stream and boulder—contained a spirit, then why should a human corpse be otherwise? Dead people lingered on in memories and dreams; how could they possibly appear to a sleeper unless they somehow still existed?

In ancient Egypt, death became a research project worthy of vast expenditure, the target of enormous amounts of human energy. The whole of ancient Egyptian society was structured obsessively around the concept of an afterlife. What particle accelerators and space probes represent to us today, death did to an Egyptian of old. The country's whole necropolis—its gods, its pyramids, its mummified pharaohs—was a kind of conceptual time machine, with immortality as its destination.

The Egyptian afterlife carried many of the best

features of this world over into the next. For the
ancient Sumerians, the afterworld was a bleak and
shadowy place, dry as dust. The Greek Hades was also
distinctly dismal and bloodless. Norsemen, on the
other hand, imagined a Valhalla where dead warriors
pursued the drinking and violence they enjoyed in
their earthly existence. Christianity progressively re-
furbished one large sector of the afterlife as a torture
chamber to punish the wicked.

Dead souls, however, did not necessarily remain in
the afterworld permanently. Plato speculated about
the transmigration of souls from one body to another.
Reincarnation forms a major strand in eastern religions, with *The Tibetan Book of the Dead* offering a
lengthy textbook guide on how to be reborn favorably.

Religions have promised blissful rewards and threatened dire punishments in the next life either as a
compensation for having to exist in an unjust world or
as a motive for ethical conduct. It is a commonplace
that in societies afflicted by poverty and inequality a
belief in afterworldly restitution for those who accept
their lot in life serves the interests of the status quo.
Paradoxically, such beliefs do not necessarily insure
social stability. Believing that the end of the world was
near, many early Christians sought death so eagerly
that the fledgling church had to stress that suicide,
and the desire for one's own death, was a mortal sin.
Both Viking berserkers of the past and Iranian berserkers of the present can wreak terror and violence
without a qualm, convinced of their reward after
death.

In more secular modern societies, many people re-
ject the traditional versions of the afterlife, yet they

have not necessarily become skeptics about the underlying principle. Purportedly nonfictional accounts of
previous lives and of near-death visions command a
wide audience. In the officially atheistic society of the
Soviet Union a widespread interest in spiritual
phenomena thrives under the rubric of parapsychology. It is, indeed, the Soviet Union that pours
state funding into enterprises which in the West are
regarded as being on the dubious fringes of science.

Meanwhile, popular horror fiction, with its panoply
of ghosts, evil spirits and dark forces, may actually
serve to reassure its audience that death, however terrifying, is not final. Nationalist politics as mediated by
Islamic clergy has now given us modern religious mar-
tyrs, while in the most advanced technological country
many millions of fundamentalist Christians view nuclear Armageddon with positive enthusiasm, for those
who believe will be "raptured" to heaven.

Those who find no consolation or place no credence
in religious or mystical promises can now speculate
about technological and biological means to defeat
death or create an afterlife. Perhaps our ailing bodies
might be frozen, then restored to life once medical
techniques are more advanced and the aging process
has been overcome. Perhaps our brains might be transplanted into a series of bodies, donning a fresh one
when the old one wears out. Perhaps the pattern of
our memories and personality might be stored in a
computer. On the one hand, physical immortality of
one kind or another begins to seem like a remote
possibility—thus evading the whole question of an
afterlife, for a few billion years at any rate. On the
other hand, some claim that consciousness may sur-

vive after death as an entirely natural phenomenon
that may be an integral part of the evolutionary process.

Curiously, science fiction, which has boldly explored so many regions, has generally shied away from
the theme of the afterlife. Physical immortality, the
prolonging of life, has proved a popular subject with
many science fiction writers; survival after death has
been far less popular as a theme.

Robert A. Heinlein's *I Will Fear No Evil* (1970)
shows us a dying man whose brain is transplanted into
the body of a young woman; her personality somehow
survives this transplant. Here, biological technology
provides the means for a kind of afterlife in this world,
but cannot save the characters from what seems a final
death at the novel's conclusion. In *The Ophiuchi Hot-
line* (1977), by John Varley, people routinely survive
death because their memories and personalities are
regularly programmed into cloned bodies held in
store. On the surface, Varley's novel is one of jaunty
acrobatics, in which nobody needs to worry too much
about being killed. Logically, though, it is a totally
materialistic book; otherwise, one might legitimately
ask where the previous consciousness has gone. Lucius
Shepard, in *Green Eyes* (1984), performs an intriguing twist on this theme by positing a project where
entirely *new* personalities are placed inside newly dead
bodies.

Occasionally science fiction writers begin with an
afterlife motif but then execute a hasty waltz sideways.
Philip José Farmer, in *To Your Scattered Bodies Go*
(1971) and its sequels, which form his *Riverworld*
series, resurrects all who have ever lived and places

them along the winding banks of a mysterious river millions of miles long. This initial, fascinating premise is often lost in the ensuing maze of plot and counter-plot, while the thread of explanation—namely, that advanced superscientists are responsible—ties itself into progressively bewildering knots.

Arthur C. Clarke, in his classic *Childhood's End* (1953), depicts the end of humanity and our subsequent racial advancement to a different order of existence. This is a "paranormal," yet natural, evolutionary progress toward a cosmic mind, an energy-being. Bob Shaw, in *The Palace of Eternity* (1969), imagines souls surviving death; they do so, however, as energy clusters that can all be physically destroyed. Interstellar "butterfly-ships" draw these souls into their engines along with other fuel particles from the void.

A genuine novel of reincarnation is Arsen Darnay's *The Karma Affair* (1978), yet here again souls can be trapped, exploited and warped by machinery. On the same topic, Robert Sheckley's *Immortality, Inc.* (1958) provides a vehicle for somewhat satirical adventure.

Inferno (1975), written by Larry Niven and Jerry Pournelle, is actually a rewriting of Dante's *Inferno*, using a science fiction writer as its narrator. Benito Mussolini takes Virgil's place as the dead man's guide, and the authors energetically mete out satiric punishments to those they regard as modern-day sinners (such as Kurt Vonnegut, whose biggest sin, in the view of the authors, was against science fiction itself).

One of the most significant science fiction stories about an afterlife is Robert Silverberg's novella "Born With the Dead" (1974). Here, people are "rekindled" after death and retain their memories of their former lives, yet remain far distant, emotionally, from those who have not died. It is as though they have become spiritually autistic, although apparently normal in every other respect.

One anthology of science fiction, *Five Fates* (1970), attempted to deal directly with the subject of the afterlife. For this book, five noted writers were asked to provide stories that commenced with the death of the protagonist, but four of the authors evaded the theme in various ways (such as by showing the death to have been an illusion, or by continuing the story with another character). Among the contributors, only Harlan Ellison, in his novella "The Region Between," wrote of an actual afterlife, and even included experimental typographics designed to involve the reader in the experience.

Science fiction by definition tends to incorporate the modern scientific worldview, even though particular examples may veer toward fantasy or the wildly improbable. Therefore, we find in it a largely skeptical or rationalizing attitude toward the notion of an afterlife. The afterlife has to be manufactured by technology, or given to us by aliens whose own superior technology will inevitably seem magical or godlike to us. Alternatively, if we look at time and space from a different perspective, then the whole Universe exists forever in a single, timeless, all-embracing moment (as it does for the aliens in Vonnegut's *The Sirens of Titan* (1959), and in his 1969 novel *Slaughterhouse Five*); therefore, death itself is an illusion. If we were to encounter an authentic afterlife, we would probably soon start tinkering with it and exploiting it, just as we tinker with everything else we come across. We would, no doubt, subject the afterlife to rational experiment of a parapsychological or metascientific kind.

What distinguishes "true" science fiction from fantasy is that the former tackles real possibilities without violating current state-of-the-art knowledge. When science fiction *does* violate what is known, which is actually fairly often, it feels obliged to offer a good set of plausible excuses, which owe just as much at bottom to rational scientific thinking as does the most "nuts and bolts" narrative. Since there is no hard evidence for any afterlife, the theme has been largely surrendered to science fiction's satirists—and to writers of fantasy and horror.

For this book, we sought stories that confront the theme of the afterlife directly. A few of the contributors have taken the idea as a given, proceeding from that point to explore what such an afterlife might be like. Others assume a natural basis for an afterlife or else speculate as to what might happen here and now if we gained the certainty that there is a life after death.

In the following pages, you will find aliens providing an afterlife and advanced human technology producing artificial resurrection. You will discover the "timeless moment," as well as vicious warfare in the godless heavens. You will spy on the passage between life and death. You will experience afterlives that are bizarre, happy, obsolete, inverted, frightening, tragic and comic.

No matter how different in their treatments of the theme, all of these stories have two things in common.

The first is an assumption that some kind of life after death is possible; these stories demonstrate the variety of ways in which science fiction can deal with this eternally provocative theme. The second is that all of these stories are, in the opinion of the editors, excellent pieces of writing.

The American Book of the Dead

JODY SCOTT

Jody Scott is a true original. Who else could create a giant alien dolphin masquerading as Virginia Woolf, a secret war to upgrade the human race by marketing a Famous Men's Sperm Kit to suburban housewives, or a 700-year-old gamin vampire? These feature in Jody Scott's science-fiction novels Passing for Human *(1977) and* I, Vampire *(1984). Her writing is hip, vivacious, ferociously satiric, and tongue-in-cheek. An earlier novel,* Cure It With Honey, *garnered a Mystery Writers of America Special Award. Another novel of the Berkeley generation,* Down Will Come Baby, *appeared as an abridged magazine serial when the book's agent became managing editor of* Escapade *and bought it. Jody Scott was herself editor of the now defunct* Circle, *which published Henry Miller, Anaïs Nin, and Tennessee Williams. She lives in Seattle.*

FOR THEODORE STURGEON
FEBRUARY 26, 1918–MAY 8, 1985

Even while she was still alive, Coriolanus hated to be pawed by strangers.

Being smashingly beautiful seemed to put you into a whole separate category. A lot of people thought it was perfectly O.K. to leer or make remarks or grab at you. Why was that? she wondered. Maybe they thought you were being elitist or something, by virtue of having been born gorgeous.

But: all that was over. She didn't care to dwell on the past. It would be morbid. An innocently healthy person, Cori had always felt that it was better to look ahead; although she could never forget how in life strangers had constantly tried to cop a feel, maybe back her into a corner and coax her into giving them their favorite kind of pain. Or rip at her knicks while grinning hungrily into her eyes. And what eyes she had. Or rather had had, in the recent past when she was "alive" (what a silly way of putting it; as if she wasn't every bit as alive now!)—her eyes had been so big and sparkling, such a luminous shade of lavender-blue, and set far apart. . . .

But all that was over.

To think.

She'd killed herself for a mere course.

She'd wanted an *A* so badly!—but now that seemed like a dumb, trivial reason.

The course was "The Craft of Dying Based on Theories of Gödel and Feinberg, with Current Anthropological Assumptions Regarding Altered States of Consciousness."

It was a quirky title. But then Prof. Eric Porlock, who gave the course, was a peculiar man. He'd been half killed on Ganymede in a kinky accident during the last war and was a bit strange. It was Porlock who had placed the notice in the *Flash* that had brought the doomed class together. The ad said:

> Join Death-ology research staff. Earn credits, help others, and terminate your unbearable existence all at the same time.

The ad brought a chuckle; and the idea of death research was thrilling. It had been a big fad in the late 1990s, but then s & m became so pervasive and so popular that it was almost totally eclipsed. Cori couldn't resist signing up, and at first everything seemed quite normal. Prof. Porlock was a little weird even by today's lax standards; but she didn't think much of it. At the first workshop he told the class about the accident that had motivated him to get into death research, and it sounded perfectly logical to Coriolanus.

"This happened many years ago on Ganymede," the Prof. said. "We were after the gold that drifts in chunks, some bigger than your head, borne along at discrete depths by microscopic sea-life of that watery moon of Jupiter. We hadn't yet learned it costs too much by far to get it out.

"At six hundred feet into an icy primordial soup, a diver hallucinates. I was wearing the normal gear for that depth; 'cumbersome' is no word for it. A pressure suit has never been designed that can match it.

"I saw a shark. A hallucination, of course; or was it? There's no life above the microorganism on Ganymede; or so we are told, over and over.

"I fought the shark. It tore into me. The equipment was ruptured. At that pressure I was already starting

to flow out the hole. Another few seconds and I would
have been a strand of human spaghetti.

"The pain was unbearable. I blacked out. I kept
wondering, 'Am I going to die? Or am I already
dead?' . . .

"Almost immediately, the submersible was able to
grapple me into the main unit. But I knew I had really
died. I was floating above my head, looking directly at
my physical body, now just an empty shell. I heard
music, incredibly beautiful harmonies, the music of
the spheres, and felt a deep serenity. There were
lights; I spoke with a deceased brother.

"I came back to consciousness on a table. The resus-
citators were humming. The faces of my teammates
were peering down at me. I told them I had been
dead. They didn't believe me.

"That experience changed me. I wanted to find out
what had happened to me. I wanted to explore the
shock syndrome, or transcendental experience, or
whatever it was, to a degree that some might call an
obsession. The rest is history, on file in the archives
where anyone can get at it, all leading directly to this
class; to this very day.

"Now. What you kill yourself for must be valid and
important. Trivial reasons will not be accepted."

He explained that it would be a simulation of a
near-death event and perfectly harmless, of course,
but as close to the real thing as they could achieve.
Then he swore the class to secrecy.

"Nothing we discuss must go beyond this room," he
said.

One thing worried Coriolanus. How did Prof. Porlock get a permit to have the ceiling cameras turned
off? No ordinary citizen ever got that kind of permit.

The Prof. must have a politician friend, or some kind of pull that wouldn't quit.

He had a deeply lined, thin face and was tall and gaunt and not at all trendy, wearing slightly passé chainmail with worn satin knicks, spats, sash and black varnished topper; plain-enough garments. But he had a powerful gaze that verged on the hypnotic. He scared Coriolanus. She knew it was silly, but he did.

Still, as the days flew by Cori learned many things. The subject had been well documented by Death-ologists, doctors whose patients had presumably been "dead" for several minutes but then recovered and were able to tell what they knew about the experience.

She loved the two coursebooks, *The Tibetan Book of the Dead* and *The Egyptian Book of the Dead*. They were ancient tomes full of quaint words that had been written many, many centuries ago. What a good idea, to have a handbook for when you died! Other-wise, how would you know what to do at that critical moment when the energy field known as the VITAL-X or "soul" departed from your body?

Americans had never had such a guidebook. They had no coaching at all. They were expected to die blindly, to just go ahead and stumble into whatever was going to happen next. Coriolanus felt that this was highly unfair. She'd love to be the one to write a popular book for Americans on the subject.

"What to Do When You Die" was a title she liked. Or to sell better maybe it should be, "The Power of Death: How You Can Use It to Get Everything You Want." The course notes said there was an *American Book of the Dead* written years ago, but it was basi-cally an update of the Tibetan one. There was no truly up-front, scientific, modern American handbook as far as Cori could tell. Of course, she was just a beginner; she had a lot to learn. And at the moment she was absolutely convinced that she had killed herself.

Had she really killed herself? Or was it just another fantasy? Porlock had said:

"During the moments of death, various misleading illusions occur. On the first day all is sweetness and light. The Muslim has a soothing vision of Mohammed and Allah taking his hands and leading him beside the still waters. The American Indian sees the Happy Hunting Ground spread out around him in full, colorful detail.

"But after the first rosy glow, your own mental condition will begin to pull other images in upon you. Examples: on the thirteenth day the disturbed Tibetan will see the Red Pukkase holding coils of intestines in the right hand and putting them into her mouth with the left. The Tibetan will also see the Dark-Green Ghasmari holding a blood-filled skull, stirring it with a *dorje*, then drinking it with majestic relish. He will see the Yellowish-White Tsandhali tearing a head off a corpse, the right hand holding a heart, the left putting the corpse into her mouth.

"The first day is all pastoral scenery, calm and serene; but what frightful visions an untrained, upset American will see on the thirteenth day we have no idea. That is precisely what we are here to find out.

"To repeat: on the first day the Jew meets Abraham and Moses and perhaps Groucho and Mel Brooks as well, while the Catholic meets the Virgin and St. Peter. It depends entirely on one's training and expectations. For example, if I were to repeat over and over that upon dying you will be greeted by the Horse-

necked King and the red Hoopoo-headed Desire Goddess, and the Wrathful Goddess Rich in Space, as the
Tibetans did, that is precisely what would occur.

"The universal fact seems to be that all of us enter
a pretty landscape, see various lights, and greet our
departed friends. This is why the death phenomena
must be studied long before death takes place, while
the subject is in excellent physical condition, as readouts show you all are."

The class grinned at each other; Porlock continued.

"When the untrained VITAL-X gets out of the
body the first thing it does is look around and say 'Am
I dead or alive?' and it doesn't know which. The dead
can see and hear everything that goes on. They see
their friends crying, their body being wheeled away.
They see the mortician who embalms them. They also
see lights, rays and other things, and hear sounds.

"This can be upsetting, grotesque, even terrifying.
It can also be fatiguing. But you must accustom yourself to this state just as a newborn must accustom itself
to our world.

"It takes three or four days to realize that, yes, you
are really dead. At first there is that wonderful, liberating feeling of sheer bliss we've all heard about. Now
the purpose of this course is to enable you to hold onto
that desirable state. Our goal is to be 'calm and timeless' rather than 'oppressed and exhausted.' It's purely
a matter of practice. As in learning any skill we must
drill, drill, and drill some more."

Porlock smiled and continued.

"Trained in self-discipline, you can do it. Just remember to stay calm, don't panic, and whatever you
do don't get caught in the motivational traps of jeal-

ousy, revenge or greed. If you do you'll only slip right back into the darkness of ego-demands, a pit of nightmare we may well call 'hell.'

"My job is to help you avoid this sort of thing. Don't be attached to joys or sorrows, and at all costs avoid jealous fury or extreme fear; they will set you back."

"You mean no more spookshows?" someone asked.

Porlock frowned, opened the book and read, " 'If you are to be born on a higher plane, the vision of that plane will be dawning upon you.' Whether you wish to retain that state of bliss is your decision."

Well, that kind of advice was all very fine, but how was Coriolanus supposed to hold onto that state, or any state, when she was so darned mixed up? She tried to think clearly and remember exactly what happened. Let's see . . .

She thought she had turned on the gas, in the kitchen of the unit she shared with Ted, her CIAO*U* partner. Then she placed her head on the bottom shelf of the oven on a soft, fluffy towel newly purchased from Field's; an apricot-colored Cannon bathtowel with a beige border. The towel was there so she'd be comfortable while making the transition.

The transition came sooner than expected. It often does. Like many suicides, Coriolanus had hoped, up to the very last instant, that Ted would smell the gas and come rushing in and say, "Cori—please don't do it! I'll be the aggressor. I'll hurt you any way you like. I swear by the Divine Marquis," getting down on his knees and crying, "Please, Cori, please."

Or even, "Cor, baby, don't leave me. I'll never masoch with anyone else, never, I swear it. It'll be just you, me, and Chip."

Chip of course was the computer chip everyone had implanted at birth in his or her brain for full mental health. It induced the CIAO*U* of every hidden secret sexual fantasy in the closedinaround-orgasming*you*, the intensely marvelous foreplay leading to frenzies of exquisite shudders like nothing else could do. CIAO*U* produced a come-together version of the fulfillment *you* most desired. It was used to offset boredom. Boredom could be a killer in today's world, where people had been so bombarded with loud noises, crime, violence, other people's sex, and frenzied images of paranoia that they could no longer experience certain parts of life without boosters. That's why there were all these quirky courses and pain sessions, and why up to the last minute Cori had hoped that Ted would take her into his arms and rush her to the hospital where she'd be quickly revived, as she'd often been before.

But no such luck. Before she knew what had happened, the Wrathful Goddess Rich-in-Space was saying with a merry smile:

"Welcome and congratulations, Coriolanus! Here we are again, my dear, in a prenatal existence."

Now just a darn minute! All this was happening too fast. She had to sort all this stuff out. Prof. Porlock had talked so fast it was hard to take notes. In stirring tones, he had read from the Egyptian book:

" 'Your soul lives and your veins are firm. You breathe the air and emerge into the light of day like a god.' And that, class, was recited by the priest to the mummy, before burial.

"The book was written on a roll of papyrus. It described going through the portals of the other world. My point is, thousands of years ago these people already knew what we've only recently discovered about what happens at the moment of death.

"Now: we can define an ordinary sequence D: n_1, n_2, n_3 and so on, so there's no general way of telling in a finite number of steps whether a given positive integer is or is not D. Should one then regard D as clearly defined? . . . Question?"

Lowering her hand shyly, Coriolanus quavered, "What does the D stand for?"

"At the moment we are attempting to define death," Porlock said gravely. "Statements can be formulated which can neither be proved nor disproved within the system. Not everything can be measured with a ruler. This is where Gödel comes into the picture. To step outside the system we call 'death' will be quite a trick, will it not?"

The most brilliant student in the class, whose name was Daniel Berg, asked, "Is this in the nature of an occult hype, Prof., or are we actually being asked to step outside the system?"

Porlock scowled. He sometimes ignored Berg's questions. Berg was flippant. The Prof. disliked disrespect, laughter, and interruptions. At times he even sank into gloom and wouldn't speak.

He had a trick of inserting both hands under his sash, tipping back his head and gazing at a student with the most withering, scornful, devastating, but strangely compelling and provocative look Coriolanus had ever seen. Even Ted never looked that sinister when they were deep in their Chips and exploring the most excruciating $CIAOU$ a person could hope to orgasm wildly over.

Porlock took his time about answering. His voice was loaded with impeccable scorn.

"Would you call a giant steel womb of unjammable channels a hype, Mr. Berg?"

"Hardly, but I don't see—"

"This is a difficult course. You can't just skate through it, relying on what you seem to consider your elitist status. You can't keep your nose in the air here, Mr. Berg."

"I never intended to—"

"We have several million dollars' worth of micro-equipment in this lab," Porlock went on. "Fifty years ago you'd have been hooked up to outlandish and cumbersome equipment, blood-monitoring devices, ultrasonic scanners, tubes going in and out, electroencephalographs and all the rest of it. I'd be photographing your body aura by old Kirlian methods, and measuring your brainwave signals in microvolts and on and on. Today I'm doing all this without a touch, without an imposition. Is the mere lack of *mass* a reason to take what I'm saying lightly? Does the fact that we are at this moment measuring the colonic spasms caused by your unexpressed fear upset you unduly—say, to the point where you'd be willing to drop this class?"

Berg hastily said no, no, of course not, and Porlock went on, reading from *The Tibetan Book of the Dead.*

" 'Maybe those old lamas really caught a glimpse of the fourth dimension and twisted the veil from the greatest of life's secrets.

" 'Both Jung and the Druids taught us, "To learn to die is a science most profitable, and passing all other sciences." We've been brought to a standstill by Freudianism and our own backward biological ideas, but now Western man must awaken from his long slumber of ignorance and confront the incredible mass of evidence which tells us that, dying, we don't go out like so many candles, nor do we find ourselves in an old-fashioned heaven or hell.

"The living come from the dead, as Socrates intuitively perceived as he was about to drink the hemlock and experience death. Tell me, how many of you would welcome such an opportunity?"

A few tentative hands went up.

Porlock said, "Thank you, ladies and gentlemen. Obviously you understand that the exploration of Man's Demise, in a manner truly scientific, is incomparably more important than the exploration of outer space.

"We know that you will experience a psychic thrill, a glimpse of Pure Truth, 'subtle, sparkling, bright, dazzling, glorious and radiantly awesome.' This is the radiance of your own nature. Understand that and all goes well. Otherwise . . .

"If you see something that upsets you, such as friends arguing over your belongings or your will, do not fly into a rage. You've been told this many times. Buddha said it; Jesus said it; now hear it once again, in equally poetic language.

"If you don't master your emotions, you will wander into the abodes of the devas and be drawn into the whirl of the six *Lokas*. You will see the dull bluish-yellow light from the human world. If you follow it you will be born in the brute-world again and will suffer birth, age, sickness and death, and be stuck in the quagmire of worldly existence. Whirled round and round, you'll be made to taste the suffering thereof. But on that first day . . .

"Does something strike you as funny, Mr. Berg?"

"No, not at all." Berg grinned. Porlock went on:

"On that first day the terrifying karmic illusions, which are your own thought-forms, have not yet dawned. Nor have the frightful apparitions or experiences caused by the Lords of Death. Again: the purpose of this course is to teach you how to confront these demons, knowing they come from yourself, and go on to the pure Paradise Realms. None of this is to be taken literally, of course, but I know of no other way to express the transcendental. Questions?"

There were no questions.

"I want you to face death heroically. Please get the word 'hero' defined. It will be on the exam."

Porlock was passing around a paper for everyone to sign. It was a Hold Harmless contract that said whatever happened to you in this workshop was your own fault, and you could sue neither the Prof. nor the college for it. Well, that seemed fair enough; Coriolanus signed it. But she wouldn't let anyone poke needles into her arm, or play with her mind, or her body either, without express permission.

All in all, Cori was enthralled. It could have been grouptrance, but she both loved and hated this Prof. at the same time; it was as if she knew him from long ago. She yearned to ask questions but didn't want to sound dumb in front of the class, so when the others had gone she went up and told him how confused she was. If he insulted and belittled her when they were alone, as he sometimes did to Daniel Berg, it wouldn't matter.

"I'm a hopeless dope," she smiled, lowering her gaze, "but I still don't see what you mean by D being a round trip in the Gödel sense or what you mean by all this stuff about visions and illusions."

The eyes were suave and cool, maybe a bit sardonic.

He uncoiled his long legs from the chair and wrote a reading list so that she could learn more about tachyons and deteriorating sequences and so on. In particular, he said, she should concentrate on these questions: Does the body lose a significant amount of mass when the VITAL-X separates off? And if atoms and molecules are not involved, what exactly accounts for this weight loss? He spoke of experimentation and the scientific method, and varying one thing at a time.

He looked straight into her eyes. The whites of his own eyes were discolored and bloodshot. He advised, "When we know more of the dead it will be time to pursue the living."

Trying to remember what happened next, Cori got confused. All she could think of was her own funeral, and friends who came up to Ted and asked, "But why? Why did she do it, Ted? I just can't understand it. She had everything to live for."

Cori agreed, wholeheartedly. She did have everything to live for, so how could she possibly have bumped herself off? Ted said it was because she was in love with a certain professor who spurned her. He showed a note that Cori had written this professor, whose name was Eric Porlock.

"When I get my hands on Porlock I'll knock his teeth out," Ted said.

That was nice of Ted, but he was wrong. Cori didn't love Porlock and the note was definitely forged. In fact, she was almost certain that the idea of suicide was a mere fantasy; something on the order of seeing Jesus waiting at the end of a long tunnel of light. Porlock said everyone's mind had been so filled with dramatized concepts of death, and religious fables, and the ideas of other people, that these confusions occurred as a matter of course.

One thing was for sure. When you made the transition, time became scrambled.

She tried to figure out the correct sequence, which went something like this:

Cori stayed unconscious right up to the morning of the funeral, a dreary and squalid little affair she was thankful to forget. Then for about a week all she did was hang around that small, unimpressive plastic tombstone, lost in a labyrinth of other little fake-marble tombstones, and whimper inaudibly because she had not only lost a gorgeous body but had gone neither to heaven nor to hell nor out like a candle. She still existed. Imagine that. But she felt so stupid and wretched about the whole thing that she almost forgot her purpose in dying, which was to get an *A* in Porlock's course.

Or even . . . and she hardly let herself think about this part any more; but: it was to take detailed notes of everything that happened and write *The American Book of the Dead* so that (was it still possible?) millions of others wouldn't be as confused by this crazy business as she was.

But then another problem came up. A rap group called Cryptanon (for crypts anonymous) was being formed for the benefit of newly deceased men and women, so they could learn to cope during this difficult and sudden adjustment period. Cori thought of not joining; she needed to be alone and think things out, but the others talked her into it.

"You have so much to offer," they pointed out.

She needed a little flattery after her recent bereavement, so she agreed to join. At the first session she met some interesting people and was amazed to find that a few of them had even been in Porlock's Death-ology class. Each member of Cryptanon got to tell his or her own special and particular loss, grief, joy, pain or gain, and discuss those of the others.

The consensus was that, yes, you certainly did see lights, hear voices and travel down a wide long tunnel full of blazing light; and you did speak with old friends and meet fictional characters like Scrooge, Madame Bovary and Charlie Brown, and that right at the start came a glorious sense of freedom and release known as "that first fine careless rapture."

Unfortunately, it was only a transitional phase. It kicked into the deteriorating sequence D_1, D_2, D_3, which turned out to be the old, familiar sequence of denial, bargaining, grief, anger, propitiation and so on, along with sheer frustration over the fact that no matter how hard you tried you simply could not get rid of yourself permanently. And while they were discussing it, the group captain came in. His name was the Horse-necked King.

"Many people when they die seem to fumble around blindly, grab the first available infant body and get born in a hurry," the Horse-necked King told them. "This group bypassed that syndrome, for reason or reasons unknown. Either you lack an obsessive need to get back into the game, or something else is going on. Any ideas?"

Everyone expressed confusion. Cori was in her glory taking all these terrific notes as fast as she could write. Death. The most simple, most natural phenomenon known to Man. Why fear it? There is nothing to it. You hardly even know it's happening. And the Horse-necked King was a genial host who kept them laughing.

"In terms of quantum mechanics it's important to find God, but we're not ready for that. Is this a true or false question? Let's see a show of hands."

And yet, something strange was going on here. Cori wished she could figure out what it was. She noticed that at least four other people besides herself, including Daniel Berg, all of whom had been in Porlock's death class, were now here. What did that mean? What was going on? Something nagged her; something she'd forgotten. Was this a field trip or something? What was it? She almost had it; then it slithered away.

The Horse-necked King said: "Don't let those Orientals get ahead of you. Show a little Yankee ingenuity. The Tibetans didn't have the last word. Let's get practical here. If someone tells you revenge is to be avoided, maybe he's got a reason. Maybe he or she wants to escape *your* revenge. Ever think about that? Maybe that person was trying to elude a just and rightful punishment."

He spoke of the stress of impinging on the 3DU, making your thoughts visible to the living, and sending out the trace filaments that get imprinted on the 3DU, which are the source of all matter and which come before a maneuver called "Making the jump out of the dreamworld into a womb of flesh and blood."

What did that mean? "Selling yourself on the idea of getting back into the rough-and-tumble game," is how the Horse-necked King put it. All this crazy stuff triggered something in Coriolanus, or reminded her of something, she couldn't think what. But she was sure it had something to do with Prof. Eric Porlock.

The red Hoopoo-headed Desire Goddess spoke next. She explained that "time" happens all at once. "Now" is only a viewing-slot.

She asked for testimonials and up jumped Brad, a former lead singer for a New York hong band. Brad said that he had gone to the veterinarian's in a dog suit and asked to be put to sleep. He was motivated by boredom, due to a blow on the head which happened at a concert and which destroyed his Chip. After an exchange of credits, the vet obliged, and here Brad was.

"Congratulations and welcome," smiled the red Hoopoo-headed Desire Goddess. Everyone applauded, and she again called on the Horse-necked King to give an inspirational talk.

The Horse-necked King advised them to get a mind-scissor on their former enemies.

"Always play over your head. Do things nobody else dares to do. And don't ever be intimidated. Play from a position of power. There are over ten billion of us dead people and only four billion of those others, so don't let them push you around. We outnumber them nearly three to one."

While Coriolanus was taking notes and getting more and more excited, it suddenly hit her. She never put her head in any oven! And she never wrote any notes to Porlock. What really happened was, she had been murdered by Porlock and then forgot, having been in the state of amnesia and shock which death produces.

Leaping up, she cried out: "That man killed me! He wasn't doing it for research at all. He was just a sadistic creep. He said he was inducing a harmless trance and

I should take notes. Then he murdered me and made it look like suicide."

There was pandemonium. The Death-ology class was going through paroxysms of stupefaction, amazement and fury. Daniel Berg, convulsed with rage, stamped and shouted over and over, "That pervert killed me! He gave me an after-dinner mint and started reading the death services and that's the last I knew. My parents think I committed suicide! I can't stand it!"

By now the whole class was there. Angry words flew.

"Porlock must think he can do whatever he likes with human life."

"Not Porlock, the government. He's just a tool."

"What was it, a blood sport? Is he insane?"

They compared notes. Each had been given an after-dinner mint. It happened at the last lab session of the course. Cori ate her mint, thinking it was only a friendly gesture because this was the final night. They were all sitting around laughing and joking; then they lay on their slabs. No, not slabs. Scales.

Porlock said, "Remember, you must be scientist enough to take your own mental pulse through each step of the mock biological death which the mints you have eaten will produce. Please relax completely. Take a deep breath. Now another. And another."

A crackle of impending excitement hung in the air. The class lay back calmly, naked and smiling and thrilled with anticipation.

Soon Cori's body was glistening with sweat.

Porlock began reciting:

"O nobly-born students, that which is called 'death' is coming to you now. Now thou art experiencing the

Radiance of the Clear Light of Pure Reality. Recognize it. Thine own intellect is now voidness, but not the voidness of nothingness, but the intellect itself, unobstructed, shining, thrilling, and blissful. The naked consciousness now enters the realm of Clear Light.

"The man blinded by the darkness of ignorance, the fool caught in the meshes of his own actions and the illiterate man, by listening to this Great Tantra, are released from the bonds of karma."

Cori noted that she was paralyzed but had no pain. Porlock's voice droned on.

"As for the common worldly folk, what need is there to mention them! By fleeing, through fear, terror, and awe, they fall over the precipices into the unhappy worlds and suffer." He had begun moving around, attaching cylinders to the prone bodies; Cori felt the touch of metal on her eyelids, underarms, scalp, belly and genitals. She heard Porlock reciting, "Do not be attracted towards the dull blue light of the brute-world, where stupidity predominates and where you will again suffer the illimitable miseries of slavery and dumbness and stupidness, and it will be a very long time before you can get out."

She tried to scream but no sound came. There was a terrible pain in her throat, an agonized squeezing; she had become blind, then totally paralyzed. Then there was a blur of rushing sound followed by blackness.

Next thing she knew, she was out of her body and hovering somewhere near the ceiling. Was it autosuggestion, or grouptrance, as Porlock had said? She noticed how dusty the light fixture was. She didn't want to look at what was going on below. Porlock was doing unspeakable things while he recited, "And now, embark upon the perilous ocean, and pray for the Divine Hand to guide you in your Great March to the Beyond."

She went into a tunnel. The inside was so luminous it blinded her to look at it. She heard soothing music and saw people everywhere. Her grandparents were there. Her Aunt Ivy and Uncle Chester, who had died last year in a shuttle crash, came up to say hello. Then Natalie Wood took both her hands, smiled, and said, "Welcome and congratulations."

Truman Capote laughed and gave her a little hug. Bobby Kennedy gave her a big hug, and Philip K. Dick said he liked her style. Even John Wayne waved from across the tunnel, and she got a glimpse of the sainted Boy George who died leading an uprising on Titan years before she was born. All this kind attention was wonderful. Cori was in her glory meeting all these dead celebrities, and it helped her to fully understand, deep down where it really counted, that she too was dead, and had been so ever since that incredible day in Prof. Porlock's classroom. And it struck her with furious force how angry she was at Porlock.

"What a sadist that man is! He's crazy!" she cried out.

The red Hoopoo-headed Desire Goddess rapped for silence, proclaiming: "I want to thank all of you for sharing that with us, but would like to point out an important fact. The anger you are experiencing must be resolved, or else it will turn inward and fester. And the only way you can resolve it is through revenge." She called on the Horse-necked King, who said:

"We'll take a vote, but I can see some of you aren't too sure about this. Here's a point to consider: a revenge motive will give you an interesting project and take your mind off your self-created phantoms."

Berg said he liked the idea.

Cori said. "But I feel guilty about wanting to harm Porlock."

"Those are normal moral delinquencies. Don't worry about them."

"I've got to be able to live with myself."

"Can you do it, knowing that Porlock remains un-punished?"

They took the vote. Everyone agreed that the evil professor should be destroyed, except Cori who was still uncertain.

The Horse-necked King said: "Do you want to be responsible when he does the same thing to the next class?"

So she agreed. "But how? Do the dead have any power over the living?"

"Murderers are tampering with forces they don't fully understand. Setting up a guilt trap is a simple matter."

"And Porlock is a psychoshrimp," someone said.

"Don't forget, from the legal point of view we died of ill-treatment," said Berg. "In view of the facts, it is incumbent upon us to be judge, jury and execu-tioner."

The Horse-necked King said, "What we do is, we give him a vision. No; give him a super-vision. Poison his life with an unknown horror, then ram it home."

Hands waved. "I got it. The best and surest way is to—"

"Hang a dead rat around his neck," said Berg.

"Come again?"

"The Rhyme of the Ancient Mariner," Berg said,

excited. "Coleridge wrote that poem to make the supernatural seem real, and it was. The mariner killed the pet albatross with his crossbow; the superstitious sailors hung the dead albatross around his neck—"

"I think you've got it!" cried the Wrathful Goddess Rich in Space, elated. "Back in the past where I come from, if a farmer had an animal that killed chickens, what he'd do is, he'd hang a dead chicken around that animal's neck for about a week. After that it would never kill another chicken. I vote we hang a dead Daniel Berg around this fiend's neck. How many like it?"

They all, except Berg, liked it a lot.

"Give him geological eyes," said the red Hoopoo-headed Desire Goddess. "Give him images he can't refuse. Just you watch, you new people, as we smoke this killer out."

"There are many abuses to correct," agreed the Horse-necked King, "and it's too complicated to calculate, so watch how it works."

Daniel Berg said: "Hold on. Let's not use my body, it wouldn't be effective. I yield the honor to Cori here. We'll hit Porlock right between the eyes and use Cori's body. That's bound to upset him a lot more."

They started slow. In Porlock's classroom, a door swung open silently. Behind it lurked Cori, her eyes wide and staring, and then the group immediately peppered him with scenes from his own past: the childhood home, yesterday's breakfast, kindergarten, the day he made full professor, an embarrassing moment or two.

Porlock fled to his cabin in the forest preserve, where fireflies spelled out the word *MURDER*. He shook his fist at them.

"You aren't real!" he screamed. "I'm on Ganymede in a damp, fetid ocean cave and I'll be rescued any minute now."

The Horse-necked King said: "Couldn't be better. He's being choked to death by his own guilt. If we handle the entire execution this well, Porlock will never be alive again in any sense of the word."

For a dozen dreams they had the Prof. climb a twisting path that wound up a long, bleak, windswept hill. He was bedeviled by dim voices. He couldn't make out what they said. Each time when he was just about to reach the summit, he would stumble on Cori's body hidden under a heap of leaves and wake up chewing his fingers in a cold sweat.

He turned to his Chip for comfort. Porlock's fantasy was a mild one, nothing but a hollow-cheeked woman who wore boots and put clothespins on his nipples and penis; but while he was enjoying his CIAOU and getting a little bit of relief, they turned the hollow-cheeked woman into Cori's dead body.

Next Coriolanus became an elusive shadow in the classroom. Weird music and vaporizing clouds were produced with pressure-codes tied into the inertia of his own guilt.

They made a new gravity envelope for his front head and played horror movies inside his brain. They installed a tiny corpse, Coriolanus, bumping at the inside of his chest. They analyzed his case in group discussion and came to some interesting conclusions.

Like most mass-murderers, Porlock had been on the verge of collapse for a long time. Satisfied desire only brought on the feverish pursuit of new victims. A recent one was Cori, now propped in her usual seat in the middle row in a moderate state of decay.

She also visited him every night; but Porlock was a man of extraordinary toughness, with a clever mind and the courage of the demented. He woke up yelling, "This is deceptive. A temporary malady only," and went on about his business.

They used Porlock for target practice—Bang! you're a lost soul—pumping adrenalin through his bloodstream but being careful not to grant him the easy escape of cardiac arrest. They sent brimstone, whimpers and grinding noises that seemed to arise from inside his groin. Then they took a few days off.

"It works better if the criminal thinks he's been given a reprieve," said the red Hoopoo-headed Desire Goddess. "Remember, it's not enough to kill his body; we've got to kill *him*."

Vacation over, Porlock walked to his desk and picked up the day's mail. A miasma of dead fish, wet logs and methane, rotten smells of tomb-ish, fetid, organic, bloodrooty Coriolanus melted and spread out, sending Porlock spinning. He was flung with the force of a superheated energy bolt, then picked up just as carefully and set on his feet.

Although the floor was moving he ran outside to where a terrible sun climbed a terrible sky and shed its terrible rays on a terrible landscape. Small monsters rained down on the top of his aircar. He yanked open the door, hoping to drive away to safety. But Cori's body lay sprawled in the back seat.

"Come play with me, Eric dear," said her cold and bloodless lips.

The only part still intact was her lovely, flowing hair, which was as pretty as ever. She stretched out decaying arms to the Professor, who screamed and fled down street after street for hours like a crazy man, then walked for several hours and finally calmed down.

"There's a certain amount of satisfaction in doing it well," remarked the Wrathful Goddess Rich in Space.

Porlock turned toward home. A pale mass detached itself from a snowy hedge and followed him. It was Cori's body. She touched his shoulder with a dead hand. A chunk of tissue fell off.

He shrieked.

Another few minutes and they'd have him.

Porlock ran upstairs. There was Cori's body in the hallway. He ran and slammed the elevator door. And there was Cori's body in the elevator. She smiled at him with a badly decomposed face. He went berserk.

A burst of laughter from behind a potted palm.

Suffering from acute mental exhaustion, Porlock let himself into the apartment. With trembling hands and weak knees he wiped his face, poured himself a shot of *Io* and tossed it off. Then he sat down to write a note; but a fire broke out under the desk.

With a howl Porlock ran to the big porcelain antique stove that had cost him a small fortune (a luxurious cavern in which to terminate an unbearable existence) and turned on the gas. On the lower shelf he placed a fluffy, soft new apricot-colored towel that had a beige border. Then he drew up a chair, put his head on the towel and began sobbing brokenly.

The transition took eight minutes, give or take a few milliseconds. The sobs gradually died away; then Cori grew impatient and asked, "Why isn't the Professor here?"

"Because this is an execution. You were on the jury that agreed that no good end can be served by allow-ing the fiend to continue his miserable existence in any sense of the word."

"But I didn't mean permanently," she cried.

"Of course you did," the Horse-necked King assured her.

"But that can't be," she argued. "Remember the ordinary sequence D: n_1, n_2, n_3 and so on. It proves death is a simple, natural phenomenon and the Professor will surely be joining us in a few minutes."

"See for yourself." The Horse-necked King shrugged and pointed to the porcelain stove.

Cori smelled gas and saw the apricot-colored towel, the head, then Porlock's ghastly expression. His eyes were wide open. They stared at her with a fixed, hideous glare.

"Don't be angry, Professor!" she smiled. "We only want to congratulate and welcome you."

But the Horse-necked King had been correct.

Prof. Eric Porlock was no longer alive, in any sense of the word.

Time of Passage

J. G. BALLARD

J. G. Ballard's autobiographical novel, Empire of the Sun *(1984), was hailed by critics as one of the great books of the twentieth century. A story of the Japanese occupation of Shanghai—where Ballard was interned in World War II during his formative boyhood years—*Empire of the Sun *is a definitive novel about the dislocation of "normal" life and also a climax to Ballard's writing career to date.*

For over twenty years he has been known as one of the genuinely innovative science-fiction writers. His many story collections, such as The Terminal Beach, Low-Flying Aircraft, *and* Myths of the Near Future, *and his novels, such as* The Drowned World, Crash, High-Rise, *and* The Unlimited Dream Company, *are at once hallucinatory and contemporary, surrealistic yet clinical—and always beautifully crafted. Typically, they have concerned "inner" rather than "outer" space, dealing with the psychological, almost Jungian impact of the modern technological landscape. They evoke the new archetypes of the late twentieth century—computers, automobiles, eco-catastrophe, megalopolis—as they affect us psychically, even erotically.*

In a deeper sense, perhaps all of Ballard's works have

been strategies by which he could come to terms imaginatively with those early, disorienting days in Shanghai. One might say that Ballard's unique vision was liberated in Shanghai, and after focusing prismatically through that glass of strangeness upon the postwar world of motorways, moon rockets, disasters and media delirium, it returned at last to its source in Empire of the Sun, *where the adult Ballard became once more a boy.*

"Time of Passage" is the haunting story of a similar kind of return.

S unlight spilled among the flowers and tombstones, turning the cemetery into a bright garden of sculpture. Like two large gaunt crows, the gravediggers leaned on their spades between the marble angels, their shadows arching across the smooth white flank of one of the recent graves.

The gilt lettering was still fresh and untarnished.

JAMES FALKMAN
1963–1901
"The End is but the Beginning"

Leisurely they began to pare back the crisp turf, then dismantled the headstone and swathed it in a canvas sheet, laying it behind the graves in the next aisle. Biddle, the older of the two, a lean man in a black waistcoat, pointed to the cemetery gates, where the first mourning party approached.

"They're here. Let's get our backs into it."

The younger man, Biddle's son, watched the small procession winding through the graves. His nostrils scented the sweet broken earth. "They're always early," he murmured reflectively. "It's a strange thing, you never see them come on time."

A clock tolled from the chapel among the cypresses. Working swiftly, they scooped out the soft earth, piling it into a neat cone at the grave's head A few minutes later, when the sexton arrived with the principal mourners, the polished teak of the coffin was exposed, and Biddle jumped down onto the lid and scraped away the damp earth clinging to its brass rim.

The ceremony was brief and the twenty mourners, led by Falkman's sister, a tall white-haired woman with a narrow autocratic face, leaning on her husband's arm, soon returned to the chapel. Biddle gestured to his son. They jerked the coffin out of the ground and loaded it onto a cart, strapping it down under the harness. Then they heaped the earth back into the grave and relaid the squares of turf.

As they pushed the cart back to the chapel the sunlight shone brightly among the thinning graves.

Forty-eight hours later the coffin arrived at James Falkman's large gray-stoned house on the upper slopes of Mortmere Park. The high-walled avenue was almost deserted and few people saw the hearse enter the tree-lined drive. The blinds were drawn over the windows, and huge wreaths rested among the furniture in the hall where Falkman lay motionless in his coffin on a mahogany table. Veiled by the dim light, his square, strong-jawed face seemed composed and unblemished, a short lock of hair over his forehead making his expression less severe than his sister's.

A solitary beam of sunlight, finding its way through the dark sycamores which guarded the house, slowly

traversed the room as the morning progressed, and
shone for a few minutes upon Falkman's open eyes.
Even after the beam had moved away a faint glimmer
of light still remained in the pupils, like the reflection
of a star glimpsed in the bottom of a dark well.

All day, helped by two of her friends, sharp-faced
women in long black coats, Falkman's sister moved
quietly about the house. Her quick deft hands shook
the dust from the velvet curtains in the library, wound
the miniature Louis XV clock on the study desk, and
reset the great barometer on the staircase. None of the
women spoke to each other, but within a few hours
the house was transformed, the dark wood in the hall
gleaming as the first callers were admitted.

"Mr. and Mrs. Montefiore . . ."

"Mr. and Mrs. Caldwell . . ."

"Miss Evelyn Jermyn and Miss Elizabeth . . ."

"Mr. Samuel Banbury . . ."

One by one, nodding in acknowledgment as they
were announced, the callers trooped into the hall and
paused over the coffin, examining Falkman's face with
discreet interest, then passed into the dining room
where they were presented with a glass of port and a
tray of sweet-meats. Most of them were elderly, over-
dressed in the warm spring weather, one or two obviously ill at ease in the great oak-paneled house, and all
unmistakably revealed the same air of hushed expec-
tancy.

The following morning Falkman was lifted from his
coffin and carried upstairs to the bedroom overlooking
the drive. The winding sheet was removed from his
frail body dressed in a pair of thick woolen pajamas.
He lay quietly between the cold sheets, his gray face

sightless and reposed, unaware of his sister crying softly on the high-backed chair beside him. Only when Dr. Markham called and put his hand on her shoulder did she contain herself, relieved to have given way to her feelings.

Almost as if this were a signal, Falkman opened his eyes. For a moment they wavered uncertainly, the pupils weak and watery. Then he gazed up at his sister's tear-marked face, his head motionless on the pillow. As she and the doctor leaned forward Falkman smiled fleetingly, his lips parting across his teeth in an expression of immense patience and understanding. Then, apparently exhausted, he lapsed into a deep sleep.

After securing the blinds over the windows, his sister and the doctor stepped from the room. Below, the doors closed quietly into the drive, and the house became silent. Gradually the sounds of Falkman's breathing grew more steady and filled the bedroom, overlaid by the swaying of the dark trees outside.

So James Falkman made his arrival. For the next week he lay quietly in his bedroom, his strength increasing hourly, and managed to eat his first meals prepared by his sister. She sat in the blackwood chair, her mourning habit exchanged for a gray woolen dress, examining him critically.

"Now, James, you'll have to get a better appetite than that. Your poor body is completely wasted."

Falkman pushed away the tray and let his long slim hands fall across his chest. He smiled amiably at his sister. "Careful, Betty, or you'll turn me into a milk pudding."

His sister briskly straightened the eiderdown. "If

you don't like my cooking, James, you can fend for yourself."

A faint chuckle slipped between Falkman's lips. "Thank you for telling me, Betty, I fully intend to."

He lay back, smiling weakly to himself as his sister stalked out with the tray. Teasing her did him almost as much good as the meals she prepared, and he felt the blood reaching down into his cold feet. His face was still gray and flaccid, and he conserved his strength carefully, only his eyes moving as he watched the ravens alighting on the window ledge.

Gradually, as his conversations with his sister became more frequent, Falkman gained sufficient strength to sit up. He began to take a fuller interest in the world around him, watching the people in the avenue through the French windows and disputing his sister's commentary on them.

"There's Sam Banbury again," she remarked testily as a small leprechaunlike old man hobbled past. "Off to the Swan as usual. When's he going to get a job, I'd like to know."

"Be more charitable, Betty. Sam's a very sensible fellow. I'd rather go to the pub than have a job."

His sister snorted skeptically, her assessment of Falkman's character apparently at variance with this statement. "You've got one of the finest houses in Mortmere Park," she told him. "I think you should be more careful with people like Sam Banbury. He's not in your class, James."

Falkman smiled patiently at his sister. "We're all in the same class, or have you been here so long you've forgotten, Betty."

"We all forget," she told him soberly. "You will

too, James. It's sad, but we're in this world now, and
we must concern ourselves with it. If the church can
keep the memory alive for us, so much the better. As
you'll find out though, the majority of folk remember
nothing. Perhaps it's a good thing."

She grudgingly admitted the first visitors, fussing
about so that Falkman could barely exchange a word
with them. In fact, the visits tired him, and he could
do little more than pass a few formal pleasantries.
Even when Sam Banbury brought him a pipe and
tobacco pouch he had to muster all his energy to thank
him and had none left to prevent his sister from making off with them.

Only when the Reverend Matthews called did Falkman manage to summon together his strength, for
half an hour spoke earnestly to the parson, who listened with rapt attention, interjecting a few eager
questions. When the Reverend left he seemed refreshed and confident, and strode down the stairs with
a gay smile at Falkman's sister.

Within three weeks Falkman was out of bed, and
managed to hobble downstairs and inspect the house
and garden. His sister protested, dogging his slow
painful foot-steps with sharp reminders of his feeble-
ness, but Falkman ignored her. He found his way to
the conservatory, and leaned against one of the orna-
mental columns, his nervous fingers feeling the leaves
of the miniature trees, the scent of flowers flushing his
face. Outside, in the grounds, he examined everything
around him, as if comparing it with some Elysian
paradise in his mind.

He was walking back to the house when he twisted

his ankle sharply in the crazy paving. Before he could cry for help he had fallen headlong across the hard stones.

"James Falkman, will you never listen?" his sister protested, as she helped him across the terrace. "I warned you to stay in bed!"

Reaching the lounge, Falkman sat down thankfully in an armchair, reassembling his stunned limbs. "Quiet, Betty, do you mind," he admonished his sister when his breath returned. "I'm still here, and I'm perfectly well."

He had stated no more than the truth. After the accident he began to recover spectacularly, his progress toward complete health accelerating without a break, as if the tumble had freed him from the lingering fatigue and discomfort of the previous weeks. His step became brisk and lively, his complexion brightened, a soft pink glow filling out his cheeks, and he moved busily around the house.

A month afterward his sister returned to her own home, acknowledging his ability to look after himself, and her place was taken by the housekeeper. After re-establishing himself in the house, Falkman became increasingly interested in the world outside. He hired a comfortable car and chauffeur, and spent most of the winter afternoons and evenings at his club; soon he found himself the center of a wide circle of acquaintances. He became the chairman of a number of charitable committees, where his good humor, tolerance and shrewd judgment made him well respected. He now held himself erect, his gray hair sprouting luxuriantly, here and there touched by black flecks, jaw jutting firmly from suntanned cheeks.

Every Sunday he attended the morning and evening services at his church, where he owned a private pew, and was somewhat saddened to see that only the older people formed the congregation. However, he himself found that the picture painted by the liturgy became increasingly detached from his own memories as the latter faded, too soon became a meaningless charade that he could accept only by an act of faith.

A few years later, when he became increasingly restless, he decided to accept the offer of a partnership in a leading firm of stock brokers.

Many of his acquaintances at the club were also finding jobs, forsaking the placid routines of smoking room and conservatory garden. Harold Caldwell, one of his closest friends, was appointed Professor of History at the university, and Sam Banbury became manager of the Swan Hotel.

The ceremony on Falkman's first day at the stock exchange was dignified and impressive. Three junior men also joining the firm were introduced to the assembled staff by the senior partner, Mr. Montefiore, and each presented with a gold watch to symbolize the years he would spend with the firm. Falkman received an embossed silver cigar case and was loudly applauded.

For the next five years Falkman threw himself wholeheartedly into his work, growing more extrovert and aggressive as his appetite for the material pleasures of life increased. He became a keen golfer; then, as the exercise strengthened his physique, played his first games of tennis. An influential member of the business community, his days passed in a pleasant round of conferences and dinner parties. He no longer attended the church, but instead spent his Sundays escorting the more attractive of his lady acquaintances to the race tracks and regattas.

He found it all the more surprising, therefore, when a persistent mood of dejection began to haunt him. Although without any apparent source, this deepened slowly, and he found himself reluctant to leave his house in the evenings. He resigned from his committees and no longer visited his club. At the stock exchange he felt permanently distracted, and would stand for hours by the window, staring down at the traffic.

Finally, when his grasp of the business began to slip, Mr. Montefiore suggested that he go on indefinite leave.

For a week Falkman listlessly paced around the huge empty house. Sam Banbury frequently called to see him, but Falkman's sense of grief was beyond any help. He drew the blinds over the windows and changed into a black tie and suit, sat blankly in the darkened library.

At last, when his depression had reached its lowest ebb, he went to the cemetery to collect his wife.

After the congregation had dispersed, Falkman paused outside the vestry to tip the gravedigger, Biddle, and compliment him on his young son, a cherubic three-year-old who was playing among the headstones. Then he rode back to Mortmere Park in the car following the hearse, the remainder of the cortege behind him.

"A grand turnout, James," his sister told him approvingly. "Twenty cars altogether, not including the private ones."

Falkman thanked her, his eyes examining his sister

with critical detachment. In the fifteen years he had
known her she had coarsened perceptibly, her voice
roughening and her gestures becoming broader. A dis-
tinct social gap had always separated them, a division
which Falkman had accepted charitably, but it was
now widening markedly. Her husband's business had
recently begun to fail, and her thoughts had turned
almost exclusively to the subjects of money and social
prestige.

As Falkman congratulated himself on his good
sense and success, a curious premonition, indistinct
but nonetheless disturbing, stirred through his mind.

Like Falkman himself fifteen years earlier, his wife
first lay in her coffin in the hall, the heavy wreaths
transforming it into a dark olive-green bower. Behind
the lowered blinds the air was dim and stifled, and
with her rich red hair flaring off her forehead, and her
broad cheeks and full lips, his wife seemed to Falkman
like some sleeping enchantress in a magical arbor. He
gripped the silver foot rail of the coffin and stared at
her mindlessly, aware of his sister shepherding the
guests to the port and whisky. He traced with his eyes
the exquisite dips and hollows around his wife's neck
and chin, the white skin sweeping smoothly to her
strong shoulders. The next day, when she was carried
upstairs, her presence filled the bedroom. All afternoon he sat beside her, waiting patiently for her to
wake.

Shortly after five o'clock, in the few minutes of light
left before the dusk descended, when the air hung
motionlessly under the trees in the garden, a faint
echo of life moved across her face. Her eyes cleared
and then focused on the ceiling.

Breathlessly, Falkman leaned forward and took one of her cold hands. Far within it, the pulse sounded faintly.

"Marion," he whispered.

Her head inclined slightly, lips parting in a weak smile. For several moments she gazed serenely at her husband.

"Hello, Jamie."

His wife's arrival completely rejuvenated Falkman. A devoted husband, he was soon completely immersed in their life together. As she recovered from the long illness after her arrival, Falkman entered the prime of his life. His gray hair became sleek and black, his face grew thicker, the chin firmer and stronger. He returned to the stock exchange, taking up his job with renewed interest.

He and Marion made a handsome couple. At intervals they would visit the cemetery and join in the service celebrating the arrival of another of their friends, but these became less frequent. Other parties continually visited the cemetery, thinning the ranks of graves, and large areas had reverted to open lawn as the coffins were withdrawn and the tombstones removed. The firm of undertakers near the cemetery which was responsible for notifying mourning relatives closed down and was sold. Finally, after the gravedigger, Biddle, recovered his own wife from the last of the graves the cemetery was converted into a children's playground.

The years of their marriage were Falkman's happiest. With each successive summer Marion became slimmer and more youthful, her red hair a brilliant diadem that stood out among the crowds in the street when she came to see him. They would walk home arm in arm, in the summer evenings pause among the willows by the river to embrace each other like lovers.

Indeed, their happiness became such a byword among their friends that over two hundred guests attended the church ceremony celebrating the long years of their marriage. As they knelt together at the altar before the priest, Marion seemed to Falkman like a demure rose.

This was the last night they were to spend together. Over the years Falkman had become less interested in his work at the stock exchange, and the arrival of older and more serious men had resulted in a series of demotions for him. Many of his friends were facing similar problems. Harold Caldwell had been forced to resign his professorship and was now a junior lecturer, taking postgraduate courses to familiarize himself with the great body of new work that had been done in the previous thirty years. Sam Banbury was a waiter at the Swan Hotel.

Marion went to live with her parents, and the Falkmans' apartment, to which they had moved some years earlier after the house was closed and sold, was let to new tenants. Falkman, whose tastes had become simpler as the years passed, took a room in a hostel for young men, but he and Marion saw each other every evening. He felt increasingly restless, half conscious that his life was moving toward an inescapable focus, and often thought of giving up his job.

Marion remonstrated with him. "But you'll lose everything you've worked for, Jamie. All those years."

Falkman shrugged, chewing on a stem of grass as they lay in the park during one of their lunch hours. Marion was now a salesgirl in a department store.

"Perhaps, but I resent being demoted. Even Montefiore is leaving. His grandfather has just been appointed chairman." He rolled over and put his head in her lap. "It's so dull in that stuffy office, with all those pious old men. I'm not satisfied with it any longer."

Marion smiled affectionately at his naïveté and enthusiasm. Falkman was now more handsome than she had ever remembered him, his suntanned face almost unlined.

"It's been wonderful together, Marion," he told her on the eve of their thirtieth anniversary. "How lucky we've been never to have had a child. Do you realize that some people even have three or four? It's absolutely tragic."

"It comes to us all, though, Jamie," she reminded him. "Some people say it's a very beautiful and noble experience, having a child."

All evening he and Marion wandered around the town together, Falkman's desire for her quickened by her increasing demureness. Since she had gone to live with her parents Marion had become almost too shy to take his hand.

Then he lost her.

Walking through the market in the town centre, they were joined by two of Marion's friends, Elizabeth and Evelyn Jermyn.

"There's Sam Banbury," Evelyn pointed out as a firework crackled from a stall on the other side of the market. "Playing the fool as usual." She and her sister clucked disapprovingly. Tight-mouthed and stern, they wore dark serge coats buttoned to their necks.

Distracted by Sam, Falkman wandered off a few steps, suddenly found that the three girls had walked away. Darting through the crowd, he tried to catch up with them, briefly glimpsed Marion's red hair.

He fought his way through the stalls, almost knocking over a barrow of vegetables, and shouted at Sam Banbury:

"Sam! Have you seen Marion?"

Banbury pocketed his crackers and helped him to scan the crowd. For an hour they searched. Finally Sam gave up and went home, leaving Falkman to hang about the cobbled square under the dim lights when the market closed, wandering among the tinsel and litter as the stall holders packed up for home.

"Excuse me, have you seen a girl here? A girl with red hair?"

"Please, she was here this afternoon."

"A girl . . ."

". . . called . . ."

Stunned, he realized that he had forgotten her name.

Shortly afterward, Falkman gave up his job and went to live with his parents. Their small red-brick house was on the opposite side of the town; between the crowded chimney pots he could sometimes see the distant slopes of Mortmere Park. His life now began a less carefree phase, as most of his energy went into helping his mother and looking after his sister Betty. By comparison with his own house his parents' home was bleak and uncomfortable, altogether alien to everything Falkman had previously known. Although kind and respectable people, his parents' lives were circumscribed by their lack of success or education. They had no interest in music or the theater, and Falkman found his mind beginning to dull and coarsen.

His father was openly critical of him for leaving his job, but the hostility between them gradually subsided as he more and more began to dominate Falkman, restricting his freedom and reducing his pocket money, even warning him not to play with certain of his friends. In fact, going to live with his parents had taken Falkman into an entirely new world.

By the time he began to go to school Falkman had completely forgotten his past life, his memories of Marion and the great house where they had lived surrounded by servants altogether obliterated.

During his first term at school he was in a class with the older boys, whom the teachers treated as equals, but like his parents they began to extend their influence over him as the years passed. At times Falkman rebelled against this attempt to suppress his own personality, but at last they entirely dominated him, controlling his activities and molding his thoughts and speech. The whole process of education, he dimly realized, was designed to prepare him for the strange twilight world of his earliest childhood. It deliberately eliminated every trace of sophistication, breaking down, with its constant repetitions and brain-splitting exercises, all his knowledge of language and mathematics, substituting for them a collection of meaningless rhymes and chants, and out of this constructing an artificial world of total infantilism.

At last, when the process of education had reduced him almost to the stage of an inarticulate infant, his parents intervened by removing him from the school, and the final years of his life were spent at home.

"Mama, can I sleep with you?"

Mrs. Falkman looked down at the serious-faced little boy who leaned his head on her pillow. Affectionately she pinched his square jaw and then touched her husband's shoulder as he stirred. Despite the years between father and son, their two bodies were almost identical, with the same broad shoulders and broad heads, the same thick hair.

"Not today, Jamie, but soon perhaps, one day."

The child watched his mother with wide eyes, wondering why she should be crying to herself, guessing that perhaps he had touched upon one of the taboos that had exercised such a potent fascination for all the boys at school, the mystery of their ultimate destination that remained carefully shrouded by their parents and which they themselves were no longer able to grasp.

By now he was beginning to experience the first difficulties in both walking and feeding himself. He tottered about clumsily, his small piping voice tripping over his tongue. Steadily his vocabulary diminished until he knew only his mother's name. When he could no longer stand upright she would carry him in her arms, feeding him like an elderly invalid. His mind clouded, a few constants of warmth and hunger drifting through it hazily. As long as he could, he clung to his mother.

Shortly afterward, Falkman and his mother visited the lying-in hospital for several weeks. On her return Mrs. Falkman remained in bed for a few days, but gradually she began to move about more freely, slowly shedding the additional weight accumulated during her confinement.

Some nine months after she returned from the hospital, a period during which she and her husband thought continually of their son, the shared tragedy of his approaching death, a symbol of their own imminent separation, bringing them closer together, they went away on their honeymoon

Of Space-Time and the River

GREGORY BENFORD

*Gregory Benford has two faces: a respected profes-
sional physicist, specializing in extra-galactic plasma
jets, and a fiction writer with remarkable literary skill.
In the creation of his characters and locations, Benford
searches for authentic tones and colors just as keenly
as he studies astronomical X-ray plates. Conversely, his
portrayal of the actual business of science sounds genuine notes which are usually absent from the stories of
"literary" writers describing scientists at work. All of
which combines to make his award-winning Time-
scape (1980) an excellent novel by any standards, as
well as a thrilling science-fiction story and a daring
speculation about the nature of time and those hypo-
thetical faster-than-light particles, tachyons. Benford
has also written many noteworthy stories, one of the
finest of which is "Of Space-Time and the River."*

*He was born in Alabama and is now a professor at
the University of California at Irvine. An international-
ly-known scientist and author, he may be found in
Moscow one day delivering a paper on relativity, and
in Yorkshire, England, the next as guest of honor at a
science-fiction convention.*

MONDAY, DECEMBER 5, 2048

We took a limo to Los Angeles for the 9:00 A.M. flight, LAX to Cairo.

On the boost up we went over 1.4 G, contra-reg, and a lot of passengers complained, especially the poor thins in their clank-shank rigs, the ones that keep you walking even after the hip replacements fail.

Joanna, seasoned traveler that she is, slept through it all, and I occupied myself with musing about finally seeing the ancient Egypt I'd dreamed about as a kid, back at the turn of the century.

> If thou be'st born to strange sights,
> Things invisible to see,
> Ride ten thousand days and nights
> Till Age snow white hairs on thee.

I've got the snow powdering at the temples and steadily expanding waistline, so I guess John Donne applies. Good to see I can still summon up lines I first read as a teenager. There are some rewards to being a Prof. of Comp. Lit. at UC Irvine, even if you do have to scrimp to afford a trip like this.

The tour agency said the Quarthex hadn't interfered with tourism at all—in fact, you hardly noticed them, they deliberately blended in so well. How a seven-foot insectoid thing with gleaming russet skin can look like an Egyptian I don't know, but what the hell, Joanna said, let's go anyway.

I hope she's right. I mean, it's been fourteen years since the Quarthex landed, opened the first diplomatic interstellar relations, and then chose Egypt as the only place on Earth where they cared to carry out what they called their "cultural studies." I guess we'll get a look at that, too. The Quarthex keep to themselves, veiling their multi-layered deals behind diplomatic dodges.

As if six hours of travel weren't numbing enough, including the orbital delay because of an unannounced Chinese launch, we both watched a holoD about one of those new biotech guys, called *Straight from the Hearts*. An unending string of single-entendre jokes. In our stupefied state it was just about right.

As we descended over Cairo it was clear and about 15 degrees C. We stumbled off the plane, sandy-eyed from riding ten thousand days and nights in a whistling aluminum box.

The airport was scruffy, instant third-world hubbub, confusion and filth. One departure lounge was filled exclusively with turbaned men. Heavy security everywhere. No Quarthex around. Maybe they do blend in.

Our bus across Cairo passed a decayed aqueduct, about which milled men in caftans, women in black, animals eating garbage. People, packed into the most unlikely living spots, carrying out peddler's business in dusty spots between buildings, traffic alternately frenetic or frozen.

We crawled across Cairo to Giza, the pyramids abruptly looming out of the twilight. The hotel, Mena House, was the hunting lodge-cum-palace of nineteenth-century kings. Elegant.

Buffet supper was good. Sleep came like a weight.

DEC. 6

Joanna says this journal is good therapy for me, .night even get me back into the habit of writing again. She says every Comp. Lit. type is a frustrated author and I should just spew my bile into this diary. So be it:

> Thou, when thou return'st, wilt tell me
> All strange wonders that befell thee.

World, you have been warned.

Set off south today—to Memphis, the ancient capital lost when its walls were breached in a war and subsequent floods claimed it.

The famous fallen Rameses statue looks powerful still, even lying down. Makes you feel like a pigmy tiptoeing around a giant, *à la* Gulliver.

Saqqara, principal necropolis of Memphis, survives 3 km. away in the desert. First Dynasty tombs, including the first pyramid, made of steps 5 levels high. New Kingdom graffiti inside are now history themselves, from our perspective.

On to the Great Pyramid—by camel! The drivers proved even more harassing than legend warned. We entered the pyramid of Khefren; slightly shorter than that of his father, Cheops. All the 80 known pyramids were found stripped. These passages have a constricted vacancy to them, empty now for longer than they were filled. Their silent mass is unnerving.

Professor Alvarez from UC Berkeley tried to find hidden rooms here by placing cosmic ray detectors in the lower known rooms, and looking for slight increases in flux at certain angles, but there seem to be none. There are seismic and even radio measurements of the dry sands in the Giza region, looking for echoes of buried tombs, but no big finds so far. Plenty of echoes from ruins of ordinary houses, etc., though.

No serious jet lag today, but we nod off when we can. Handy, having the hotel a few hundred yards from the pyramids.

I tried to get Joanna to leave her wrist-comm at home. Since her breakdown she can't take news of daily disasters very well. (Who can, really?) She's pretty steady now, but this trip should be as calm as possible, her doctor told me.

So of course she turns on the comm and it's full of hysterical stuff about another border clash between the Empire of Israel and the Arab Muhammad Soviet. Smart rockets versus smart defenses. A draw. Some things never change.

I turned it off immediately. Joanna's hands shook for hours afterwards. I brushed it off.

Still, it's different when you're a few hundred miles from the lines. Hope we're safe here.

DEC. 7

Into Cairo itself, the Egyptian museum. The Tut Ankh Amen exhibit—huge treasuries, opulent jewels, a sheer wondrous plenitude. There are endless cases of beautiful alabaster bowls, gold-laminate boxes, testifying to thousands of years of productivity.

I wandered down a musty marble corridor and then, coming out of a gloomy side passage, there was the first Quarthex I'd ever seen. Big, clacking and clicking as it thrust forward in that six-legged gait. It ignored me, of course—they nearly always lurch by humans as though they can't see us. Or else that distant, distracted gaze means they're ruminating over strange, alien ideas. Who knows why they're intensely studying ancient Egyptian ways, and ignoring the rest of us? This one was cradling a stone urn, a meter high at least. It carried the black granite in three akimbo arms, hardly seeming to notice the weight. I caught a whiff of acrid pungency, the fluid that lubricates their joints. Then it was gone.

We left and visited the oldest Coptic church in Egypt, supposedly where Moses hid out when he was on the lam. Looks it. The old section of Cairo is crowded, decayed, people laboring in every nook with minimal tools, much standing around watching as others work. The only sign of really efficient labor was a gang of men and women hauling long, cigar-shaped yellow things on wagons. Something the Quarthex wanted placed outside the city, our guide said.

In the evening we went to the Sound & Light show at the Sphinx—excellent. There is even a version in the Quarthex language, those funny sputtering, barking sounds.

Arabs say, "Man fears time; time fears the pyramids." You get that feeling here.

Afterwards, we ate in the hotel's Indian restaurant; quite fine.

DEC. 8

Cairo is a city being trampled to death.

It's grown by a factor of 14 in population since the revolution in 1952, and shows it. The old Victorian homes that once lined stately streets of willowy trees are now crowded by modern slab-concrete apartment houses. The aged buildings are kept going, not from a sense of history, but because no matter how run-down they get, somebody needs them.

The desert's grit invades everywhere. Plants in the courtyards have a weary, resigned look. Civilization hasn't been very good for the old ways.

Maybe that's why the Quarthex seem to dislike anything built since the time of the Romans. I saw one running some kind of machine, a black contraption that floated two meters off the ground. It was laying some kind of cable in the ground, right along the bank of the Nile. Every time it met a building it just slammed through, smashing everything to frags. Guess the Quarthex have squared all this with the Egyptian gov't., because there were police all around, making sure nobody got in the way. Odd.

But not unpredictable, when you think about it. The Quarthex have those levitation devices which everybody would love to get the secret of. (Ending sentence with preposition! Horrors! But this is vacation, dammit.) They've been playing coy for years, letting out only a trickle of technology, with the Egyptians holding the patents. That must be what's holding the Egyptian economy together, in the face of their unrelenting population crunch. The Quarthex started out as guests here, studying the ruins and so on, but now it's obvious that they have free run of the place. They *own* it.

Still, the Quarthex haven't given away the crucial devices which would enable us to find out how they do it—or so my colleagues in the physics department tell me. It vexes them that this alien race can master space-time so completely, manipulating gravity itself, and we can't get the knack of it.

We visited the famous alabaster mosque. It perches on a hill called The Citadel. Elegant, cool, aloofly dominating the city. The Old Bazaar nearby is a warren, so much like the movie sets one's seen that it has an unreal, Arabian Nights quality. We bought spices. The calls to worship from the mosques reach you everywhere, even in the most secluded back rooms where Joanna was haggling over jewelry.

It's impossible to get anything really ancient, the swarthy little merchants said. The Quarthex have bought them up, trading gold for anything that might be from the time of the Pharaohs. There have been a lot of fakes over the last few centuries, some really good ones, so the Quarthex have just bought anything that might be real. No wonder the Egyptians like them, let them chew up their houses if they want. Gold speaks louder than the past.

We boarded our cruise ship, the venerable *Nile Concorde*. Lunch was excellent, Italian. We explored Cairo in mid-afternoon, through markets of incredible dirt and disarray. Calf brains displayed without a hint of refrigeration or protection, flies swarming, etc. Fun, especially if you can keep from breathing for five minutes or more.

We stopped in the Shepheard's Hotel, the site of many Brit spy novels (Maugham especially). It has an excellent bar—Nubians and Saudis, etc. putting away decidedly non-Islamic gins and beers. A Quarthex was sitting in a special chair at the back, talking through a voicebox to a Saudi. I couldn't tell what they were saying, but the Saudi had a gleam in his eye. Driving a bargain, I'd say.

Great atmosphere in the bar, though. A cloth banner over the bar proclaims,

Unborn tomorrow and dead yesterday,
why fret about them if today be sweet.

Indeed, yes, ummm—bartender!

FRIDAY, DEC. 9, MOSLEM HOLY DAY

We left Cairo at 11 P.M. last night, the city gliding
past our stateroom windows, lovelier in misty radiance
than in dusty day. We cruised all day. Buffet breakfast
& lunch, solid eastern and Mediterranean stuff, passa-
ble red wine.

A hundred meters away, the past presses at us,
going about its business as if the Pharaohs were still
calling the tune. Primitive pumping irrigation, don-
keys doing the work, women cleaning gray clothes in
the Nile. Desert ramparts to the east, at spots sending
sand fingers—no longer swept away by the annual
flood—across the fields to the shore itself. Moslem
tombs of stone and mud brick coast by as we lounge
on the top deck, peering at the madly waving children
through our binoculars, across a chasm of time.

There are about fifty aboard a ship with a capacity
of a hundred, so there is plenty of room and service
as we sweep serenely on, music flooding the deck,
cutting between slabs of antiquity; not quite decadent,
just intelligently sybaritic. (Why so few tourists?
Guide guesses people are afraid of the Quarthex.
Joanna gets jittery around them, but I don't know if
it's only her old fears surfacing again.)

The spindly, ethereal minarets are often the only
grace note in the mud brick villages, like a lovely idea
trying to rise out of brown, mottled chaos. Animal
power is used wherever possible. Still, the villages are
quiet at night.

The flip side of this peacefulness must be boredom. That explains a lot of history and its rabid faiths, unfortunately.

DEC. 10

Civilization thins steadily as we steam upriver. The mud brick villages typically have no electricity; there is ample power from Aswan, but the power lines and stations are too expensive. One would think that, with the Quarthex gold, they could do better now.

Our guide says the Quarthex have been very hard-nosed—no pun intended—about such improvements. They will not let the earnings from their patents be used to modernize Egypt. Feeding the poor, cleaning the Nile, rebuilding monuments—all fine (in fact, they pay handsomely for restoring projects). But better electricity—no. A flat no.

We landed at a scruffy town and took a bus into the western desert. Only a kilometer from the flat flood-plain, the Sahara is utterly barren and forbidding. We visited a Ptolemaic city of the dead. One tomb has a mummy of a girl who drowned trying to cross the Nile and see her lover, the hieroglyphs say. Nearby are catacombs of mummified baboons and ibises, symbols of wisdom.

A tunnel begins here, pointing SE toward Akhena-ton's capital city. The German discoverers in the last century followed it for forty kilometers—all cut through limestone, a gigantic task—before turning back because of bad air.

What was it for? Nobody knows. Dry, spooky atmo-sphere. Urns of dessicated mummies, undisturbed. To duck down a side corridor is to step into mystery.

I left the tour group and ambled over a low hill—
to take a pee, actually. To the west was sand, sand,
sand. I was standing there, doing my bit to hold off
the dryness, when I saw one of those big black con-
traptions come slipping over the far horizon.
Chuffing, chugging, and laying what looked like pipe
—a funny kind of pipe, all silvery, with blue facets
running through it. The glittering shifted, changing to
yellows and reds while I watched.

A Quarthex riding atop it, of course. It ran due
south, roughly parallel to the Nile. When I got back
and told Joanna about it she looked at the map and
we couldn't figure what would be out there of interest
to anybody, even a Quarthex. No ruins around. Nothing. Funny.

DEC. 11

Beni Hassan, a nearly deserted site near the Nile. A
steep walk up the escarpment of the eastern desert,
after crossing the rich flood plain by donkey. The rock
tombs have fine drawings and some statues—still left
because they were cut directly from the mountain and
have thick wedges securing them to it. Guess the
ancients would steal anything not nailed down. One
thing about the Quarthex, the guide says: they take
nothing. They seem genuinely interested in restoring,
not in carting artifacts back home to their neck of the
galactic spiral arm.

Up-river, we landfall beside a vast dust plain, which
we cross in a cart pulled by a tractor. The mud brick
palaces of Akhenaton have vanished, except for a bit
of Nefertiti's palace, where the famous bust of her was
found. The royal tombs in the mountain above are

defaced—big chunks pulled out of the walls by the priests who undercut Akhenaton's monotheist revolution, after his death.

The wall carvings are very realistic and warm; the women even have nipples. The tunnel from yesterday probably runs under here, perhaps connecting with the passageways we see deep in the king's grave shafts. Again, nobody's explored them thoroughly. There are narrow sections, possibly warrens for snakes or scorpions, maybe even traps.

While Joanna and I are ambling around, taking a few snaps of the carvings, I hear a rustle. Joanna has the flashlight and we peer over a ledge, down a straight shaft. At the bottom something is moving, something big.

It takes a minute to see that the reddish shell isn't a sarcophagus at all, but the back of a Quarthex. It's planting sucker-like things to the walls, threading cables through them. I can see more of the stuff further back in the shadows.

The Quarthex looks up, into our flashlight beam, and scuttles away. Exploring the tunnels? But why did it move away so fast? What's to hide?

DEC. 12

Cruise all day and watch the shore slide by.

Joanna is right; I needed this vacation a great deal. I can see that, rereading this journal—it gets looser as I go along.

As do I. When I consider how my life is spent, ere half my days, in this dark world and wide . . .

The pell-mell of university life dulls my sense of wonder, of simple pleasures simply taken. The Nile has a flowing, infinite quality, free of time. I can *feel* what it was like to live here, part of a great celestial clock that brought the perpetually turning sun and moon, the perennial rhythm of the flood. Aswan has interrupted the ebb and flow of the waters, but the steady force of the Nile rolls on.

> Heaven smiles, and faiths and empires gleam,
> Like wrecks of a dissolving dream.

The peacefulness permeates everything. Last night, making love to Joanna, was the best ever. Magnifique!

(And I know you're reading this, Joanna—I saw you sneak it out of the suitcase yesterday! Well, it *was* the best—quite a tribute, after all these years. And there's tomorrow and tomorrow . . .)

> He who bends to himself a joy
> Does the winged life destroy;
> But he who kisses the joy as it flies
> Lives in eternity's sunrise.

Perhaps next term I shall request the Romantic Poets course. Or even write a few stanzas myself . . .

Three Quarthex flew overhead today, carrying what look like ancient ram's-head statues. The guide says statues were moved around a lot by the Arabs, and of course the archeologists. The Quarthex have negotiated permission to take many of them back to their rightful places, if known.

DEC. 13

Landfall at Abydos—a limestone temple miraculously preserved, its thick roof intact. Clusters of scruffy mud huts surround it, but do not diminish its obdurate rectangular severity.

The famous list of Pharaohs, chiseled in a side corridor, is impressive in its sweep of time. Each little entry was a lordly Pharaoh, and there is a whole wall jammed full of them. Egypt lasted longer than any comparable society, and the mass of names on that wall is even more impressive, since the temple builders did not even give it the importance of a central location.

The list omits Hatchepsut, a mere woman, and Akhenaton the scandalous monotheist. Rameses II had all carvings here cut deeply, particularly on the immense columns, to forestall defacement—a possibility he was much aware of, since he was busily doing it to his ancestors' temples. He chiseled away earlier work, adding his own cartouches, apparently thinking he could fool the gods themselves into believing he had built them all himself. Ah, immortality.

Had an earthquake today.

We were on the ship, Joanna dutifully padding back and forth on the main deck to work off the opulent lunch. We saw the palms waving ashore, and damned if there wasn't a small shockwave in the water, going east to west, and then a kind of low grumbling from the east. Guide says he's never seen anything like it.

And tonight, sheets of ruby light rising up from both east and west. Looked like an aurora, only the wrong directions. The rippling aura changed colors as it rose, then met overhead, burst into gold, and died. I'd swear I heard a high, keening note sound as the burnt-gold line flared and faded, flared and faded, spanning the sky.

Not many people on deck, though, so it didn't cause

much comment. Joanna's theory is, it was a rocket exhaust.

An engineer says it looks like something to do with magnetic fields. I'm no scientist, but it seems to me whatever the Quarthex want to do, they can. Lords of space/time, they called themselves in the diplomatic ceremonies. The United Nations representatives wrote that off as hyperbole, but the Quarthex may mean it.

DEC. 14

Dendera. A vast temple, much less well-known than Karnak, but quite as impressive. Quarthex there, digging at the foundations. Guide says they're looking for some secret passageways, maybe. The Egyptian gov't. is letting them do what they damn well please.

On the way back to the ship, we passed a whole mass of people, hundreds, all dressed in costumes. I thought it was some sort of pageant or tourist foolery, but the guide frowned, saying he didn't know what to make of it.

The mob was chanting something even the guide couldn't make out. He said the rough-cut cloth was typical of the old ways, made on crude spinning wheels. The procession was ragged, but seemed headed for the temple. They looked drunk to me.

The guide tells me that the ancients had a theology based on the Nile. This country is essentially ten kilometers wide and seven hundred kilometers long, a narrow band of livable earth pressed between two deadly deserts. So they believed the gods must have intended it, and that the Nile was the center of the whole damned world.

The sun came from the east, meaning that's where things began. Ending—dying—happened in the west, where the sun went. Thus they buried their dead on the west side of the Nile, even 7,000 years ago. At night, the sun swung below and lit the underworld, where everybody went finally. Kind of comforting, thinking of the sun doing duty like that for the dead. Only the virtuous dead, though. If you didn't follow the rules . . .

> Some are born to sweet delight,
> Some are born to endless night.

Their world was neatly bisected by the great river, and they loved clean divisions. They invented the 24-hour day but, loving symmetry, split it in half. Each of the 12 daylight hours was longer in summer than in winter—and, for night, vice versa. They built an entire nation-state, an immortal hand or eye, framing such fearful symmetry.

On to Karnak itself, mooring at Luxor. The middle and late Pharaohs couldn't afford the labor investment for pyramids, so they contented themselves with additions to the huge sprawl at Karnak.

I wonder how long it will be before someone rich notices that for a few million or so he could build a tomb bigger than the Great Pyramid. It would only take a million or so limestone blocks—or much better, granite—and could be better isolated and protected. If you can't conquer a continent or scribble a symphony, pile up a great stack of stones.

> L'éternité,
> ne fut jamais perdue.

The light show tonight at Karnak was spooky at times, and beautiful, with booming voices coming right out of the stones. Saw a Quarthex in the crowd. It stared straight ahead, not noticing anybody but not bumping into any humans, either.

It looked enthralled. The beady eyes, all four, scanned the shifting blues and burnt-oranges that played along the rising columns, the tumbled great statues. Its lubricating fluids made shiny reflections as it articulated forward, clacking in the dry night air. Somehow it was almost reverential. Rearing above the crowd, unmoving for long moments, it seemed more like the giant frozen figures in stone than like the mere mortals who swarmed around it, keeping a respectful distance, muttering to themselves.

Unnerving, somehow, to see—

     . . . a subtler Sphinx renew
    Riddles of death Thebes never knew.

DEC. 15

A big day. The Valleys of the Queens, the Nobles, and finally of the Kings. Whew! All are dry washes (wadis), obviously easy to guard and isolate. Nonetheless, all of the 62 known tombs except Tut's were rifled, probably within a few centuries of burial. It must've been an inside job.

There is speculation that the robbing became a needed part of the economy, recycling the wealth, and providing gaudy displays for the next Pharaoh to show off at *his* funeral, all the better to keep impressing the peasants. Just another part of the socio-economic machine, folks.

Later priests collected the Pharaoh mummies and

hid them in a cave nearby, realizing they couldn't protect the tombs. Preservation of Tuthmosis III is excellent. His hook-nosed mummy has been returned to its tomb—a big, deep thing, larger than our apartment, several floors in all, connected by ramps, with side treasuries, galleries, etc. The inscription above reads,

> You shall live again forever.

All picked clean, of course, except for the sarcophagus, too heavy to carry away. The pyramids had portcullises, deadfalls, pitfalls, and rolling stones to crush the unwary robber, but there are few here. Still, it's a little creepy to think of all those ancient engineers planning to commit murder in the future, long after they themselves are gone, all to protect the past. Death, be not proud.

An afternoon of shopping in the bazaar. The old Victorian hotel on the river is atmospheric, but has few guests. Food continues good. No dysentery, either. We both took the EZ-Di bacteria before we left, so it's living down in our tracts, festering away, lying in wait for any ugly foreign bug. Comforting.

DEC. 16

Cruise on. We stop at Kom Ombo, a temple to the crocodile god, Sebek, built to placate the crocs who swarmed in the river nearby. (The Nile is cleared of them now, unfortunately; they would've added some zest to the cruise. . . .) A small room contains 98 mummified crocs, stacked like cordwood.

Cruised some more. A few km. south, there were

gangs of Egyptians working beside the river. Hauling blocks of granite down to the water, rolling them on logs. I stood on the deck, trying to figure out why they were using ropes and simple pulleys, and no powered machinery.

Then I saw a Quarthex near the top of the rise, where the blocks were being sawed out of the rock face. It reared up over the men, gesturing with those jerky arms, eyes glittering. It called out something in a halfway human voice, only in a language I didn't know. The guide came over, frowning, but he couldn't understand it, either.

The laborers were pulling ropes across ruts in the stone, feeding sand and water into the gap, cutting out blocks by sheer brute abrasion. It must take weeks to extract one at that rate! Further along, others drove wooden planks down into the deep grooves, hammering them with crude wooden mallets. Then they poured water over the planks, and we could hear the stone pop open as the wood expanded, far down in the cut.

"That's the way the ancients did it," the guide said kind of quietly. The Quarthex towered above the human teams, that jangling, harsh voice booming out over the water, each syllable lingering until the next joined it, blending in the dry air, hollow and ringing and remorseless.

(note added later)

Stopped at Edfu, a well preserved temple, buried 100 feet deep by Moslem garbage until the late nineteenth century. The best aspect of river cruising is pulling along a site, viewing it from the angles the river affords, and then stepping from your stateroom directly into antiquity, with nothing to intervene and break the mood.

Trouble is, this time a man in front of us goes off a way to photograph the ship, and suddenly something is rushing at him out of the weeds and the crew is yelling—it's a crocodile! The guy drops his camera and bolts.

The croc looks at all of us, snorts, and waddles back into the Nile. The guide is upset, maybe even more than the fellow who almost got turned into a free lunch. Who would introduce crocs back into the Nile?

DEC. 17

Aswan. A clean, delightful town. The big dam just south of town is impressive, with its monument to Soviet excellence, etc. A hollow joke, considering how poor the USSR is today. They could use a loan from Egypt!

The unforeseen side effects, though—rising water table bringing more insects, rotting away the carvings in the temples, rapid silting up inside the dam itself, etc.—are getting important. They plan to dig a canal and drain a lot of the incoming new silt into the desert, make a huge farming valley with it, but I don't see how they can drain enough water to carry the dirt, and still leave much behind in the original dam.

The guide says they're having trouble with it.

We then fly south, to Abu Simbel. Lake Nasser, which claimed the original site of the huge monuments, is hundreds of miles long. They enlarged it again in 2008.

In the times of the Pharaohs, the land below these waters held villages, great quarries for the construction of monuments, trade routes south to the Nubian king-doms. Now it's all under water.

They did save the enormous temples to Rameses II —built to impress aggressive Nubians with his might and majesty—and to his queen, Nefertari. The colos-sal statues of Rameses II seem personifications of his egomania. Inside, carvings show him performing *all* the valiant tasks in the great battle with the Hittites —slaying, taking prisoners, then presenting them to himself, who is in turn advised by the gods—which include himself! All this, for a battle which was in fact an iffy draw. Both temples have been lifted about a hundred feet and set back inside a wholly artificial hill, supported inside by the largest concrete dome in the world. Amazing.

"Look upon my works, ye Mighty, and despair!"

Except that when Shelley wrote *Ozymandias*, he'd never seen Rameses II's image so well preserved.

Leaving the site, eating the sand blown into our faces by a sudden gust of wind, I caught sight of a Quarthex. It was burrowing into the sand, using a silvery tool that spat ruby-colored light. Beside it, floating on a platform, were some of those funny pipe-like things I'd seen days before. Only this time men and women were helping it, lugging stuff around to put into the holes the Quarthex dug.

The people looked dazed, like they were sleep-walk-ing. I waved a greeting, but nobody even looked up. Except the Quarthex. They're expressionless, of course. Still, those glittering popeyes peered at me for a long moment, with the little feelers near its mouth twitching with a kind of anxious energy.

I looked away. I couldn't help but feel a little spooked by it. It wasn't looking at us in a friendly way. Maybe it didn't want me yelling at its work gang.

Then we flew back to Aswan, above the impossibly narrow ribbon of green that snakes through absolute bitter desolation.

DEC. 18

I'm writing this at twilight, before the light gives out. We got up this morning and were walking into town when the whole damn ground started to rock. Mud huts slamming down, waves on the Nile, everything.

Got back to the ship but nobody knew what was going on. Not much on the radio. Cairo came in clear, saying there'd been a quake all right, all along the Nile.

Funny thing was, the captain couldn't raise any other radio station. Just Cairo. Nothing else in the whole Middle East.

Some other passengers think there's a war on. Maybe so, but the Egyptian army doesn't know about it. They're standing around, all along the quay, fondling their AK 47s, looking just as puzzled as we are.

More rumblings and shakings in the afternoon. And now that the sun's about gone, I can see big sheets of light in the sky. Only it seems to me the constellations aren't right.

Joanna took some of her pills. She's trying to fend off the jitters and I do what I can. I hate the hollow look that comes into her eyes.

We've got to get the hell out of here.

DEC. 19

I might as well write this down, there's nothing else to do.

When we got up this morning the sun was there all right, but the moon hadn't gone down. And it didn't, all day.

Sure, they can both be in the sky at the same time. But all day? Joanna is worried, not because of the moon, but because all the airline flights have been cancelled. We were supposed to go back to Cairo today.

More earthquakes. Really bad this time.

At noon, all of a sudden, there were Quarthex everywhere. In the air, swarming in from the east and west. Some splashed down in the Nile—and didn't come up. Others zoomed overhead, heading south toward the dam.

Nobody's been brave enough to leave the ship—including me. Hell, I just want to go home. Joanna's staying in the cabin.

About an hour later, a swarthy man in a ragged gray suit comes running along the quay and says the dam's gone. Just *gone*. The Quarthex formed little knots above it, and there was a lot of purple, flashing light and big crackling noises, and then the dam just disappeared.

But the water hasn't come pouring down on us here. The man says it ran *back the other way*. South.

I looked over the rail. The Nile was flowing north.

Late this afternoon, five of the crew went into town. By this time there were fingers of orange and gold zapping across the sky all the time, making weird designs. The clouds would come rolling in from the north, and these radiant beams would hit them, and they'd *split* the clouds, just like that. With a spray of ivory light.

And Quarthex, buzzing everywhere. There's a kind of high sheen, up above the clouds, like a metal boundary or something, but you can see through it.

Quarthex keep zipping up to it, sometimes coming right up out of the Nile itself, just splashing out, then zooming up until they're little dwindling dots. They spin around up there, as if they're inspecting it, and then they drop like bricks, and splash down in the Nile again. Like frantic bees, Joanna said, and her voice trembled.

A technical type on board, an engineer from Rockwell, says *he* thinks the Quarthex are putting on one hell of a light show. Just a weird alien stunt, he thinks.

While I was writing this, the five crewmen returned from Aswan. They'd gone to the big hotels there, and then to police headquarters. They heard that TV from Cairo went out two days ago. All air flights have been grounded because of the Quarthex buzzing around and the odd lights and so on.

Or at least, that's the official line. The Captain says his cousin told him that several flights *did* take off two days back, and they hit something up there. Maybe that blue metallic sheen?

One crashed. The others landed, although damaged.

The authorities are keeping it quiet. They're not just keeping us tourists in the dark—they're playing mum with everybody.

I hope the engineer is right. Joanna is fretting and we hardly ate anything for dinner, just picked at the cold lamb. Maybe tomorrow will settle things.

DEC. 20

It did. When we woke, the Earth was rising.

It was coming up from the western mountains, blue-white clouds and patches of green and brown, but mostly tawny desert. We're looking west, across the Sahara. I'm writing this while everybody else is running around like a chicken with his head chopped off. I'm sitting on deck, listening to shouts and wild traffic and even some gunshots coming from ashore.

I can see further east now—either we're turning, or we're rising fast and can see with a better perspective.

Where central Egypt was, there's a big, raw, dark hole.

The black must be the limestone underlying the desert. They've scraped off a rim of sandy margin enclosing the Nile valley, including us—and left the rest. And somehow, they're lifting it free of Earth.

No Quarthex flying around now. Nothing visible except that metallic blue smear of light high up in the air.

And beyond it—Earth, rising.

DEC. 22

I skipped a day.

There was no time to even think yesterday. After I wrote the last entry, a crowd of Egyptians came down the quay, shuffling silently along, like the ones we saw back at Abu Simbel. Only there were thousands.

And leading them was a Quarthex. It carried a big disk-like thing that made a humming sound. When the Quarthex lifted it, the pitch changed.

It made my eyes water, my skull ache. Like a hand squeezing my head, blurring the air.

Around me, everybody was writhing on the deck, moaning. Joanna, too.

By the time the Quarthex reached our ship I was the only one standing. Those yellow-shot, jittery eyes peered at me, giving nothing away. Then the angular head turned and went on. Pied piper, leading long trains of Egyptians.

Some of our friends from the ship joined at the end of the lines. Rigid, glassy-eyed faces. I shouted, but nobody, not a single person in that procession, even looked up.

Joanna struggled to go with them. I threw her down and held her until the damned eerie parade was long past.

Now the ship's deserted. We've stayed aboard, out of pure fear.

Whatever the Quarthex did affects all but a few percent of those within range. A few crew stayed aboard, dazed but ok. Scared, hard to talk to.

Fewer at dinner.

The next morning, nobody.

We had to scavenge for food. The crew must've taken what was left aboard. I ventured into the market street nearby, but everything was closed up. Deserted. Only a few days ago we were buying caftans and alabaster sphinxes and beaten-bronze trinkets in the gaudy shops, and now it was stone cold dead. Not a sound, not a stray cat.

I went around to the back of what I remembered was a filthy corner cafe. I'd turned up my nose at it while we were shopping, certain there was a sure case of dysentery waiting inside . . . but now I was glad to find some days-old fruits and vegetables in a cabinet.

Coming back, I nearly ran into a bunch of Egyptian

men who were marching through the streets. Spooks.

They had the look of police, but were dressed up like Mardi Gras—loincloths, big leather belts, bangles and beads, hair stiffened with wax. They carried sharp spears.

Good thing I was jumpy, or they'd have run right into me. I heard them coming and ducked into a grubby alley. They were systematically combing the area, searching the miserable apartments above the market. The honcho barked orders in a language I didn't understand—harsh, guttural, not like Egyptian.

I slipped away. Barely.

We kept out of sight after that. Stayed below deck and waited for nightfall.

Not that the darkness made us feel any better. There were fires ashore. Not in Aswan itself—the town was utterly black. Instead, orange dots sprinkled the distant hillsides. They were all over the scrub desert, just before the ramparts of the real desert that stretches—or did stretch—to east and west.

Now, I guess, there's only a few dozen miles of desert, before you reach—what?

I can't discuss this with Joanna. She has that haunted expression, from the time before her breakdown. She is drawn and silent. Stays in the room.

We ate our goddamn vegetables. Now we go to bed.

DEC. 23

There were more of those patrols of Mardi Gras spooks today. They came along the quay, looking at the tour ships moored there, but for some reason they didn't come aboard.

We're alone on the ship. All the crew, the other tourists—all gone.

Around noon, when we were getting really hungry and I was mustering my courage to go back to the market street, I heard a roaring.

Understand, I hadn't heard an airplane in days. And those were jets. This buzzing, I suddenly realized, is a rocket or something, and it's in trouble.

I go out on the deck, checking first to see if the patrols are lurking around, and the roaring is louder. It's a plane with stubby little wings, coming along low over the water, burping and hacking and finally going dead quiet.

It nosed over and came in for a big splash. I thought the pilot was a goner, but the thing rode steady in the water for a while and the cockpit folded back and out jumps a man.

I yelled at him and he waved and swam for the ship. The plane sank.

He caught a line below and climbed up. An American, no less. But what he had to say was even more surprising.

He wasn't just some sky jockey from Cairo. He was an astronaut.

He was part of a rescue mission, sent up to try to stop the Quarthex. The others he'd lost contact with, although it looked like they'd all been drawn down toward the floating island that Egypt has become.

We're suspended about two Earth radii out, in a slowly widening orbit. There's a shield over us, keeping the air in and everything—cosmic rays, communications, spaceships—out.

The Quarthex somehow ripped off a layer of Egypt and are lifting it free of Earth, escaping with it. Nobody had ever guessed they had such power. Nobody Earthside knows what to do about it. The Quarthex who were outside Egypt at the time just lifted off in their ships and rendezvoused with this floating platform.

Ralph Blanchard is his name, and his mission was to fly under the slab of Egypt, in a fast orbital craft. He was supposed to see how they'd ripped the land free. A lot of it had fallen away.

There are silvery pods under the soil, he says—must be enormous anti-grav units. The same kind that make the Quarthex ships fly, that we've been trying to get the secret of.

The pods are about a mile apart, making a grid. But between them, there are lots of Quarthex. They're building stuff, tilling soil and so on—upside down! The gravity works opposite on the underside. That must be the way the whole thing is kept together— compressing it with artificial gravity from both sides. God knows what makes the shield above.

But the really strange thing is the Nile. There's one on the underside, too.

It starts at the underside of Alexandria, where *our* Nile meets—met—the Mediterranean. It then flows back, all the way along the underside, running through a Nile valley of its own. Then it turns up and around the edge of the slab, and comes over the lip of it a few hundred miles upstream of here.

The Quarthex have drained the region beyond the Aswan dam. Now the Nile flows in its old course. The big temples of Rameses II are perched on a hill high above the river, and Ralph was sure he saw Quarthex working on the site, taking it apart.

He thinks they're going to put it back where it was, before the dam was built in the 1960s.

Ralph was supposed to return to Orbital City with

his data. He came in close for a final pass and hit the shield, the one that keeps the air in. His ship was damaged.

He'd been issued a suborbital craft, able to do re-entries, in case he could penetrate the airspace. That saved him. There were other guys who hit the shield and cracked through, guys with conventional deep-space shuttle tugs and the like, and they fell like bricks.

We've talked all this over but no one has a good theory of what is going on. The best we can do is stay away from the patrols.

Meanwhile, Joanna scavenged through obscure bins of the ship, and turned up an entire case of Skivaa, a cheap Egyptian beer. So after I finish this ritual entry —who knows, this might be in a history book some-day, and as a good academic I should keep it up—I'll go share it out in one grand bust with Ralph and Joanna. It'll do her good. It'll do us both good. She's been rocky. As well,

> Malt does more than Milton can
> To justify God's ways to man.

DEC. 24

This little diary was all I managed to take with us when the spooks came. I had it in my pocket.

I keep going over what happened. There was nothing I could do, I'm sure of that, and yet . . .

We stayed below decks, getting hungry again but afraid to go out. There was chanting from the distance. Getting louder. Then footsteps aboard. We retreated to the small cabins aft, third class.

The sounds got nearer. Ralph thought we should stand and fight but I'd seen those spears and hell, I'm a middle-aged man, no match for those maniacs.

Joanna got scared. It was like her breakdown. No, worse. The jitters built until her whole body seemed to vibrate, fingers digging into her hair like claws, eyes squeezed tight, face compressed as if to shut out the world.

There was nothing I could do with her, she wouldn't keep quiet. She ran out of the cabin we were hiding in, just rushed down the corridor screaming at them.

Ralph said we should use her diversion to get away and I said I'd stay, help her, but then I saw them grab her and hold her, not rough. It didn't seem as if they were going to do anything, just take her away.

My fear got the better of me then. It's hard to write this. Part of me says I should've stayed, defended her —but it was hopeless. You can't live up to your ideal self. The world of literature shows people summoning up courage, but there's a thin line between that and stupidity. Or so I tell myself.

The spooks hadn't seen us yet, so we slipped overboard, keeping quiet.

We went off the loading ramp on the river side, away from shore. Ralph paddled around to see the quay and came back looking worried. There were spooks swarming all over.

We had to move. The only way to go was across the river.

This shaky handwriting is from sheer, flat-out fatigue. I swam what seemed like forever. The water wasn't bad, pretty warm, but the current kept pushing us off course. Lucky thing the Nile is pretty narrow there, and there are rocky little stubs sticking out. I grabbed onto those and rested.

Nobody saw us, or at least they didn't do anything about it.

We got ashore looking like drowned rats. There's a big hill there, covered with ancient rock-cut tombs. I thought of taking shelter in one of them and started up the hill, legs wobbly under me, and then we saw a mob up top.

And a Quarthex, a big one with a shiny shell. It wore something over its head. Supposedly Quarthex don't wear clothes, but this one had a funny rig on. A big bird head, with a long narrow beak and flinty black eyes.

There was madness all around us. Long lines of people carrying burdens, chanting. Quarthex riding on those lifter units of theirs. All beneath the piercing, biting sun.

We hid for a while. I found this diary, in its zippered leather case, made it through the river without a leak. I started writing this entry. Joanna said once that I'd retreated into books as a defense, in adolescence—she was full of psychoanalytical explanations, it was a hobby. She kept thinking that if she could figure herself out, things would be all right. Well, maybe I did use words and books and a quiet, orderly life as a place to hide. So what? It was better than this "real" world around me right now.

I thought of Joanna and what might be happening to her. The Quar

new entry

I was writing when the Quarthex came closer. I thought we were finished, but they didn't see us.

Those huge heads turned all the time, the glittering black eyes scanning. Then they moved away. The chanting was a relentless, sing-song drone that gradually faded.

We got away from there, fast.

I'm writing this during a short break. Then we'll go on.

No place to go but the goddamn desert.

DEC. 25

Christmas.

I keep thinking about fat turkey stuffed with spicy dressing, crisp cranberries, a dry white wine, thick gravy—

No point in that. We found some food today in an abandoned construction site, bread at least a week old and some dried-up fruit. That was all.

Ralph kept pushing me on west. He wants to see over the edge, how they hold this thing together.

I'm not that damn interested, but I don't know where else to go. Just running on blind fear. My professorial instincts—like keeping this journal. It helps keep me sane. Assuming I still am.

Ralph says putting this down might have scientific value. If I can even get it to anybody outside. So I keep on. Words, words, words. Much cleaner than this gritty, surreal world.

We saw people marching in the distance, dressed in loincloths again. It suddenly struck me that I'd seen that clothing before—in those marvelous wall paintings, in the tombs of the Valley of Kings. It's ancient dress.

Ralph thinks he understands what's happening. There was an all-frequencies broadcast from the Quarthex when they tore off this wedge we're on. Nobody understood much—it was in that odd semispeech of theirs, all the words blurred and placed wrong, scrambled up. Something about their mission or destiny or whatever being to enhance the best in each world. About how they'd made a deal with the Egyptians to bring forth the unrealized promise of their majestic past and so on. And that meant isolation, so the fruit of ages could flower.

Ha. The world's great age begins anew, maybe— but Percy Bysshe Shelley never meant it like this.

Not that I care a lot about motivations right now. I spent the day thinking of Joanna, still feeling guilty. And hiking west in the heat and dust, hiding from gangs of glassy-eyed workers when we had to.

We reached the edge at sunset. It hadn't occurred to me, but it's obvious—for there to be days and nights at all means they're spinning the slab we're on.

Compressing it, holding in the air, adding just the right rotation. Masters—of space/time and the river, yes.

The ground started to slope away. Not like going downhill, because there was nothing pulling you down the face of it. I mean, we *felt* like we were walking on level ground. But overhead the sky moved as we walked.

We caught up with the sunset. The sun dropped for a while in late afternoon, then started rising again. Pretty soon it was right overhead, high noon.

And we could see Earth, too, farther away than yesterday. Looking cool and blue.

We came to a wall of glistening metal tubes, silvery

and rippling with a frosty blue glow. I started to get woozy as we approached. Something happened to gravity—it pulled your stomach as if you were spinning around. Finally we couldn't get any closer. I stopped, nauseated. Ralph kept on. I watched him try to walk toward the metal barrier, which by then looked like luminous icebergs suspended above barren desert.

He tried to walk a straight line, he said later. I could see him veer, his legs rubbery, and it looked as though he rippled and distended, stretching horizontally while some force compressed him vertically, an egg man, a plastic body swaying in tides of gravity.

Then he started stumbling, falling. He cried out— a horrible, warped sound, like paper tearing for a long, long time. He fled. The sand clawed at him as he ran, strands grasping at his feet, trailing long streamers of glittering, luminous sand—but it couldn't hold him. Ralph staggered away, gasping, his eyes huge and white and terrified.

We turned back.

But coming away, I saw a band of men and women marching woodenly along toward the wall. They were old, most of them, and diseased. Some had been hurt —you could see the wounds.

They were heading straight for the lip. Silent, inexorable.

Ralph and I followed them for a while. As they approached, they started walking up off the sand— right into the air.

And over the tubes.

Just flying.

We decided to head south. Maybe the lip is different there. Ralph says the plan he'd heard, after the generals had studied the survey-mission results, was to try to open the shield at the ground, where the Nile spills over. Then they'd get people out by boating them along the river.

Could they be doing that, now? We hear roaring sounds in the sky sometimes. Explosions. Ralph is ironic about it all, says he wonders when the Quarthex will get tired of intruders and go back to the source —*all* the way back.

I don't know. I'm tired and worn down.

Could there be a way out? Sounds impossible, but it's all we've got.

Head south, to the Nile's edge.

We're hiding in a cave tonight. It's bitterly cold out here in the desert, and a sunburn is no help.

I'm hungry as hell. Some Christmas.

We were supposed to be back in Laguna Beach by now.

God knows where Joanna is.

DEC. 26

I got away. Barely.

The Quarthex work in teams now. They've gridded off the desert and work across it systematically in those floating platforms. There are big tubes like cannon mounted on each end and a Quarthex scans it over the sands.

Ralph and I crept up to the mouth of the cave we were in and watched them comb the area. They worked out from the Nile. When a muzzle turned toward us I felt an impact like a warm, moist wave smacking into my face, like being in the ocean. It drove me to my knees. I reeled away. Threw myself further back into the cramped cave.

It all dropped away then, as if the wave pinned me to the ocean floor and filled my lungs with a sluggish liquid.

And in an instant was gone. I rolled over, gasping, and saw Ralph staggering into the sunlight, heading for the Quarthex platform. The projector was leveled at him so that it no longer struck the cave mouth. So I'd been released from its grip.

I watched them lower a rope ladder. Ralph dutifully climbed up. I wanted to shout to him, try to break the hold that thing had over him, but again the better part of valor and all that. I just watched. They carried him away.

I waited until twilight to move. Not having anybody to talk to makes it harder to control my fear.

God I'm hungry. Couldn't find a scrap to eat.

When I took out this diary I looked at the leather case and remembered stories of people getting so starved they'd eat their shoes. Suitably boiled and salted, of course, with a tangy sauce.

Another day or two and the idea might not seem so funny.

I've got to keep moving.

DEC. 27

Hard to write.

They got me this morning.

It grabs your mind. Like before. Squeezing in your head.

But after a while it is better. Feels good. But a buzzing all the time, you can't think.

Picked me up while I was crossing an arroyo. Didn't have any idea they were around. A platform.

Took me to some others. All Egyptians. Caught like me.

Marched us to the Nile.

Plenty to eat.

Rested at noon.

Brought Joanna to me. She is all right. Lovely in the long draping dress the Quarthex gave her.

All around are the bird-headed ones. Ibis, I remember, the bird of the Nile. And dog-headed ones. Lion-headed ones.

Gods of the old times. The Quarthex are the gods of the old time. Of the great empire.

We are the people.

Sometimes I can think, like now. They sent me away from the work gang on an errand. I am old, not strong. They are kind—give me easy jobs.

So I came to here. Where I hid this diary. Before they took my old uncomfortable clothes I put this little book into a crevice in the rock. Pen too.

Now as I write it helps. My mind clears some.

I saw Ralph, then lost track of him. I worked hard after the noontime. Sun felt good. I lifted pots, carried them where the foreman said.

The Quarthex-god with ibis head is building a fresh temple. Made from the stones of Aswan. It will be cool and deep, many pillars.

They took my dirty clothes. Gave me fresh loin-cloth, headband, sandals. Good ones. Better than my old clothes.

It is hard to remember how things were before I came here. Before I knew the river. Its flow. How it divides the world.

I will rest before I try to read what I have written in here before. The words are hard.

DAYS LATER

I come back but can read only a little.

Joanna says You should not. The ibis will not like if I do.

I remember I liked these words on paper, in my days before. I earned my food with them. Now they are empty. Must not have been true.

Do not need them any more.

Ralph, science. All words too.

LATER

Days since I find this again. I do the good work, I eat, Joanna is there in the night. Many things. I do not want to do this reading.

But today another thing howled overhead. It passed over the desert like a screaming black bird, the falcon, and then fell, flames, big roar.

I remembered Ralph.

This book I remembered, came for it.

The ibis-god speaks to us each sunset. Of how the glory of our lives is here again. We are one people once more again yes after a long long time of being lost.

What the red sunset means. The place where the dead are buried in the western desert. To be taken in death close to the edge, so the dead will walk their last steps in this world, to the lip and over, to the netherworld.

There the lion-god will preserve them. Make them live again.

The Quarthex-gods have discovered how to revive

the dead of any beings. They spread this among the stars.

But only to those who understand. Who deserve. Who bow to the great symmetry of life.

One face light, one face dark.

The sun lights the netherworld when for us it is night. There the dead feast and mate and laugh and live forever.

Ralph saw that. The happy land below. It shares the sun.

I saw Ralph today. He came to the river to see the falcon thing cry from the clouds. We all did.

It fell into the river and was swallowed and will be taken to the netherworld where it flows over the edge of the world.

Ralph was sorry when the falcon fell. He said it was a mistake to send it to bother us. That someone from the old dead time had sent it.

Ralph works in the quarry. Carving the limestone. He looks good, the sun has lain on him and made him strong and brown.

I started to talk of the time we met but he frowned.

That was before we understood, he says. Shook his head. So I should not speak of it.

The gods know of time and the river. They know.

I tire now.

AGAIN

Joanna sick. I try help but no way to stop the bleeding from her.

In old time I would try to stop the stuff of life from leaving her. I would feel sorrow.

I do not now. I am calm.

Ibis-god prepares her. Works hard and good over her.

She will journey tonight. Walk the last trek. Over the edge of the sky and to the netherland.

It is what the temple carving says. She will live again forever.

Forever waits.

I come here to find this book to enter this. I remember sometimes how it was.

I did not know joy then. Joanna did not.

We lived but to no point. Just come-go-come-again.

Now I know what comes. The western death. The rising life.

The Quarthex-gods are right. I should forget that life. To hold on is to die. To flow forward is to live.

Today I saw the Pharaoh. He came in radiant chariot, black horses before, bronze sword in hand. The sun was high above him. No shadow he cast.

Big and with red skin the Pharoah rode down the Avenue of the Kings. We the one people cheered.

His great head was mighty in the sun and his many arms waved in salute to his one people. He is so great the horses groan and sweat to pull him. His hard, gleaming body is all armor for he will always be on guard against our enemies.

Like those who fall from the sky. Every day now more come down, dying fireballs to smash in the desert. All fools. Black rotting bodies. None will rise to walk west. They are only burned prey of the Pharaoh.

The Pharaoh rode three times on the avenue. We threw ourselves down to attract a glance. His huge glaring eyes regarded us and we cried out, our faces wet with joy.

He will speak for us in the netherworld. Sing to the undergods.

Make our westward walking path smooth.

I fall before him.

I bury this now. No more write in it.

This kind of writing is not for the world now. It comes from the old dead time when I knew nothing and thought everything.

I go to my eternity on the river.

Out of My Head

JAMES GUNN

The past decade has seen a huge upsurge of involvement in science fiction on the part of academics, at hundreds of campuses, who are now teaching, researching, and critically analyzing science fiction. Of course science fiction—"the only relevant literature of today," in the words of J. G. Ballard—deserves such attention. Yet cynics might suggest—given the necessity of a doctoral thesis and publication credits, along with the exhaustion of more "traditional" thesis topics—that science fiction has been seized upon as a career lifeline; that the encounter between science fiction and academia is less a passionate tryst than a marriage of convenience.

James Gunn is a different case. As an academic at the University of Kansas he long ago pioneered the teaching of science fiction. His Alternate Worlds: The Illustrated History of Science Fiction *is noteworthy among books on the subject, and his four-volume, million-word* The Road to Science Fiction *is a landmark. Gunn also began practicing the art of science fiction as early as 1949 (in* Startling Stories*). He knows whereof he speaks. He has himself erected some of the major signposts along that road: notably* The Listeners,

about radio contact with extra-terrestrial civilizations;
The Joy Makers; and The Immortals, *which became*
a television movie and later a series. James Gunn's tales
frequently concern organizations in which individuals
are compelled to cooperate. Mix this with the notion
of immortality, and we come up with an inconvenient
but hilarous form of afterlife.

R oddy came out of anesthesia feeling
like a hairy mammoth thawing. Lights overhead were
like splinters of ice, and his head felt as if it had
already been stuffed for display in some natural history
museum. It *was* stuffed, he soon realized, but with
voices—angry, petulant, loud, soft, strident, whiny
voices. And they were arguing.

"Move over! Give someone else a bit of space!"

"Move over yourself. You're the one hogging everything."

"Can't we keep it down in here? We're all in this
together."

"Why doesn't everybody just shut up!"

Yes, Roddy agreed. Everybody shut up!

"Well, I'm not going to shut up until I get my fair
share. Some people are just pigs!"

"Now, it's going to be all right. The change always
makes us edgy."

"Shut up, Grandpa! I'm the one who's got a right
to complain!"

"You! You're the one who got us into this mess!"

"How was I to know the gun was loaded?"

"We all told you: don't fool around with another
man's wife!"

"Who even saw a weapon like that outside a museum!"

"He's an antiquarian, we said. He's got old-fashioned ideas, we told you. Besides which, he's always secretly hated us, we said."

"I mean, after all, this is 2093—"

"Shut up!" Roddy shouted. A passing nurse looked in, shocked, as Roddy sat up alone in his starched, white hospital bed, holding his head between his hands as if they were the jaws of a vise. Nausea churned his stomach and burned the back of his throat.

"That's gross!" a voice complained.

"Somebody's got to do something about this boy. What's his name? Roddy? What kind of name is that?"

"It was his mother's idea."

"Kick his frontal lobe, Sam, you're closest. Teach him to show some respect for his elders."

Sam, Roddy thought confusedly, was his father's name.

"We're all in this together, and we've got to—"

"Shut up, Grandpa!"

"Shut up!" Roddy screamed. "I can't stand it!" And then, as the voices momentarily fell silent, he said, "What are you doing in there?"

The voices all began to speak at once. It was like a Tower of Babel rising up through the top of Roddy's skull.

"One at a time!" Roddy pleaded, holding his head again.

"You speak, Grandpa. You're the oldest."

"That's better," said the voice that Roddy was beginning to identify as Grandpa. "A proper respect for age and wisdom is the beginning of a good relationship."

"Bullshit!" said the voice that kept telling everybody to shut up. The voice seemed painfully familiar.

"You're new at this," Grandpa said patiently, "and you'll just have to learn patience and protocol. Now, Roddy, this first experience is difficult. A partial amnesia is not an uncommon symptom, but memory comes back fast if you let it. Remember?"

Roddy clutched his head and stared up at the glittering ceiling. God help him, he *was* beginning to remember.

It should be understood that Greta was a liberated young woman. At the age of fifteen she had her own conapt, her own income, her own sense of values and her own last name, chosen when she was twelve and changed each month since. Roddy had forgotten her patronym if he ever knew. He had never met Greta's parents. For all he knew she had none. Greta had her own close friends, her own circle of acquaintances and her own way of life.

Roddy understood all that. The problem, as he saw it, was that Greta was not liberated with him. For Greta was beautiful. She had blond hair and blue eyes that opened wide, when she was pleased, to reveal the largest, blackest pupils. But they had never looked that way at Roddy. Instead, ever since they had met at a party, Roddy had deluged Greta with calls and letters, flowers and gifts, and all he got in return was a look from narrowed eyes that said, "You're too young."

"You're too young," she had said that very evening.

"But I'm seventeen," he had protested, "and you're fifteen."

"I'm an old fifteen," she said as if stating an indisputable fact, "and you're a young seventeen."

"That doesn't make sense," he said. They were standing outside her conapt door where he had half-accompanied, half-followed her, from the sensorium concert where they had accidentally (intentionally on his part) met. The door kept murmuring questions that Roddy did not understand because his senses were reeling in a way the sensorium had not achieved. Greta was not only beautiful, she was nubile, and Roddy's skin prickled with passion, and more than a little lust.

"It does to me," she said. "Besides, you probably want to involve me in something serious."

"No, no," he protested. "Nothing like that. Nothing sordid and long-term. Brief ecstasy, that's all."

"Well . . . ," she began.

He did not know whether this was the beginning of surrender or the continuation of refusal, because it was then that a bright light dazzled his eyes and a voice that lacked not only humanity but any trace of compassion asked, "Roddy Wilson?" But the voice already knew the answer, because it belonged to a robot waiting in the glassy street on its plastic treads for an answer that Roddy could not give. Then, in the brief confusion the door had opened and shut and Greta was gone, and his one opportunity to be immortal if only for a few moments was gone with her. He turned on the robot with teenaged fury. "Now see what you've gone and done!" he said with magnificent inarticulateness.

But the robot had already identified him by telltale
i.d. button and features, and an extensible arm shot
out to grab his wrist in its padded fingers. Roddy was
pulled, protesting, to a seat in front of the robot's
vision plate. "Roddy Wilson," it said. "Emergency."

"See here," Roddy said, already being trundled
through the lighted streets toward an unknown destination, " 'a robot may not injure a human being, or,
through inaction . . .' "

"You have not been injured," the robot said, swivel-
ing on its treads at an intersection and heading off at
right angles in a direction that seemed to lead toward
a large, glowing building in the distance.

"You have no idea," Roddy mourned.

Neither did the physician. "We regret the need to
summon you so abruptly," it said, though it was clear
that real regret was not involved, "but your father is
dying. . . ."

"My father?"

". . . and there wasn't time."

Roddy hadn't seen his father for years—except, of
course, for annual inspections and ceremonial occa-
sions. He remembered his father as a tall, forbidding
presence, whose face was sometimes hairy and sometimes not. Roddy preferred it hairy because then he
couldn't see the features that he found so terrifying,
but the change was frightening, too, and he could
never be sure that any bearded stranger might not be
his father. His father was a wealthy and powerful man
who spent his time manipulating other people, and
Roddy had learned that it was better to be forgotten
by such people. Finally he realized that he had his
father mixed up with God. That must have been

about the time his father developed doubts; he would pause as if listening to internal voices.

Roddy had stopped listening to the physician, who was a different kind of robot, all clear plastic and efficient stainless steel. Now he heard the physician say, "There's no hope for recovery. The cerebellum has suffered irreparable damage, and it is only a matter of hours, perhaps minutes, before death occurs. We can keep him alive only until transfer."

"Transfer?" Roddy echoed.

"His body was found in a waste disposal chute, apparently abandoned for dead, but the sensor detected life and rejected the body. With his last conscious breath, Mr. Wilson invoked parental rights."

"Parental rights?" Roddy said.

It was all coming back to him now, the struggle with the come-along robot in the sterile white hallway, the physician's forefinger extended toward him like God's to Adam as Roddy yelled, "I'm too young! I'm only seventeen! I've got my own life to live!" And then the forefinger touched his and brought not life but paralysis. In a strangely detached condition that Roddy associated with death, he watched himself being disrobed, wrapped in a hospital gown, placed on a robot gurney, and rolled down that long white corridor into an operating room whose low ceiling lights were cold and bright.

"It doesn't hurt, you know," the physician said, looming over Roddy as he attached electrodes to his head with a sticky fluid and suction devices. When Roddy's head was turned to the left he saw another gurney beside him. On it was a man with his head wrapped in bandages, his face pale, his eyes closed, tubes leading in and out of his body, an apparatus around his chest doing his breathing for him. A moment later Roddy recognized the face—unhairy now. It was his father, looking shrunken and ungodlike.

No! Roddy protested silently. *I don't want God inside me!* But it was useless. He could neither speak nor move, and the process continued as inexorably as the glaciers. And when the current was turned on it was as if the glaciers had rolled over him, turning the overhead lights into glittering ice crystals that broke into a million shards of darkness descending. . . .

"Out!" Roddy groaned. "Out of my head!"

"Now you remember!" Grandpa said. "And we can't get out. We're in here for good—or for bad, however you make it for yourself."

"Oh, stop pampering the boy," the harsh voice said. Roddy recognized it now. It was his father's voice. It was the voice of God. "I didn't make this much fuss when it happened to me."

"You were sixty when it happened, Sam," Grandpa said, "and there was money involved, a great deal of it."

"And now the boy gets it all—so what?" Sam said.

"That's not so clear, Sam. You're a lawyer, you ought to know that. You may have stranded us without funds. We may have to start all over because of your unorthodox departure."

Another voice broke in, "If you'd just taken care of the succession matter at an appropriate time of life, the boy would be a more suitable age. But no—you didn't want to be bothered."

"Now we have to suffer through adolescence again," said a fourth voice. "It's all your fault, Sam."

"Might as well let up on that," Grandpa said. "We're stuck with each other, and we'd better stick to each other."

"Oh, God!" Sam said. "I can't stand it!"

"And let up on the boy, too," Grandpa said. "He just never had a chance to get used to the idea."

"And I'm not going to get used to it either," Roddy said.

But he did. At least he and the voices managed to work out a method for surviving in concentration-camp circumstances. He began to sort out the voices: his father, of course, he recognized all too well, and Grandpa, who wasn't his grandfather or even his father's grandfather, but Roddy's great-great grandfather, George Wilson, who had been the first member of the family to take advantage of—no, seize upon—the new Loudon process for personality transference. George had persuaded his son, William—persuasion was necessary in those days—to accept the transfer or lose the considerable amount of money that George had accumulated over his lifespan of ninety-five years. By the time William Wilson had reached the latter part of his life—then one hundred and five—he and George, putting their heads together, so to speak, had pyramided William's inheritance into a true fortune, and William's son, John, had not been hard to persuade to accept William/George. Of course John at that time was already ninety and had grown used to the domination of William/George and the financial support that went along with it.

By then a legislature already salted with conglomer-ates, or with those who either had ambitions to start their own successions or had been bought with con-

glomerate-controlled money, had regularized the laws
of personality transfer to accommodate the powerful
gestalts that had already transformed the nature of
society and commerce. It became not only a son's duty
to accept his father's personality (or a daughter, her
mother's) when the exigencies of life called upon him
to do so, but his father's inherited personalities as well.

One result was an upsurge in psychosis, and the
practice of psychiatry soared. This was only a problem
for production controllers, however, since psychiatry
had become entirely computerized. The treatment of
multiple personalities improved markedly. Philoso-
phers developed an ethics of transfer and an ethics of
personality relationships. One of their principles was
that transferred personalities could advise but not
compel. Drugs had been developed to discipline un-
ruly guest personalities, with a final weapon—electro-
shock—held in reserve for the worst offenders. Some
psychologists speculated that schizophrenia and multiple personalities, and perhaps even possession, had
been no more than natural processes mechanized by
Loudon's electronic apparatus.

Some stubborn holdouts, including a number of
human lawyers, insisted that the entire concept was a
hoax, in spite of feats of recall inevitably flawed by
time and sometimes senility. For that reason many
conglomerates contained at least one lawyer. Sam,
Roddy's father, was the Wilsons' legal representative.

All of this had been part of Roddy's ambient world
since his birth, but like all young people he had never
related it to himself. Personality transfer, like old age,
was for people like his father who had already lived
their lives. Roddy was only in the process of discover-
ing what it was all about.

The Wilson corporation lawyer was a silky smooth man who wore a conservative one-piece blue suit. On its surface it had random electric patterns in a lighter blue that kept shifting hypnotically as Roddy watched them. The lawyer's name was Fred Lewandowska, and he had requested an appointment to discuss the settlement of Roddy's father's estate.

Roddy sat uneasily in the bobbing chair behind the broad, shining, uncluttered desk watching the shifting patterns while Lewandowska said smoothly, "Your father's will leaves the corporation and all its assets to you, his only son—having first made a settlement on his former wife and her heirs—if . . . ," Lewandowska paused for emphasis, "the Loudon process has been consummated."

"The son-of-a-bitch doesn't dare deny the existence of the will," Sam said bitterly, "since other copies exist."

"Wait a minute," Grandpa said. "Fred is up to something."

"Unfortunately," Lewandowska continued, "your father died suddenly and unexpectedly, and so there is some question about your rights of inheritance."

"Well . . . ," Roddy began, shifting uneasily in the penthouse office of the Wilson tower with its panoramic view of the Flint Hills. He had not yet managed to get the hang of the magnetically supported chair, and it threatened to pitch him out onto the floor.

"Wait a minute," Grandpa said. "Maybe he doesn't really know whether transfer was completed, and he's trying to goad us into telling him."

"The son-of-a-bitch!" Sam said.

"Of course," Lewandowska said silkily, "the best

tactic might be to maintain that a last-minute transfer did occur. . . ."

"Ah-hah!" said Grandpa.

"The son-of-a-bitch!" said Sam.

"But . . . ," Roddy began.

". . . and let whoever wishes to contest the will prove otherwise," Lewandowska finished.

"But," Roddy began again, and was surprised to find himself uninterrupted, "transfer did occur."

Lewandowska smiled. "You're a very bright young man, and I am sure you will be a match for any vicious cross-examiner. Meanwhile I trust that you will allow Lewandowska/Lewandowska/Lewandowska to represent you as we did your father for so many years, and his father before him."

"The son-of-a-bitch!" Sam said. "Watch him! He's a crook."

"But don't watch those patterns!" Grandpa said. "That's his watch-my-patterns-not-my-eyes suit that he uses on susceptible juries."

"If you knew he was a crook," John said, "why did you keep him on?"

"He was my crook," Sam said.

"How can I think?" Roddy said, screwing up his face.

"What did you say?" Lewandowska asked.

"What do you think?" Roddy said.

"It would be better, of course," Lewandowska said, "if transfer of assets had occurred before—uh, transfer of personalities—as is customary in such situations, but since death was accidental, I think the course you have chosen is the wise one. If you need any coaching . . ."

"Coaching?" Roddy said.

"I mean, of course, therapy," Lewandowska said smoothly. "I would be happy to recommend people with whom we have had good success in the past. Sometimes integration of memories can be a problem."

"The son-of-a-bitch!" Sam said.

"If you will just sign these papers," Lewandowska said casually, coming around the corner of the shining desk to put down a sheaf opened to the last page, "I will file the will for probate."

"Don't sign anything!" Sam said.

"Tell him to leave the papers and you'll call him when they're ready," Grandpa said.

"Paperwork is so boring," William said. "Can't we go have some fun?"

"All you want to do is get drunk so you won't have to listen to Grandpa," John said, "and the rest of us hate getting drunk."

Roddy noted that. Maybe he could work something out with William.

"Not on your life," John said.

"Not Willie," Grandpa said.

"Just sign the papers," Lewandowska said. "The sooner you sign the sooner you can start enjoying your fortune."

"How soon?" Roddy asked, reaching for the stylus.

"Lewandowska/Lewandowska/Lewandowska could advance you—say a million—against the successful probate of your father's will."

"Don't sign anything!" Grandpa said. "You'll regret it!"

"We'll all regret it," John said. "All the money we've worked for into that slimy character's pocket. Can't you see he's trying to cheat you?"

"The son-of-a-bitch!"

But Roddy was tired of listening to the voices in his head. Maybe if he had a million Greta would take him seriously. He picked up the stylus defiantly and poised it above the dotted line before it fell from his suddenly limp fingers. "That's illegal!" he protested.

"No, no," Lewandowska said. "Perhaps I got hold of the wrong papers."

"You'll never prove a thing," Grandpa said. "Fred clearly is recording this whole interview, but if it is ever presented in court it will be cleverly and illegally edited."

As Lewandowska whisked the papers away, Roddy caught a glimpse of the title on the top. It read "Power of Attorney."

"Well," Lewandowska said, "as your father's attorney of record, I can simply proceed to file the will for probate."

"Lewandowska / Lewandowska / Lewandowska?" Roddy said dazedly.

"Yes," Lewandowska said, "yes, and yes."

"The sons-of-bitches!" Sam said.

For perhaps the first time Roddy realized that he was in a world of conglomerates. He felt weak and afraid.

"Don't worry," Grandpa said. "You've got us."

"Yes," William said, "and we've been more than a match for all those bastards for the past century and a half."

But why did his father keep calling Lewandowska a son-of-a-bitch?

"Don't you know?" asked Grandpa.

"He's the son-of-a-bitch who shot me!" Sam said.

"Whom may I announce?" the door asked.

"Nobody," Roddy said. "I don't want to see Greta." It was the first time since he had met her that he'd been able to say that.

"Nonsense, my boy," Grandpa said. "You've got responsibilities now."

"First things first," said William.

"I thought you wanted to get drunk," Roddy said cruelly.

"That, too." Roddy had a mental image of the moist lip of a glass against his followed by the sliding bite of alcohol across his mouth and against his palate, and a sensation of burning all the way down to his stomach, where it curled around like a cat settling down. Roddy gagged.

"Whom may I announce?" the door repeated.

"Go ahead!" John said. "We've had this discussion before, and we're all agreed. This is something you've got to take care of. Look at what happened in your case because your father neglected his responsibilities."

"See here!" Sam said. "I'm tired of being held up as a bad example to my son."

It was better, Roddy thought, than not being an example at all—to being unimaginable!

"Son, son," Sam said sorrowfully.

"I didn't agree!" Roddy wailed. He felt like a fool standing in front of Greta's insistent front door holding an insane colloquy with himself and unable to tell the door who he was and what he wanted.

"You did, you know," Grandpa said.

"You said that if we quit bothering you, you'd take care of it," John said.

"I didn't say when," Roddy said. The realization

had come to him, when his uninvited guests had found the image of Greta in his memory, that their presence had changed the situation.

"She'll understand," Grandpa said soothingly. "Things will go much smoother than you expect."

And they did. Partly it was because Roddy was distracted by the voices in his head, and didn't have time to get knotted up and incomprehensible. Partly it was Greta, who seemed different, who did understand.

"I understand," she said. "My mother told me all about such things."

"That's better than my mother did," Roddy said glumly, holding her warm, supple hand in his as they sat upon her living-room couch. "Or my father, either. It's all been a terrible shock."

"I'd have talked to you about it in time, boy," Sam said.

"I expect to do my duty when the time comes," Greta said bravely, her lovely chin pointed at the corner of the mirrored ceiling. "Just think! I'll have all the memories not only of my mother but of her mother before her and her mother and her mother before her."

"You're a fifth generation, too?"

"Yes," she said. "And tradition is important."

"Kiss her!" Grandpa said.

"Go ahead," Sam said. "Kiss her!"

"I can't," Roddy said. The thought had suddenly occurred to him that making love to Greta was going to be done with an audience.

"Not an audience," John said. "A cheering section."

"What did you say?" Greta asked, her blue eyes widening but her pupils tiny.

"I'm sorry," Roddy said. "I'm not used to all this conversation."

"Well," Greta said, offended, "if you don't like the way I talk. . . ."

"Kiss her, dummy!" Sam said. "Quick!"

Roddy found himself kissing her. Later he could not remember how it had happened, but he suspected that it had not been his volition. As a consequence the kiss was a bit clumsy at first, but it adjusted and shaped itself into something very satisfying indeed.

"My goodness!" Greta said, opening her blue eyes even wider, pupils included. He had the feeling that it was the first time she had seen him.

"Kiss her again!" John said. "She's just getting warmed up."

Roddy kissed her again. She was just getting warmed up. More than warm, Roddy thought. In fact, things got rather hot for a while, and one thing led to another, Roddy forgot his audience, and he soon found himself involved more deeply than he had imagined possible. His senses all adrift, his voice and actions taken over, it seemed, by strange forces, he heard himself saying, "Let's get married."

"What?" she asked indignantly.

"Let's get married," he repeated. "I want to make you happy," he heard himself saying. "You're so beautiful, so wonderful, I can't bear to think of us apart."

"Well," she said.

"I want to lay all my wealth at your feet. I want to lay the world at your feet."

"Well . . . ," she said more thoughtfully.

Afterwards he was silent. Finally she said, "Why don't you say something?"

"I think I've said too much already," he said. First he had lost exclusive occupancy of his head, then of his bed. He might never be alone again. Then he looked at the reflection of himself and Greta in the overhead mirror and smiled. There were compensations.

"Tell her the terms," Grandpa said.

They talked about contracts and living arrangements.

"My mother and father don't live together, you know," she said.

"Neither do mine."

"They don't get along," she continued.

"Neither do mine."

"I mean they really don't get along," she said. It didn't seem to bother her. She seemed to Roddy not only a very attractive person but a very sensible one as well. It was a combination he liked. Grandpa liked it, too. Everybody liked it. Roddy wondered how he had gotten so lucky. "But I think we should," Greta said.

"Get along?"

"Well, that too. But live together. I mean, we shouldn't run out of things to say, not with all the different people to talk to."

There was that, too, Roddy thought.

"Tell her the terms," Grandpa said again.

"All I ask," Roddy said, "is a boy for me."

"And a girl for me," Greta said.

She kissed him. She was a sensible person. And beautiful.

"You handled yourself very well, too," Sam said.

"Thanks," Roddy said. Maybe his father wasn't such a bad sort after all.

"You don't have to thank me," Greta said, "but I like it."

He pulled her close to him. It was his own idea, and it was a good one.

The door announced, "Your father is calling," but it was too late. The door shattered with a dying gurgle and a man lunged into the room. He was waving an old-fashioned pistol wildly in the air.

"Son-of-a-bitch!" Sam said. "It's happening again!"

"What's going on here?" the intruder shouted, pointing the gun at Roddy.

The man was Lewandowska.

It was an old-fashioned courtroom done in stainless steel and clear plastic, with an old-fashioned judge. He was a white-haired robot with a face that looked as if Solomon himself had sat for it. In front of the bench and to the judge's left sat Roddy. To the right sat Lewandowska and Greta. There was no space for an audience, but cameras made it possible for the interested or the simply curious to watch from their own living rooms.

The judge turned to Lewandowska. "What is the reason for your presence here?"

"As the lawyer for the Wilson Corporation. . . ," Lewandowska began smoothly.

"He's not my lawyer!" Roddy said. But it was Sam who spoke.

". . . I am here to represent the interests of the corporation's employees in case the will shall be held invalid."

"Hah!" said Sam through Roddy's mouth.

"In addition," Lewandowska said, "I am here representing my daughter, who has an interest in the Wilson estate, since she is clearly a minor."

"Hah!" said Roddy. That was why, he realized now, Lewandowska had burst in on them. Perhaps he had even been spying on them. Roddy had always been suspicious of that mirrored ceiling. Perhaps it was why Lewandowska had burst in on his wife and Sam, not in an old-fashioned defense of honor but as a calculated attack upon the Wilson family fortune. Waving his gun he had persuaded Roddy to sign a marriage contract giving Greta community property rights before the wedding. And then he had forbidden the marriage.

Roddy looked wistfully at Greta, and Greta looked wistfully at him.

"The son-of-a-bitch can't lose," Sam said. "If we lose he controls the corporation, and if we win he controls half of its assets."

The world had closed in upon Roddy like a pack of wolves, led by Lewandowska, nipping at his corporate flanks, eager to pull down the crippled giant. Roddy was served with writs and subpoenas until he could scarcely see over the desk that had been so efficiently and proudly bare. "At least we'll have each other," he had said.

"Don't be stupid!" Sam had said.

"What good is mere existence?" John had asked.

"Without even a host when the time comes?" William had added.

"Greta wouldn't desert me," Roddy had said, but a rising inflection revealed his lack of confidence. Did he really know Greta? All he knew was that at times their interests coincided.

"Without money," Sam had said, "Greta is as unobtainable as she was before we joined you."

"Without money," John had said, "even succession is doubtful."

"Without money," William had added, "life can be more pain than joy."

"Now, now," Grandpa had said, "let's not be hard on the boy. He's doing his best for us. Right? Greta's not the problem; it's her father. And we're responsible for Fred. So let's dig in."

Roddy had found his hands reaching for documents, his eyes scanning unfamiliar words, his fingers writing alien memoranda, his voice barking strange words into stranger orifices. He even began remembering events he had never experienced, as his forefathers' memories began leaking into his. It was all too complicated for Roddy, but not for his new tenants. They enjoyed the struggle for its own sake, and made the inside of his head untenable. He could only tune them out with thoughts of Greta, and so he had arrived, without being aware of it, in the courtroom.

The legal business went on without him. Lewandowska talked and then Sam talked through Roddy. Grandpa prompted Sam occasionally, and William and John provided an infrequent nudge. Roddy, when he could, looked at Greta and wondered, idly, what she would look like in five years or twenty.

Lewandowska brought in a psychiatrist as an expert witness on the Loudon transfer. Sam cross-examined it ruthlessly. Sam brought in an expert witness for the Wilson gestalt, and it was ruthlessly cross-examined by

Lewandowska. Lewandowska brought in half a dozen of Sam's former colleagues and so-called friends to testify that they had brought up certain matters to which Roddy had been unable to respond, and Sam brought in former colleagues and friends to testify that they were confident that Sam and his guest personalities were all faithfully ensconced in Roddy's skull.

Sam called his final witness—the robot physician who had presided at the Loudon transfer.

"I object," Lewandowska said.

"On what grounds?" the judge asked.

"A machine can testify on matters of fact, but not on matters of opinion, and whether the Loudon transfer was completed is a matter of opinion."

"It is a matter," the judge said, "that will be fact as soon as I reach an opinion."

But in the end the only fact allowed into the record was that Sam was alive when transfer was attempted.

"It is clear," the judge said, "that we will not be able to reach a verdict today. We will take the matter under advisement." He was not using the royal "we." All the precedents, all the statutes, all the opinions ever delivered were recorded in the computer files to which he had access.

"Your honor," Sam said through Roddy, "justice delayed is justice deferred. Especially in this instance."

Lewandowska had won. Collectively they hated the silky smile on his face. "He must have outbid us for the judge," Grandpa complained.

"Greta's mother," Roddy said.

"Did you say something?" the judge asked.

"Greta's mother," Roddy repeated. "Greta has a mother."

"Of course she has," the judge said. "Every human has a mother."

"What our junior colleague is saying," Sam said, as smoothly as Lewandowska could have done it, "is that we wish to call Greta's mother as a witness."

It took an hour before Greta's mother was located and brought to the courtroom. She was at least as beautiful as her daughter, and Roddy felt a bit of Sam's passion for her.

"I give my consent to my daughter's marriage to Mr. Wilson," she said.

"I object," said Lewandowska, no longer so smooth.

"Since the person in question is a female," the judge said, "the mother has jurisdiction. Objection overruled."

"I appeal," Lewandowska said, looking ruffled.

"The judgment of the lower court is affirmed," the judge said promptly. He contained his own appeal process.

"There's nothing like an honest judge," Grandpa said.

"Events in this courtroom," the judge said, "have also demonstrated that the Loudon transfer has indeed been effected, and I therefore hold that Roderick Wilson is the legal heir to the Wilson estate."

"I . . . ," Lewandowska began.

"What's more," Sam said, "I accuse this man of murder." He pointed Roddy's finger dramatically at Lewandowska.

"You can't prove a thing," Lewandowska said.

"And I will call, as witness, Mrs. Lewandowska," Sam continued inexorably.

"Everything would have been lost without you," Sam said as Roddy clasped Greta to him in the corridor outside the courtroom. They made a friendly little group, Greta, Greta's mother, and Roddy and his tenant personalities. "You are going to be a great addition to the Wilson family," Sam said fondly.

For the first time Roddy felt like a son. It felt good. In fact, everything felt good. Greta felt good. His head felt good. Everything felt so good he began to wonder what could go wrong.

Until he realized he felt a certain atavistic yearning for Greta's mother.

A Work of
Art

JAMES BLISH

*James Blish, who died in 1975, was a paradox as a
writer. He was both a rationalist and a romantic. He
had an impeccable scientific background (in microbi-
ology), and pioneered the literary use of the "softer"
science of biology; yet he also gave a convincing scientific explanation for telepathy, in which he personally
did not believe, and passionately addressed religious
and demonic themes about which he was highly skeptical. He could be called a kind of atheistic Jesuit.*

*Blish was considered an "intellectual" among
science-fiction writers. He was an expert on James
Joyce, Ezra Pound, and the music of Richard Strauss,
yet he also novelized many* Star Trek *episodes. He
could be frugal, recycling his own material, yet could
produce on an heroic scale (as with his* Cities in Flight
saga). He wasn't one to balk at a challenge: in Black
Easter *he let all the devils out of hell and brought world
history to a resounding, apocalyptic halt. Then, when
his editor amazingly asked for a sequel to the end of
the world, Blish produced* The Day After Judgment,
*which reaches a magnificent climax with pages of blank
verse in the style of Milton's* Paradise Lost.

Blish was a pessimist about human nature, the future

and any form of immortality. But he also possessed wonderful verve, lively curiosity, and courage: within days of major surgery he would be talking about music, science or Finnegans Wake *over many pints of draft Guinness.*

The Triumph of Time *was the title of the final volume of his* Cities in Flight; *and in "A Work of Art" we encounter triumph over the tragedy of time.*

Instantly, he remembered dying. He remembered it, however, as if at two removes—as though he were remembering a memory, rather than an actual event; as though he himself had not really been there when he died.

Yet the memory was all from his own point of view, not that of some detached and disembodied observer which might have been his soul. He had been most conscious of the rasping, unevenly drawn movements of the air in his chest. Blurring rapidly, the doctor's face had bent over him, loomed, come closer and then had vanished as the doctor's head passed below his cone of vision, turned sideways to listen to his lungs.

It had become rapidly darker, and then, only then, had he realized that these were to be his last minutes. He had tried dutifully to say Pauline's name, but his memory contained no record of the sound—only of the rattling breath, and of the film of sootiness thickening in the air, blotting out everything for an instant.

Only an instant, and then the memory was over. The room was bright again, and the ceiling, he noticed with wonder, had turned a soft green. The doctor's head lifted again and looked down at him.

It was a different doctor. This one was a far younger

man, with an ascetic face and gleaming, almost fey eyes. There was no doubt about it. One of the last conscious thoughts he had had was that of gratitude that the attending physician, there at the end, had not been the one who secretly hated him for his one-time associations with the Nazi hierarchy. The attending doctor, instead, had worn an expression amusingly proper for that of a Swiss expert called to the deathbed of an eminent man: a mixture of worry at the prospect of losing so eminent a patient, and complacency at the thought that, at the old man's age, nobody could blame his doctor if he died. At eighty-five, pneumonia is a serious matter, with or without penicillin.

"You're all right now," the new doctor said, freeing his patient's head of a whole series of little silver rods which had been clinging to it by a sort of network cap. "Rest a minute and try to be calm. Do you know your name?"

He drew a cautious breath. There seemed to be nothing at all the matter with his lungs now; indeed, he felt positively healthy. "Certainly," he said, a little nettled. "Do you know yours?"

The doctor smiled crookedly. "You're in character, it appears," he said. "My name is Barkun Kris; I am a mind sculptor. Yours?"

"Richard Strauss."

"Very good," Dr. Kris said, and turned away. Strauss, however, had already been diverted by a new singularity. *Strauss* is a word as well as a name in German; it has many meanings—an ostrich, a bouquet; von Wolzogen had had a high old time working all the possible puns into the libretto of *Feuersnot*. And it happened to be the first German word to be spoken either by himself or by Dr. Kris since that twice-removed moment of death. The language was not French or Italian, either. It was most like English, but not the English Strauss knew; nevertheless, he was having no trouble speaking it and even thinking in it.

Well, he thought, *I'll be able to conduct* The Loves of Danae *after all. It isn't every composer who can première his own opera posthumously.* Still, there was something queer about all this—the queerest part of all being that conviction, which would not go away, that he had actually been dead for just a short time. Of course medicine was making great strides, but . . .

"Explain all this," he said, lifting himself to one elbow. The bed was different, too, and not nearly as comfortable as the one in which he had died. As for the room, it looked more like a dynamo shed than a sickroom. Had modern medicine taken to reviving its corpses on the floor of the Siemanns-Schuckert plant?

"In a moment," Dr. Kris said. He finished rolling some machine back into what Strauss impatiently supposed to be its place, and crossed to the pallet. "Now. There are many things you'll have to take for granted without attempting to understand them, Dr. Strauss. Not everything in the world today is explicable in terms of your assumptions. Please bear that in mind."

"Very well. Proceed."

"The date," Dr. Kris said, "is 2161 by your calendar —or, in other words, it is now two hundred and twelve years after your death. Naturally, you'll realize that by this time nothing remains of your body but the bones. The body you have now was volunteered for your use. Before you look into a mirror to see what it's like, remember that its physical difference from the one you were used to is all in your favor. It's in perfect health, not unpleasant for other people to look at, and its physiological age is about fifty."

A miracle? No, not in this new age, surely. It was simply a work of science. But what a science! This was Nietzsche's eternal recurrence and the immortality of the superman combined into one.

"And where is this?" the composer said.

"In Port York, part of the State of Manhattan, in the United States. You will find the country less changed in some respects than I imagine you anticipate. Other changes, of course, will seem radical to you; but it's hard for me to predict which ones will strike you that way. A certain resilience on your part will bear cultivating."

"I understand," Strauss said, sitting up. "One question, please; is it still possible for a composer to make a living in this century?"

"Indeed it is," Dr. Kris said, smiling. "As we expect you to do. It is one of the purposes for which we've —brought you back."

"I gather, then," Strauss said somewhat dryly, "that there is still a demand for my music. The critics in the old days—"

"That's not quite how it is," Dr. Kris said. "I understand some of your work is still played, but frankly I know very little about your current status. My interest is rather—"

A door opened somewhere, and another man came in. He was older and more ponderous than Kris and had a certain air of academicism; but he too was wearing the oddly tailored surgeon's gown, and looked upon Kris's patient with the glowing eyes of an artist.

"A success, Kris?" he said. "Congratulations."

"They're not in order yet," Dr. Kris said. "The final proof is what counts. Dr. Strauss, if you feel strong enough, Dr. Seirds and I would like to ask you some questions. We'd like to make sure your memory is clear."

"Certainly. Go ahead."

"According to our records," Kris said, "you once knew a man whose initials were RKL; this was while you were conducting at the Vienna *Staatsoper*." He made the double "a" at least twice too long, as though German were a dead language he was striving to pronounce in some "classical" accent. "What was his name, and who was he?"

"That would be Kurt List—his first name was Richard, but he didn't use it. He was assistant stage manager."

The two doctors looked at each other. "Why did you offer to write a new overture to *The Woman Without Shadows* and give the manuscript to the city of Vienna?"

"So I wouldn't have to pay the garbage removal tax on the Maria Theresa villa they had given me."

"In the backyard of your house at Garmisch-Partenkirchen there was a tombstone. What was written on it?"

Strauss frowned. That was a question he would be happy to be unable to answer. If one is to play childish jokes upon oneself, it's best not to carve them in stone, and put the carving where you can't help seeing it every time you go out to tinker with the Mercedes. "It says," he replied wearily, "*Sacred to the memory of Guntram, Minnesinger, slain in a horrible way by his father's own symphony orchestra.*"

"When was *Guntram* premièred?"

"In—let me see—1894, I believe."

"Where?"

"In Weimar."

"Who was the leading lady?"

"Pauline de Ahna."

"What happened to her afterwards?"

"I married her. Is she . . ." Strauss began anxiously.

"No," Dr. Kris said. "I'm sorry, but we lack the data to reconstruct more or less ordinary people."

The composer sighed. He did not know whether to be worried or not. He had loved Pauline, to be sure; on the other hand, it would be pleasant to be able to live the new life without being forced to take off one's shoes every time one entered the house, so as not to scratch the polished hardwood floors. And also pleasant, perhaps, to have two o'clock in the afternoon come by without hearing Pauline's everlasting, *"Richard—jetzt komponiert!"*

"Next question," he said.

For reasons which Strauss did not understand, but was content to take for granted, he was separated from Drs. Kris and Seirds as soon as both were satisfied that the composer's memory was reliable and his health stable. His estate, he was given to understand, had long since been broken up—a sorry end for what had been one of the principal fortunes of Europe—but he was given sufficient money to set up lodgings and resume an active life. He was provided, too, with introductions which proved valuable.

It took longer than he had expected to adjust to the changes that had taken place in music alone. Music was, he quickly began to suspect, a dying art, which would soon have a status not much above that held by flower-arranging back in what he thought of as his own century. Certainly it couldn't be denied that the trend toward fragmentation, already visible back in his own time, had proceeded almost to completion in 2161.

He paid no more attention to American popular tunes than he had bothered to pay in his previous life. Yet it was evident that their assembly-line production methods—all the ballad composers openly used a slide-rule-like device called a Hit Machine—now had their counterparts almost throughout serious music.

The conservatives these days, for instance, were the twelve-tone composers—always, in Strauss's opinion, a dryly mechanical lot but never more so than now. Their gods—Berg, Schoenberg, Webern—were looked upon by the concert-going public as great masters, on the abstruse side perhaps, but as worthy of reverence as any of the Three B's.

There was one wing of the conservatives, however, which had gone the twelve-tone procedure one better. These men composed what was called "stochastic music," put together by choosing each individual note by consultation with tables of random numbers. Their bible, their basic text, was a volume called *Operational Aesthetics,* which in turn derived from a discipline called information theory; and not one word of it seemed to touch upon any of the techniques and customs of composition which Strauss knew. The ideal of this group was to produce music which would be "universal"—that is, wholly devoid of any trace of the composer's individuality, wholly a musical expression of the universal Laws of Chance. The Laws of Chance seemed to have a style of their own, all right; but to Strauss it seemed the style of an idiot child being

taught to hammer a flat piano, to keep him from
getting into trouble.

By far the largest body of work being produced,
however, fell into a category misleadingly called
"science-music." The term reflected nothing but the
titles of the works, which dealt with space flight, time
travel, and other subjects of a romantic or an unlikely
nature. There was nothing in the least scientific about
the music, which consisted of a *mélange* of clichés and
imitations of natural sounds, in which Strauss was
horrified to see his own time-distorted and diluted
image.

The most popular form of science-music was a nine-
minute composition called a concerto, though it bore
no resemblance at all to the classical concerto form;
it was instead a sort of free rhapsody after Rach-
maninoff—long after. A typical one—"Song of Deep
Space" it was called, by somebody named H. Valerion
Krafft—began with a loud assault on the tam-tam,
after which all the strings rushed up the scale in unison, followed at a respectful distance by the harp and
one clarinet in parallel 6/4's. At the top of the scale
cymbals were bashed together, *forte possibile,* and the
whole orchestra launched itself into a major-minor,
wailing sort of melody; the whole orchestra, that is,
except for the French horns, which were plodding
back down the scale again in what was evidently supposed to be a countermelody. The second phrase of
the theme was picked up by a solo trumpet with a
suggestion of tremolo; the orchestra died back to its
roots to await the next cloudburst, and at this point
—as any four-year-old could have predicted—the
piano entered with the second theme.

. . .

Behind the orchestra stood a group of thirty women, ready to come in with a wordless chorus intended to suggest the eeriness of Deep Space—but at this point, too, Strauss had already learned to get up and leave. After a few such experiences he could also count upon meeting in the lobby Sindi Noniss, the agent to whom Dr. Kris had introduced him, and who was handling the reborn composer's output—what there was of it thus far. Sindi had come to expect these walkouts on the part of his client, and patiently awaited them, standing beneath a bust of Gian Carlo Menotti; but he liked them less and less, and lately had been greeting them by turning alternately red and white like a toti-potent barber pole.

"You shouldn't have done it," he burst out after the Krafft incident. "You can't just walk out on a new Krafft composition. The man's the president of the Interplanetary Society for Contemporary Music. How am I ever going to persuade them that you're a contemporary if you keep snubbing them?"

"What does it matter?" Strauss said. "They don't know me by sight."

"You're wrong; they know you very well, and they're watching every move you make. You're the first major composer the mind sculptors ever tackled, and the ISCM would be glad to turn you back with a rejection slip."

"Why?"

"Oh," said Sindi, "there are lots of reasons. The sculptors are snobs; so are the ISCM boys. Each of them wants to prove to the others that their own art is the king of them all. And then there's the competition; it would be easier to flunk you than to let you into the market. I really think you'd better go back in. I could make up some excuse—"

"No," Strauss said shortly. "I have work to do."

"But that's just the point, Richard. How are we going to get an opera produced without the ISCM? It isn't as though you wrote theremin solos, or something that didn't cost so——"

"I have work to do," he said, and left.

And he did: work which absorbed him as had no other project during the last thirty years of his former life. He had scarcely touched pen to music paper—both had been astonishingly hard to find—when he realized that nothing in his long career had provided him with touchstones by which to judge what music he should write *now*.

The old tricks came swarming back by the thousands, to be sure: the sudden, unexpected key changes at the crest of a melody; the interval stretching; the piling of divided strings, playing in the high harmonics, upon the already tottering top of a climax; the scurry and bustle as phrases were passed like lightning from one choir of the orchestra to another; the flashing runs in the brass, the chuckling in the clarinets, the snarling mixtures of colors to emphasize dramatic tension—all of them.

But none of them satisfied him now. He had been content with them for most of a lifetime, and had made them do an astonishing amount of work. But now it was time to strike out afresh. Some of the tricks, indeed, actively repelled him: where had he gotten the notion, clung to for decades, that violins screaming out in unison somewhere in the stratosphere was a sound interesting enough to be worth repeating inside a single composition, let alone in all of them?

And nobody, he reflected contentedly, ever approached such a new beginning better equipped. In addition to the past lying available in his memory, he had always had a technical armamentarium second to none; even the hostile critics had granted him that. Now that he was, in a sense, composing his first opera —his first after fifteen of them!—he had every opportunity to make it a masterpiece.

And every such intention.

There were, of course, many minor distractions. One of them was that search for old-fashioned score paper, and a pen and ink with which to write on it. Very few of the modern composers, it developed, wrote their music at all. A large bloc of them used tape, patching together snippets of tone and sound snipped from other tapes, superimposing one tape on another, and varying the results by twirling an elaborate array of knobs this way or that. Almost all the composers of 3-V scores, on the other hand, wrote on the sound track itself, rapidly scribbling jagged wiggly lines which, when passed through a photocell-audio circuit, produced a noise reasonably like an orchestra playing music, overtones and all.

The last-ditch conservatives who still wrote notes on paper did so with the aid of a musical typewriter. The device, Strauss had to admit, seemed perfected at last; it had manuals and stops like an organ, but it was not much more than twice as large as a standard letter-writing typewriter, and produced a neat page. But he was satisfied with his own spidery, highly legible manuscript and refused to abandon it, badly though the one pen nib he had been able to buy coarsened it. It helped to tie him to his past.

Joining the ISCM had also caused him some bad moments, even after Sindi had worked him around the political roadblocks. The Society man who examined his qualifications as a member had run through the questions with no more interest than might have been shown by a veterinarian examining his four thousandth sick calf.

"Had anything published?"

"Yes, nine tone poems, about three hundred songs, an—"

"Not when you were alive," the examiner said, somewhat disquietingly. "I mean since the sculptors turned you out again."

"Since the sculptors—ah, I understand. Yes, a string quartet, two song cycles, a—"

"Good. Alfie, write down 'songs.' Play an instrument?"

"Piano."

"Hm." The examiner studied his fingernails. "Oh, well. Do you read music? Or do you use a Scriber, or tape clips? Or a Machine?"

"I read."

"Here." The examiner sat Strauss down in front of a viewing lectern, over the lit surface of which an endless belt of translucent paper was traveling. On the paper was an immensely magnified sound track. "Whistle me the tune of that, and name the instruments it sounds like."

"I don't read that *Musiksticheln*," Strauss said frostily, "or write it, either. I use standard notation, on music paper."

"Alfie, write down 'Reads notes only.'" He laid a sheet of greyly printed music on the lectern above the ground glass. "Whistle me that."

"That" proved to be a popular tune called "Vangs, Snifters and Store-Credit Snooky" which had been written on a Hit Machine in 2159 by a guitar-faking politician who sang it at campaign rallies. (In some respects, Strauss reflected, the United States had indeed not changed very much.) It had become so popular that anybody could have whistled it from the title alone, whether he could read the music or not. Strauss whistled it and, to prove his bona fides, added, "It's in the key of B flat."

The examiner went over to the green-painted upright piano and hit one greasy black key. The instrument was horribly out of tune—the note was much nearer to the standard 440/cps A than it was to B flat —but the examiner said, "So it is. Alfie, write down, 'Also reads flats.' All right, son, you're a member. Nice to have you with us; not many people can read that old-style notation anymore. A lot of them think they're too good for it."

"Thank you," Strauss said.

"My feeling is, if it was good enough for the old masters, it's good enough for us. We don't have people like them with us these days, it seems to me. Except for Dr. Krafft, of course. They were *great* back in the old days—men like Shilkret, Steiner, Tiomkin, and Pearl . . . and Wilder and Jannsen. Real goffin."

"*Doch gewiss,*" Strauss said politely.

But the work went forward. He was making a little income now, from small works. People seemed to feel a special interest in a composer who had come out of the mind sculptors' laboratories; and in addition the material itself, Strauss was quite certain, had merits of its own to help sell it.

It was the opera which counted, however. That grew and grew under his pen, as fresh and new as his new life, as founded in knowledge and ripeness as his long full memory. Finding a libretto had been troublesome at first. While it was possible that something existed that might have served among the current scripts for 3-V—though he doubted it—he found himself unable to tell the good from the bad through the fog cast over both by incomprehensibly technical production directions. Eventually, and for only the third time in his whole career, he had fallen back upon a play written in a language other than his own, and —for the first time—decided to set it in that language.

The play was Christopher Fry's *Venus Observed*, in all ways a perfect Strauss opera libretto, as he came gradually to realize. Though nominally a comedy, with a complex farcical plot, it was a verse play with considerable depth to it, and a number of characters who cried out to be brought by music into three dimensions, plus a strong undercurrent of autumnal tragedy, of leaf-fall and apple-fall—precisely the kind of contradictory dramatic mixture which von Hofmannsthal had supplied him with in *The Knight of the Rose*, in *Ariadne at Naxos*, and in *Arabella*.

Alas for von Hofmannsthal, but here was another long-dead playwright who seemed nearly as gifted; and the musical opportunities were immense. There was, for instance, the fire which ended act two; what a gift for a composer to whom orchestration and counterpoint were as important as air and water! Or take the moment where Perpetua shoots the apple from the

Duke's hand; in that one moment a single passing reference could add Rossini's marmoreal *William Tell* to the musical texture as nothing but an ironic footnote! And the Duke's great curtain speech, beginning:

> *Shall I be sorry for myself? In Mortality's name*
> *I'll be sorry for myself. Branches and boughs,*
> > *Brown hills, the valleys faint with brume,*
> > *A burnish on the lake . . .*

There was a speech for a great tragic comedian, in the spirit of Falstaff; the final union of laughter and tears, punctuated by the sleepy comments of Reedbeck, to whose sonorous snore (trombones, no less than five of them, *con sordini?*) the opera would gently end. . . .

What could be better? And yet he had come upon the play only by the unlikeliest series of accidents. At first he had planned to do a straight knockabout farce, in the idiom of *The Silent Woman*, just to warm himself up. Remembering that Zweig had adapted that libretto for him, in the old days, from a play by Ben Jonson, Strauss had begun to search out English plays of the period just after Jonson's, and had promptly run aground on an awful specimen in heroic couplets called *Venice Preserv'd*, by one Thomas Otway. The Fry play had directly followed the Otway in the card catalogue, and he had looked at it out of curiosity; why should a twentieth-century playwright be punning on a title from the eighteenth?

After two pages of the Fry play, the minor puzzle of the pun disappeared entirely from his concern. His luck was running again; he had an opera.

. . .

Sindi worked miracles in arranging for the performance. The date of the première was set even before
the score was finished, reminding Strauss pleasantly of
those heady days when Fuerstner had been snatching
the conclusion of *Elektra* off his worktable a page at
a time, before the ink was even dry, to rush it to the
engraver before publication deadline. The situation
now, however, was even more complicated, for some
of the score had to be scribed, some of it taped, some
of it engraved in the old way, to meet the new techniques of performance; there were moments when
Sindi seemed to be turning quite grey.

But *Venus Observed* was, as usual, forthcoming
complete from Strauss's pen in plenty of time. Writing the music in first draft had been hellishly hard
work, much more like being reborn than had been
that confused awakening in Barkun Kris's laboratory,
with its overtones of being dead instead; but Strauss
found that he still retained all of his old ability to score
from the draft almost effortlessly, as undisturbed by
Sindi's half-audible worrying in the room with him as
he was by the terrifying supersonic bangs of the rockets that bulleted invisibly over the city.

When he was finished, he had two days still to spare
before the beginning of rehearsals. With those, fur-
thermore, he would have nothing to do. The techniques of performance in this age were so completely
bound up with the electronic arts as to reduce his own
experience—he, the master *Kapellmeister* of them all
—to the hopelessly primitive.

He did not mind. The music, as written, would
speak for itself. In the meantime he found it grateful
to forget the months'-long preoccupation with the
stage for a while. He went back to the library and

browsed lazily through old poems, vaguely seeking texts for a song or two. He knew better than to bother with recent poets; they could not speak to him, and he knew it. The Americans of his own age, he thought, might give him a clue to understanding this America of 2161; and if some such poem gave birth to a song, so much the better.

The search was relaxing and he gave himself up to enjoying it. Finally he struck a tape that he liked: a tape read in a cracked old voice that twanged of Idaho as that voice had twanged in 1910, in Strauss's own ancient youth. The poet's name was Pound; he said, on the tape:

> . . . the souls of all men great
> At times pass through us,
> And we are melted into them, and are not
> Save reflexions of their souls.
> Thus I am Dante for a space and am
> One François Villon, ballad-lord and thief
> Or am such holy ones I may not write,
> Lest Blasphemy be writ against my name;
> This for an instant and the flame is gone.
> 'Tis as in midmost us there glows a sphere
> Translucent, molten gold, that is the "I"
> And into this some form projects itself:
> Christus, or John, or eke the Florentine;
> And as the clear space is not if a form's
> Imposed thereon,
> So cease we from all being for the time,
> And these, the Masters of the Soul, live on.

He smiled. That lesson had been written again and again, from Plato onwards. Yet the poem was a history of his own case, a sort of theory for the metempsychosis he had undergone, and in its formal way it was moving. It would be fitting to make a little hymn of it, in honor of his own rebirth, and of the poet's insight.

A series of solemn, breathless chords framed themselves in his inner ear, against which the words might be intoned in a high, gently bending hush at the beginning . . . and then a dramatic passage in which the great names of Dante and Villon would enter ringing like challenges to Time. . . . He wrote for a while in his notebook before he returned the spool to its shelf.

These, he thought, are good auspices.

And so the night of the première arrived, the audience pouring into the hall, the 3-V cameras riding on no visible supports through the air, and Sindi calculating his share of his client's earnings by a complicated game he played on his fingers, the basic law of which seemed to be that one plus one equals ten. The hall filled to the roof with people from every class, as though what was to come would be a circus rather than an opera.

There were, surprisingly, nearly fifty of the aloof and aristocratic mind sculptors, clad in formal clothes which were exaggerated black versions of their surgeon's gowns. They had bought a block of seats near the front of the auditorium, where the gigantic 3-V figures which would shortly fill the "stage" before them (the real singers would perform on a small stage in the basement) could not but seem monstrously out of proportion; but Strauss supposed that they had taken this into account and dismissed it.

There was a tide of whispering in the audience as the sculptors began to trickle in, and with it an under-current of excitement the meaning of which was un-known to Strauss. He did not attempt to fathom it, however; he was coping with his own mounting tide of opening-night tension, which, despite all the years, he had never quite been able to shake.

The sourceless, gentle light in the auditorium dimmed, and Strauss mounted the podium. There was a score before him, but he doubted that he would need it. Directly before him, poking up from among the musicians, were the inevitable 3-V snouts, waiting to carry his image to the singers in the basement.

The audience was quiet now. This was the moment. His baton swept up and then decisively down, and the prelude came surging up out of the pit.

For a little while he was deeply immersed in the always tricky business of keeping the enormous orches-tra together and sensitive to the flexing of the musical web beneath his hand. As his control firmed and be-came secure, however, the task became slightly less demanding, and he was able to pay more attention to what the whole sounded like.

There was something decidedly wrong with it. Of course there were the occasional surprises as some bit of orchestral color emerged with a different *Klang* than he had expected; that happened to every com-poser, even after a lifetime of experience. And there were moments when the singers, entering upon a phrase more difficult to handle than he had calculated, sounded like someone about to fall off a tightrope (although none of them actually fluffed once; they were as fine a troupe of voices as he had ever had to work with).

But these were details. It was the overall impression that was wrong. He was losing not only the excitement of the première—after all, that couldn't last at the same pitch all evening—but also his very interest in what was coming from the stage and the pit. He was gradually tiring; his baton arm becoming heavier; as the second act mounted to what should have been an impassioned outpouring of shining tone, he was so bored as to wish he could go back to his desk to work on that song.

Then the act was over; only one more to go. He scarcely heard the applause. The twenty minutes' rest in his dressing-room was just barely enough to give him the necessary strength.

And suddenly, in the middle of the last act, he understood.

There was nothing new about the music. It was the old Strauss all over again—but weaker, more dilute than ever. Compared with the output of composers like Krafft, it doubtless sounded like a masterpiece to this audience. But he knew.

The resolutions, the determination to abandon the old clichés and mannerisms, the decision to say something new—they had all come to nothing against the force of habit. Being brought to life again meant bringing to life as well all those deeply graven reflexes of his style. He had only to pick up his pen and they overpowered him with easy automatism, no more under his control than the jerk of a finger away from a flame.

His eyes filled; his body was young, but he was an old man, an old man. Another thirty-five years of this? Never. He had said all this before, centuries before. Nearly a half-century condemned to saying it all over again, in a weaker and still weaker voice, aware that even this debased century would come to recognize in him only the burnt husk of greatness?—no; never, never.

He was aware, dully, that the opera was over. The audience was screaming its joy. He knew the sound. They had screamed that way when *Day of Peace* had been premièred, but they had been cheering the man he had been, not the man that *Day of Peace* showed with cruel clarity he had become. Here the sound was even more meaningless: cheers of ignorance, and that was all.

He turned slowly. With surprise, and with a surprising sense of relief, he saw that the cheers were not, after all, for him.

They were for Dr. Barkun Kris.

Kris was standing in the middle of the bloc of mind sculptors, bowing to the audience. The sculptors nearest him were shaking his hand one after the other. More grasped at it as he made his way to the aisle, and walked forward to the podium. When he mounted the rostrum and took the composer's limp hand, the cheering became delirious.

Kris lifted his arm. The cheering died instantly to an intent hush.

"Thank you," he said clearly. "Ladies and gentlemen, before we take leave of Dr. Strauss, let us again tell him what a privilege it has been for us to hear this fresh example of his mastery. I am sure no farewell could be more fitting."

The ovation lasted five minutes, and would have gone another five if Kris had not cut it off.

"Dr. Strauss," he said, "in a moment, when I speak a certain formulation to you, you will realize that your name is Jerom Busch, born in our century and with a life in it all your own. The superimposed memories which have made you assume the mask, the *persona*, of a great composer will be gone. I tell you this so that you may understand why these people here share your applause with me."

A wave of assenting sound.

"The art of mind sculpture—the creation of artificial personalities for aesthetic enjoyment—may never reach such a pinnacle again. For you should understand that as Jerom Busch you had no talent for music at all; indeed, we searched a long time to find a man who was utterly unable to carry even the simplest tune. Yet we were able to impose upon such unpromising material not only the personality, but the genius, of a great composer. That genius belongs entirely to you—to the *persona* that thinks of itself as Richard Strauss. None of the credit goes to the man who volunteered for the sculpture. That is your triumph, and we salute you for it."

Now the ovation could no longer be contained. Strauss, with a crooked smile, watched Dr. Kris bow. This mind sculpturing was a suitably sophisticated kind of cruelty for this age; but the impulse, of course, had always existed. It was the same impulse that had made Rembrandt and Leonardo turn cadavers into art works.

It deserved a suitably sophisticated payment under the *lex talionis:* an eye for an eye, a tooth for a tooth —and a failure for a failure.

No, he need not tell Dr. Kris that the "Strauss" he had created was as empty of genius as a hollow gourd. The joke would always be on the sculptor, who was incapable of hearing the hollowness of the music now preserved on the 3-V tapes.

But for an instant a surge of revolt poured through his bloodstream. *I am I,* he thought. *I am Richard Strauss until I die, and will never be Jerom Busch, who was utterly unable to carry even the simplest tune.* His hand, still holding the baton, came sharply up, though whether to deliver or to ward off a blow he could not tell.

He let it fall again and, instead, at last, bowed—not to the audience, but to Dr. Kris. He was sorry for nothing, as Kris turned to him to say the word that would plunge him back into oblivion, except that he would now have no chance to set that poem to music.

The Rapture

TOM DISCH

Tom Disch is the poetic incarnation of Thomas M. Disch, prose stylist and ironist, author of such classics as Camp Concentration, 334, On Wings of Song *and* The Businessman. *"The Rapture" takes off from a firmly held belief among born-again Christians, that nuclear apocalypse is just around the corner—and will be a blessing. Christ and his angels will appear in the sky prior to the thermonuclear fireballs and "rapture" true believers directly up to heaven, stark naked, from wherever they are, leaving an empty suit of clothes in the driver's seat of a car, an empty pair of shoes on the sidewalk. And thus the afterlife commences, for the faithful.*

This bizarre concept has inspired Tom Disch with a lyric poem, representing his own brand of fundamentalist piety.

Suddenly it is all clear
I am this naked body here
Hung like a bulb upon the tree
Of Earth's exploded history

My flesh as from a sauna glows
And see how my erection grows
The world's become a single flame
And I am naked without shame

It is salvation to be lost
In such a happy holocaust
Embraced by the apocalypse
Of flesh and fire come to grips

Bomb Rome and ravish South St. Paul
Make every damned Episcopal
Pay for all the days they've seized
Burn like the sun and be well pleased

From every living cell release
Its prisoners to cloudy peace
Redeem destroy and fill with joy
All Africa and Illinois

Lift us higher make us see
The vistas of Eternity
How the godless squirm in hell
Their meat napalmed into a gel

How the blessed are whirled and tossed
Broiled by flames of Pentecost
And how at last I'm made to feel
That these bones live and I am real

Wood

MICHAEL N. LANGFORD

"Wood" is Michael Langford's first published story. Born in 1954 in Alabama, he now lives near Atlanta, Georgia. In his senior year in high school he was part of a full-scale simulation, with NASA support, of a moon-landing; and later, at the University of Georgia, he wrote and directed a locally popular film parody of Japanese monster movies, featuring a cast of eighteen Asian students and a hermit crab, which he taught to climb a model of the Eiffel Tower. His other activities have included helping to observe and analyze eclipsing binary star systems, hosting a radio talk show about the future, announcing for a classical radio station and undertaking graduate cinema studies in California. But his most meaningful experience, he tells us, was working with international students at the University of Southern California's American Language Institute.

He is particularly interested in altered states of consciousness, paranormal phenomena, and near-death experiences. None of which quite prepares you for the haunting tale that follows. . . .

Many people, including colleagues, students, friends, and former friends, have wondered aloud and in private why I dropped out, why I ended a long association with a major university, why I stopped publishing in the psychiatric journals, why I curtailed a lucrative private practice just as it was beginning, why I did or didn't do this or that. I have dealt with the rumors, which have ranged from premature male menopause to religious enlightenment, and I haven't even minded having my face splattered all over page twelve of some supermarket tabloid. I do, however, draw the line at exposés of my research institute in unauthorized paperbacks, crammed between the witchcraft manuals and the UFO testimonies, and I want to set the record straight.

For three years I have been a codirector of the Institute for Primal Sciences, which has set for itself the lofty goal of achieving, through traditional and nontraditional scientific methods, a more complete understanding of the role that paranormal phenomena may have played in the evolution of human consciousness. Our laboratory experimentation is conducted in a thoroughly systematic and rigorous fashion. Nevertheless, a few have chosen to brand me as some kind of bizarre neo-druid, so I will make a small confession: In some of the more ancient European forests, I have, on occasion, spent time examining and photographing tree trunks and fallen branches. These activities have been only a small part of my search for evidence to support a hypothesis derived from an unexpected, personal experience that very drastically shaped the evolution of my own consciousness.

Whatever you care to call that foundation that holds you steady while the wild winds of insanity blow —a worldview, a belief system, a comfortable set of rationalizations—whatever it is, mine came apart, fell apart, blew apart completely after meeting a very simple little man, whom I will call Bill.

Bill wandered into my office one day about seven years ago with no physician's referral and no appointment. He explained that he had been troubled for several months with a recurring dream and expressed the usual guilt about not having sought professional help before then. I was immediately taken by his soft-spoken and sincere manner and, having no further appointments that day because of a couple of cancellations, I agreed to talk with him about his dream. What follows are partial transcripts of my three sessions with Bill, spaced a week apart, during which he gradually brought his dream to the surface.

THE FIRST SESSION

Q: Bill, I just want you to relax. Take a couple of deep breaths. Let your mind relax. I'm going to ask you some questions, and I just want you to say whatever comes into your mind. Now tell me a little about your job. What do you do for a living?

A: I'm a temporary. Maybe I'll get a permanent position someday soon, but right now I'm a temporary. The people at the temporary service send me to a new plant on a different industrial boulevard every couple of days. One time they sent me to Technology Park. I mostly do light industrial.

Q: Do you enjoy your work?

A: Well, I guess so. It's just picking up boxes mostly. Taking boxes off the line. Stacking them up. The boxes are usually real heavy, but they still call it light industrial.

Q: What's in the boxes?

A: Depends on what plant it is. Sometimes I don't even know what's in them. They're just heavy boxes.

Q: What do you do when you come home from work?

A: Well, when I come home at night I'm usually real tired. I usually don't want to do nothing but watch TV, but sometimes Chuck and Steve say, "Let's party." The three of us live together. Chuck and Steve watch TV most nights, but sometimes they get a little crazy and say, "Let's party," and stuff. Then they usually drink a lot of beer and play music real loud. We listen to bands like REX. Chuck used to play in a band himself. He says REX is a good band, so we listen to a lot of their albums. One time we had some girls over, but we didn't get nothing. I remember one time I almost got something, but usually we just drink beer and stuff when we party.

Q: What sorts of things did you enjoy doing as a child?

A: Well, when I was a kid, I used to do something you might think was kind of weird. I used to collect newspapers and magazines. But not brand new from the store. I'd go around to trash dumps and pick them up. I had stacks and stacks of pulp magazines, slick magazines, and regular newspapers. Sometimes I'd find old Sears catalogs. Anything with pictures. I'd look at the pictures and try to read some of the words. I never could read very good. I got that thing that makes you see words backwards, so I'd just make up my own stories about the pictures. I used to like to do that. I'd spend hours and hours looking at all those newspaper pictures and magazine pictures and living the lives of all those people. I got some Scotch tape and put them up on my wall, so I could look at them all the time. Sometimes I'd run my hand along the wall just to feel all that smooth, crisp paper.

Q: It didn't bother you that you couldn't read the words?

A: No. Not really. I figured other people could read the words, and that was enough. I knew most everybody could read. . . . You know it's kind of funny how words can tell all kinds of people everywhere stories about all kinds of things. That's pretty wild. . . . If you think about it, I mean. It's kind of like all those pieces of paper have got lives of their own, because they got all those little marks that make words and stories. It's almost like all that paper could be thinking and living. But living sort of with a purpose, because it's carrying around those words and pictures like it really was all that stuff. . . . I don't know. You know, I hadn't thought about that in a long time. I used to think about some weird things when I was a kid.

Q: What sorts of things?

A: Oh, stuff like what dogs and cats and trees really think about. How ants talk to each other. Stuff like that.

Q: Did you have many dreams when you were a kid?

A: Well. . . . I don't know. I can't really remember.

Q: What about now? Do you dream a lot now?

A: No. Not a lot of dreams. Just that one over and

over. I mean I'll have that dream maybe one night, and then the next night I might dream it again.

Q: You never have any other dreams?

A: Well, not yet, I guess. You see, that's really the only dream I ever had. I used to go to sleep at night and never dream. I remember wondering for a long time what dreaming was. A little while back I started wishing I could have some kind of dream so I could just see what dreaming is like. After that, I started remembering a dream I had a long time ago, but I couldn't really remember all of it. Then I started dreaming the dream and dreaming it just about every night.

Q: All right. Now I want you to relax and try to describe, in as much detail as you can, exactly what happens in the dream.

A: That's the whole thing. I don't know. I can't really make myself remember too much of it. It's something about working but not in a plant like where I usually work. It's something about working outside where there's a lot of stuff going on.

Q: How did the dream make you feel?

A: Well, seems like working outside and not cooped up inside a plant all day would make me feel pretty good, but that's what was weird. This dream ain't so nice. At all.

Q: Does it make you feel uncomfortable or unhappy about something?

A: Well, it just makes me feel kind of funny, I guess. I was telling Chuck a little bit about it, and he said it was weird.

Q: What else makes you feel funny in the same way?

A: Well.... It makes me feel funny sometimes when I go to a new plant on the first day.

Q: Tell me about that.

A: Well, lately I been working at this plant that makes TV's. The first day I was there, the lady at the front desk told me I had to wait for a guy to come show me in. So I waited. Finally the guy came walking up. He didn't look at me or anything. He just asked the lady at the desk, "This the new temporary for QC?" She said, "Yeah." And then he just walked off real quick. I figured I better go with him because I must be the new temporary for QC, whatever that is. I went with him, and he showed me where to go and everything. But it made me feel real funny that he didn't say anything. Nothing like, "Hi," or even look at me or anything. But I just put it out of my mind. I figured he was real busy. People are almost always real busy at plants like that, and you got to be real businesslike, especially at a new plant on the first day.

Q: Did you ever find out what QC is?

A: Yeah. Quality control. That's a real important department. QC's job is to make sure all the TV's are the highest quality. That's not so easy. The guys in QC tell me it takes lots of testing to have quality control.

Q: What is your job in the QC department?

A: Well, I usually take some boxed-up TV's off the line, carry them over to QC, and unpack them. Then the QC testers do all their QC tests. Sometimes they look at lots of test patterns. Sometimes they hit and drop and shake the TV's. The QC guys say all the tests are to make sure every customer gets all he can from his TV. When all the testing is over, I repack the TV's in boxes, put them back on the line, and take some more off the line for QC.

THE SECOND SESSION

Q: Have you begun to remember any more of your dream?

A: Yeah. . . . But it's getting real weird. And I only remember like . . . the feel of it. Like last Tuesday at work. I was awake. But then it was like I was dreaming. All of a sudden.

Q: Where were you working then?

A: I was at that same plant that makes TV's. The one I told you about.

Q: All right. Why don't you try to tell me exactly what you were doing that day. Take your time.

A: Well, QC got ahead of the game, so they sent me to another part of the plant where they do most of the packing. They had lots of boxes all stacked up to put TV's in. They'd just brought a big load down from the warehouse. They told me to stack all the empty boxes against the wall to get them out of the way for the time being. That was no trouble because the boxes were real light. I took my time and watched all the people working on all the lines. It was kind of interesting, all the different stuff going on. There was a lot going on all the time, and nobody seemed to notice me much. The empty boxes were so light I started to think about how this job was *real* light industrial for a change. That seemed kind of funny. I started laughing. Then some supervisor guy saw me and said to get busy, and if I didn't have anything to do that I better look busy. I almost laughed at that, too, but then everything seemed to get real funny all of a sudden. Somehow I knew it was a lot like that dream. The box I was holding started to feel kind of weird. It was almost the same, but weird. . . . I can't explain it.

Q: You're doing fine, Bill. Please continue. . . . What were you thinking when the box started to feel weird?

A: Well. . . . I was just thinking different. Maybe I was thinking like in the dream. Something was pushing and pulling me for a while. At the same time. I couldn't move, like I was in a vise. I saw everything around me in a real special kind of way. It was like I was seeing things for the first time ever in my life. I ran my hand along all the stacks of boxes. Maybe five hundred boxes. They felt so square and hard and kind of dry to my hands. I guess my hands were chapped and dry, but it was like the cardboard was, too. It was like my hands were made out of dry cardboard. Then the inside of my mouth started to feel all dry around my tongue. It felt kind of square and hard up in the roof of my mouth the more I thought about it. Then I just stood there looking at all the boxes. I finally picked up another box like I was going to try to get back to work, but I started feeling kind of sorry and scared for that box because it was an empty box and couldn't quit being an empty box. . . . It was all so weird.

Q: Did the feelings continue after that?

A: No. . . . It was over, and I just tried to put it all out of my mind. I kept on stacking boxes against the wall. Pretty soon QC started getting a little behind the game, and I was real glad when a supervisor sent me back over to QC.

Q: Is there anything else about boxes, or anything that looks like a box, that makes you have the same feelings and thoughts?

A: No. I don't think so. . . . But I been thinking a lot about boxes. I started trying to remember things. Then I remembered going to my mee maw's funeral. I was about five, I guess. I remember I couldn't see inside the box, so my daddy held me up in his arms and showed me. It was Mee Maw. I couldn't believe she was in that box all still and cold. Then they put the box in a deep hole and filled the hole up with dirt and left it that way.

Q: How did that make you feel?

A: I just kept thinking about what they had done, and I couldn't believe it. I remember riding home that night with Daddy and staring out the car window at all the dark country along the highway. Daddy tried to explain about how you go to heaven and live with God and all that when you die. I was listening to him, but all I could think about was Mee Maw inside that box under the ground. I could almost believe all that stuff about heaven. But I kept thinking it must be some kind of imaginary self that goes to heaven. I knew your real self had to stay there under the ground. And what I mostly worried about was what would you do there under the ground? Would you just have to lay there in all the dark and quiet and just be bored for years and years? Then I'd say to myself, no, it couldn't be like being bored, because you wouldn't even be alive. You wouldn't be doing anything. Not even thinking. Then I started trying to imagine what it's like not to even think. I tried to quit thinking about anything. Then I realized I was thinking about not thinking. I guess you really can't ever quit thinking. You keep on thinking even when you're asleep. Maybe even when you're dead. . . . Maybe that's what dreaming is. Maybe it's all that thinking you do when you're asleep. Or when you're dead and alone. And stuck in the dark. When you're not really alive anymore and don't have anything to do except remember things and think about how you'll never really be part of the world ever again. . . . It's funny how all that stuff about not being alive reminds me of that dream. A lot. And that's so damn weird because I can't even really remember much about what happens in the dream. Like I won't let myself remember it. But it's like all these memories and stuff are around me all the time. Almost like that dream is reaching out to me.

THE THIRD SESSION

Q: All right, Bill. You indicated on the phone that you'd made a lot of progress in remembering the dream. . . .

A: I'm remembering the whole thing.

Q: Did it help you to set your alarm clock like I—?

A: No. You don't understand. I don't have to try to remember it anymore. It remembers itself. I can see it in my mind. I can see the whole thing. Right now.

Q: When did you remember the dream?

A: Monday. I been up just about every night since. I'm almost even afraid to go to sleep. I don't think

I ever want to have that dream again. It's bad enough just walking around thinking about it.

(Bill's extreme state of anxiety at this point made it difficult to continue. Another major concern at this time was to avoid his slipping back into repression. Since he had shown a high degree of suggestibility in previous tests, I decided to place him under hypnosis for a few minutes. This enabled me to give Bill a post-hypnotic suggestion that reduced his fears to a manageable level and allowed us to continue.)

Q: . . . Beginning now you will be able to tell me every detail. Everything that happens in your dream will become clear. I want you to say whatever comes to mind without hesitation.

A: Okay. It's hard to. . . .

Q: Where were you working this week? Was it in that plant that produces television sets?

A: No. It was a lumberyard. That was the first morning the temporary service sent me to work at a big lumberyard.

Q: Did that make you uneasy?

A: Well, yeah. I felt a little funny like I always do on the first day. But pretty soon I started moving lumber and stuff around and forgot all about it. There was lots of lumber in lots of piles. It was all on pallets and lying alongside a whole bunch of train tracks that all ran side by side. I never saw so many train tracks. And they looked real familiar like I'd seen it all before. . . . Lots of workmen were moving around from one pile of wood to another all the time. And lots of flatcars would come in and go out on different tracks. There was a lot going on all the time.

Q: Tell me more about the trains and the tracks. Anything that comes to mind. Any particular feelings about those trains?

A: Yeah. All those trains coming in and going out. And the tracks don't ever really cross or come together. At least not that I can see. It just looked so familiar. . . . I guess it makes me think about how people don't really connect, but we just think we do. We think our lives and brains are all connected together. We think everything'll stay that way, and everybody'll live together forever and ever. Then somebody dies. Or maybe just moves away. Then you realize for a while how we're not really connected. We don't really ever know what's in other people's heads. . . . When somebody dies, it's like you almost understand how we're never really part of each other. We're not really thinking or feeling the same things. We're not living in the same skin. We're all completely separate and loose. Sometimes one of the pieces gets lost. Everything gets lost sooner or later. But then you forget. Or maybe just worry about it less and less till you almost forget. Then you go back to imagining you'll never die and nobody dies and nothing changes and people really understand each other and everybody is sort of connected and part of each other.

Q: Can you tell me exactly when you first made these associations? When did train tracks first give you these ideas?

A: It was whenever I first started having that dream, I guess. All that was in the dream, but I didn't

remember any of it till I saw all those tracks at the
lumberyard. . . . It was kind of like remembering
something in a quick little flash with a picture to
go with it. All that day more and more dream stuff
kept coming back to me like that. Like commercials in your head for a movie that's going to come
on later that day. But I tried to put it all out of
my mind. I wanted to keep on working.

Q: Exactly what were your duties at the lumberyard?

A: I had to move piles of lumber around on pallets
with a pallet jack so they would be in position for
loading on flatcars.

Q: Did you have any problems with the work?

A: Well, things got a whole lot busier and noisier the
later it got. Nobody paid much attention to me.
I guess they figured I was just a temporary, and I
was doing my job okay. Having no trouble. But
late in the day things got real hectic. Lots of cars
were lining up on the tracks. I couldn't keep up
and got confused. I didn't know which pallet to
put beside which flatcar. Or which one to move
first. I asked this guy for help, but I guess he was
too busy right then. But I was still kind of confused. I waited a bit and called for help again.
Nobody seemed to hear me. I figured they
couldn't hear me for the noise. I yelled a little
louder to a guy near me, but he just walked right
on by. It was real strange. I started to feel kind of
invisible, so I finally just stopped trying to do
anything. I was kind of disgusted by then, I guess.
I sat down on a stack of four-by-eight plywood
sheets. I was figuring, if things back up maybe
they'll come looking for me and maybe help me
figure out what I'm supposed to be doing. So I just

sat there. Soon I got to looking at the grain in the plywood. I never thought about it much, I guess. About how wood has all those swirls and whorls and knotholes. They look kind of like pictures. Some can look like fingerprints or designs. I started looking at some of the other stacks of wood. I wanted to see all the pictures I could find, and I found some that looked a little like faces. But twisted kinds of faces. I ran my hand across a plywood sheet that had this kind of big spiral on it. It looked a lot like a face. That's when the dream started trying to come true. Like before. . . . My fingers touched the wood. It was all hard. And dry. And my mouth was real dry. I tried to swallow, but I couldn't. The inside of my mouth and my tongue felt all square. Just like that other time. Then I saw everything. . . .

Q: What do you mean by everything?

A: All the train tracks and everything. I saw it like I was high up in the air looking down. I thought I was outside of myself, like I was dead or something. But I knew I was still alive, because I was seeing everything like I was still down there on the ground, too. All those workmen kept on being real busy. They didn't see me. They didn't see me anymore than the flatcars or piles of lumber did. . . . Right about then I was walking by this stack of plywood. I was still looking for any patterns I could see. Then a face jumped out. I stared at that face for a while, and I could almost see a mouth. It was in the middle. In the very inside whorl. It was like a kind of mashed circle. It looked like it was making a sound. Maybe a holler or scream. But I knew it had to be a real permanent and silent sort of scream. . . . Then it all came back to me real clear. I could see the whole dream wide awake. Like watching a movie.

Q: What's the very first thing you see?

A: I start to see all these things around me. I can see lots of people and things moving around me all the time. All these trains are moving in and moving out all the time in between all the real businesslike people and all the piles of paper and stacks of boxes and crates and piles and stacks of wood. Then I start to realize. I'm in the very middle of all this stuff, but nobody notices me. And I'm so busy watching all this stuff I'm not even noticing myself. . . . So then I start to see the things near me. It's just piles of wood. I can see the wood all around me. Lots of wood real close to me. And that's all I can see. Then I realize it all of a sudden. I'm a piece of wood! . . . No wonder nobody heard me or noticed me. How could anybody ever know what I'm thinking or ever know anything at all about my real inside self? And who would want to? Who's going to waste time talking to a two-by-four? . . . I start to realize I don't have any arms or legs. I couldn't walk around. Or even move. Or pick up anything. I couldn't even touch anybody to just get their attention. . . . In the dream, about that time, I start to get this real powerful, helpless, scared feeling. Like when you're in church, and the preacher is preaching about hell, and you start to think about being there with no let-up at all ever. . . . Then I know I'm stuck. I know I'm stuck forever being this thing that can't be alive but is. Right then I know I'm really nothing, and I know I'll be thinking about that and get reminded about

it over and over by everything that's anything at
all, forever and ever.

Q: What did you do then, after remembering all this?

A: I just kept on standing there. I felt tired and kind
of numb. I kept looking at all those rows and rows
of stacks of wood and all the people running up
and down and around all the time. I decided to try
and keep on working the best I could a little
longer. Quitting time finally came, and I left. I
don't guess I had done a whole lot of work, but I
felt real tired.

Q: Did you speak to anyone before leaving?

A: I thought about it, but I didn't see much need.
Nobody noticed me being confused about the job,
and I know they sure didn't want to hear about
any daydreams. But it was okay, I guess. They
were real busy that day. And I was just there to
help out the best I could.

Q: You've made excellent progress, Bill. Remembering the details of the dream was very important.
You overcame what is called the repression of
dream memory. Now we must identify the con-
flict and devise a means of resolving it. . . . So now
that you remember exactly what happens in the
dream, how do you feel about it?

A: Well, the dream don't seem too much like a
dream anymore. It's almost like a door to something else. A door to some place. Like that place
you go when they put you to sleep for an operation. After the operation, you try to wake up, but
you can't. This dream is getting that way. I'm
thinking weird, and I can't get out of it. I'm in
that lumberyard for maybe an hour after I wake
up. My mind keeps thinking that way and won't

stop. I can feel the acres and acres of lumber, trains, tracks, workmen. All spread out and stacked up in neat square angles. Everything square and busy all the time. . . . It's in my room when I wake up. In the mirror when I'm trying to brush my teeth. And it's not like I'm just seeing it or remembering it. It's like I'm living it. And every second is this lonesome, hopeless thing that just hangs there.

Q: Could there be anything else that comes to mind, anything at all, that you associate with wood in any significant way? What do you think of when you think about wood?

A: Well, I've thought about that a lot. I went home that night after work, and I just sat and looked at the walls. I have this paneled room, and I just sat and looked at the walls. It was like being in a cemetery or something. I could just almost feel the people, the life in the walls. I remembered about Mee Maw dying. And Paw Paw. I felt like they were in the wall just looking at me. And lots more, too. Like the walls were just full of faces and people from way, way back. And everything, the air even, seemed like it was just full of life. I could almost hear it crying out, if I would just stop and be quiet for a little bit. It's like the world was alive, and I was the only one that really knew it. Like I was the only one in the world that knew all this life was all around and crying out to be noticed.

Q: Do you have the same feelings about other wooden objects?

A: Well, I been noticing how a lot of stuff looks like wood, but it's not. Furniture and stereos and kitchen stuff and even cars. They all got these plastic and metal strips that look like wood. . . . It's kind of like we want to have all this stuff that looks like wood around us all the time to tell us things are okay. It's like we're ashamed of all our plastic and metal stuff. We don't really believe in all that plastic and metal stuff. It don't seem real. It's cold and phony, so we cover it up with phony wood that's really plastic and metal. We cover it up with more cold, unreal stuff that looks real, so we won't be ashamed or uncomfortable. . . . Sometimes I think we're trying to get back to some kind of pioneer time or something. Back when just about everything was wood. Log cabins and wood tables and chairs. Stoves and fireplaces burned real wood. People could talk to each other then. They had time. I wonder if we want all these wood things around so we won't forget about being together and warm in those cabins with all that wood a long time ago.

Q: What about the pictures that you see in the grain? Why do you think they're there?

A: Maybe all those lines in the grain are like some kind of current. Or waves in some kind of frozen ocean. Or like fossils maybe. . . . Maybe they're just things from a real long time ago. Maybe before we were born. That's it. Maybe they're like frozen memories from some kind of ocean your mind was in before you were born. It's like all those real and solid things we used to be part of a long time ago, but we lost it. So now we want all this wood around us to remind us about it.

Q: What do you think that long ago ocean was like?

A: I don't know. But maybe we got to get back to that, whatever it was. Even if it's strange and lonely and cold and hard for a while. Maybe that's the way it's got to be, because maybe what could happen soon is worse. Maybe we'll blow each other up or just forget how to look at each other or something. Maybe we got to go way, way back and remember all that stuff before it's too late. We got to remember how to be real. Even if it means going backwards to something weird and horrible. Even if it means going back to that world where things aren't alive, but they used to be and maybe will be again.

At the end of our third session, I strongly recommended that Bill try to take some time off from work as soon as possible. When I offered to call the temporary service and request that they find him a different work assignment, Bill assured me that he had tried the same thing and found that there were currently no other assignments available. He nervously explained that the job was only intended to last a few more days and that he would like to see it through. Having worked out his bizarre philosophy about life and lumber, he seemed much more composed, but I credited this to a dangerous confidence in his own delusions. I tried to warn him to take it easy. He merely smiled a very uneasy smile, accepted my prescription for some Valium, and made an appointment with my secretary to see me again on the following week.

Three days later I received a call. There was a great deal of noise in the background, and it took me some time to determine that it was Bill. He was at first apologetic about calling, and through the noise, I eventually heard him say that he had just remembered the experience of his own birth and some additional things about his dream. He wanted to meet me right away, if possible, at the lumberyard. Since he sounded very disturbed, I immediately jotted down the address, even though I knew this would mean canceling an appointment.

On arriving at the lumberyard, I quickly recognized the intense, systematic chaos to which Bill had reacted so strongly. While searching for someone in authority, I found myself staring at all the massive amounts of lumber in stack after towering stack. It was an even more imposing scene than I had expected from Bill's description. With such a large operation, it was immediately apparent that I would probably never locate Bill without some kind of assistance, so I stopped the nearest worker. A sunburned, middle-aged man in overalls said that he didn't know anybody by that name and directed me to the foreman, a slightly younger man with a deep tan.

I introduced myself and asked if I could speak briefly with Bill. The foreman frowned and, slowly pushing back his hard hat, stepped over to a clipboard that was nailed to a post. After flipping roughly through a couple of pages, he announced confidently that no such person was working at his lumberyard. When I asked if there could somehow be a mistake, all I got was a grumbling remark about how you never know with temps, the way they come and go.

Turning, I began to walk back toward my car and then remembered the tangle of streets I had hurriedly crossed to get to this place. I wondered if I had the right lumberyard. Had I misunderstood Bill and written down the wrong address? Hoping to catch sight of him somehow, I stopped next to a chainlink fence and looked back at the small city of people and lumber products.

Desperation was gripping me, almost as if I were beginning to succumb to Bill's dream myself. I truly wanted to say something or do something that might stop his hell in midflight, but he was not to be found.

As I reluctantly turned to leave, I tripped and fell across a low stack of plywood sheets. My hands and elbows touched the rough surface. For a moment my body described a kind of prostrate crucifix. And my eyes instantly found his familiar face, wildly distorted but unmistakably there, deep in the pattern of the grain.

A Woman's Life

W. WARREN WAGAR

*For the past decade and a half Warren Wagar has been
Professor of History at the State University of New
York at Binghamton. He has a string of nonfiction
titles to his credit, ranging from* H. G. Wells and the
World State *(1961) to his latest,* Terminal Visions, *a
study of the "world's end" theme in science fiction.
However, he has also been writing poetry and fiction on
the sly since childhood. Only when he turned fifty did
he begin to submit stories, and he has since been published in* Isaac Asimov's Science Fiction Magazine
and The Magazine of Fantasy & Science Fiction.

*The story that follows was inspired by Wagar's own
experience during a recent episode of open-heart surgery. It suggests that the best guidebook to the afterlife
may be Darwin's* Origin of Species, *with its struggle for
survival conducted by a Nature red in tooth and claw.
If that is how the natural world evolves, then perhaps
the supernatural world follows suit.*

The forever woman lay dying.
Death was not something that could happen to Bess

Merton. To anyone else, perhaps, but not to her. The gods had long ago condemned her to life.

She thought again of the patron at the library, the old man with the Slavic accent. His voice had been so shrill and insistent.

"Please, but I could not help to notice."

She had stared up at him, almost frightened.

"I mean, your name. Not to be afraid. I saw your name on desk, your name Bess Merton. In Russian, we say *bessmertnii*. That means, you know, immortal."

She had just continued staring.

"Please, not to be afraid! It's good luck. You are, in English, how can I say, the forever woman. You will never die."

In time it became a sour joke she told on herself.

Bess was a strong-looking woman of sixty, leathery and tall and heavy-boned, but her strength was all in her silences, which people misread. In fact she was shy, afflicted with that awful shyness that binds the tongue and bows the head.

She had no family, hardly any friends. Dogged, quiet, anxious, poor old Bess. The kind of gray soul who stays the same for as long as anyone can remember, immune to the raptures or ravages of time.

But now somebody half her age thought she was dying.

"Tell me," she said.

Dr. Herring gave her only a bleak smile.

"It's that bad?"

He searched for the right words. "I just wish you had come in a little sooner."

Bess looked away at the pale blue wall, then at the lamp in the ceiling. It was easier to confront lamps than faces, especially strange faces. Better burn yourself blind in the noonday sun than lock eyes with a stranger. She lay on the table, afraid to speak.

"Well, Bess," he said softly, "the angiogram we've just done shows you do have a problem. You're really lucky to be here."

She dug her teeth into her upper lip.

Lucky?

Bess Merton, the forever woman, librarian in the suburbs for thirty-five years, never sick, never late, the Doric pillar of her community, who used to think that old age was a punishment for drabness, suddenly wanted nothing more than to be a drab old woman. To live. Persian cats, herbal teas, African violets, till the end of time. Please!

In the beginning was the will, and the will was with life, and the will was life.

Something fluttered, like a bat opening its wings, like two bats, or three. Small and dark, with eyes glinting.

But they were not bats, and they had no eyes.

Only hunger.

Dr. Herring fidgeted with his notes.

"You're about 90 percent obstructed in the right coronary artery, with significant blockage in the posterior branches. We also found multiple lesions in the left circumflex system. What all this means is that the blood just isn't getting through. Your heart is starving for oxygen."

Bess tried to raise her head.

The cardiologist gently restrained her.

"Remember, you have to keep your head down after the catheterization. Just for the next few hours."

She swallowed.

"What comes next?" she asked, still looking at the lamp in the ceiling.

"Well, I would recommend bypass surgery, and preferably tomorrow morning. Your angina is so unstable, I just don't think you want to wait."

He paused to touch her hand.

"Naturally, I'll consult with Dr. Metcalfe, my partner. It never hurts to get a second opinion, although I'm sure he's going to agree."

Bess gave him a quick glance. His face was firm and young, his lips almost red.

"What about a surgeon?" she asked.

"Oh, we have a couple of good people we work with, and I think the best is still available for tomorrow. Dr. Vasilew. He's done hundreds of bypasses.

"The only problem we may have is your low ejection fraction. That's how we measure your heart's pumping capacity. Yours is lower than normal, which gives us just a bit of concern. It depends. I'll have Dr. Vasilew check out your angiogram this evening."

All the doctor talk was somehow relaxing. It reduced living and dying to mechanical processes, like overhauling a car. Bess had a moment's picture of Dr. Herring with an oilcan in one hand, a trusty wrench in the other. Just a prosaic tune-up.

But then the oilcan sprayed blood. The wrench changed to a knife, slicing the tender flesh between her breasts.

No.

Think again, Bess. Women were raised to listen to men, listen to all their explanations and their opinions and their swollen purple egos, and say yes, sir, yes, do whatever you need to do.

"I don't think I can go through with it," she said, staring resolutely at the lamp.

Dr. Herring cleared his throat. His hand touched hers again, and pressed.

"Bypass surgery is no picnic, I grant you. But a successful operation will save your life. The way your chest pains have been acting up these last few weeks, who can tell? Judging from the angiogram, I'd say you were overdue for a heart attack. It could easily be fatal, Bess."

She took a long slow breath. "I'm not ready. Let me go home for a day or two and get things sorted out."

He looked vaguely unhappy. "I couldn't take that kind of responsibility."

"I'm not asking you to. I'll just go."

"Please listen to me, Bess," he began.

"No!" she said, between hard-clenched teeth. "I'm not listening to anybody. Don't you see? I'm sixty years old. I'm not a little girl. Just give me a few days to think."

He walked over to a chair and sat down, not looking at her directly. "I'm sorry. Believe me, I'm truly sorry. But you must stay. Stay at least overnight, until we've had a chance to see if we can stabilize this thing."

Why did he have to be so reasonable?

Why did she have to die?

Why anything?

From the caverns high outside the world came the bats. Their wings spun round and round, armed with vibrating blades.

First to arrive near the widening hole was Thutmose. He slashed through the ether, trying to clear his mind.

His hunger surged as he flew. He needed a home

soon. A day or two, as the inside world measured time, and his pattern would be too weak to cohere. The energy stored from his last nesting was almost spent.

Now Bronwen dropped in from above, still freshly charged. She felt the presence of a fellow-pattern and banked sharply to repel him. The edges of their blades touched in a moment's phosphorescent agony. Thutmose veered off howling.

He was older, shrewder, stealthier, but also wearier. He might have to settle for another home, if he could find one in time.

Random visions crowded his mind, like moths dancing in the dusk. He tried to remember who he had been just before his last death.

The thought would not form.

But for an instant he glimpsed one of his long-past victims, a bejewelled young rani in her bright green royal dress, so easy to take as she lay panting with fever on her bed. After Thutmose nested in her, she had grown into a skillful seducer and poisoner. A sweet, sad, violent life.

The image whirled away, a scrap of memory lost in the void.

In the beginning was the will.

Bess pulled herself together, tightening her lips.

"I suppose I can stay until morning," she said. "I have to get back to the library, though. I'm what they call a fixture."

Dr. Herring smiled. "I'll stop by this evening after supper."

"It's not necessary." She looked at him briefly. "I don't feel a thing."

"If I can track down Dr. Vasilew, will you talk to him?"

She tried to raise her head, remembered, and let her muscles relax.

"I'm sure he has better things to do with his time," she said.

"Okay, but when he looks at your angiogram, Bess, I have an idea he'll want to see you."

The thought of the surgeon's eyes boring into her chest, even into pictures of her chest, was painful. A macabre magic lantern show, brought up to date. Surgical pornography. She shuddered.

Hours later, after picking absentmindedly at the meal on her tray and watching part of the network news, she got back to the serious business of dying.

The pain started low in her stomach, a dull ache that spread leftward and up.

She rang the nurse to ask for an antacid, but before help arrived she already knew it wasn't gastritis. Something was crushing her chest, like the foot of an elephant. She broke out in a sick sweat.

"Hang in there, honey," said the nurse. "I've paged Dr. Herring."

Bess was losing touch. Why didn't they give her a nitro? She had a full bottle in her purse when she came to the hospital that morning, but they had made her check it before she was admitted.

She tried to think about tomorrow, at the library. The director wanted to reorganize the children's section, make things more attractive, easier to reach. She had some ideas.

Another doctor was in the room now. Another nurse. Bess closed her eyes.

. . .

As Thutmose waited for the psychons in his wounded blades to cluster again, more visions of old lives plucked at him, stinging and caressing at the same time.

Processions of priests and peasants. Long hours in distant fields. A white-livered janissary in the court of Sultan Mustafa; Thutmose had seized the man as he bled from a would-be assassin's blade. The dusty years in the office in Hamburg, scratching letters to customers with a feathered pen that bobbed up and down, tirelessly.

He could not choose his memories.

Then he saw his latter-day favorite, a tubercular dandy of no account in fin-de-siècle Paris. Charming! He reeled along the rue Royale clutching a leather-bound copy of Baudelaire's Fleurs du mal, *eager for the death that makes life worthwhile. Thutmose would let him find another café, and another, and another, until he drowned.*

The visions stopped. Thutmose roused himself. The ether was warming, and a new prize waited below.

He knew only that he must be quick. What happened when many patterns gathered in their hunger and fury at the same hole, he could not forget. Each did whatever was required to gain the victory. Whatever had to be done. Hurt or maim or kill. Gladly.

Czeslawa arrived, wheeling and diving deliriously. She carried a high charge, higher even than Bronwen's, but she had centuries less experience. Her blades clattered noisily, a mark of the novice.

She bit Bronwen's rear, but not hard enough to prevent her opponent from turning in midsoar and giving her a deep cut.

Czeslawa dropped like a stone, falling through fathoms of ether, out of control. Later she might come back, but her psychons needed time to reassemble.

Everywhere the continuum was of the densest black, lit briefly by sparks of pain when patterns touched. Thutmose drowsed.

But not for long.

In the beginning, and always, and ever after, was the will.

Bess did not respond well to her medication. She hurt somewhere in her chest, and she knew that the nurses and the young intern who had joined them were trying everything they could.

The intern mumbled. ". . . pulse in the 20s . . . and she's really perspiring . . ."

They had to improvise in the absence of the Great Man.

Then she heard the familiar baritone of Dr. Herring. She hated herself for feeling relieved.

"How's it going?" he asked, almost jauntily.

She tried to speak, but nothing came. She could not open her eyes. Was she even awake?

Wake up, Bess. They're sharpening the knives. Come on, girl.

She sensed a distant rustle of wings, as if from another world. She wanted so much to rise to the surface, open her eyes, let the doctors know she was still there, still guarding her chest.

But the painkillers pumping through her blood carried her away again. She had a slow morphine dream of disembodied male voices, each deeper, more resonant, more paternal. The voices were dancing a solemn pavane.

"Did you locate Dr. Vasilew?" someone asked.

Bess strained to hear.

". . . on his way . . . daughter's graduation . . . told him . . ."

". . . has to sign . . ."

Has to sign?

Yes. The knives and needles could not slice and sew without her consent. But they would scare her into giving it, if they could.

She was stubborn, as cowards are stubborn. When they had offered her the director's job, and Willis Morris had begged her to step aside because he needed the extra money to put his kids through college, she said, no, it wasn't fair to her. No, she would not step aside.

He had come to her apartment that night with a box of flowers and talked her out of it.

What else could she do?

But when Willis left only a year later, the board decided to hire a younger woman with an M.L.S.

Bess had gone to the board and talked of quitting, but it was no good. Wouldn't Bess try to understand their point of view? The new library association guidelines. Unusually well-qualified candidate. A rare opportunity for the township. But if she couldn't see her way clear . . . ?

Just as the axe—oh, speaking metaphorically—was about to fall, Bess had seen her way clear.

Yes, sir. Thank you for hearing me out. I'll do my best.

The new director, with her M.L.S., was all business, and Bess had done her best.

She opened her eyes for a moment. A nurse bent over her, lifted her head, and adjusted her pillow.

"There. You'll be more comfortable now."

Her mouth felt too dry to make an answer.

The nurse smiled at her. "Dr. Vasilew will be here soon," she said cheerily. "You'll like him. He's sweet."

Bess swallowed, tried to speak.

"What is it, honey?" the nurse cooed.

Bess forced the words out. "I won't . . . sign."

"Oh, now, you wait till you've seen the doctor, honey. You just wait. Everything will be fine, you'll see."

Bess stopped listening.

It was just like the proposal. There had been only one. He was a skinny young law student with a ragged moustache and bright black eyes. So ugly and yet so vulnerable in his need.

They had met in the campus coffee shop on a rainy afternoon. He took her out a few times. Long before anything made any sense, he proposed.

No, I couldn't, no, you don't want me.

One chance at the brass ring, and she had been too shy to grab it.

Bess, you don't have the right instincts. Bess, you're not a killer.

Yes, but they won't kill me!

Come on, girl, wake up!

The psychic ether trembled now with the swarming of patterns. Some scouted the hole at the center and sniffed and flew off. Males who hated being female, even for one life. Fledglings who had died young and could not brook the insults of old age. Veterans who doubted that the victim would survive.

But the first arrivals clung to their purpose.

Thutmose hovered out of range, biding his time.

Czeslawa came back up and used her energy recklessly, diving this way and that, so fast that Bronwen could not catch her. But there was method in Czeslawa's frenzy, because each wild loop brought her closer to the warm hole at the center.

Bronwen was not fooled.

She took a shrewd guess and plunged into Czeslawa's path from above. Czeslawa dodged and spiralled away, losing her momentum. But she did not give up. Her reflexes were as quick as ever.

Thutmose took careful note, but kept his distance. He mused, haphazardly, on Czeslawa's youth. From her vibrations he sensed that a century had passed, no more, since her first life, and afterward, how many kills? No counting. She was a noisy thing, strong and reckless.

A few of his own kind remained, artful ancients of Egypt and Sumer and the Dynasty of Chou. This, too, he remembered. They knew how to wait, his kind. They could be deathly still.

Then, all at once, without forethought or mercy, they struck.

Yet only a few from his times were left. Not in a thousand years had he flown against a pattern of the older ages still, the ages of stone and cave. All gone now. Starved or slain, psychons scattered for eternity.

And some day?

Intimations of mortality seized him, shook him, sharpened his appetite.

In the final reckoning, there was no difference. Old or young, the single goal of all patterns was the same. To be incarnate. To merge pattern with brain, to move flesh, to feel blood, to link desire to memory to ego. The I! The I-who-am is reborn!

In the beginning was the will.

Bess opened her eyes, surprising even herself.

"Hello, Bess," a dark voice rumbled. "I'm Dr. Vasilew. We need to talk."

She turned her head slightly, and a man's face slowly took shape, a face with heavy brows and thick lips, a faraway look in his eyes.

At least he was not loud.

She listened.

The doctors had brought her heart rate up again with atropine. She was not dying. Or not yet. But she had to have the surgery. Had to have it.

"So you agree with Dr. Herring?" Bess asked.

The surgeon allowed himself a faint smile. "My only quarrel with Dr. Herring is whether we should operate tonight or tomorrow morning."

"And you—?"

"I'd rather go for tonight," he said, still with the smile, "but Dr. Herring thinks he can keep you ticking until I've had a good night's rest. We usually do a better job in the morning."

Bess closed her eyes, not wanting to think about anything.

The surgeon went on talking. Arteries. Plaque. Angina. Veins carved from her legs to make the grafts. God, it would be like a butcher shop.

"But I want to emphasize, Bess, this is not an operation designed to leave you a cripple. With any luck you'll be one hundred percent again. You'll be able to lead a completely normal life, go back to work if you wish within five weeks."

His voice was deep and soothing.

"To be frank, your chances will be far better on the operating table than they have been for the past twenty-four hours. Hearts are just not built to run on empty."

Back to the old auto mechanic metaphors. Bess conjured up endless rows of men in sea-green surgeon's uniforms with a gas pump in every rubber-gloved right hand.

Her will power was dissolving.

She hated herself, hated the flabby thing deep inside her, the spineless spinster who could not say yes and could not say no. All she had ever managed in life was to frighten babies with her bigness and her square face.

Willis Morris had not been frightened. The skinny young law student had not bothered to ask again.

Why fight now, just for the privilege of dying?

She shriveled on her bed, letting the sap of her resistance sink until she was like dry timber.

She signed the release.

She shut off her mind for the night.

The hole in the continuum widened steadily. Thutmose twitched and hungered. The victim's pattern, he could feel, was in its direst state, in that split-open time when the will is dead, and bats must bite—or move on.

A vision brushed his mind, unbidden, of his life as the Parisian boulevardier, addicted to champagne and oysters and sick rhymes. His hunger changed momentarily to a driving thirst.

For Pommery. For Taittinger. For the foaming wares of Charles Heidsieck and Pol Roger and Louis Roederer, silver blood to replenish the red that his victim had coughed into a basin every long sweaty night.

Then he braced himself.

There was only one way to be the I-who-am again.

As even the boulevardier liked to say, quoting the latest fashionable wisdom from across the Rhine, beware of pity. *Pity for the Higher Man is the last snare set in the path of the I-who-would-be-I.*

Czeslawa was whirling round the hole. Each snap of her swing brought her measurably nearer.

Swoop. Swoop. Swoop.

Bronwen tried again to intercept her, but Czeslawa was ready. She braked for the slightest instant, avoiding her opponent's blade and raking her as she passed. The ether erupted in scintillas of white-hot pain.

Thutmose prowled close by.

Swoop. Swoop. Swoop.

One rearward edge of Czeslawa's pattern grazed the hole. It was finally wide enough for entry. Unless someone stopped her now, she would hook and plummet.

Out of the black Bronwen flew headfirst.

Czeslawa had not expected her. Collisions could be fatal. But Bronwen's speed was too great for braking or dodging.

The Welsh noblewoman and the Polish peasant girl, stripped to their warrior-souls, clashed in the pitchy ether for the prize of living again. Thutmose winced.

Somehow, the patterns missed slamming together, core to core. But their blades meshed and disassembled. Showers of fire filled the continuum.

Holes opened wide enough for no longer than a scream.

With his last reserve of strength, the wily Egyptian threw himself at his target, fell in, hooked, and pounced.

Behind him the ether sealed impenetrably shut.

The victim's pattern was soft and stupid.

It stiffened at the first slash of his blade. Then it hunched into a corner and went limp with terror.

Thutmose tore and ripped. He had no time to waste. He drilled open the core of the pattern, before it could stiffen again, and spat out a million mewling psychons.

They would never regather.

In an instant, Thutmose shredded the rest of the pattern. Psy-tissue sprayed in all directions as he worked.

Then his new home was clean. He slipped into the empty nest comfortably. Every notch locked in place.

He turned on. Memories of the XVIIIth Dynasty and two hundred stolen afterlives trooped into line, all at his command. The memories of his new hostess waited meekly in front. Her life would be simple and lazy. A sweet suburban idyll.

Three days after the operation, Dr. Vasilew dropped by. Bess took his hand and held it tightly.

"Thank you, thank you, Doctor," she purred. Although her lungs were still partially collapsed from the open heart surgery, and her pulse pounded loud and fast in her ears, she felt whole again.

"You won't forget your exercises, now?" Dr. Vasilew asked.

They wanted her to take lots of deep breaths and cough as hard as she could, to help her lungs inflate. Otherwise, there was a risk of pneumonia.

"Every hour on the hour, Doctor!"

"Not sorry we went in there, are you?"

She laughed. "You know what all the shrinks say about us old maids. Scared to death of men because our daddies beat us."

She patted Dr. Vasilew's arm. Her eyes glistened.

"I was just being silly," she said. "Who wants to creep around gumming nitros? Not me. I'm a reformed character, Doctor. From now on, my heart goes out to you any time!"

He chuckled.

"I wish you could see how much you've changed," he said.

She laughed again. "So give me a mirror, and I'll check it out."

"No, I mean your frame of mind. Bypass operations sometimes do that to a person. When your heart's not running on empty, you have more energy, more get-up-and-go."

Bess looked him in the eye. "Well, just say the word and I'm got-up-and-gone out of here, believe me. I can't wait to start living again."

She took the deepest gulp of air she could manage and on her palate it tasted like a fine *blanc de blancs* champagne, poured icy cold from a magnum at Maxim's.

Dr. Vasilew beamed at her.

"You look like a new woman," he said.

In the beginning was the will.

Into That Good Night

JAMES STEVENS

James Stevens lives in Puerto Rico, where he works as a creative consultant in the advertising business. He writes, produces, and directs television commercials; composes and produces commercial jingles; acts; and is a voice-over announcer. He also writes, and his stories have appeared in Worlds of If, Tomorrow Today, Generation, Isaac Asimov's Science Fiction Magazine, *and elsewhere. A firm believer in keeping many irons in the fire, Stevens is plainly a master of all trades, as the following story testifies.*

"Do not go gentle into that good night . . . / "Rage, rage against the dying of the light," wrote Dylan Thomas. But should we take the poet's advice?

Cassie was dictating the script for her weekly thinkpiece on Trans/World/Cable's highly rated *VideoMag*—a contemplation of Jean-Paul Sartre's existential philosophy with a commentary on how his notion that "hell is other people" still applied to Western man in 2023—when Lázaro came back from the dead.

His face looked pale and puffy, with an unhealthy greenish cast that told her he'd been barreling flat out on no sleep for at least a couple of days. One look at him and you knew that here was a man in a hurry. Except for the eyes. They looked serene, almost exalted. And, somehow, haunted.

He started talking with no preliminaries—no embrace, no kiss, no hello. "Listen sharp, Cassie. You're going to have to make the toughest decision of your life with what I'm going to spiel you, and I won't have time to do it more than once. It won't take them long to figure out where I've holed."

"Who?"

He shushed her. "Caribbean Cryogenics' security goons. Kill the questions. Just let me talk, ah?" Cassie bit back her curiosity and nodded.

"I saw Alba."

Cassie couldn't stop herself from blurting out, "But she's dead."

Lázaro nodded. "So was I."

"Your brains are loose," Lázaro said to Raúl Betances, the president of Caribbean Cryogenics. "I get paid *not* to get croaked."

"Your death would be only temporary," Betances said. "The process works. We guarantee it."

Lázaro laughed. Betances frowned. "Skysurfer's joke," Lázaro explained. " 'Should this parafoil prove defective, we will cheerfully replace it.' "

"Mr. Odonojiú," Betances said stiffly, "my father founded this company twenty-six years ago. We have successfully maintained something in excess of twenty thousand clients in that time."

Caribbean Cryogenics had started in Puerto Rico in

1997 as Rebirth Unlimited, a company offering the terminally ill the opportunity to be frozen right after death and thawed out and revived when medical science had progressed enough to cure the disease that had killed them. In an era of social upheaval, in which multitudes expected the Second Coming momentarily, those who tried to cheat death by choosing the ice were ridiculed as emotional infants, lacking the maturity to cope with life.

"Cryobabies," Lázaro said.

"That is what some people called our first clients, yes." Betances pursed his lips disapprovingly. "Comics made jokes. But the expression went out of fashion at least twenty years ago."

Lázaro grunted. "I'm a hotbed of nostalgia."

Lázaro thought Betances's desk and chair seemed small, and it occurred to him that they had been deliberately chosen to make the bearlike man loom even larger in contrast. The piney scent of Peruvian candlewood tickled the nostrils, and hidden speakers barely whispered a spare arrangement of the Cole Porter classic, "Miss Otis Regrets."

"You've heard of Dr. Ana María Baralt, of course."

"I doubt there's a Maori tribesman or a *jívaro* left in the Mato Grosso who doesn't know that name."

"Well," Betances continued, "the regeneration techniques that won her the Nobel have enabled us finally to . . . revive some of our clients."

Lázaro's eyes sparkled with sudden interest. "You've brought deaders back?"

"We don't call them that," Betances said with barely masked annoyance. Then he softened his voice. "But, yes, we have resuscitated and cured some of our clients."

"But that's incredible! Why haven't you done any drumbeating? I've seen nothing on the DV."

"There have been certain unforeseen . . . complications."

Lázaro's excitement subsided. "Oh. Your reborns croaked."

"They did not 'croak,' Mr. Odonojiú." Betances leaned across the desk, tired, incredulous, bewildered. "They killed themselves."

Three people had been resurrected—a man and two women—and each had committed suicide at the first opportunity.

"And we do not know why," Betances said.

"Wake another and ask."

"We cannot. Our contract guarantees we will revive no client unless we are certain beyond a reasonable doubt he or she will survive. That, obviously, is no longer the case."

Lázaro nodded. "So that's why you want me to. . . ."

"Let us kill you. And resurrect you a week later. So you can tell us why."

"But why me? You say the death and resurrection process is risk-free, and I'm a man who makes his living taking risks. Why don't you use one of your own people?"

"Because there *is* a risk. . . ."

Understanding spread over Lázaro's features. ". . . that after you awaken me, I may croak myself. . . ."

Betances nodded grimly.

Cassie glared at Lázaro. "Why do you keep shoving your life into mine? I'm not your wife, lover and confidante anymore. You've got plenty of femmies hanging off you. Why don't you go irk one of them?"

"They don't mean squirt to me, and you know it. The divorce was your pet, not mine. As far as I'm concerned, we're still a pair. We just live apart."

Cassie sighed, exasperated. "Well, I always figured you'd kill yourself with one of your damned stunts, but never on purpose."

"You know I never shoot a gag if I don't figure I've got the odds. Lax Odonojiú backs no long shots."

Cassie coldvoiced him. "Like with Alba?"

Lázaro looked like he wanted to kick her face in. "You never miss a chance, do you? You just can't let her rest in peace, can you?"

"She was only nine years old, Laz!"

"I know that!" He slapped the tabletop so hard that for an instant Cassie feared the oak might crack. His hand stung, but his face didn't show it. "I know she'd've been twelve two weeks from tomorrow. I know you can't make another little. And I know you fault me." He drew a ragged breath. "But, for Cristo's sake, Cassie, don't you know I hurt too? Don't you know I loved my baby? Don't you know I wish every day it'd never happened?" He shoved his crow-black hair angrily off his forehead. "But it was an accident. It wasn't my fault. That's what an accident is, Cassie. Some terrible thing that isn't anybody's fault."

Usually Cassie left it there. But not tonight. She looked at him coldly, because although she didn't doubt his sincerity, she knew how selfish he was. When it came to the stunts, to the risks, to testing a suborbital bailout pod or piloting a prototype one-man sub to the floor of the Milwaukee Deep, he never considered the havoc a small misjudgment would wreak on others' lives. If he liked the odds he went with them, and he never understood that in the long run you can't beat the house. Sure, he'd lost bad only once, but that time he'd been gambling with Alba's life.

"When you killed her," Cassie said deliberately, "you killed the most important part of me."

Stung, Lázaro looked up. She'd never taken it this far before. "Look," he said, his voice taking on an edge, "she *wanted* to do it. She'd done it a million times without a glitch. I taught her to fly those foils like an angel. Better than me, better than anyone. You know that. You two were linked."

"But her skill made no difference in the end, did it? What you gave her couldn't save her."

Anger branded his cheeks. But it was the pain in his eyes that shook her. *My God*, Cassie thought, *he still loves me. He hates me, but he really does still love me.*

But she was vindictive enough to use his pain against him. Because he owed her for The Nightmare, and for the nameless dread that flooded her when she least expected it, and for the scalding emptiness only Alba could fill but never would again. Because the pain he'd caused her would never stop, and she was too selfish to let him share it.

But most of all, because he was part of her hell. And she part of his.

"That's unfair," he said.

"You sent her up in poor weather."

"The weather was *acceptable.*"

"But it wasn't *good!*"

Lázaro opened his mouth angrily, but gritted it shut without speaking.

"And when you saw the camera helo tossed straight

at her by the updraft," Cassie said, biting off each
word, "and you saw her sucked into the helo's blades
in spite of her frantic struggles—"

"God *damn* you, stop!" He stalked out onto the
balcony and glared down at the traffic seventy-eight
stories below. Ozone bite rose from the rush-hour of
electricars.

Cassie followed him, breathing heavily. "I know
exactly what she felt, you know, because we were
linked. But what I've always wanted to know is . . .
what did *you* feel?"

A look she'd never seen hardened his face, and it hit
her that she'd finally taken it too far. For a long moment, he said nothing. "I felt . . . ," he murmured, and
she started to interrupt, but the pain in his eyes
stopped her. He sat down wearily on a woodweave
loveseat. "I wished it were me instead of her."

Cassie felt suddenly ashamed. *God,* she thought,
sitting next to him and hugging his shaggy head to her
breast, *this poor man. This crazy, lonely, aching man.*

After a while, she said, "So this is your chance to
eat your cake and have it too, ah?" He wrinkled his
nose questioningly. "Make your death wish come true
and live to spiel about it. Your ultimate fantasy made
flesh."

"Is that what you figure?" he said angrily. She nodded sadly. "Well . . . I just know it's a got-to."

"It's always a got-to," Cassie said with a touch of
sarcasm. She released his head, sighed. "You wouldn't
be you, would you?"

He scratched the side of her arm like a puppy paw-
ing at a door. "I love you, Cassie. You're the only one
who's ever really known me."

"I know."

"And you're the only one I've ever really loved."

That didn't mean he hadn't made love to others. Or lied to her about it. Just that there'd been no permanent emotional links. And he'd never known she knew.

"Me too," she said.

"Still fault me for Alba?" he whispered.

"Yes." He jerked away, tense with rage again. "Though I figure you've suffered for it." *But not enough.* "When?" Cassie said.

"Tomorrow."

"You don't give much warning."

"They called only this morning. They need it yesterday. I'll be gone a week. Be like a business trip."

Only this trip, Cassie thought, *there'll be no femmies.* She'd discovered he liked them busty, big-boned and blonde. Like her. She supposed she might have taken it as a compliment, but she hadn't. And now she was icy scared. What if Laz didn't come back from this gag?

"Do you want to love?" she said.

He looked up, flabbergasted. "You sure swing freeze to fry."

Later, she cradled him like a child until he slept. She studied the scars on his face, the pink patch on his temple and cheek where they'd covered the burn from the wreck of the ramjet Porsche with nuflesh. She remembered when he'd crashed his trike into a tree to impress her, and opened a gash across his forehead that took fifteen staples to close. It had been just one of numberless cuts, wounds, tears, abrasions, breaks and fractures he would eventually suffer. Though he'd been only three years old, he'd treated the injury with the stoic disdain which became his trademark as an adult.

Cassie had just moved in next door, the little *gringa* from the Mainland, and he'd done it because she was two years older and she'd called him a baby who couldn't do squirt. Sneering through the blood on his face, he'd said, "Now you!" When Cassie refused the challenge, he'd grinned through the streaming blood and said, "Won."

Even then, young as she was, Cassie'd thought it a silly victory. But it had set the pattern. He took up each challenge; she stood by and watched. He grabbed life's reins and made it jump through hoops; she was happy just to hang on for the ride. And, he'd succeeded in his intention. She'd been impressed. And, yes, in a funny way, attracted to this mad little boy.

Then, just a day shy of his eighteenth birthday, he'd brought home Puerto Rico's first gold ever in the World War Games, becoming at the same time the youngest medal winner ever in suborbital dogfighting, a distinction he still held. Two million people, more than half the island's population, mobbed Greater San Juan's avenues and expressways to cheer his triumphant return. That's when the media had fallen in love with Lázaro Odonojiú, and he'd become a T-shirt, a Saturday morning kidvid adventure series and a programmable play-action figure ("some assembly required").

They'd loved his colorful hispanicized Irish surname, and his nickname, *El Gallito*, the Fighting Cock, which he'd earned because like those fierce fighters of his island home, he packed enormous courage and aggressiveness into a tiny body.

They'd loved, too, his shameless *fuerza de cara* (the Puerto Rican equivalent of *chutzpah*), and they'd simply gone crazy when he'd dropped his pants on live DV and mooned the world to show off the face of anarchic '70s actor-comic John Belushi he'd just had tattooed on his ass.

Now Lázaro lay still, breathing hardly at all, and in the soft moonlight filtering into Cassie's bedroom his face became a silver deathmask.

She ached to put things right between them, but knew it was hopeless. Something sick inside her took twisted pleasure in speaking angry words when understanding was wanted, in hurting when healing was needed.

She swallowed the two morphex beads which sometimes blessed her with a dreamless night's sleep, and sent up a silent prayer that tonight they'd work. An old joke flitted into her head as she finally drifted into sweet oblivion. *Women: can't live with them, can't live without them.* How perfectly that applied to Laz.

Her last waking thought was of Sartre. *Oh God, yes, hell* is *other people.*

When Alba said, "Toy," and toddled off toward her room, Belkis, the Dominican cleaning lady, thought nothing of it. Alba could amble pretty ably for a two-year-old. She was constantly popping into closets to try on Mommy's nuleather mocs, opening kitchen cabinets to clatter cookware across the floor tiles.

As she whisked garbage into the disposal, Belkis smiled at the tot's growing independence. The child insisted on soaping herself in the whirlpool, walking unassisted down any steps she encountered. The disposal set up a terrible racket, and Belkis made a mental note to remind Cassie to call the repairer as soon as she got back from market.

Five minutes later, Belkis suddenly registered that Alba hadn't come back.

Alba's room didn't open onto the pool area, but Cassie and Laz's room did. And the two bedrooms adjoined. Alba loved the water and needed no coaxing to leap in when Cassie or Laz were there to pluck her out splashing and laughing.

Or even when they weren't. And Alba couldn't swim.

"Alba?" Belkis called. No answer. "Alba." Again silence.

Praying she was frightening herself for no reason, Belkis rushed out to poolside as fast as she could without actually running. She hadn't heard a splash, but then the clatter of the disposal had been almost deafening. Now the day seemed deadly silent, and the Chattahoochee pebbles covering the surface of the walkway crunched with exaggerated loudness beneath her sandals. *Alelí* blossoms perfumed the air, but Belkis was too worried to appreciate them. Despite the burning sun, her flesh felt cold.

The pool came into view, and she breathed a sigh of relief. The child was nowhere in sight and, thank God, the water was undisturbed.

She took two more steps. And screamed.

Alba lay at the bottom of the pool, still as death under a fathom and a half of water.

Belkis didn't stop to think. The water was chilly and dragged at her clothes, and the chlorine Cassie had mixed in only a half hour earlier stung her eyes. But struggle as she might, she couldn't get close enough to reach the child because she had never learned to swim and every time she dove under, the water choked her.

A heavy splash, like a depth charge. Cassie was in the pool, arrowing for the drain that held her baby pinned to the bottom. Thanking God, Belkis retreated to the underwater bench at the shallow end and sat in water up to her breasts, gasping and coughing.

Beneath the surface, Cassie was almost crazed with fear and grief. She had experienced the drowning through her link with Alba just as she was selecting some fresh deep-sea salmon for that night's sushi dinner. Weeping and crying out incoherently, she had rushed home from the seafood shop sixteen blocks away, lashed by a feeling of desperate helplessness, for though she was aware of her little girl's terror, she could do nothing to save her.

And their link was crumbling.

Now, she finally managed to grab a chubby forearm and buoy the baby up and out of the pool.

Pressure on the back. Water mixed with fluids gushed from the child's nose and mouth. Repeat pressure. More fluids. When finally no more came, Cassie switched to mouth-to-mouth. Blow in, press down; blow in, press down. Over and over, endlessly.

But Alba's lungs refused to breathe, her heart refused to beat. Cassie wept, cursed, pounded with her fist on the child's chest. Fruitlessly.

Time was running out. Oh, Lord, she should have thought of it sooner! "Belkis," she cried. "¡Rápido! Call the rescue squad!" *Too late, oh, Lord, too late!* Her self-control was slipping away. Then, from deep in the back of her brain a steely voice said, *Calm down. Stop. Think.*

Belkis had rushed inside. Alba lay sprawled like a

corpse. Fighting desperation, Cassie breathed deeply, cleansing her lungs, her mind. *Discipline.* She forced herself to turn inward, shut everything out, *concentrate.* She crooned her mantra, over and over. And at last a sense of peace enveloped her.

She tried her link with Alba. Nothing. Dead air. She tried to probe deeper, and for the first time— perhaps because Alba's consciousness wasn't there to block her—broke through to another level and became suddenly aware of something she had never sensed before: a kind of *life force.*

Alba's body was still alive. The heart had stopped beating, the blood flowing, the brain thinking, but the aura of life still clung to every organ, every system, every cell.

Cassie felt as though she had suddenly sprouted invisible hands with which she could reach inside Alba's body and feel, and sense, and . . . and here was the heart, lying like a lump in her "hands!" Without thinking, she squeezed it.

And felt it spasm.

She squeezed again. And again. Rhythmically. Squeeze, release, squeeze, release. Over and over. And the heart jerked and fluttered, started and stopped, coughed and died, like an early auto fighting a crank-start.

Oh, Lord, she prayed, not understanding how she was doing this but knowing it was her baby's only hope, *please help me.*

And suddenly the heart leapt and began beating and the child cried out and a rush of unutterable relief washed over Cassie.

Belkis burst back, wailing, "I can't find the rescue squad's number!" Then she took in the scene, let loose a shriek—"*¡Milagro, milagro!*"—and swept up the baby in her sturdy arms and began consoling her.

Cassie's legs turned to butter and her body began shaking. She sank to her knees, weeping and laughing. But even as she rejoiced, fear coated her belly with a sheet of ice.

She had learned the terrible price she would pay should she ever lose her daughter.

The day Lázaro went off to die dawned bright and blue-skied. He slipped out before Cassie awoke, but left a note on his pillow. He'd scrawled, "I shall return," followed by *X*'s and *O*'s. She smiled wistfully and slipped the folded sheet into the drawer of her nighttable.

The smell of the grilled bacon-and-mushroom-on-whole-wheat sandwiches he'd fixed himself for breakfast still lingered in the kitchen. Cassie nibbled the nub of a sour pickle Laz had left unfinished and turned on the air extractor.

She decided she wouldn't think about Lázaro until he came back. But that was as easy, she discovered, as obeying her old meditation master's command: "Don't think of a white rabbit."

It became progressively more difficult when Lázaro didn't turn up after twelve, thirteen, fourteen days. A dozen times she picked up the phone to call the Caribbean Cryogenics people, a dozen times she reconsidered and hung up. She was concerned, yes, but she didn't want *him* to know it. With increasing frequency, she found herself having to use her mantra just to keep body and soul on an even keel.

Then he burst back into her life, trying to convince her to kill herself.

. . .

And this is the tale he told:

They'd killed him by inducing double pneumonia, knowing they could easily cure him when they thawed him out. Death, Lázaro discovered, wasn't unpleasant. It was, as Dylan Thomas had described, a "dying of the light." And when that final blackness swallowed him, Lázaro felt himself rising, soaring, breathlessly whizzing up an ebony shaft. Far above glowed a strange new light, soft and white. It swelled to fill the universe and he plunged soundlessly into it.

And through.

And found himself in a great field that rippled soft and golden to the horizon. A vast cloud crowded the sky, filtering through a silken light that cast no shadows and painted all colors pastel. A cool breeze brought the sweet scent of apples.

Three people awaited him. A pale halo outlined the head and body of each. Lázaro stood at the center of the golden living sea and watched them approach. He felt safe, serene.

They came neither quickly nor slowly, and they smiled, happy to see him. His father, short and stocky, no longer with the broken nose from his boxing days but still with the eyes that missed nothing, looked about twenty-six years old. His mother, all chicken-wing arms and drumstick legs, fragile but filled with wiry strength, looked twenty-six. And Alba, full-grown and lovely, with the face of the woman she would have become, Alba too looked twenty-six. Dead at sixty-eight, seventy-four, nine years of age—all now forever young.

One by one, they embraced him. Lázaro felt encompassed in kindness. Love glowed like a sun at the center of his soul. They had come to welcome him and escort him from the field of living gold to a place beyond the horizon where he would meet the Being of Light.

Where he would look upon the Face of God.

But when they left, Lázaro couldn't follow. Something prevented him. So they returned.

"Ah," his mother said, "you are one of those still bound to the flesh. You cannot accompany us until you are released."

Still, they stayed and joined with him in a union not unlike Lázaro's idea of what Cassie and Alba's link had been, and shared with him their thoughts and memories and love. During that timeless interval, he neither thirsted, nor hungered, nor tired. His body felt young and strong, bursting with energy and desperately eager to move beyond this golden field to whatever next awaited.

A cold lurch in his belly and an irresistible tug as of an unseen umbilical cord warned him recall had begun. Back in the laboratories of Caribbean Cryogenics the liquid nitrogen had been drained from his cryopod, and the resurrection of Lázaro Odonojiú, dead seven days from pneumonia, was under way. More than anything he'd ever desired, Lázaro wanted to stay. The pain of exile from this place promised to be unbearable.

His mother said, "Lázaro, don't be afraid. We will be here when you return."

Pain like molten lead melting his bones flooded his body, and invisible hooks impaled him and dragged him writhing and screaming in agony back down the endless ebony shaft.

The light of heaven fled, and finally there was no pain, save the shredding of his soul. . . .

The front door blew in off its hinges. Sulfur-stench stung Cassie's nostrils. Men in uniform crowded shouting into her apartment.

The head honcho barked, "Grab him!"

But Lázaro was too quick. Before anyone could reach him, he had plunged through the airscreen out onto the balcony and scrambled up on the railing. There he balanced nimbly, a highwire artist unperturbed by the seventy-eight-story drop to Avenida Piñones behind him.

"Come at me and I'm gone," Lázaro said. "You won't be able to rebirth what you scrape off the street."

"He's bluffing," one of the uniforms sneered, and started forward.

"¡No seas idiota, López!" the head honcho shrieked, too late.

"Cassie," Lázaro said urgently, "I'd have done this three days ago, but for you." Calmly he turned away and stepped off into air. His last words were: "Don't be long."

Cassie and the uniforms rushed out onto the balcony. Lázaro had flipped belly down, arms and legs extended in the skysurfer's flying X. In perfect control, he swooped across the teeming avenue and disappeared into the darkness of a construction site that was abandoned for the night. Seconds later, they heard a pulpy thud. Cassie felt sick.

All the King's horses and all the King's men, echoed through her stunned mind. *All the King's horses and all the King's men. . . .*

"This whole scenario's out of bounds," Cassie said angrily. "Crashing my space, killing my husband, snatching me!"

She sat in an uncomfortable plastic chair in an interrogation room in the Caribbean Cryogenics compound. She could taste a hint of ether in the chilled air, and in the background she could just make out the faint strains of an instrumental version of a sixties rock ballad called "Endless Sleep."

Raúl Betances eyed her coldly. "It is all quite legal. The Industrial Security Act of 2017. You have had illicit access to corporate secrets."

"Whale *mierda.*"

Betances's brow furrowed, but he retained his composure. "Your former husband was in our employ when he died. He had important information for which we paid him in advance. He absconded with that information three days ago, and we know you are the only person he had contact with." Betances looked as if he would have enjoyed slicing up her brain and riffling through it. "What did he tell you?"

Ignoring the question, Cassie said, "You are in deep drek."

Betances did a double take. "We?" He laughed, a fat choking wheeze.

"I'm an accredited digital video journalist. I've got freedom of information rights. And I work for a bigger corp than yours. You don't manhandle Trans/World/ Cable personnel."

"I am certain they would understand the special circumstances," Betances said. But he looked worried.

"You bank on it."

Betances's deskcom chirrupped. "Betances," he

growled, slapping on the privacy barrier so Cassie heard nothing more. As he listened, his flesh paled. Finally, he flicked off the barrier and eyed Cassie unhappily.

"Problems?" she suggested.

"A T/W/C security squad. They demand your instant release. Or else."

Cassie's interest perked up. "Or else what?"

"They did not say." Betances swallowed his frustration. "How could they have known?"

Cassie showed him the ghost scar on the underside of her left wrist where the medicos had implanted her distress beeper.

"Lucky guess."

Betances closed his eyes and massaged his temples. "My dear Mistress Darcel, let me be frank. We know what Odonojiú must have told you."

"Then why the melodrama? Why was he on the run from you?"

"He wanted to communicate his experience to you. For personal reasons, he said. We wished otherwise." Betances pursed his lips. "Are you going to satellite this information?"

Things fell into place for Cassie. Her eyes widened. She was just beginning to perceive the magnitude of the matter, its possible impact on the future of human life itself. *Lord,* she thought, *the social and religious repercussions.* . . .

"Wait a minute," she said. "If Laz is right . . ."

Betances nodded unhappily. "We would have the moral obligation to thaw out our clients and let their deaths become final. To . . . free their souls. We would, of course, be in breach of contract. We would in all likelihood be sued by every surviving relative and his brother. And we would most certainly go out of business."

But Cassie was thinking of bigger things. If Laz's Other Side were real, if people believed that taking their lives was a quick ticket to heaven, what would prevent them from committing suicide, one and all? Of course, looked at from a different perspective, if the Other Side were as Laz described it, what would it matter if they did? They wouldn't be destroying themselves, only moving on to a better life.

Hadn't that been precisely the Church's problem in the Middle Ages? Doomed to misery by reason of birth, with no hope for improvement or escape from his lot, why should any serf have been willing to endure his preordained lifetime of wretchedness and pain? Ah, said the Church, because you will be rewarded when you die.

Well, then, a shrewd serf might have thought, if I just end it all now, I could avoid a lot of unnecessary suffering and reap that lovely reward that much sooner, right? Uh-uh, not so fast, buddy, said the Church, ready with a catch that anticipated just this smart-ass line of reasoning. If you kill yourself, you not only lose out on heaven, you have to go to hell, which means even worse misery, only this time forever.

Well, that sure put the screws to the poor bastard in the worst way, but it was necessary. Otherwise, who would stick around to do the shitwork that kept the nobles and clergy living high on the hog? So maybe this whole notion of having to earn your way into heaven wasn't actually God's very own personal directive, but just a dose of good old politijive, just a whopping slice of that stale old pie in the sky.

"But if Laz is wrong . . ."

"Then thawing them out would deny them their chance at rebirth. It would be the cruelest thing we could do. With all the same legal and financial fall-out."

If Laz was wrong and she put out the story *and people believed her and acted on that belief,* then she'd be the most heinous of genocidal monsters, worse than Vlad Tepes, worse than Hitler, worse than Pol Pot, worse than Synghman Wu.

"What are you going to do?" Betances said.

Cassie shook her head wearily. "I don't know," she said.

"When I was fifteen years old," Cassie said to Juanma Saavedra, "I died on the operating table."

Saavedra had been sent with the T/W/C security unit in case legal counsel were needed. Cassie was grateful for the presence of an old friend. He'd handled the building maintenance crew that replaced Cassie's door and he'd calmed the building manager and Cassie's neighbors. Saavedra's looks leaned toward the craggy, and a bushy moustache and a crooked nose added to the ruggedness of his face, but a wistful look in his eyes prompted people to unburden themselves unbidden to him. Women in particular.

"When I was ten, Laz broke my nose with a stinger to first which I lost in the late afternoon sun," Cassie said. "So a couple of years later, I had to have this deviated septum straightened. And while I was under, my heart stopped. Just like that.

" 'An extremely rare occurrence,' the chief surgeon called it later. It took the surgical team five minutes and forty-seven seconds to restart me, five minutes and forty-seven seconds in which I was, medically, dead."

Cassie poured more Chilean cabernet sauvignon. Its crisp bouquet tickled the nostrils. "And you know what?" She sipped. The rich red tasted a lot smoother now that it had had time to breathe. "Nothing happened."

"Nothing?"

"No 'life-after-life experience.' No 'out-of-body' sensations, no warm reception by spirits of dead relatives, no communion with 'beings of light.' Nothing." She shook her head emphatically. "Well, hey, if that was death, buddy, then little Cassie Darcel didn't want to play; because what *I* found on the 'Other Side' scared the hell out of me."

"What?" Saavedra said. He watched her intently.

Cassie looked into his eyes, looked away, troubled. "Souls die."

She took a deep shuddering breath. "Now Laz says different. And backs it to the bone. So. Who do I believe? Me? Or Laz?" She forced a laugh and tried to toss off a joke. "The way he tells it, heaven sounds like a helluva place."

An awkward pause. Then, Saavedra said, "Are you going public with this?"

Cassie shook her head.

Saavedra cocked his head quizzically, like a dog puzzling something. "Are you going to kill yourself?"

Cassie shrugged.

"But you're thinking about it."

"It *is* on my mind," Cassie said drily.

Saavedra regarded her tensely for a moment. "Suicide's a sin," he said. "A one-way ticket to hell."

Cassie looked stricken, the understanding she'd expected rudely withheld.

"I'm sorry," he said. "I didn't mean to fright you. But that's what I believe. Life is sacred. If you shoot this out over the DV, you'll be responsible for every glitchhead who kills himself on your say-so. You know that."

He gave her a hard look. *It's too big a weight, too big a weight,* her mind cried out, but just when she thought she'd burst into tears, his expression softened.

"And as for you," he said, "please don't think about death." He slipped his arms around her waist and gently kissed her. "Think about life."

It was unexpected and kind of corny, but it was just what she needed. For a moment, she felt safe, and could look with longing into his eyes and say, "Oh, God, Juanma, don't let me think about anything."

Sex is fun and life-affirming as hell, and if it's good it can make you forget what you want to forget—while it lasts. But no matter how good it is, when you wake up weeping in the middle of the night with the sour taste of nightmare in your mouth and your lover lies sleeping unaware, you realize nothing's changed. It all comes back down to you, alone with your seething brain in the dark. And so in the stark, chilling hours before dawn, Cassie confronted herself.

The more she weighed them, the more convincing she found Lázaro's claims. The man had killed himself without hesitation, secure in his convictions. What more proof did she need?

But still her own experience nagged at her. Dead for five minutes and forty-seven seconds, why hadn't she seen the things Laz reported? *Because souls die*, she thought. But she didn't want to believe that.

Maybe she hadn't been "dead enough" for her soul to slip out on her, ah? Maybe it took more time for the "life force" to abandon the body. Hadn't she found its aura still clinging to Alba almost ten minutes after the child had drowned?

Or maybe Cassie'd gone through the whole show, just like Laz described, but she'd forgotten or blocked it out when she'd re-embodied. Sleep studies proved people dream every night, but that few dream memories survive waking. Maybe locked deep in her subconscious, an afterlife memory lurked, prodding her now to take Laz's word.

She did so want to believe him. . . .

Like anyone else, she didn't want to die. She wanted to live forever. But she did, desperately, want her daughter back. She wanted her mother, too. And Laz. And all the others who'd left her before she could tell them one last time how much she loved them. She wanted to be with them, to love them and be loved back, to be cleansed and complete again.

And, Lord, she wanted an end to nightmares and nameless dread.

If only Laz were telling the truth. But he'd lied to her so often, been unfaithful so damn much. And the voice in her head kept whimpering, *Souls die.* . . .

She remembered his last words: " 'I'd have done this three days ago, but for you. Don't be long.' " And then his leap of faith.

No doubts. The man *believed*.

He was either crazy or right, and she knew him far too well not to know the difference.

The question was, Did *she* believe?

Did she trust him?

As the question echoed inside her head, her eyes slowly closed and, without realizing it, she slipped hungrily back into sleep. And found The Nightmare waiting.

Alba swept across the sky like a silver gull, sliding off thermals into swooping dives, looping back up in arcs achingly beautiful. Sunlight glinted on bright blue ocean swells and fireballed off Alba's outstretched foils. Swimmers and sunbathers along Vacia Talega beach watched her work out, dazzled.

Cassie was used to it. Even as a baby, Alba had turned heads. Utter strangers exclaimed over her corn-silk hair and darkfringed olive eyes. When she smiled, they cried, "What a sweet child," and patted her head, or caressed her cheek, or affectionately brushed the tip of her tiny nose with a finger, as though touching could somehow rub a trace of her magic off on them.

By the time she was four years old, Alba was quite the little coquette, dimpling demurely, coyly batting her eyelashes, seeking and getting the attention of everyone she met. Yet somehow she avoided becoming a prima donna, a spoiled brat. And that, too, was part of her charm.

Sometimes Alba would find *trova* music on the radio and demand that Cassie dance with her. Then the two would cavort together with a shake of hips and a hurly-whirl of limbs that left them both laughing breathlessly. And Cassie would secretly marvel at her child's perfect body, at her lovely face, at the endearing little person who inhabited them.

They loved each other in a way beyond the usual

mother-daughter bond. Cassie had felt the first in-klings of their linkage with the baby's first stirrings in her belly. Warmth. Floating. Timelessness. Cozy con-tentment. And she had shared the shock of birth from Alba's point of view. Distress, terror, the trauma of cold, light, sound. Alba, in turn, had experienced the pain of labor, and the glorious relief of at long last pushing the baby out into the world, and the inexpres-sible strangeness and joy of finally nestling the child of your belly against your breast.

It had been their secret, shared only with Lázaro. Cassie had no yen to have scientists turn her daughter and her into lab dogs.

But though they shared this special communica-tion, they remained two entirely different persons, and in many ways Alba was more her father's child. She relished the same kind of roughhousing, displayed the same disdain for injury, sought the same challenge of leaning farther out over the edge than the next guy.

And Laz loved her like a rock. He taught her to roller skate and bike without training wheels before she was three, to foil fly before she was four. In her he saw himself, and it puffed him into the proud papa, eager to help her stretch beyond his limits. Like Laz, Alba hungered for the adrenalin rush and the height-ened sense of life danger brought, and they shared a special rollicking camaraderie that excluded Cassie and made her jealous.

Still, Cassie harbored dreams for her daughter. Alba would be a ballerina, supple and sleek, with Laz's long muscles and Cassie's expressive face. She'd be star striker of Team USA's first World Cup champions, tough enough to run all day and still have the stamina to back-kick the winning goal in the final seconds while billions watched on DV. She'd be a poet, a classical keyboardist, an electronics whiz. She'd converse with dolphins, run conglomerates, bear beautiful babies.

She'd make Cassie proud. And oh, how they would love each other!

Cassie lay in the sand, letting the sun burnish her skin while she watched Alba's aerial ballet through polarized lenses. Surf pounded the shoreline and a salt mist floated on the February air. The sand seemed incandescent.

Alba, this graceful child of the wind, knew everyone below was watching, and reveled in their attention. For a time she hotdogged to awed *oohs* and *aahs*, and then, at the peak of one great arc, suspended on her back between sky and sea, she suddenly folded her foils, dropped her head and plummeted like an eagle shotgunned.

All along the beach, people jerked upright. Something was wrong! This was a death dive.

Cassie felt everything Alba felt. Her breath stopped. Her heart tympanied in her ears. The swells below turned to slick stone. But there was no fear. Only the hot thrill of danger.

"Alba!" Cassie screamed just as the child crashed.

And suddenly the huge foils umbrellaed, trapping great scoops of salty air, freezing Alba's fall amid the foam of breakers. A flash of silver and she was flying level with the whitecaps, like a pelican in pursuit of lunch. A soft moan of relief escaped the watchers. And then, as Alba soared triumphantly aloft, a wave of applause.

My six-year-old daredevil, Cassie thought wistfully. Her heart ached with love.

Then, as it always did, the dream went sour.

The sky turned leaden and a helo clattered into view, trailing a dark vortex. Alba, suddenly nine years old, sailplaned above the chopper, strutting her stuff for the DV cameras. They were getting terrific footage in spite of the dodgy weather when a sudden updraft hoisted the helo higher than rehearsed, and the trailing edge of the vortex tagged Alba just as she was closing the second loop of a Cuban 8 and sucked her into the spinning blades.

Alba bucked and fought all the way in, calling on every trick Laz had taught her. But nothing worked. And Cassie lived it all with her, right up to the terrible moment when the blades bit into her baby.

Their link snapped, and it was as though someone had burned out Cassie's eyes. But what stabbed her through the heart were Alba's last words: "Daddy! Oh, Daddy!"

"If you'd found her sooner, maybe," the medico said. "But the brain's gone. When brain cells die, goodbye."

"There must be something you can do, Dr. Ogawa," Saavedra said.

Ogawa sighed and assumed a patient air. "In a way, morphex is like aspirin. People use it because it works, but they have no idea *how* it works. Morphex is not a sedative, narcotic or hypnotic, okay? Morphex acts directly on your brain waves, makes them nice and regular and smooth. That's why you go to sleep. But you can't kill yourself with an overdose. You can flatten your brain waves to a faretheewell. But that just kills the brain. The body keeps chugging right along. Brain needs the body, body doesn't need the brain."

"What about the Baralt techniques?"

"I'm sorry. The applications are still limited. Under certain conditions now, we can regenerate liver tissue, the stomach lining, damaged alveoli. An article in the current issue of the *Lancet* reports that they've been able to regrow a severed finger in South Africa. But I'm afraid brain tissue's still a good many years down the road."

"Can't you freeze her till then?"

" 'Let us ship you to the future'?" Ogawa said, ironically quoting Caribbean Cryogenics' current advertising slogan.

No, Cassie cried out, but her throat made no sound.

"Yes," Saavedra said.

"Did she leave specific written instructions to that effect?"

"I don't know."

"Are you a relative?"

"No."

"Can't do it, then."

"You'll let her die?"

"It's not a question of that. That's a healthy body. You'd have to put a bullet through the heart to kill it." Ogawa sighed. "We've got a whole garden of vegetables just like her in this ward."

Saavedra was ready to settle for even a crumb. "Well, where there's life, there's hope."

Ogawa's eyes went icy. "Mr. Saavedra, forgive me if I sound heartless, but I assure you the case is quite the contrary. The fact is this woman is dead. Yet because the law forces us to keep her hooked up to these high tech gizmos as a 'precautionary measure,' someone else who, given access to this equipment might live, won't, while this . . . this *corpse* fakes it."

Saavedra flushed scarlet. "Dr. Ogawa," he said, barely keeping his rage in rein, "this woman tried to take her life. If she dies without regaining consciousness and repenting, she will spend all eternity in hell. Do you want that on your conscience?"

Ogawa took a deep breath, then looked at him levelly. "I'm afraid I don't share your religious convictions. However, isn't it another tenet of your faith that God's will be done?"

"Well . . . yes. . . ."

"Good. So here's what we'll do. I won't kick her out of the hospital or pull the plug on the life support. Let's let Him work out the rest."

Cassie's heart throbbed, thrusting rich blood through hearty arteries. Her diaphragm tensed and relaxed in slow rhythm, pumping oxygen into pretty pink lungs. Her kidneys sucked wastes from her system, her endocrine glands manufactured their magical enzymes, her hair grew, her fingernails lengthened. Each organ functioned to perfection. The blind retinas of her eyes registered sharp images, her deaf eardrums vibrated sympathetically to the rumble of voices and the mechanical murmur of expensive machinery. Sparked by high technology, Cassie's body marvelously simulated living.

But trapped inside a dead brain, the fragment of immortality that called itself Cassie Darcel sensed everything, controlled nothing.

She had made her choice. *Her* choice. She'd made no attempt to persuade anyone else to ape her course of action, because what others might or might not do given her situation was neither her concern nor her responsibility. She couldn't even say if she'd made the right decision.

What she did know for certain was that the only man she'd ever loved had overcome enormous obstacles—good Lord, he'd come back from the dead!—to ask her to do something that, stripped to the bare bone, translated into the desperate plea: trust me.

Trust me.

She'd wanted very badly to trust him, to believe in him. Always. Perhaps more than anything else. If only he'd made it possible, it might have made all the difference.

And now, when she'd least expected it, this chance, this one last opportunity, had come eerily knocking. All she'd had to do was bet her life on it. The definitive put up or shut up.

In the end, as hard as it was for her, she'd decided she had to borrow a leaf from Lázaro's book, she *had* to take the ultimate gamble. Because, in a funny way, she figured she had the odds. And the stakes were worth the risk.

Only now she'd trapped herself in this unexpected and terrible cul-de-sac.

She felt as though she were slowly smothering, and that this feeling would never stop. Time was endless, as ponderous in its passing as glaciers.

She was only thirty-eight years old and wonderfully fit. They might keep her body going for decades. Eventually, of course, nature would claim it. But in the meantime, caged in this gross flesh, she'd go slowly mad, yearning in mounting desperation for Alba and Laz, cruelly tormented by her helplessness.

Year after endless year of living hell.

It wasn't fair. Oh, Lord, it wasn't right. Her thoughts skittered hither and yon, seeking an out. There had to be one. *Had to.*

She knew she was panicking, but couldn't control herself.

She tried desperately to escape, to tear her soul free from its prison of flesh. She was a madwoman in a lightless cell, crashing against padded walls that yielded but would never crack.

The nurse who was replacing Cassie's depleted glycogen pack gasped at the life support readout.

Heart: trip-hammering.

Blood Pressure: sky high.

Respiration: rapid and heavy.

The systems monitor automatically paged Ogawa, who charged into the room only moments later.

"*¡Qué pasa!*" he barked at the nurse.

She pointed to the data raging across the CRT screens.

His almond eyes went almost round. He swore softly in Japanese. Then, to the nurse, "We've got to trank her, Duarte. A crash dose. *Rápido.*"

Somewhere inside Cassie's terrified soul, a steely spark of reason still blazed. *Calm down, stop, think.* She began to hum her mantra.

She shut everything from her consciousness but the fluid Hindu words with their bell-like resonance. . . .

. . . *om mani padme* . . . *om mani padme* . . . *om mani padme.* . . .

. . . and a strange thing happened. Just as her desperation had somehow panicked her body, these soothing emotional vibrations now began to calm it.

She felt as though she had once again sprouted the "invisible hands" with which she had massaged Alba's drowned heart back to life. She considered this new and unexpected development. Then, after a moment, she "reached" tentatively inside her own body and with an assurance that took her by surprise began to apply the healer's comforting touch.

She continued chanting steadily, focusing her entire being into what she was trying to do. Her "hands" encircled the thrashing dove of her heart, felt its throbbing terror. At first she simply held it tight, letting it absorb her strength and calm. It fought her, but she kept a firm, reassuring grip until it seemed to sense she meant it no harm.

Then she began stroking it. Gently, gently, her hands caressed and quieted. And slowly, then faster, the tide of fear receded.

Nurse Duarte hustled back with the sleepshot. But by then peace had reclaimed the screens.

"What happened?" Duarte said.

Ogawa shook his head. "Beats the hell out of me."

But Cassie knew. She'd found the key that could set her free. She had only to locate the lock. And now she had a plan.

"Check the readouts every quarter hour," Ogawa instructed Duarte. "Page me at once if anything out of the ordinary happens again."

He left, shaking his head. Duarte took a final look at the now peaceful screens and crossed herself, murmuring "*Virgen de la Providencia, protégenos,*" on her way out.

Alone at last, Cassie gathered herself to make her bid for freedom. And was frozen by another thought. She had come to believe without reservation in Laz. But what if Juanma were right, too? What if there *were* a hell for suicides? Laz wouldn't have known when he came back for her. *He* hadn't killed himself the first time. But if Juanma were right, then Laz hadn't leapt back to heaven. He'd plunged from the balcony of her apartment straight into pools of eternal fire.

Where she would join him if she succeeded in pulling off her own bizarre escape attempt.

Oh, Lord, why hadn't she thought of this sooner? She had acted too hastily, goaded by her desperate need to believe in the man she loved. Her soul raged bitterly at the monumental unfairness of it.

After a time, her rage subsided. She strove to consider the alternatives calmly. Maybes. She was penned in by maybes. Maybe Lázaro was right and death would rocket her to heaven. Maybe Juanma was right and it would blast her to hell. Or maybe death was the final blackness that blotted you out as though you had never existed: Souls die.

There were only two things she could really be sure of: that what life remained to her would be spent as a vegetable, and that wherever death took her, Laz had gone there first.

The truth was, she no longer believed souls die. Lázaro had persuaded her otherwise. And even if it did prove to be true, well, she wouldn't be around to regret it, would she?

Which left heaven. Or hell. The lady or the tiger.

And suddenly she didn't care. In either case, she'd be with Laz. And even being in hell with Laz would surely be preferable to being in heaven with a God so cruel as to make a hell.

When she'd gobbled the handfuls of morphex beads, she'd felt herself really in control of her fate for the first time. Like Laz, she'd finally seized life's reins, getting an almost physical rush from knowing exactly what she was doing and why. Sadly, she'd botched it, but now she thought she saw one final chance to finish the thing cleanly after all. She would do what she thought she should, and pay the price if she had to, and the Devil take Juanma Saavedra and his fear-filled faith.

Duarte popped in for the first of the periodic check-ups ordered by Dr. Ogawa. Cassie waited while the nurse examined the terminal screens and the printed readouts. Everything registered normal. Duarte gave Cassie's comatose body a quick, professional once-over, then left to continue her rounds.

Cassie acted.

She chanted her prayer in ancient Hindu, and her mantra's soothing aura slowly permeated her body, and after a time she was able once again to reach inside herself and nestle her nervous bird of a heart in her "invisible hands." She petted it, stroking away the fear, slowing it, lull-lull-lulling it to sleep, to sleep. Her plan was working.

Her heart slowed . . .

. . . and slowed . . .

. . . and slowed . . .

. . . and . . .

. . . at last . . .

Stopped.

And went berserk!

Her plan had failed. Adrenalin gushed into Cassie's bloodstream. Her pulse rocketed. Her fingers twitched. Her lips groaned.

Cassie struggled to regain control, but her body fought with unexpected ferocity. The soul may be immortal, but the flesh knows the worms await and when push comes to shove will not go gentle into that good night.

So without understanding just how she did it, but because she so desperately needed to, Cassie "clenched" her invisible hands.

And strangled her heart.

Cassie's soul sang as it soared up and up, shooting through an ebon shaft toward a warm white glow.

Laz, O Laz, you told me true!

In the golden field, Lázaro awaited, a newly minted man. And with him, Cassie's mother, again a gay young girl. And dear Alba, smiling.

Cassie felt the warmth of their love envelop her and she trembled. Then Alba reached out, and the touch of her haloed hand sent shivers through Cassie's soul, erasing the pain, finally closing the wounds that had refused to heal, making her whole again.

Cassie understood so much now that she was here. The mere *thought* of going back was unbearable, yet for her sake Laz had borne the unendurable anguish of exile those three days he'd spent dodging Caribbean Cryogenics' goons. How deep had been his love for her, and how wrong she'd been to punish him for her pain.

But past was past and, if nothing else, it served to make this new life by comparison all the sweeter. She had dared stake everything on her trust in Laz, she had finally taken up the mad little boy's challenge—" 'Now you!' "—and won.

Pure joy, pure love flowed through her, for here she was linked not just with Alba, but with everyone. And suddenly Cassie laughed out loud. She had momentarily merged minds with her beloved Monsieur Sartre himself and briefly shared the shock that had greeted the poor *penseur* upon his arrival.

"*C'est vrai, ma chérie,*" the great philosopher chuckled ruefully, "I was mistaken. *Heaven* is other people."

Prometheus's Ghost

CHET WILLIAMSON

Since 1981 Chet Williamson has acquired a notable list of credits in such magazines as Twilight Zone, The Magazine of Fantasy & Science Fiction, Playboy, The New Yorker, *and* Alfred Hitchcock's Mystery Magazine. *His first novel,* Soulstorm, *and his second,* Ash Wednesday, *will soon be published. Now a free-lance writer, Williamson used to earn his living by writing and directing industrial publicity films for a firm of flooring manufacturers.*

In the following story, strange things rise from floors . . . .

On Fifth Avenue, the old man howled. He lifted his black and weathered face, empty eyes glaring at cathedral spires, and howled long and loud. David Ormond stopped walking and turned to look. Usually Ormond ignored the street crazies, but the blind man had been on Fifth Avenue for so many years that Ormond thought of him as an institution. Winters and summers Ormond saw the man and his dog, a mixed breed that reminded him of a large bear cub. The sign the man bore on his back was nearly as creased and stained with years as the man's face. *Here but for the grace of God go thee. Buy a pencil.*

"What's *wrong* with you people?" Ormond was close enough to see the yellowed teeth, the dark holes where others were missing. The blind man's nose was running, and moisture clotted his untrimmed moustache. "*I* know! *I* know! You're all *ghosts!* This city is fulla ghosts! I *hear* you—I hear you walkin' and talkin'—but you don't buy no pencils no more, I ain't heard no fuckin' plunkin' in my goddam cup. . . ." The words rushed out, the irregular puffs of vapor making a frenzied smokestack of the man. Ormond caught his balance as someone jostled him from behind, and decided to move again.

He walked down Fifth, listening to the old man's cries of "*Ghosts!* Goddam *ghosts!*" diminish, swallowed up by traffic and voices and the scuff of shoes on cement. He did not look back, but the old man stayed beside him, becoming in Ormond's mind another old man, his father.

Ormond counted the months and came up with seven. It surprised him that so much time had passed, but then he supposed that the experience would always seem near, even if he grew old. His father had been so sad at the end, so full of despair at leaving a life that had never been very good to him. Burdened with various cancers since his fifties, he had fought back and held on long enough to see his ever-healthy wife die of a stroke just before their fortieth wedding anniversary. Even then, with machines doing the work of half his sundered organs, he feared death more than he hated what he'd become. He'd not been comforted by pastoral words, nor from his only son's lying assurances that soon he and his wife would be reunited. A few nights before he died in pain, not being granted the grace of coma, he had held Ormond's hand in his, squeezed with what little strength remained, said, "If only I knew, Davey, if only I knew, I wouldn't be so scared," and they had both cried. Ormond had thought that cry his father's own, but later he realized that it was that of each bit of humanity damned with the unwanted leisure to slide slowly into the dark rather than fall headlong. If only we knew, he thought again as he walked.

Then the two previously disparate concepts collided within him. The blind man had cried of ghosts, and his father had wished for life. And what were ghosts if not some evidence of the survival of life?

It was Saturday. Ormond walked past Saks, where he'd intended to buy some shirts, and continued down Fifth until he came to the main library. The subject catalogue on "Ghosts" was impressive, and after an hour of consideration and browsing, he withdrew four books: two on parapsychology and related fields, an older volume on ceremonial magic and a thin chapbook on ghostly folklore and traditions. He spent all afternoon reading, gathering snippets of spectral lore and making notations on a yellow pad.

When he finally glanced out his window, Ormond was surprised to find that night had fallen. He had not realized how deeply he had been immersed in the books. It was as if for the past several hours someone other than himself had been controlling his actions, encouraging his dilettantism in the field of the supernatural. He had never had any interest in the subject before; he didn't care for horror movies, and even as a child the ghost stories the other children shivered at had left him bored, impressed only by their silliness. Why, after forty years, was he now seeking out such tales?

The answer was simple, and it came to him simply. He was haunted, not by ghosts, but by death itself, by its reality and its finality, by its might and surety in claiming his father. Yet it was not for his father that he was now seeking some spectral sign of assurance, but for himself. He'd thought a thousand times, not only since the death, but since his father had contracted his first, gentle carcinoma, about the hereditary aspects of cancer, the other death that might be waiting for *him* in the years ahead, years that might not prove as long as he would wish. At times he thought it inevitable that the genes bequeathed to him should someday turn rebel and devour their fellows. And then he would tell himself that death was inevitable for *everyone*, that it was the price one paid for the experience of life. But that knowledge did not comfort him. The only thing that could do that, he realized, was the knowledge that what he had been reading about was real.

Ormond poured himself a double scotch and looked out to the lighted windows of the apartments opposite. The liquor warmed him, and he began to wonder if he were serious, if he were willing to make the search in earnest. Dim forms passed behind glass or curtains. He wondered what those people were looking for tonight, what they were planning, what they wanted to learn or acquire. Money that would eventually be left to relations or the state? Position that could be snatched away long before death? Sex that would not matter a jot when he was shrunken and withered, she dry and barren in the earth? Those things made his own quest seem not nearly so absurd as he had first considered it. He looked for nothing more nor less than the calm certainty of immortality, the ability to face death in peace, and surely such a search was worth time and money.

He sat down and looked at the pages of notations he had made. Medieval superstitions, backwoods legends, parapsychological theories were all there, and running through them was a unity, a sense of purpose, a message he could not ignore. *Seek and ye shall find* was the essence. To open oneself, to be willing to listen and believe, was essential. *Self-delusion*, he thought. *Hallucinations. You expect to see ghosts and you will, but only the ghosts of your own mind. That's why most apparitions are horrible, because we're afraid of them and we project that fear.* He told himself that he had to retain doubt, if only to avoid creating his own ghosts. He could not afford to lose his disbelief. He would have to see a ghost *in spite* of his lack of faith. That was the only way in which he could believe in one.

But where, for God's sake?

Then he thought of Mallory Stewart, his father's partner. Mal had taken over the real estate business a few weeks after the funeral, paying Ormond a healthy sum for all the years and energy his father had sunk into it. In truth, Mal had been the strong one, doing the lion's share of work once the first illness had claimed his partner. Ormond had felt guilty taking the money, but Mal had insisted, and told him that if he ever needed anything to let him know. Perhaps Mal could help him now.

When he called, Mal sounded as jovial as ever. "Davey, good to hear from you. What's up?" The voice was harsh from years of Camels, but that was the only effect that the four decades of nicotine had had.

"Well, I was wondering if you were going to be home tomorrow. Thought I might drop by."

"Just happen to be in the neighborhood of Utica?" Ormond heard good-humored irony in Mal's voice. There was no reason to dissemble.

"There *is* something I'd like to talk about."

"Sure. We'll be around. Anytime after one."

Ormond arrived early the next afternoon. He chatted with Mal and his wife for a bit until Mal stood up. "Shall we talk turkey?" he asked.

Ormond nodded. He and Mal put on jackets and went outside, where they strolled in a fair-sized reproduction of an old English garden, Mal's favorite spot on earth. It was where Ormond had played cowboys and Indians with Mal and his children, now grown and moved away, and it was where Mal had made Ormond the offer for his father's half of the business. The narrow paths through the faded beds and brown vines were rich with memories. It was a place Ormond thought of often. "You should've been here a week ago," Mal said. "I still had some bleeding hearts."

"So late?"

"Mild autumn. Had roses almost till October." He stopped and turned to Ormond. "So what did you want to talk to me about?"

Ormond sighed. "This is going to sound strange."

"Try me."

"Have you ever come across any houses that were supposed to be haunted?"

"Haunted?" Mal smiled gently. "What brought this on, your dad?"

They sat on a bench, and Ormond tried to explain

as best he could, suspecting that every word he said sounded like that of a lunatic trying very hard to act normal. But Mal did not laugh, and, when Ormond finished, he looked intently at the younger man, leaned back and lit one of his Camels.

"Okay," he said, "you came up here to ask me a question and I'll answer it. But first just let me say something." He made a slow, broad gesture, leaving ash droppings on the dirt. "I think I've learned things from this garden. I mean, every year I see all these things die, and every year they come back to life again. Now I go to church, and I think I believe what I hear there, but all *this* is what makes me sure."

"People aren't plants," Ormond said softly.

They sat in silence for a while. "So you want to see a ghost," Mal finally said. "You figure if you see a ghost, then you'll know."

"Yes."

"I'll tell you the truth, Davey. I've got no haunted houses listed. I've been in realty for a helluva long time, and I've never even heard of one. Ghost stories aren't real life, kiddo. I don't know how many hundreds of houses I've been in and sold and tried to sell, and people had died in them, sure, and there were some where people were murdered or went crazy and killed themselves, but no ghosts, Davey, not even a hint of it, not in any of them. I'm sorry."

"Maybe you just didn't know how to look."

"Why would I *want* to look?"

"How about an *old* house then? One that's been around for a while, one that a lot of people have lived in over the years."

"Davey . . ."

"Mal, you said if I ever needed your help . . ."

"All right. Jesus." Mal threw down the butt, stomped it out, then field-stripped it, slipping the paper into a jacket pocket. "Oldest place I've got listed now is a place a little north of Remsen. Old farmhouse from the mid eighteen hundreds. It's beat to hell. Been up for almost three years, heirs in Syracuse want too much for it. Eighty-five-five, and it'd be at least another thirty to fix it up. If you want, I'll give you the key." He shook his head. "But there aren't any ghosts. When you want it, this week?"

"No more vacation days. How about next Saturday?"

"Stop by the office. I'll be there till two or so. Just tell me one thing. When you don't see anything—and you won't—you gonna give up? You gonna admit it's stupid and forget it?"

Ormond smiled. "I don't think I'll forget it. But I'll probably give up."

He passed the following week without the impatience he had anticipated, as if the knowledge that the search was coming was enough. Often he considered just what steps he would take once he was inside the house. Try as he might, he was unable to imagine himself drawing pentagrams on the floor, or chanting unpronounceable names. The spells for raising the dead were grisly and time-consuming, calling for the "operator" to spend days in graveyards and dress in clothing that had been worn by corpses.

But he did not want to raise the dead, had no wish to see some moldering corpse by the side of its grave, waiting zombielike for orders. He wished only to see a ghost, a revenant, a spiritual souvenir of a soul that had passed on to some higher plane. He decided he would simply go to the house with some candles, remain there overnight, and keep himself open to whatever might choose to manifest itself.

Mal Stewart was out showing a house when Ormond arrived at his office late the following Saturday morning, but a secretary gave Ormond the key and directions. In another forty-five minutes he was pulling off the two-lane onto a long driveway of loose stones. The house itself sat back two hundred yards from the road. Distance made it look grander than it was, and by the time Ormond was halfway down the lane he could see the immense disrepair into which the place had fallen. Shutters hung cockeyed, paint had vanished from most of the woodwork, and more shingles were missing and askew than were in their proper place. But the house itself seemed sturdy, constructed of large red stones that glowed warmly in the October sun. Aside from the cosmetic deficiencies, it appeared to be worth the price asked, especially if the surrounding land went with it.

Once inside, however, Ormond thought Mal's thirty-thousand-dollar repair estimate was low. A damp dust not far from mildew coated the building's interior, and it took a long while for him to get used to the smell. Boards creaked wherever he walked, even when he merely shifted weight, and those which did not creak felt spongy beneath his feet. Small piles of cracked and fallen plaster dotted the floors like old droppings in a beast's cage. The windows were unbroken but filthy, turning day into twilight, and Ormond returned to the car for the Coleman lantern he had bought that week in SoHo.

He went through the first floor, and found the

kitchen to be the only room with a recognizable function. An old Kelvinator sat in one corner, its once-white finish yellowed. A large double sink was near it, rusty pipes visible beneath. There were no cabinets, no counters, and Ormond wondered who could have lived in the place only—what had Mal said?—three years before.

Ormond tried the cellar next, and found only a large room, seemingly bare of anything but an ancient coal furnace and an equally aged water pump and heater. The floor was divided into quadrants by thick lines of dust and debris, as if there had once been walls there. He was about to return upstairs when he noticed in one corner a yellowish lump which proved to be a pile of newspapers roughly two feet high. Ormond blew the dust off the top of the stack and found himself looking into the grim face of the Ayatollah Khomeini. The issue of *The Utica Press* was from 1980, and announced the freeing of the Iranian hostages. So, Ormond thought with satisfaction, someone *had* been there just a few years before.

Gingerly he looked through the papers, dropping one on top of the other as he read the headlines; the events were self-dating. Whoever had saved them had saved only special issues. There was a bicentennial Fourth of July issue, whose red and blue masthead was uniformly green with mold; there was the Nixon resignation; the Bobby Kennedy and King assassinations; four issues on Jack Kennedy's death and burial; the Cuban missile crisis; and more. They went back to Korea, to V-E and V-J Days, D-Day, Pearl Harbor, repeal of prohibition, Roosevelt's election, and the stock market crash. The issue on the bottom of the pile announced the Armistice. It was stiff and board-like, and when Ormond tried to unfold it, it cracked into large chunks, enveloping him in a choking cloud of flakes.

Coughing, he dropped the pieces and went back upstairs. Only when he went outside in the autumn chill was he able to stop. Nevertheless, he was glad he had found the papers. It told him the house had had long-term residents and, if he was correct in assuming that the issues had been collected by one man, a resident of age and determination, continuing his collection as he had for over sixty years. He wondered briefly if that determination might extend as well to things of life and death. And then, as quickly as the thought had come, Ormond smiled at it. Already he was projecting, wishing too much. In another minute he might make himself see an old man in bib overalls rocking on the porch, reading a crisp, brand new *Utica Press* from the 1920s. He cautioned himself to be careful. The place was atmospheric, and he felt sure that men wiser and saner than himself had allowed themselves the luxury of seeing things that weren't there.

He resumed his examination on the second floor. There were seven rooms, each as empty and neglected as the rest of the house. Wallpaper hung in damp strips, and he saw, above the broken plaster of the ceiling, support joists like the skeleton beneath the skin. Dirt was everywhere. Ormond opened the closets in each room, and was startled by a mouse that skittered past him and into the hall. *Maybe that was a ghost,* he thought, smiling. *Maybe I've seen one now, so I ought to just get the hell out of here.* He made himself laugh, and slammed the closet door.

In the last second-floor room he entered, what he

assumed was the closet door was wider than the others he had seen. When he opened it he found, instead of a wall two feet away, a winding staircase going up, which he followed. The attic was high-ceilinged and as vacant as the rest of the house, but the smell of dampness was not nearly as strong. Ormond looked about, went back downstairs and waited for evening.

He stayed in his car, trying to read a book, afraid that he wouldn't have enough fuel for his lantern to last the night if he remained inside the house. When he analyzed his feelings, he realized that while he'd been in the house he had felt nothing. There was no sensation of a presence, there were no cold spots on the stairs, no areas where his lantern flickered, no sounds—other than those he made himself—of creaking boards or shifting foundations. It was as if the house had done all its shifting years before, as if it were permanently settled and was now just waiting.

When darkness came, he did not go inside right away, but sat in the car and waited until the moon had moved through an hour of arc. At ten o'clock he entered the house and stood for some time in what he had guessed was the living room before he decided how to proceed. By his lantern light he lit three candles and let them drip on the floor boards until the puddle of wax could hold them upright. Then he sat on the floor, back against the wall. He left the lantern burning for a few minutes more before he allowed himself to admit that it was fear that kept it lit. Finally he turned the knob and the white-hot light blinked out, leaving him in the pale yellow glow of the three candles.

Suddenly he felt unbearably alone, as if the house were in the center of some unpopulated continent, thousands of miles from the nearest living being. All the specters that had failed to haunt him in childhood returned, frightening him now that he knew what they meant, now that he knew what death entailed—its horror and finality. And he thought, quite rationally it seemed, that the ghosts in which he now believed were born of *will*, of a desire for immortality so strong as to transcend the mundane facts of worn-out cells and cold flesh—born of will and the energy that survived corporeal death. He looked down at the floor between his knees, not wanting to look up where the flickering candles made the shadows move on the rotted ceiling, the tattered walls.

The fear passed slowly, like a cloak of ice melting away: its weight lifted, but the feel of it, like cold water, remaining all about him. He looked up and saw nothing but the candles, the bare walls, the dark doorway to the rooms beyond. Gazing into the flame, he waited longer, and then, thinking that what he sought and dreaded was not in this room, pried the candles loose from their bed of wax and moved through the next room into the kitchen at the back of the house. There he sat and watched and waited, and his candles burned down until he took new ones from his pocket and lit them from the stubs of the old.

Just as he had finished the process and was sitting down once more, something at the window caught his eye—a quick, small movement on the other side of its dusty surface. His insides grew cold. He did not turn his head, only his eyes, but saw no movement, only the dull reflection of the flames off the filthy glass. He watched a moment longer, then turned away quickly. Just as quickly the movement came again, and now he twisted his head toward the pane, giving a small

squeak of terror, and saw what appeared to be three
fingers twitching against the glass. He froze, his eyes
locked on the three pale appendages beating a soft
tattoo that he could now hear, hear and *recall*, not as
the sound of fingers on glass, but rather—

The wings of a moth. He breathed, laughed, gulped
down great draughts of air, laughed again. "Moth," he
said aloud, watching the wings flutter, the thick thorax
beat against the glass, forming traceries in the dust.
"Moth," he said. A moth seeing the candles, seeking
the light, and wasn't that what *he* was doing, seeking
the light as well? "Hello, little brother," he said, smiling, feeling foolish, tapping gently on the pane. The
moth stopped its fluttering, clung to the glass, moved
its wings slowly in and out as though breathing, and
disappeared into the darkness.

He was about to move into another room, perhaps
upstairs, he thought, when he heard a new sound. It
seemed to come from beneath him, and the first thing
that came to mind was rats scrabbling about in the
cellar. But after listening for a moment, he concluded
that it did not have the intermittent rhythm that he
would expect animals to make, but was rather a continuous rustling, crackling sound. The moth had put
him into a kind of dulled ease, and he walked to the
cellar stairs, two candles in one hand, and opened the
door. The sound grew louder.

It *was* coming from below, he was sure of it—a
noise of newspaper whirling over a sidewalk on a
windy day. He wondered if he had not noticed that
a window was open down below, and if now a breeze
was stirring the old papers he'd left on the floor. He
walked down the steps, waiting to feel a slight rush of
air from below, but his candles did not flicker, his hair

did not stir. Arriving at the bottom, he held the candles out and up, knowing that it must be mice making the papers rustle, no doubt taking bits and pieces for a nest. Of course—he could see the paper moving on the floor now, wiggling and twitching in places as though it were alive. He walked closer, intending to kick the fragile pile and watch the animals scuttle away, but two feet from it something made him stop. It was not the movement of several small rodents under the brittle sheets, but rather of the whole mass of paper shifting at once, bunching together, gathering toward the center, growing in height.

And as he watched, as he realized, very slowly, what was truly happening, the wads of newspaper coalesced, merged, took on form and shape and character, until there stood before him a snowman made of rotting paper, but with none of a snowman's roundness or levity. Instead it was gaunt, thin, composed of boluses of wadding. There were no legs, only layers joined together with no regard for anatomy. Torn strips of colored comics, now uniformly yellow, stuck out from the torso, a parody of arms, with even thinner ripped shreds for fingers.

The head and face formed last, as small clumps of mildewed paper rolled upward over the carcass and united on its top with a wet, slapping sound like that of papier-mâché being formed, sending off a sour odor that would have gagged Ormond had he been able to breathe. Then smaller pieces, dry and brittle, seemed to float into place, somehow sticking to the whole, and he found himself gazing into a face of torn and wrinkled paper, black print on yellow, its thin shadows deepened by the flames of his candles.

Ormond stood frozen, unable to move or speak.

Even thought seemed to have retreated for his sanity's sake. The face looked into his, and his strength faded until the clenched fingers still holding the candles relaxed, opened, and the lights fell to the dirt floor and winked out. Though he could not close his eyes against what he saw, the darkness closed them for him.

He came to life then, letting some of the fear escape in a tense cry that stayed mostly within. He swung around and ran blindly toward where the stairs had been, tripped once, ran again, banged his ankle into the first step, ignored the sharp pain, scrambled sobbing up the stairs on hands and knees, fell across the kitchen threshold, pulled himself to his feet and bounced off walls and doorways, forging a madman's path to the front door, finding the knob, leaping off the porch, fumbling for keys as he ran to his car, the car turning over, then catching, starting, the clutch flying out, tires kicking up the stones of the lane, turning on the lights and not slowing down until he was out on the two-lane, not stopping until he saw up ahead the bright neon of the truck stop.

Finally, seated on the counter stool, he nestled in the diner's warmth, inhaled the smell of early morning bacon frying, let his fingers keep time to the country-western song on the jukebox. He did this for ten minutes, eating a donut and drinking coffee, before he allowed himself to think about what he had experienced. And when he did, all else faded. He could not hear the music, smell the bacon, feel the heat that stuck his shirt tight against his ribs. There was room for nothing in his mind but the thing he had seen.

He *had* seen it. Of that much he was certain. He

knew that he did not possess the grim unpleasantness of imagination necessary to concoct a hallucination of such originality. A shrouded man or a shapeless white Halloween haunt were all he would have come up with. Thus it followed that what he had seen existed.

But how? Paper did not live, did not build itself into a mockery of humanity to frighten off interlopers. That meant, he concluded, that there must have been some animating force behind it, and what could that force have been if not a ghost?

He nearly laughed. Ghost, revenant, call it what he would, still it was a survivor, a remnant of life once lived. It was enough, wasn't it? It proved that there was something after, didn't it? *Didn't it?*

"Mister?"

Ormond looked up. The waitress was eyeing him from over the top of her glasses. "Yes?"

"You okay?"

"Yes." She offered more coffee and he refused, thinking that he had blown it after all. What had the books said, every single one of them? *Ask.* Ask it what it wants, why it has returned, where it is bound, where is the treasure, and it is impelled to answer. But he had asked nothing, when he could conceivably have bridged the abyss between life and death. Instead, he had run like a terrified schoolboy from a county-fair funhouse.

What else could I have done? he asked himself. The sight of the thing had literally frozen him, stopped his voice as well as everything else. He thought of returning, but knew that if he did there would be no change. One cannot grow used to the Inferno, and that, he felt, was what he had seen—a face and form from the deepest wells of, if not a literal Hell, then the Inferno of man's darkest fears. He could not accept it, could not bring himself to speak to it. No one could, no one who could see it.

No, he thought. *No one who could see it.*

Ormond reached down, rubbed the aching shin he had bumped on the cellar steps, then asked the waitress for more coffee. He sat there for over an hour before driving back to New York.

"You want to make ten dollars?"

The blind man's head twitched birdlike toward Ormond. "Who you?" His voice was suspicious, unfriendly. His dog raised its head from its paws and looked up, wary but without malice.

"My name's David Ormond. I want to buy you a cup of coffee. Talk to you about something. Ten dollars just to listen. Coffee's on me."

"You try and mess with me, Mister, my dog'll bite your white ass."

Ormond frowned. "How do you know I'm white?"

"Shit, don't you try that, next you'll be throwin' a fist in my face to make me duck. You *sound* white, boy, you sound like a necktie and a briefcase's what you sound like." The man chuckled. It was an unpleasant sound, deep and filled with phlegm. "You gimme the ten bucks first." Ormond handed over two fives. "*Singles,* Jack, you think I was born fuckin' yesterday?" Ormond went into a luggage store, where a frowning clerk broke his fives.

"Here," he said, rejoining the blind man and placing them in his hand.

The man counted the bills slowly, then pocketed them. "Where we go?"

"Horn and Hardart," Ormond replied. "Should I . . . take your arm or anything?"

"Just walk, Jack. Shit, I could lead *you.*" Ormond had no idea how the old man separated his footfalls from the hundreds of others around them, but when he sat down at a table, the man was there across from him, the dog at his feet giving a low whine. An assistant manager in white shirt and string tie started over, but Ormond held up a hand and shook his head quickly, and the man stalked away, looking doubtful. "Muhthuhfucker was gonna throw me out, wasn't he?"

"Maybe, not anymore. Look, are you really blind?"

"You look at these, man," the old man said, opening his eyes wide and leaning toward Ormond, who drew back from the fetid breath. "You think these is contact lenses or some shit?"

The eyes were red, full of lesions, the pupils a pale gray. Ormond had not previously noticed the puckered skin of the eyelids. "Okay," he said placatingly. "Okay, I'm sorry. What's your name?"

"John."

"John?"

"You expectin' a Leon or a Mustafa or a Willie? My mama named me John."

"John what?"

"John Washington Wilson. That's more like it now, ain't it, *Mister* Ormond? Now what you want to talk to this poor old blind nigger about?"

Ormond got them coffee, and then he told Wilson as clearly and simply as he could, offering him three hundred dollars to come along and speak to the apparition when Ormond's voice froze in fear, with an extra two hundred if it responded. When Ormond had finished, he sipped his coffee, now only lukewarm, and watched Wilson's broad, black features. The man started to chuckle deep in his throat, then actually laughed in a loud, wet bark that turned half the heads in the room. Even the dog looked up.

"Dave, you is somethin'! This a joke, right? You got boys watchin' me, right? Waitin' to see my eyes pop out 'n my hair stand up like Willie Best, huh?"

"No joke, Mr. Wilson. I'm very serious."

Wilson's smile faded, hiding the ruined teeth. "Goddam," he said softly. He finished his coffee in one gulp. "You know, when I was a kid I *liked* Willie Best. Willie Best and Rochester. I didn't give a shit they was servants or nothin'. They made me laugh. They was funny. I could see back then." His face swung toward Ormond's again, and had Ormond not been sure of the blindness, he would have sworn Wilson was glaring at him. "How I know you be straight with me? How I know you not gonna kill me or nothin'?"

"Bring the dog along. Or we can tell your friends where we're going."

"My daughter. We tell my daughter. When you wanta go?"

"Next weekend? Saturday?"

"Not weekends. Weekends I spend with my daughter."

"Look, Mr. Wilson, I'm paying you . . ."

"No weekends."

The voice was like stone. Ormond decided to fake a sick day at the office. "All right. This week then. Wednesday."

"That be all right. Now I got one more question.

How come me? Why didn't you go to the Blind Institute and get somebody classy?"

"Well . . . I . . ."

"Never mind, I know. They'd thrown you out on your ass. Guess I oughta be glad. I can use the money."

"I thought you could. I heard you once . . . saying that everybody was a ghost. Because no one was buying any pencils."

"I said that? Crazy nigger. Forget that shit. Sometimes I get pissed. Forget that shit."

The following Wednesday Ormond picked up John Wilson on the corner of Fifth and Fiftieth at three in the afternoon. The signboard went in the trunk, the dog in the back seat, where he sat watching the street with a greater amount of interest than Ormond had ever seen him display. "Lousy day," Wilson said, lighting a Lucky. "People damn cheap. Maybe in a few weeks when Christmas decorations start goin' up."

"Your dog trained?" Ormond asked. "Seeing-eye?"

"Nah, not really. He know when the lights is green or red, 'n what they mean. Won't let nobody hurt me neither. He's fuckin' smart." They got out of the city, headed north. "What you wanta do this for anyway? You really see a ghost?"

"I saw something. Something that scared me so much I couldn't talk. I think anybody who saw it would've felt the same."

"But I won't see it."

"That's right. That's why you do the talking."

"Jes' ask it what it wants."

"That's right."

"You still ain't said why."

"Hell, Wilson, don't *you* want to know?"

"Know what?"

"Know what comes after. After you die."

"What the fuck do I care? I be dead. Maybe I be with Jesus. I sure as shit ain't goin' to no hell, I up to here with that shit right here on earth. Like them boys who been in Vietnam. Like I hear their jackets say."

"Well, maybe you'll find out anyway. Maybe tonight. That bother you?"

"We ain't gonna find nothin'. I gonna take your money, but you ain't gonna find nothin'."

It was growing dark when they arrived at the house. Ormond had called Mal the previous Sunday and asked to keep the key for another week. Mal had hesitated, but agreed. Ormond and Wilson ate some sandwiches Ormond had brought, and drank some coffee from a Thermos. Wilson let the dog out of the car and fed him a sandwich. The old man swallowed the last of his food, washed it down with a final sip of coffee, then sniffed the air. "Smells clean," he said, "but there's somethin' else." As if he understood the words, the dog raised his head and sniffed too. "Musty. Musty smell. That the house?"

"That's it." Ormond could detect no smell, but there was nothing else around that it could have been. "Let's go in."

They walked into the house, Wilson holding Ormond's arm. Ormond watched the dog closely to see how he would react, if the supposed heightened sensitivity of animals to spirits would prove to be true. But the dog seemed at ease, following them steadily as they went through the door.

Ormond found the lantern where he had left it

when he had fled the house, put more fuel into it, and lit it. Its mantles blazed brightly, bringing light and warmth to the dark, chilly room. "The cold bother you?" Ormond asked the old man.

"Shit, I stand outside all winter with them winds tryin' to blow me down. This is nothin'."

"All right. We'll go in the cellar now. That's where I saw it. Now remember . . ." Ormond heard his voice shaking and stopped talking for a moment, thinking, *Control. Get hold of it. You'll never make it if you're this scared this soon.*

"Remember what?"

"Remember I'll have hold of your arm. If I squeeze it hard, you'll know it's there. Or if I stop talking. Or if you feel me stiffen or freeze. That'll mean it's there. We'll go into the cellar. The steps are steep."

Ormond led the way, Wilson's hand on his shoulder. The dog trailed behind. Near the bottom of the stairs, Ormond thought that if he'd have to run up them now, he'd have the blind man and the dog to go through first. Then he told himself he would not run. This time he would not run.

The cellar stank of foulness. Was it worse since he'd been there, Ormond wondered. The dog whined softly. "Hush up," Wilson said. "You smelled worse'n this." The old newspapers lay disordered on the dirty floor. The long strips and torn shreds told Ormond that he had not imagined it all. He felt vindicated, but at the same time more frightened now that the last natural explanation—hallucination—was gone. He kept walking until he was only a few feet away from the pile.

"We there?" Wilson asked.

"We're there."

"Now what?"

"Now we wait." Ormond set the lantern near the wall and went back to where Wilson and the dog stood. He took Wilson's arm and watched the mound of paper on the floor, alert for the slightest bit of movement.

The dog was the first to notice. His head twitched, his ears went up, his eyes opened wider, as if looking for what he had heard. "What's 'at?" barked the old man.

"What?" Ormond asked, his voice thick.

"Noise. Somethin' rubbin'."

It was several more seconds before Ormond heard it. Paper, wet and dry, moving against itself. "Oh God . . . ," he said, less in awe than if to see if he could still speak.

"What's *happ*'nin'?"

"It's . . . coming," Ormond whispered. "Forming." A large mass heaved up amidst the rest, and Ormond knew his voice was gone. He could only watch spellbound as the clumps of paper joined and grew, colliding wetly, rising higher, rolled papers lurching sluglike up the trunk, strips slithering behind them, the whole growing, growing, even more terrifying in the harsh beam of the lantern than in the candle's feeble glow, for there were no shadows now to soften and disguise, but only the blazing light, so that he could not deny what stood constantly higher before him.

He heard Wilson speak, but only understood the last few words, ". . . you think you're going? Git back down here, you . . ." and he realized the dog was gone. But the face formed, and then he couldn't remember the dog at all. It was worse this time, for the depressions, which had before been only empty sockets, were now filled with eyes, two egg-sized balls of paper whose *whiteness* stunned Ormond with their incongruity in that field of yellow. Two bits of black, torn from thick headline letters, drifted over the white balls and stopped dead center, ragged pupils that fixed him as no human eyes ever could. There was a sharp rip, and a mouth, wide and seeping, dropped open, a cloud of must bursting from it, reaching his own face in an instant and clogging his throat with its vileness. The jaw did not close, but hung sagging like a rotted limb as, just above, a wad pushed outward in which two dark holes were poked as by some invisible hand, forming nostrils which expelled two puffs of moist, sour air, along with tiny fragments of powdery paper. The face was complete.

Ormond had expected it, but the expectation in no way diminished the shock. He was stunned, immovable as rock, and only the irrevocable commands of his body kept him breathing. He thought later that he would have stood there forever, staring into the face, had Wilson not spoken, playing his part, doing as he'd been instructed. The blind man's voice intruded only dimly into Ormond's smothered consciousness, but he heard, and understood the words.

"Who are you? What you want?"

The yellow, rotting head swiveled until the thing was looking at Wilson. Sweat coated the old man's face, giving him the sheen of onyx, and now Ormond could hear his breathing, heavy and labored. Suddenly Wilson groaned deep within, then grunted again and again, as though he were being repeatedly struck by blows, or wracked by tubercular coughing. The final grunt, instead of dropping away, began to soar in an ascending cry, and the blind man howled as he had that day when he'd shouted of ghosts on the streets of New York, howled so high and so long that Ormond, not seeing him, could imagine blood streaming upward from his throat, could almost see it splashing the horror in front of him, deep red drops on the yellow-gray paper.

The howl ceased, and Wilson sank to the earth as gently as if hands had lowered him. At the same time the upright tower of paper crumbled, falling upon itself layer by moldering layer, the face descending in lurches toward the floor, but turning, turning to once more face Ormond, keeping its newsprint eyes on him as it sank and dissolved into damp shreds, the jaw twisting as if in an effort to shape some expression prohibited by its very composition. As it fell, Ormond's fear fell with it, so that he detected in its dissolution a sense of purpose fulfilled, not from anything he saw, but rather from what he felt.

He didn't know how long he stood looking down at the pile of rubbish on the dirt floor, but after a while he heard low growls interspersed with high whinings. At last he looked away and saw that the dog had returned. It had Wilson's shirt collar in its mouth, and was slowly dragging him backward, away from the musty pile. The sight broke the spell that had been laid on Ormond, and he leaned down to help, the dog yielding when it realized he meant no harm. Wilson's bubbling breathing told Ormond he was still alive, and when he had pulled him several more feet from the remnants of the apparition, he shook him gingerly until the blind eyes opened and the wide, trembling mouth could speak.

"Where are we? We still there?" The voice was cracked and shaking.

"In the cellar. Yes." They were the first words Ormond had spoken since the thing's coming, and he was surprised to hear how calm he sounded.

"Get me outa here," Wilson said, stumbling to his feet. "For the luvva Jesus, get me outside. . . ."

They went up the stairs together, the dog trailing solicitously, Wilson muttering, "Oh Jesus, oh Jesus," in a litany as they went. At the top of the stairs Wilson turned to Ormond. "Where is it?" he asked.

"It's gone. Fallen apart. Gone." He tightened his grip on Wilson's arm. "What happened?" he asked. "What did it say? What did it tell you?"

"Get me outside. In the car. Outa here."

They got to the car and climbed in. "You want to go?" asked Ormond. "Shall we leave now?"

"No. Let's just set a while."

From somewhere in his voluminous coat Wilson drew a pint bottle of Kessler, took a long pull, and offered it to Ormond, who drank without wiping the neck. "All right," he said, handing it back, "now tell me. Why did you pass out?"

Wilson hacked up phlegm, shook his head. "It hit me too strong. Like all at once it just started comin'. And I couldn't hold it all, like it'd been keepin' it back for so long it just all poured out at once, and I couldn't hold it."

"But did it *tell* you anything? Before you blacked out?"

Wilson's face seemed far away, and his eyes looked as if they could see again. "It told me. All it wanted to. All I could hold."

"Was it a ghost then?"

"Yeah."

"Then . . ." He struggled to voice the thought,

because now it was no longer theory, but truth. "Then there *is* life after death."

"But not for him." Wilson sounded sad.

"What?"

"Not the life the rest of 'em have. Not that good life."

"I don't understand. . . ."

"There's a good life, but he don't got it. He stuck here. 'Cause he tried to come back." Wilson shook his craggy head. "They don't *want* us to know. And he tried to come back to tell. And they didn't like that. He told me. How'd he look anyway? Bad? Really ugly?"

Ormond nodded, remembered Wilson was blind, said, "Yes."

"I thought, he felt bad. Couldn't help it. I think he was glad you brought me to ask. I don't think he coulda told nothin' if nobody'd asked."

"We're too afraid to," Ormond said softly.

"What?"

"We're too afraid to ask, so we never know." He said nothing for a while, thinking it through. "Even if there are some who *want* to tell us," he went on, slowly, cautiously, "who want to come back to comfort us, they can only come back as horrors. As things that frighten us away from the truth. And who wants to seek *that* out? So it stays a secret. Or becomes the stuff of legend."

"I think we crazy, but I think you right. I was scared, scared as hell, but I felt sorry too. Sorry for that thing."

"It's trapped," Ormond said. "Trapped between life and death for trying to tell the truth." They sat in silence until Ormond finally spoke. "Was there anything else?" he asked Wilson. "Anything you can remember."

"No. Just . . ." Wilson's face twisted, trying to recall. "There was a song, like a little tune. I mean, he didn't sing it to me or nothin' like that, it's just like I remember that it was there. Now how did that go? . . ." And Wilson hummed a snatch of melody that Ormond had not heard for many years, and only remembered one man ever singing. "That's all," Wilson said. "That's all she wrote."

He leaned back and rubbed his dog's head, and Ormond dug into his pocket for the car keys, filled with a new knowledge that he could never share and that no one would ever believe, filled with a new, burning lust to know what distant Zeus, so needful of faith, would chain an immortal to a rock on which the vulture of man's fear would gnaw forever at his generous, misunderstood soul.

"Wonder who it was," Wilson said. "Wonder just who that poor bastard was."

"My father," said Ormond, turning the key to make the engine spark and start. "Prometheus. My father."

Small Change

URSULA K. LE GUIN

The roll call of Ursula K. Le Guin's publications and awards is well known, and her pre-eminence as a major literary figure is so well established that it seems like strange and ancient history to disinter a first edition of one of her earliest novels, City of Illusions, *and discover the packaging of this 50¢ Ace Book from 1967 posing the question: "Was he a human meteor or a time-bomb from the stars?" No publisher today would advertise a title by Ursula Le Guin in quite that way.*

She—and science fiction—have moved onward and upward, the latter in no small part thanks to the influence of her writings.

Another slice of ancient history is the time when Playboy *magazine insisted that her story "Nine Lives" appear under the byline U. K. Le Guin, since Playboy's male readers wouldn't readily accept a science-fiction story written by a woman. Science fiction by women authors has long since transcended that moment—again, no small thanks to Ursula Le Guin.*

Nowadays Le Guin finds some areas of the contemporary science-fiction landscape "all hard and gray and martial and threatening," while in the workshops the youngest writers are turning out frightened, nuclear-

holocaust stories. Thus in her own recent writing, Ursula Le Guin has come back down to Earth from the murderous stars. A recent project, Always Coming Home, *is set in a far-future northern California, land of her childhood: a loving evocation of the earth, song, culture and life.*

"Small Change" is also, in its way, a slice of ancient history: a haunting, elegiac death and afterlife in the mode of classical Greece—and uniquely in the mode of Ursula Le Guin.

"Small change," my aunt said as I put the obol on her tongue. "I'll need more than that where I'm going."

It is true that the change was very small. She looked exactly as she had looked a few hours before, except that she was not breathing.

"Good-bye, Aunt," I said.

"I'm not going yet!" she snapped. I always tried her patience. "There are rooms in this house I've never even opened the door of!"

I did not know what she was talking about. Our house has two rooms.

"This obol tastes funny," she said after a long silence. "Where did you get it?"

I did not want to tell her that it was a good-luck piece, a copper sequin, not money though it was round like a coin, which I had carried for a year or more in my pocket, ever since I picked it up by the gate of the brickmaker's yard. I had rubbed it clean, of course, but my aunt had a keen tongue, and it was trodden mud, dog turds, brick dust, and the inside of my pocket that she was tasting, along with the dry-blood taste of copper. I pretended that I had not understood her question.

"A wonder you had it at all," my aunt said. "If you have a penny in your pocket after a month without me, I'll be surprised. Poor thing!" She would have sighed if she had been breathing. I had not known that she would continue to worry about me after she died. I began to cry.

"That's good," my aunt said with satisfaction. "Just don't keep it up too long. I'm not going far, now. I just want very much to find out what room that door leads to."

She looked younger when she got up, younger than she was when I was born. She went across the room lightly and opened a door I had not known was there.

I heard her say in a pleased, surprised voice, "Lila!" Lila was the name of her sister, my mother.

"For goodness' sake, Lila," my aunt said, "you haven't been waiting in here for eleven years?"

I could not hear what my mother said.

"I'm very sorry about leaving the girl," my aunt said. "I did what I could, I tried my best. She's a good girl. But what will become of her now!"

My aunt never cried, and now she had no tears; but her anxiety over me made me cry again in alarm and self-pity.

My mother came out of that new room in the form of a lacewing fly and saw me crying. Tears taste salt to the living but sweet to the dead, and they have a taste for sweets, at first. I did not know all that, then. I was just glad to have my mother with me even as a tiny fly. It was a gladness the size of a fly.

That was all there was left of my mother in the house, and she had got what she wanted; so my aunt went on.

The room she was in was large and rather shadowy, lighted only by a skylight, like a storeroom. Along one wall stood distaffs full of spun flax, in a row, and in the place where the light fell from the skylight stood a loom. My aunt had been a notable spinster and weaver all her life, and was sorely tempted now by those rolls of fine, even thread, as well spun as any she had ever spun herself; the loom was warped, and there lay the shuttle ready. But linen weaving is a careful art. If she began a shroud now she would be at it for a long time, and much as she wanted a proper shroud, she never had been one to start a job and then drop it unfinished. So it was that she kept worrying about what would become of me. But she had already made up her mind to leave the housework undone (since housework is never done anyhow), and now she admitted that she must let other people see to her winding sheet. She hoped she could trust me to choose a clean sheet, at least, and a well-patched one. But she could not resist picking up the end thread of one of the distaffs and feeding out a length between her thumb and finger to test it for evenness and strength; and she kept the thread running between thumb and finger as she walked on.

It was well that she did so, as the new room opened onto a corridor along which were many doorways, each one leading to other halls and rooms, a maze in which she would certainly have lost her way but for the thread of flax.

The rooms were clean, a little dusty, and unfurnished. In one of them my aunt found a toy lying on

the floor, a wooden horse. It was crudely carved, the
forelegs all of a piece and the hind legs the same, a
kind of a two-legged horse with round, flat eyes, which
she thought she remembered, though she was not
sure.

In another long, narrow room many unused kitchen
tools and pans lay on a counter, and three horn buttons in a row.

At the end of a long corridor into which she was
drawn by a gleam or a reflection at the far end, there
stood an engine of some kind, which was certainly
nothing my aunt had ever seen before.

In one small room with no skylight an intense,
pungent smell hung in the air, filling up the room like
a living creature caught in it. My aunt left that room
hurriedly, upset.

Though her curiosity had been roused by finding all
these rooms she had not known in her house, her
explorations, and the silence, brought on her a sense
of oppression and unease. She stood for a moment
outside the door of the room where the strong smell
was, making up her mind. That never took her long.
She began to follow the thread back, winding it about
the fingers of her left hand as she took it up. This
process needed more attention than the paying out,
and lifting her eyes from a tangle in the thread she was
puzzled to find herself in a room which she did not
recall passing through, but could hardly have crossed
without noticing, for it was very large. The walls were
of a beautiful fine-grained stone of a pale grey hue, in
which certain figures like astrologers' charts of the
constellations, fine lines connecting stars or clusters of
stars, were inlaid in gold wire. The ceiling was light
and high, the floor of worn, dark marble. It was like

a church, my aunt thought, but not a religious church (that is what she thought). The patterns on the walls were like the illustrations in books of learning, and the room itself was like the hall of the great library in the city; there were no books, but the place was majestic and reposeful, having about it a collected stillness very pleasant to the spirit of my aunt. She was tired of walking, and decided to rest there.

She sat down, since there was no furniture, on the floor in the corner nearest the door to which the thread had led her. My aunt was a woman who liked a wall at her back. The invasions had left her uneasy in open spaces, always looking over her shoulder. Though who could hurt her now? as she said to herself, sitting down. But, as she said to herself, you never can be sure.

The lines of gold wire on the walls led her eye along them as she sat resting. Some of the figures they made seemed familiar. She began to think that these figures or patterns were a map of the maze which she was in, the wires representing passages and the stars, rooms; or perhaps the stars represented the doors into rooms, the walls of which were not outlined. She could pretty certainly retrace the first corridor back to the room of the distaffs; but on the far side of that, where the old part of our house ought to be, the patterns continued, looking a good deal more like the familiar constellations of the sky in early winter. She was not certain she understood the map at all, but she continued to study it, to let her mind follow the lines from star to star, until she began to see her way. She got up then, and went back, pursuing the flaxen thread and taking it up in her left hand, till she came back.

There I was in the same room still crying. My mother was gone. Lacewing flies wait years to be born, but they live only a day. The undertaker's men were just leaving, and I had to follow them, so my aunt came along to her funeral, though she did not want to leave the house. She tried to bring her ball of thread with her, but it broke as she crossed the threshold. I could hear her swear under her breath, the way she always did when she broke a thread or spilled the sugar —"Damn!" in a whisper.

Neither of us enjoyed the funeral at all. My aunt grew panicky as they began to throw the dirt back into the grave. She cried aloud, "I can't breathe! I can't breathe!"—which frightened me so much that I thought it was myself speaking, myself suffocating, and I fell down. People had to help me get up, and help me get home. I was so ashamed and confused among them that I lost my aunt.

One of the neighbors, who had never been particularly pleasant to us, took pity on me, and behaved with much kindness. She talked so wisely to me that I got up the courage to ask her, "Where is my aunt? Will she come back?" But she did not know, and only said things meant to comfort me. I am not as clever as most people, but I knew there was no comfort for me.

The neighbor made sure I could look after myself, and that evening she sent one of her children over with dinner in a dish for me. I ate it, and it was very good. I had not eaten anything while my aunt was away in the other part of the house.

At night, after dark, I lay down all alone in the bedroom. At first I felt well and cheerful, because of the food I had eaten, and I pretended my aunt was there sleeping in the same room, the way it had always been. Then I got frightened, and the fright grew in the darkness.

My aunt came up out of the floor in the middle of the room. The red tiles humped up and cracked apart. Her hair and her head pushed through the tiles, and then her body. She looked very dark, like dirt, and she was much smaller than she had been.

"Let me be!" she said.

I was too terrified to speak.

"Let me go!" my aunt said. But it was not truly my aunt; it was only an old part of her that had come back underground from the graveyard, because I had been wanting her. I did not like that part of her, or want it there. I cried, "Go away! Go back!" and hid my head in my arms.

My aunt made a little creaking sound like a wicker basket. I kept my eyes hidden so long that I nearly fell asleep. When I looked, no one was there, or only a kind of darker place in the air, and the tiles were not cracked apart. I went to sleep.

Next morning when I woke up the sunlight was in the window and things were all right, but I could not walk across that part of the floor where my aunt had come up through the tiles.

I was afraid to cry after that night, since crying might bring her back to taste the sweetness or to scold me. But it was lonely in the house now that she was buried and gone. I had no idea what to do without her. The neighbor came in and talked about finding me work, and gave me food again; but the next day a man came, who said he had been sent by a creditor. He took away the chest of clothes and bedding. Later that day, in the evening, he came back, because he had

seen that I was alone there. I kept the door locked this
time. He spoke smoothly at first, trying to make me
let him in, and then he began saying in a low voice
that he would hurt me, but I kept the door locked and
never answered. The next day somebody else came,
but I had pushed the bedstead up against the door. It
may have been the neighbor's child that came, but I
was afraid to look. I felt safe staying in the back room.
Other people came and knocked, but I never answered, and they went away again.

I stayed in the back room until at last I saw the door
that my aunt had gone through, that day. I went and
opened it. I was sure she would be there. But the room
was empty. The loom was gone, and the distaffs were
gone, and no one was there.

I went on to the corridor beyond, but no farther. I
could never find my way by myself through all those
halls and rooms, or understand the patterns of the
stars. I was so afraid and wretched that I went back,
and crawled into my own mouth, and hid there.

My aunt came to fetch me. She was very cross. I
always tried her patience. All she said was, "Come
on!" And she pulled me along by the hand. Once she
said, "Shame on you!" When we got to the riverbank
she looked me over very sternly. She washed my face
with the dark water of that river, and pressed my hair
down with the palms of her hands. She said, "I should
have known."

"I'm sorry, Aunt," I said.

"Oh, yes," she said. "Come along, now. Look
sharp!"

For the boat had come across the river and was
tying up at the wharf. We walked down to the wharf
among the reeds in the twilight. It was after sunset,

and there was no moon or stars, and no wind blowing. The river was so wide I could not see the other shore.

My aunt dickered with the ferryman. I let her do that, since people always cheated me. She had taken the obol off her tongue, and was talking fast. "My niece, can't you see how it is? Of course they didn't give her the fare! She's not responsible! I came along with her to look after her. Here's the fare. Yes, it's for us both. No, you don't," and she drew back her hand, having merely shown him a glimpse of the bit of copper. "Not till we're both safe across!"

The ferryman glowered, but began to loosen the painter.

"Come along, then!" my aunt said. She stepped into the boat, and held out her hand to me. So I followed her.

A Draft
of Canto CI

CARTER SCHOLZ

*Carter Scholz has written a score of stories for such
publications as* Orbit, Universe, Last Wave *and* Light
Years *and* Dark. *Among his titles are such originals as
"A Catastrophe Machine" and "The Ninth Symphony
of Ludwig van Beethoven and Other Lost Songs,"
which was a Hugo Award nominee. Scholz has also
been nominated for the Nebula Award and the John W.
Campbell Award. His first novel,* Palimpsests *(in col-
laboration with Glenn Harcourt), was published in
1984, and he is currently at work on a second entitled*
The Craft of Dying. *He lives in Berkeley, California.*

IN HIS LAST MOMENT

S napshot: the aesthetic of the accidental.

In a delta Phalos waited for dawn.

In Bangkok Phalos came in the mouth of a Thai
whore.

At a service Phalos heard Psalm 106 recited,
and at a certain line the chaplain was unable to

continue, and had to be led away.

Rotors beat back the grass around him as Phalos crouched beneath a descending copter.

An incoming shell burst a stack of body bags, and the air was filled with a charnel stench.

In the cloud-crested sky the bright dead moon sailed like a sleek craft.

He remembered the swallow-tailed wake of the transport, bringing him here, white at dusk.

At the edge of a runway Phalos huddled, shells pounding the strip, his sharp shadow rising rhythmically behind him.

In a clearing Phalos entered the court of a fallen Annamese wat. From every direction melodies rippled. An array of wind chimes hung round the margin of the court, bronze plates green with slow corrosion. He tilted his head to the sun and let it blind him, heard the wind speak.

In a canteen Phalos received for cash a packet of heroin.

At leisure Phalos read translations of poetry made by an American fifty years before. In one of these he discovered, by chance, the etymology of his name. It meant not the male organ, but the spike of a helmet, or the first green tip of a sprouting bulb. Accented differently it meant radiant, white.

In the jungle a ball of white phosphorescent gas dogged Phalos's steps.

In his dreams Phalos experienced nothing, nothing at all.

PHALOS HAD A VISION

Everything looks beautiful except there is no star in sight. It is just not visible.

Roger. Is this for star Zero One?

That's correct.

You are not getting any reflections or anything like that that would obscure your vision, are you?

Well, of course, the earth is pretty bright, and the black sky, instead of being black, has a sort of rosy glow to it, and the star, unless it is a very bright one, is probably lost somewhere in that glow, but it is just not visible. I maneuvered the reticule considerably above the horizon to make sure that the star is not lost in the brightness below the horizon. However, even when I get the reticule considerably above the horizon so the star should be seen against the black background, it is still not visible.

Roger, we copy. Stand by a minute, please.

11, this is Houston. Can you read us the shaft and trunion angle off the counters?

I will be glad to. Shaft 331.2, and trunion 35.85.

Roger, thank you.

It's really a fantastic sight through that sextant. A minute ago, during that automaneuver, the reticule swept across the Mediterranean. You could see all of North Africa absolutely clear, all of Portugal, Spain, southern France, all of Italy absolutely clear. Just a beautiful sight.

Roger, we all envy you the view up there.

But still no star.

OF A SENTENCE, STRETCHED LIKE A CLOUD-CRESTED
WAVE OF SKY

Anonymous in guttering torchlight the scribe touched style to paper. All these the products of the Earth, himself as well. He drew ideograms with care: feather, coiled rope, shepherd's staff, loaf, lyre, asp, mouth, owl, twisted rope, loaf, arm, shoulder, 3, seated woman, shepherd's staff, loaf, mouth, bolt, loaf, seated woman, vagina. He paused in the midst of his love poem, a sudden chill of fear piercing him through the summer night. She was no longer here. Yet he pursued his penisolate magics. His fear deepened into dread as he studied what he had written. The signs were not her, yet they were. The same signs differently placed would be something else. In the margin he began a sketch of her features. He was practiced and sure with the ideograms, but he had not the visual syntax to make her likeness in line. Weary, he returned to his poem and finished it, appending his sign: a human figure surmounted by an ibis-head. He extinguished the light. For a moment he regarded the moon, then unclasped his skirt and laid on the pallet, praying surcease from thought.

OVER ALL EXISTENCE: EXTENT, DURATION, KAIROS, CHRONOS:

I speak by grace of Mnemosyne. At Hellmouth, I paused: within, my love. The wind spoke through my lyre's taut strings, tuned in the Doric mode, the mode of strength and tradition. There the time-god's son spoke out of air, brandished in unseen hand the key to turn me back. There the charnel smell. But I sweetened the air with my tones, with *hypate, paramese, nete, mese, paranete, lixanos, parypate, trite*, and again *hypate*, in nines the counting, the sacred three tripled to suspend time. The god fell back. Then I passed the thin shades, who fell silent at my song. With tones I drew my love from the unpure air and led her back to the light. Then foul Aides, detuner, tempered my ninth string with his breath, the earth string, and, facing out Hellmouth, I paused and struck it. My love dissolved, and I was grief-mad, waited seven days at the riverbank for death to take me, and was refused. A second time. A second time I had lost her. So I changed all that I was, broke lyre and sang then in the new modes, unceasingly, a danger to the state as the philosopher rightly said. I took to my bed young boys. I chanted paradise, and was dismembered. But the new modes transcend death, the modes had stopped the maenads' rites, disrupted the ancient cycle, and I did not die. I realized then that *they* wanted to die. I floated on the sea, my severed head, and learned there songs of tide, *thalassa, thalassa,* came at last to rest with my tongue on foul sand, stopped. A woman came. She tongued sand from my mouth, and empty of music I spoke:—What place?

—Lesbos, she said.

THROUGH WHICH HE SWAM, TO THE EDGE OF THE
MEDIUM, TO THE VOID, OUTSIDE THE FIELD OF
METAPHOR AND FICTION,

Then Father made the cowsuit to satisfy her unnatural lust.

Then made he the labyrinth to contain the offspring.

Then made he the birdwings to free us from that secret he alone knew.

Had Minos tempered the wax sent to the workshop? It is possible. Father showed me his calculations, worked with the Phoenician marks, and the wings were sound. I trusted the figures, and flew no higher than they allowed, assuming of course the wax untempered. Minos was deep in debt with his expensive gadgets and trusted none, but I did not expect he would temper the wax. Father dwindled from roc-size to gull-size beneath me. I broke through the clouds, like a small ghost passing through a pearl, and was staggered: the sun above! Then the wings loosened. A brief superstitious fear took me, for had I not tried to mount heaven? But my eyes were open even as I fell, and there were no gods. I remember that quite clearly. There were no gods, there in the high places.

AND IN THAT HARD ICARIAN LIGHT WAS BURNED AND FELL UNNOTICED INTO WAITING SEA,

"There is so much that the United States does not know. This war is proof of such vast incomprehension, such tangled ignorance, so many strains of unknowing, I am held up, enraged by the delay needed to change the typing ribbons, so much is there that ought to be put into young America's head.

"I don't know what to put down, can't write two scripts at once. The necessary facts come in pell-mell, I try to get too much into ten minutes. Condensed form is all right in a book; saves eyesight. The reader can turn back and look at a summary.

"Maybe if I had more sense of form, legal training, God knows what, I could get the matter across the Atlantic. . . ."

Words snatched from the air by a shortwave receiver. In a ship offshore three men listened to the speech. One transcribed it in shorthand. One worked the controls of a German-made wire recorder. One smoked. They were preparing evidence for a bill of treason. It was July of 1942.

WHILE THE ENERGY OF THAT SENTENCE

Johann Gutenberg in the city of Mainz in the year
1447 oversaw the hurried printing of an astrological
calendar. An assistant stacked the sheets on drying
racks. Nearby stood a young man, moonfaced and well-
dressed, wearing a gold chain clasped with a caduceus
at his larynx. He waited to discuss with Gutenberg
a debt to his employer, Johannes Fust. He began to
speak, then stopped. He touched his lips, then his chain.

It had just occurred to him that these sheets could
be sold at market.

LEFT THE WORLD ASHEN

A student in a million-volume library wrote:

"We would like to think our work has power. We
would believe there is more to what passes our hands
than its passing, if we could, if belief itself had not
become a commodity—specific, particular, of known
value, hence limited. But power now abides in the
insensible, and the insensible world expands like a
virus in favorable medium, like the fireburst of a bomb
which forever renews its core, like the wavefront of
voices now fifty, soon a hundred light-years from
earth, receding as rapidly as the first radio broadcast
recedes into history.

"It is no longer possible to write of characters, or
groups, or aggregates, or things, or their relations; the
rate of change of their complexity defies expression.
But we cannot avoid character, unless we wish to
make text its own subject, and proceed to the breathless unphysical deserts of *le texte scriptable*, from
which none returns. If we have learned anything it is
that writing has no theory to attend it, no vehicle, no

comforts, no fixed abode—in short, no technology. That is its strength. In times when technology threatens life, it resists the threat with all the intensity, venom and understanding of a son for his father."

He stopped and peered out a tinted window into a blue sky pierced by a quarter moon, where men walked. Abode of the dead, the multitudinous commingling dead. Was it not possible that all the dead, being dead, shared some common space? Or was it merely the reluctance of language to provide separate words for the various dead which made him think now that all the dead, on dying, might share each other's thoughts? He shook his head. A conceit of the library. He forgot the moon and returned to his writing.

AS THE AFTERMATH OF TORCH TOUCHED TO FOREST,

In the cavity where invention gestates, these voices cried:

Thus they were defiled with their own works, and sent whoring with their own inventions.

And the black sky.

These are the products of the earth: metals, and plants, and those things refined from each, for instance paper and pigment. Food and all the items of commerce are of the earth, and the instruments of war, art and science. And men, too, are of the earth.

Then let us sing in the new modes, and breach technology singing as a son would sing of his father, of the loss of one's flesh.

Then the wings loosened.

For fourteen years confined. The cage.

Remember: the first signs were those of commerce.

No element is found pure. It is impurity gave birth to solid-state electronics. Invention proceeds from impurity. Bring whores for Eleusis. Let *techne* sleep with *praxis*.

Remember that the first tools for graving stone were apt also for murder.

Locked in he wrote with an ink compounded of his own blood and excrement with a sharp tool provided him for his self-destruction on the only foolscap available, namely his own body, those parts of it he could reach.

No picture is made to endure or to live with, but it is made to sell and sell quickly.

The sequence of *materia* is this: fire, air, water, earth. The sequence of life is this: water, air, fire, earth. In spirit the sequence is: earth, water, air, fire, and there is also a fifth element of the spirit: void.

Do not move. Let the wind speak.

SCIENCE TO LOVE,

Claude Garamond observed critically the craftsman's tap of the pyncheon into the type matrix. He pointed out an error in the curve of the upper case *C*, and the craftsman took down a fresh block of steel and clamped it in his vise. He began again to cut the form with his tools of tempered earth. A printer brought proofs and unfurled them proudly.

—*Maître, les formes sont bien faites. Que pensez-vous d'elles?*

—*Bien,* said Garamond, flicking his gaze over the sheets. —*Celles-ci iront bien.*

—*Et le texte? Que pensez-vous de cela?*

—*Le texte, je ne le lis pas.*

WORD TO WORLD,

In the asylum sat the poet surrounded by squirrels. The morning sun fell through trees across his shawled legs.

He peered in the direction of the Potomac. He whispered:

—Finding scarcely anyone save Monsieur de Rémusat who could understand him. . . .

The visitor, a young man with an earnest, fanatic's eye, came quietly across the tended lawn.

—Mr. Pound?

The poet jerked his head around. The squirrels fled.

A VISION CONVEYED FROM LABORATORY TO JUNGLE

Monsoon from the south had stopped the filming. The crew was dysenteric, and a month out of pocket in their salaries. The rented army equipment had returned to the capital for a revolution. The director watched the thickening rain, and thought: The accidental is the aesthetic of photography.

He arranged his actors on the steps of the wat. He summoned the lights, the cables, the cameras on their cranes hooded with clear vinyl. Rain glanced on wind chimes in the vast court. American weapons, unloaded, were shouldered by extras. He raised his arm.

One hundred blank-faced Thais waited for his arm to fall.

ITS OBSCURE CHEMISTRY ELUCIDATED IN THE WHITE
GLARE OF JELLIED FIRE

("A second time? Why? man of ill star.")

On the first day of his reenlistment Phalos led a patrol into a sector many times captured and lost. His thoughts were obscure. He walked with the dead. But it was his fear that upon returning to his country he would find it dead that had kept him here. He would bring out of this place that which he loved. So the place was the same, and yet not the same. This sector had been sprayed with defoliant days before, and the vines had rotted, the trees shed strips of their flesh, and leaves exploded underfoot, a metastasized autumn. All gave off laboratory hues and odors. At night a cool blue fire was seen here, yet not blue, in globes and streaks, as if souls fled a stinking swamp. Chatter of automatic weapons forewarned ahead. Behind him a drone typed for Phalos the aircraft approaching. He turned to see. Making a run. Payload. Such words soothed Phalos. The nomenclature of war was vivid and precise. As the craft closed he saw the markings of his country. Around him the entire squad turned, and yelled.

Fire fell from the sky. Phalos was a pyre. In his last moment Phalos had a vision of a sentence, stretched like a cloud-crested wave of sky over all existence: extent, duration, *kairos, chronos:* through which he swam, to the edge of the medium, to the void, outside the field of metaphor and fiction, and in that hard Icarian light was burned and fell unnoticed into waiting sea, while the energy of that sentence left the world ashen as the aftermath of torch touched to forest, science to love, word to world, its obscure chemistry elucidated in the white glare of jellied fire.

> "His horse's mane flowing
>   His body and soul are at peace."

Dust

MONA A. CLEE

Mona Clee was born in San Antonio, Texas, and attended Austin College and the University of Texas. She has been writing since the age of seven and is a graduate of the Clarion Science Fiction Writers' Workshop, an annual summer-long course that has produced many of the field's most important new voices. She is married to fellow Clarion graduate Mark Willard and lives near San Francisco, where she works as a tax lawyer.

"Dust" is her fifth published story, following other recent contributions, to Terry Carr's Universe 15 *and J. N. Williamson's* New Masters of Horror, *and* Fantasy & Science Fiction.

Eri had followed the main road from Ur all the way to the Euphrates River. Now she stood beside the flowing water, her eyes narrowed against the bright sun, her thoughts no less troubled than when she had left the city.

She did not want to die, although as priestess of Nannar it was her duty. She was not ready to give up her life for the shadowy existence of Kur, the afterworld, where the dead drank dust and ate ashes.

And she was afraid. There would be the procession into the pit to endure, then the farewell to the sunlight, and the closing of the tomb door. Lastly there would be the cup itself: swift-acting though the poison might be, Eri knew it would not be painless.

She gazed down at the river, hurrying to join its brother Tigris by the bitter-tasting sea to the southeast. Plumes of spray rose up where the water tripped over high rocks, and the drops sparkled and danced in the sun. The light dazzled Eri's eyes, and so she knew that Enki, the water god, must be at play in his domain.

"What should I do?" she asked Enki.

The river glittered and said nothing. Eri sighed, turned, and began to retrace her steps toward the city.

The sun blazed down on her like a ferocious living thing, but Eri turned her face up to it and smiled, for shortly she would not see it again. She walked steadily, passing field after field green with barley and emmer, threaded with irrigation ditches where peasants labored knee-deep in the water. Ahead of her, in the distance, lay the city of Ur with its great ziggurat. As always Eri was filled with wonder at the sight of it: the first wall painted black like the Netherworld, the next wall that enclosed the main temple gleaming red as blood, and above them both, at the very top, a patch of blue that was Nannar's enameled shrine—her home, her joy, her refuge.

A gust of wind washed over her from the river, carrying the smell of reeds, moist earth, and fish. At that moment life was dear to Eri, too dear to give up. She felt an impulse to flee everything: the city, the god she served, even dying Queen Pu-abi, whom she must accompany into the tomb.

The feeling passed, and she knew she would do her duty. She quickened her pace. She would go to the palace, await the Queen's death, and accompany her into the darkness of the Netherworld as she was sworn to do.

The season was over, the excavations were finished, and they were leaving Ur for the last time. Hilary walked a short distance away from her husband and his Arab workmen, gathering her thoughts to say goodbye to the city forever.

The ziggurat towered above her—what was left of it after five thousand years. The mud-brick foundations, all that remained of Ur's buildings, called to her, spots of earth still unturned promising fresh wonders if she would only stay.

But she could not. The money was gone, and there was talk in England that another great war might be approaching. She and Leonard would not be coming back; she would never see Ur again.

The dead city seemed more desolate than ever, and she wanted to cry. Next year dust storms would come and cover the foundations a little. The year after that there might be a flood to bury them further in silt. Before very long Ur would be forgotten once more, except for those moments when curious Londoners would gaze at the treasure she and Leonard were taking back to the museum.

No one would ever know Ur again as she had known it. She could feel the ghosts of its people moving in the newly-bared streets; the city scenes she pictured in her mind sometimes felt as real as her own memories of England.

As much as she knew of that lost time, she was

still leaving a mystery behind, a job unfinished, a puzzle which she now despaired of ever solving. She thought of the great burial pit inside the ziggurat, and of all the men and jewel-covered women who had walked into it one day to be covered up forever. Now she would never know why they had walked into that mass grave with such docility. Faceless and voiceless as they were, she must leave them behind with their story untold.

She surveyed the ruins, unwilling to join Leonard just yet. She was saying goodbye to ten years of her life —leaving a part of herself in Ur to be buried in blowing dust by the coming years.

Eri hurried up the palace steps, her sandals making soft sounds on the hardened mud brick. As she reached the great inner courtyard, her heart sank. Stewards, courtiers, soldiers, and slaves were gathered together in preparation for Pu-abi's funeral procession.

Until that moment, Eri had nursed some small hope that Pu-abi would not die. But now the procession was massing, and that meant there was no hope left, for to gather the mourners otherwise would have invited the worst of luck. Eri picked up her long skirt and hurried to the Queen's deathbed.

Hilary sat down on a wooden packing-box and tried to wipe her hands clean. How silly, she thought irrelevantly, to worry over a bit of Bloomsbury dirt after so many months of squatting in the unending dust of Iraq.

The basement of the decaying Georgian terrace was damp, and smelled of mildew and old papers. She stared through the grimy window into the tradesmen's area outside, thinking there was nothing like a cold, grey London day to lower one's spirits. Fog shrouded all Bloomsbury, and a dismal rain fell. The disembodied legs of strangers strode across Hilary's line of vision in a never-ending stream, coming, going, as nameless as the men and women she had brought out of the earth in Iraq.

She could not believe her great adventure was finally over. Leonard was lucky; he would be famous, his name inextricably linked with the ancients who had lived in the plain of Shinar. As for herself, there was nothing left but the remembrance of Ur.

She heard a soft knock at the door. "Lady Woolley?"

It was Mrs. Munro, the housekeeper. "Yes?" Hilary answered.

"Your husband would like to see you, if you're not busy."

"Thank you, Mary. I'll be right up."

She took a final glance around the room, wondering how they would ever bring order out of all that chaos. The prospect of all the days to come in the dark basement depressed her.

"I might as well be buried in that pit along with the others," she said aloud.

A memory flooded over her of the Iraqi sun, harsh, hot, and immediate. She closed her eyes and turned her face upward, remembering the feel of it on her skin. She shut out the mustiness of London; she drew in a breath and seemed to smell the far-off reeds and damp earth of the river.

She would have given anything right then to be back at the site. But outside the rain grew stronger, and resignedly she went up the stairs to see her husband.

Sir Leonard was standing in their office, once a drawing room. A cheerful fire had been built in the grate.

"My dear," he greeted her, "I've been wanting to ask your help. We've been asked to prepare a special display for the exhibition next month that will become part of the museum's permanent collection afterwards. Have you the time for it?"

"Yes," said Hilary, "far too much time, I'm afraid."

Sir Leonard lit a Havana cigar and sat close to the fire. "I know," he said. "Now begins the drudgery. But for this—" he looked at his cigar appreciatively—"I could never become resigned to civilization again."

"Then perhaps I should acquire the same habit."

Leonard gave her a startled look, and then laughed. "An extraordinary woman like you may do anything she pleases, Hilary. Tell me—do you know how many pictures I took of you at work on the site? There you were, never without your stockings or your little felt hat or your pillow to sit on, digging away as intently as any Arab bent on earning his *baksheesh*. I promise you one of those pictures will find its way into my book."

Hilary smiled. "I don't know what to do with myself. I'm rather at a loose end. Tell me about this display."

"The museum staff is hard at work restoring the major relics—the silver lyre, the land sledge, and those magnificent headdresses the ladies wore. But here's the problem. The museum wishes to display one of those squares of earth we brought back intact—one of those containing a crushed skull and headdress, just as we uncovered them. I think a nice exhibit of restored jewelry would temper this grisly effect, and reduce the chance of objections from our more refined patrons."

"I'll be glad to help," said Hilary, "but I must tell you, I'm not so sure this grisly effect is a bad thing. People love it. Remember how fascinated they were with Tutankhamen's tomb? Remember the talk about a curse? That's what made Carter and Carnarvon."

Leonard cleared his throat, as if uncomfortable with this revelation, and gestured to a pile of newspapers on the coffee table in front of the fire. "Look at them. 'Woolley and the Royal Death-Pit.' 'Human Sacrifice in Ur of the Chaldees.' 'The Monstrous Secret of Abraham's Birthplace.' "

Hilary laughed. "Don't fret, Leonard. They'll make your name. And I'll think of a display for the jewelry."

"How is the Queen?" Eri asked the doctor.

Simudar motioned her to a bench of costly wood, where he sat down with some difficulty. His flounced skirt was almost as long as Eri's, as befitted his rank, but he was old and stout and could not manage the garment with ease.

"I prepared a draught from the *anadishsha* plant," he said, "which I gave to the Queen, hoping it might strengthen her. But it was no use. Unless Lord Nergal releases his hold upon her, she will be dead by morning."

Eri touched his hand. "You did well. If I go to her, will she know me?"

He shook his head.

"I will go anyway. I must say farewell to her."

Simudar looked up at her. "Farewell—for a short while."

Eri rose and crossed the room to the Queen's bed-side. Pu-abi's attendants moved back so that she might sit next to the bier. "Pu-abi?" she whispered. "It is Eri."

Pu-abi's eyes did not open. Eri could scarcely feel the pulse in the old woman's wrists. Afraid she might cry, she stood up once more and replaced the Queen's hands on the bier.

"I will go to the temple now to hold vigil," she said, rejoining Simudar. "When the moon rises, I will pray to Nannar. Send word to me at once if the Queen worsens, and I will return."

Eri left the palace and made her way toward the temple. Once there she knelt, composed herself, and awaited moonrise.

Hilary managed to clear a space in the Bloomsbury basement by moving most of the expedition's para-phernalia into the pantry. She placed the ornate head-dress, just recently restored, on the table in front of her. It rested upon a wooden mount cushioned by a thick black wig. The beauty and intricacy of the work-manship amazed her—the pendants of gold shaped like leaves from a Euphrates poplar, the beads of lapis lazuli and carnelian, the headband of circlets made of beaten gold. She saw that the museum had affixed combs to the back of the wig, from which rose gold prongs crowned with rosette flowers. She shook her head; she could hardly believe that a living woman had worn this fragile thing, had taken it with her into the earth, and that now, five thousand years later, the relic rested in a chilly London basement restored to all its beauty.

What would she do with it? She must make people

stop and pay attention to all she and Leonard had done, and to the civilization that now lived again.

Inside the headdress the skull of a woman had been found, someone who had walked into the pit for a reason. Hilary wished she could see the woman's face: what would she think if she could know that her jewels and garments and all that was left of her body had been brought into the light again, five thousand years after her death?

Moonrise, at last. Eri rose from the pillow where she had knelt for so many hours and approached the looming statute of Nannar. The altar beneath it gleamed silver in the pale light, and upon this she liberally strewed oil and a magic powder, sacred to Nannar, that turned the color of flames from gold to silver. Then she took a reed and brought fire from a niche in the wall. With a quick sweep of her hand she set the oil ablaze, and the fire reared up. She stood back, raised her arms, and called to the god,

> Nannar, moon god,
> God of night and god of light,
> Hear me.

Around her the silence became complete. The shadows in the temple grew darker, the moonbeams more radiant. But Nannar did not answer, and the flames on the altar slowly died down. The fire in the little niche shrank, as if it were afraid to raise its head in the god's house.

> Nannar, dispeller of darkness,
> You who read the future that is dark,

> You who know the destinies of all,
> Hear me,
> Speak with me.

She cast a second handful of powder upon the altar and added incense. She poured out more oil, and again the silver flames leapt up, throwing dancing shadows against the blue walls. Eri thought she could feel the approaching presence of the god. She began to chant,

> Only the gods live forever under the sun,
> As for mankind, numbered are his days.
> Whatever they achieve is but the wind.
> So it must be, Lord.
> I have served you well: hear my request.

She paused and listened. There was no sound, and the image of Nannar did not move. Perhaps he knew what was in her heart and was angry that she had called him. Perhaps he would not come. But she had to try.

On impulse, Hilary put out her hands and touched the headdress. It was quite sturdy, and she found she could hold it in her hands with little fear of damaging it. She tucked her hair under the black wig, carried the headdress over to a mirror set into the wall next to the pantry, and drew in her breath. Carefully, she settled the ornament onto her head and anchored the three rosette combs at the back.

The effect was startling. Her brown eyes seemed to take on a darker cast as she gazed into the mirror, and it suddenly struck her that her coloring was just dark enough. . . .

She peered more closely into the mirror. She did not feel at all silly; neither did she feel ashamed, as if she had toyed with something grave and beautiful, or committed an act of desecration.

She reached up to steady the headdress. At the contact of her fingers, something jumped from the gold to meet her hand. Her flesh tingled. There appeared before her eyes a vision from a long-distant time. Spellbound, Hilary looked up at a piercingly bright blue sky and desert sun. She felt her body move within a cool linen dress, and felt warm dust beneath her feet. She tilted her head back and found that she was gazing up at a mighty tower—not the broken, mud-colored mound she remembered from the plain of Iraq, but a great temple reaching for the sky. She saw that the ziggurat was painted in brilliant colors: black at the base, red at the second tier, and at the very top, bluer than the sky itself.

Then the connection snapped and the vision was gone. Once more she was sitting in the cramped basement, staring at an ordinary mirror, hands raised to the headdress. She took it off and, very carefully, put it back on the table.

The god's presence grew tangible in the air. On the altar, the leaping flames collapsed into a single bright column that burned, bright and steady, without need of further feeding.

Eri looked up at the statue of Nannar and addressed him once more. "I must die soon, Lord. I have been fortunate to live twenty years, but you can read what is in my heart, and you know I would live twenty more, even as the Queen has. I am afraid of the pit, Lord, afraid of dying. I fear the dark and the land of Kur. Most of all do I fear Nergal. Counsel me, Lord."

She bowed, and stretched out her arms at knee level.

I would not be one with the dead.
I would not abide in the Netherworld.
Where dust is their food, clay their sustenance;
Where they see no light and dwell in darkness.
Where they are clad like birds with garments of
    wings,
Where over door and bolt dust has spread.

She straightened to her full height again and looked up at the altar. "Quiet my spirit, Lord. Help me let go of life. I have no child to remember me, priestess as I am. Help me not to grieve because when I am dead and covered with earth, all will forget me."

The air shivered. Eri groped for the flask of oil and poured the last of it upon the altar. Amid a great roar of moon-colored flames, she saw the flickering outlines of the god's face.

His braided hair gleamed black as jet, as did his beautifully curled and anointed beard. Nannar's eyes were black, too, though they gleamed with a cool and penetrating light, and seemed to peer straight through her flesh into her heart. On his head the god wore the horned miter of divinity, and in his ears were hung great lunate earrings which glowed with their own light.

Eri looked into his eyes and knew he heard her. She closed her eyes, folded her hands together in an attitude of reverence, and addressed him:

The thoughts of a god are as deep waters,
And not for any man to know.
Lord, give me a sign,
Give me the comfort I need.

A gust of wind swept past her, as if from an approaching storm.

A voice whispered, distant and deep, "Eri, priestess who intercedes for Ur, hear me. Only in the minds of men do the gods live forever. When a god is no longer worshipped, he too dies. When he is forgotten, he is as smoke that disappears in the wind. Thus do I understand your feeling."

"But the gods are immortal," Eri protested.

"Nothing endures forever. While Ur stands, so do its gods. Yet there will come a time when Ur is dust and naught but an empty name to all mankind. There will be no water within the city, no green plant, no living creature save the ever-hungry jackal. The sand will bury Ur. The Annunaki, the great gods themselves, will be as whispers. You wish to be remembered, my priestess: because you are faithful, I will grant your wish, as much as lies within my power.

"You go now to the grave in all your youth, but men will look upon your face when no priestess has called my name for thousands of years. A woman will summon you forth from the land of Nergal and restore to you all you have lost. And when she herself is dead, men will look upon you still, and be filled with wonder. Through you, they will remember Ur. Because of you, they will remember me. I can give you no other immortality."

The wind whipped past her and the fire went out. All was silent. She was alone.

Hilary's fingers still tingled where they had touched the headdress. She had seen the past through someone's eyes—but whose?

Not the Queen's, of that she was sure. The stone ceiling of the Queen's chamber had fallen in after the burial, crushing the body and the ornaments upon it beyond repair. This headdress had been found next to the bier, protected from much of the falling stone; perhaps it had belonged to an attendant of the Queen.

Hilary touched the headdress again. "Speak to me," she whispered. "Tell me who you were."

There came a faint tingling, once again, at the very tips of her fingers. Though the windows of the basement were closed tight against the rain, she suddenly thought she felt a draft. For an instant she smelled something sweet, like incense. She shut her eyes and caught the fleeting outlines of a moonlit room filled with a leaping fire.

Then it was gone. Hilary put her head down on the table and pulled her thoughts together. At length she rose, put on her raincoat, and left the building. She hurried down Bloomsbury toward Great Russell Street and the museum.

The moon was setting. The brilliant moonlight, by which Eri had often perused the writings on clay tablets, began to wane and pale. Then she heard the sound of feet ascending the temple steps. Simudar stood at the entrance to the sanctuary, framed in the fading light.

"Hurry," he said, "the Queen is close to death."

Together they made their way through the dark, sleeping streets of Ur back to the palace. "Is the tomb ready?" Eri asked.

"The last brick was put in place tonight, by torch-light."

"Has the steward assembled the goods Pu-abi will need on her journey? She must want for nothing."

"Yes, Lady."

"The Queen's jewels? All her belongings? Her clothes chest, her medicines?"

"All of them, Lady."

They reached the palace, and Eri hurried to the Queen and took the old woman's hand as she had done earlier that day. Little by little, as she waited, the Queen's breathing grew weaker.

All at once Pu-abi's body stiffened and, a moment later, relaxed. Her head lolled to one side and her eyelids rolled up partway, showing white crescent moons beneath. Her mouth opened and fell slack, displaying the stumps of yellowed teeth.

"The Queen is dead," said Eri. "Let us prepare the burial."

"I want to locate a box," said Hilary to Sir Arthur Keith, "a certain one that we brought back from Ur."

Sir Arthur nodded. "Just describe it, Lady Woolley, and I'll have one of the lads bring it round." He paused, and looked at her quizzically. "Just what are you looking for?"

"Do you remember the skeleton we found to one side of the Queen's bier?" asked Hilary. "The one that was so well preserved—that we took the headdress from? As I recall, we brought back the entire square of earth in which the skull was embedded. That's what I want."

Sir Arthur's eyes widened slightly, but he made no comment. "I see. It shouldn't be too difficult to locate."

"Thank you." Even though Hilary had known Arthur Keith for years, she felt awkward asking this particular favor.

"I take it this is for the display? Leonard told me you were helping him with the exhibition."

"Yes," said Hilary, "yes, that's it."

"I'll have it sent to one of the study rooms. Let me know if I can help you further. I'm something of an authority on the skulls found at Ur and Al'-Ubaid."

"Yes," said Hilary once more. "I—I'd hoped you would help me restore the skull."

Sir Arthur looked astonished. "Put it back together, you mean?"

"Yes. And then make a cast of it—or, if I could, use the skull itself. That would be much better, actually."

"To do what?"

"Reconstruct the face."

Sir Arthur considered; for a moment Hilary thought he was going to object. "That just might work," he said. "Show the woman just as she was—counterbalance the morbid effect of the crushed skull on display."

"Then you'll help me?"

"A lot of it will be guesswork," he continued. "We don't know exactly what the ancient Sumerians looked like. We have no living models to go by. I can't guarantee the likeness will be perfect."

Hilary nodded. "We'll do what we can."

"I'll get the box right now and have it brought to you."

"Make sure it's the right one," said Hilary. "It's very important."

Hours seemed to pass until, at last, she was alone with the box in a tiny museum workroom. She removed the lid and sat, motionless, staring down at the near-perfect skull on its pillow of earth. Her eyes lost their focus; slowly, she lifted her hands and ran her fingers lightly over it, forcing her mind to go blank.

It was midnight. No, long after midnight, closer to dawn. A full moon had just set, and her sandaled feet were moving down a silent street to the place where a Queen lay dying.

The midday sun beat down on the funeral party as if it wished to grind them into the clay at their feet. Eri's heart raced, and beneath her ceremonial robe her body grew clammy with sweat. Yet she tried to stay calm. All the men and women of the court would file past her shortly into the tomb, and she could not let them see she was afraid.

A horn sounded. Eri moved to the head of the procession, flanked by the priests of Enlil, chief of all the gods, father to Nannar. They stood silently as Pu-abi was carried past, draped with jewels and a fine cloak. Then the ladies in waiting went down the sloping ramp into the earth, and accepted a cup of poison from a priest. The grooms and their oxen followed, drawing the Queen's land-sledge. Lastly came the soldiers who would guard Pu-abi. Each accepted his cup with no outward sign of emotion and took up a position at the foot of the ramp.

Eri took a cup. She held her head high and walked down the ramp into the tomb, where she knelt by the side of the bier.

Outside the horn sounded once more, and everyone drank. The door to the tomb was pushed to, shutting out the light. In the dark one of the women began to cry; Eri shuddered. It was good that no one could see her face. She knelt, praying the poison would act quickly. A sensation like fire shot through her gut, and she doubled over.

"Don't go away!" whispered Hilary, as the images in her mind began to fade.

The moonlit street was gone, and in her mind's eye there was only darkness. But not, she realized gradually, the darkness of one sitting in a room with closed eyes. A deeper, older darkness.

She became aware of an almost physical silence pressing around her. The museum had become abnormally quiet. Or was she in the museum? Hilary strained to catch noises from outside, but could only hear the sound of rapid, shallow breathing—her own. Odd, she thought, how cold and tomblike the room suddenly seemed. She was aware as never before of its stone floor, stone walls, and featureless ceiling.

From far away she heard voices. They were singing, or perhaps chanting without music. The sound puzzled her, but she knew the door to her room was closed, and did not feel like getting up to open it. She did not feel like moving at all.

There was a thud and the room seemed to shake, as if a heavy door had been pushed into place. A stone door. A sharp pain cut through her middle and she bent forward, crouching over the table, struggling not to take her hands from the skull.

Outside the room she seemed to hear another thud, as if a heavy weight had been dropped to the floor. The sound was repeated once, then another time, then again. She leaned across the table and the pain intensified.

Eri's breath came fast and labored. She knew the pain would be over soon, but the tearing in her belly was all but unbearable. No longer able to hold herself upright against the bier, she slid to the dirt floor of the tomb.

All strength left her body. The heavy wig that supported the headdress felt like stone; it crushed her into the earth. The headdress itself seemed to tighten. She tried to tear it loose from her head, but her hands were too sluggish. The pressure in her skull grew worse.

She cried out. Then all at once she was through the gate. The pain was gone and she was drifting, floating, as if borne along on a bed of clouds. Strange sights passed before her eyes.

Strange, yet somehow not strange. She saw a room, dim and shadowy and somewhat frightening. A fine table was set there, and she caught sight of Pu-abi dining with kings and queens. Nannar himself played host at the head of the table.

Next to Pu-abi there was an empty chair. The Queen turned and beckoned to her.

Hilary screamed. The air in the tomb was stifling, and the headdress had become a tool of torture. In the cold and darkness, she was in agony; she was dying.

She wrenched her hands from the skull and broke the bridge to the past. She tore at her face and hair. She clawed at a wig and a headdress that were—not there.

She blinked and looked about. The light of the museum room reached her senses once more. She was sitting upright in her chair, her fingers knotted in her hair, her head no longer full of pain. She remained there for long minutes, gazing at the skull; her pulse raced with fright.

They worked at a furious pace, and the day before the exhibition, the head was finished. The skull, reinforced with plaster, was covered with a thin layer of wax tinted the color of flesh, which was then modeled to reproduce the dead woman's features. Luminous eyes of glass and black jet were then added, and color was applied to the cheeks and lips. On the head was put a wig, the design of which was taken from terracotta figures of Sumerian women, and atop this the restored headdress was anchored in all its glory. Enormous, moon-shaped earrings were affixed to the ears, and the whole was fitted to a heavy plaster bust for display.

Hilary lingered behind in the workroom after the museum closed and the staff left, putting finishing touches to the head. She had told Leonard she would be late. When she was satisfied that no one was around, she closed the door to the workroom and took a seat directly in front of her creation.

She rubbed her hands together, finding that the palms were sweaty. She was very frightened, but she had to do it. She took a deep breath, reached out, and put her hands against the wax face.

At first, nothing. Hilary held her breath as the moments ticked by. Had the link been broken? She concentrated on the face before her, trying to see the woman as a person who had walked and breathed and lived, whose spirit still existed in that shadow country the Sumerians called an afterlife. Then a bout of dizziness swept over her; a great roaring filled her head, and she became aware of the woman's presence. Hilary had experienced this feeling many times when, absorbed in her work, she suddenly would sense that someone else was in the room and raise her head to discover this was so. But the Sumerian had not physically come into the room. Her mind was there, inside Hilary's own skull, sharing her body and her consciousness.

Hilary swallowed. "Hello," she said.

There came the faintest of replies, like a whisper against her ear. "Who are you?"

"My name is Hilary."

A pause. "You must be the woman of whom Nannar spoke," the whisper said. "What place is this?"

"An island, far from Ur, the hub of a great empire."

"And what of Ur? Does my city still stand?"

Hilary hesitated, and then answered. "No. It is five thousand years since you walked into the tomb, and Ur is gone. But do not be sad. All the world comes to this island. All the world will see your face and marvel at the treasure that was in your tomb. Ur will not be forgotten."

"So," said the voice with a sigh, "Nannar was wise, and kind."

Hilary was puzzled. "Nannar?" she asked. "The moon god?"

When the reply came, there was a wry note in the

woman's voice. "Yes, the moon god. And the patron god of our city. I was Eri, his priestess."

"Where have you come from, Eri? Where were you, before I brought you to this room? What is death like?"

"I remember that the land of Kur is dark and full of shadows, just as I knew it would be. But I was not alone there. Pu-abi had made a place for me at table, just as if I were her daughter. I rested there, but I did not truly sleep. Perhaps I knew you would call me and was waiting, for I suspect that if I were to go to sleep in Kur, you could never call me back."

"Do all mortals go to the land of Kur when they die?" asked Hilary. "Will I go there?"

"I do not know," replied Eri, "but I think not. Kur is for my own people; I saw no strangers there. Perhaps the afterlife of your own fathers awaits you."

Hilary knotted her hands together, and said hesitantly, "I hope I have not angered you by calling you to this world. It cannot please you to know Ur is dead."

"No," said the voice, though it sounded sad, "I realize that everything must die—men, cities, even gods, though I would never have believed such a thing while I was the priestess of Nannar. It comforts me to know that the world remembers."

"The world will remember you," said Hilary. "Would you like to see what I have done? I have made a statue of you in wax and adorned it with all the jewelry you took into the grave."

"I cannot see anything," said Eri. "I am not yet in the world with you."

"Complete the transfer," whispered Hilary. "Trade

places with me. I think it can be done. Earlier I
seemed to see Ur through your eyes; later I felt your
pain when you took poison. Concentrate. Let us stand
in each other's places for a moment. You can walk
about in my body and see what world we have built
here in England, and I can see what death is like."

"But how will I return to Kur?"

"Put your hands on the image that looks like you
and think of me. I am sure it will work."

"Very well," said Eri.

Hilary opened her mind as best she could, letting
go of herself and her grip on England and the present.
She could feel the Sumerian hesitate. Then, suddenly,
the gap between them closed. Their spirits touched,
separated, and flowed in opposite directions. Hilary
blinked and found herself dressed in ceremonial robes
of the finest wool, her mind floating as if in a dream,
seated at a dark table amidst a gathering of shadowy
figures. Here and there a familiar face materialized in
the gloom. She realized she was very, very tired, that
her spirit was finally at peace, and that she wanted to
sleep forever.

Eri had the sensation of falling through space. She
opened her eyes and saw that she was sitting in a
strange room with impossibly smooth walls. She tilted
her head back to look up at the ceiling and gasped;
there, overhead, was a ball of glass that blazed light,
a miniature sun. Surely she must be in some fantastic
temple to Utu, the sun god, even if the woman had
told her such gods were forgotten.

She looked around and saw, on the table before her,
an almost perfect likeness of herself. This, then, was

what the woman had used to call her from the dead;
this, her own face, gazing up at her as if it, too, defied
death.

She stood to her full height and realized that she
was incredibly tall—a giantess, at least a head taller
than she had been. As she moved, she felt the body
that housed her move comfortably. She felt her bones
and found them strong. Her teeth were solid and not
the least painful. If this was the future, these people
had taken doctors away from the Annunaki themselves.

She would leave the room. The impulse swept over
her to explore whatever temple lay outside, to see this
world for an instant as the woman had bade her do.
Her courage rose. As she walked toward the door, the
body she was in remembered how to open it. From
long habit she took keys from a hook set into the wall
before stepping into the passageway.

She walked until the corridor connected to another,
larger room, and crossed that to emerge in a still larger
gallery. She found it amazing. She suspected that the
entire complex might be larger than the ziggurat of Ur
itself.

And then she came to a great central hall hung with
banners and numerous strange writings. It seemed to
be full of mysterious relics, a storehouse of the gods.
As she approached, she saw the hall was full of wooden
stands, themselves enclosed by barriers of colorless
glass.

On these stands were all-too-familiar objects: the
treasures Pu-abi had taken with her into the royal
grave, restored to life. The silver lyre with the head of
a bull was there, and the land-sledge, and the statue

of a ram caught in a thicket of gold. Half running, Eri passed case after case; when she reached the last one she stopped, fighting back tears, realizing that in truth these relics were all that was left of her world.

Then she paused and raised her head slightly, for she thought she glimpsed moonlight. Straight ahead, the enormous gallery ended in great doors of metal and wood and more glass. Beyond these doors, outside the looming temple, it was night; night, with a full moon.

Eri advanced slowly toward the doors. Her hands fitted the key automatically, and she stepped through. She seemed to have found the front of the strange edifice; a line of huge stone columns supported a roof far above her head, and the porch was open to the night sky and stars.

Overhead the moon was full. Eri looked up at it, hungrily, and found to her joy that it was the same moon, unchanged, as when she had worshipped Nannar in Ur. She felt suddenly comforted. This was her own earth still.

"Nannar?" she whispered. Her lips framed the ritual invocation to the god, and she waited long minutes for his answer. But there was no response.

Saddened, she looked away from the moon at the temple enclosure. She stared; truly, the temple around her was a mighty building, worthy of any city-state in the land of Shinar. It had a great open enclosure surrounded by what looked to be a fence of black metal spears, their points tipped with gold. Beyond that was a fine, wide street, and on the other side of that rose row after row of buildings, each as tall as her own ziggurat.

As she stood there, motionless, a swift, glowing sledge moved down the avenue before the temple, drawn by no animal she could discern. It made a strange, humming noise, and Eri feared at first it was a demon. But the city around her continued to sleep, and no one appeared to give the alarm. The apparition passed by and disappeared.

What an incredible world this was! Eri put her hands to her face, as if to reaffirm her own solidity. And then the thought occurred to her: why not stay here? Why not keep this body? She might live another twenty years. Perhaps this was the true gift Nannar had meant to confer upon her.

The thought was tempting. The lights of the city and the brilliant moonlight whispered, calling her away from the grave and the land of Kur. How easy it would be to walk away from the dark temple at her back into this new world. No one would ever know that the woman who had summoned Eri from Kur now occupied her place in that land, next to Queen Pu-abi.

Only for a moment did she really consider the deed. Then she remembered herself, and stepped back reluctantly from the moonlit porch, drawing the great doors of the temple shut behind her. She did not belong to this world. However much she wanted to live, she could not betray the god who had given her this miraculous return from the dead, the Queen who waited for her, and the woman who had called her forth. With a final glance at the moonlit courtyard and street outside, she turned and made her way through the darkened structure to the little room where her own effigy lay waiting. She shut the door behind her, locked it, and seated herself before the

waxen bust. A deep breath, and she extended her
hands toward the image.

At the first touch of fingers to wax, a shock leapt
through her hands and into her arms and body. Before
her eyes there were stars and dancing lights; then the
room grew hazy around her. She sensed the other
woman's presence in the room, as she sensed her own
spirit slipping back into the shadow land from which
it had been summoned.

"Goodbye," she called, and knew the woman had
heard her.

The dimness of Kur reappeared; she found that she
was seated once more at the great table, next to Pu-
abi. Nannar raised his cup to her, as if acknowledging
that she had come back to them, and drank.

Her arms and legs felt heavy as stone. She took her
own cup and sipped at it, finding it to be full of dust.
For a moment she wanted to jump up, flee the gray,
weary feast, and return to the lights and strangeness
of the world she had just left. But she could not. Her
place was here, at Pu-abi's side, and here she would
remain forever.

Hilary sat back in her chair, waiting for her head
to clear. Her heart hammered frantically—almost as
if it knew her spirit and body had been separated a
dangerously long time. She reached out and touched
the waxen image before her, but no shock answered
the touch. Nor, she realized, would it ever again.

She got to her feet and left the room, turning off
the light and locking up for the evening. Her feet
traced the old, familiar path out of the museum, paus-
ing for a moment on its great stone porch to look out

at the moon over Great Russell Street. A lone hansom cab passed as she watched, and she suddenly felt very glad to be back.

So she had seen Death. At least, one form of Death. Hilary knew that no shadow land of Kur awaited her in the afterlife, any more than the dead god Nannar gazed down upon her from the bright disk overhead. What lay before her was still unknown. As for the girl who had walked into the pit after her Queen—perhaps all was well with her now.

Leonard would be at home, waiting, drinking brandy, and smoking his usual Havana. She crossed beneath the stone columns of the museum facade, crossed the courtyard, and let herself out through a gate in the iron fence. She was in a great hurry to get home.

Diary of a Dead Man

MICHAEL BISHOP

In this story, the very soul of the U.S. government floats in the aftermath of Armageddon, pondering its predicament and the philosophy of Peanuts.

Bishop's other works include the novel Who Made Stevie Crye?, *about a young Southern widow and her haunted typewriter. Playful, ingenious, spooky, and funny,* Who Made Stevie Crye? *is a satire on horror and on metafiction. Its weird humor and metaphorical stylishness are characteristic of Bishop's work, also gracing both his Nebula Award-winning novel,* No Enemy but Time, *and the much-praised* Ancient of Days.

His story "Dogs' Lives" was chosen to appear in the prestigious Best American Short Stories '85.

Michael Bishop lives near Atlanta, Georgia.

Deathdate One: A short while ago, as if fulfilling the dictates of a clumsy punch line, I *woke up dead.* Forgive the italics, but the queerness of this state—postmortem consciousness—cries out for underscoring. I have no body, but I can think. On the other (nonexistent) hand, I know that I am dead because I have no body. No body, and nobody, at all. The celebrated assertion of René Descartes, "I think, therefore I am," does not apply. I refute it by pointing out that the Frenchman formulated this solipsistic law while comfortably incarnate in a (more or less) standard-issue human body. The vicissitudes of disembodiment were unknown to him—although, of course, he may be more familiar with them now.

Cogito ergo sum? I prefer "I think, therefore I'm confused," in tandem with "I'm absent, therefore I ain't."

Around me, as far as my thoughts can probe, only a glimmering ectoplasmic gray. But, to give this mother-of-pearl fog its due, the grayness may *comprise* my thoughts. I am really in no position to presume myself encompassed by it. I may be outside it, looking down. I may be under it, looking up. I may be at a remove of light-years, sensing the grayness via some kind of psychic telemetry. Or, again, I may be emitting this fog as a squid alchemizes and unfurls from itself a thalidomide plume of dreamily deforming ink. I have no body, and I am nowhere. However, the fog bank of my consciousness seems to be *moving*, and that motion holds out the hope of eventual arrival.

Where am I going?

Death, I thought, was supposed to answer that question. My next chilling realization is that maybe it will.

Dd. Two: What business have I, the disembodied consciousness of a dead man, keeping a diary? How, after all, do you date the virtually indivisible stretches of deadtime triggered by the moment of your dying? New Year's Day, Easter Sunday, the Fourth of July,

Halloween and Christmas Eve are all equally meaningless here. What year is it? What month? What
day? What cockeyed o'clock? Although I know that I
died in a certain documentable year, at a specific pin-
pointable instant, the twilight territory into which I
have died has a featurelessness—an everlasting *timelessness*—that no doubt keeps most dead people from
becoming faithful diarists. I am, in fact, the only one
I know about. You need a powerful ego to record a
chronology of undated, and undatable, non-events.
You need a powerful ego to prevent yourself from
fading into the omnipresent gray.

Maybe I have no body, but I *do* have that kind of
ego. It centers me in the fog. It arranges the non-
events of this amorphous realm into the artificial
linearity of sentences and paragraphs. Perhaps this
entry should precede the first one. Or maybe it should
make its initial appearance four or five entries down
the (artificial) line. Who am I to say? Well, like God
trying to impose order on chaos, I am trying to impose
chronology on the mist-scatter of postmortem "existence." By my lights (if no one else's), that goal gives
legitimacy to my self-appointed role as an historian of
my otherwise indistinguishable deathdays.

Dd. Three: *Cogito ergo sum.* "I think, therefore I
am." Descartes is not quite so easy to refute as I have
said. Here I am, after all, thinking in diary format, and
both my thought processes and this unlikely diary
prove that on some level I continue to exist. I think,
therefore I am. (I am, therefore I think?) If death
brings about the total annihilation of consciousness,
then obviously I have not died. However, I actually
remember dying, and the vivid ferociousness of that

event completely incinerated what used to be my body.

Could it be that death opens a door to the continuation of human consciousness by non-biological means? If so, what means? As a mind without a body, it occurs to me that these motivators must be either electromechanical or spiritual, or possibly a combination of the two, but absolutely nothing else of which I am presently aware. In other words, I am now either a piece of programmed software running in a computer or an angel sustained in the enduring dusk by the mysterious grace of God.

Which me is the true one, the electronic or the seraphic?

Dd. Four: Of course, I could be a ghost rather than an angel. If I were a ghost, my motor force would still be spiritual rather than electromechanical. Orthodox theologians deny the elevation of even death-transfigured human mortals to the ranks of the angelic hierarchy. God made the angels before He made the earth and its inhabitants. You do not inherit a pair of wings simply by dying. On the other hand, a ghost generally possesses an immaterial simulacrum of the body of its deceased "progenitor." And, as I have already noted, I have no body at all. I'm absent, therefore I am not. Am not a ghost, that is. Which somewhat reassuring conclusion leads me back to the altogether benumbing fear that I am stored on a magnetic disc inside a computer or else animated from afar by the unfathomable cogitations of God. Either way, I am the prisoner of a variety of limbo that makes me long for the release of utter oblivion.

Deprived of genuine ghosthood, I resent the fact that I am unable to haunt anyone but myself.

Dd. Five: I do not really believe that my personality has been magnetically warehoused or that I am running off at the ego inside an IBM, Apple or Radio Shack special. Computers have terminals, and terminals often have screens, and even the most complex or esoteric of programs must interface *somewhere* with consensus reality. If it did not, that program could hardly be aware of its own existence.

Well, I *know* that I exist, but not once since my deathday have I "interfaced"—being myself faceless —with any other reality but the mother-of-pearl fog impinging on every notional nerve of my disembodied consciousness. No whiz-kid hacker in wire-rimmed glasses and tennis shoes has summoned me along the link of an electronic personality preservatorium to "live" again for his and his buddies' puerile amusement. My isolation from the world on the material side of my deathday is total. I am devastatingly alone in this drifting grayness. Alone alone alone alone alone. An iambic-pentameter solitude worthy of a justly deserted Elizabethan villain.

Dd. Six: But if I am not a computer program, neither am I bona fide spiritual entity. (No question of my being an angel. Never any question.) Angels have no biological impulses because they have no biology. The bodies they occasionally assume go forth like puppets or remote-controlled robots to perform their miraculous tasks, which, nearly always, are duly sanctioned historical expressions of the will of God. The angels themselves—the irreducible *essences* constituting their being—remain in heaven, directing without participating, effecting without actually putting a finger in. They neither hunger nor thirst nor ache nor lust. Their only quasi-natural longing is for union with the Creator whose bountiful spiritual strength sustains them in existence.

Well, I am not like that. Never was. Bodiless, I continue to be buffeted by the ravening winds of biological memory.

Cut off the leg of a wounded man. Give him time to heal. Invariably, he will still experience twinges in his phantom limb.

That's me. Although wholly severed from my palate, bowels and privates, I am still a slave to the tyranny of their phantom clamor. I crave the earthy taste of potatoes and beer. I imagine cracking open the long albino legs of a snow crab and sucking from the splintery break thread after succulent thread of meat. I imagine, too, spreading the legs of a woman and nursing her brine-flavored lips with a similar greed. Are these the secret imaginings of an angel? Would a member of God's celestial militia ever contaminate itself with such calculated cupidity? Not on your life. Nor on mine, either.

Q.E.D., I'm no angel.

Dd. Seven: Besides being dead, what other possibilities present themselves? Let me catalogue them.

1. Asleep in my own room, I am having a strangely vivid nightmare. After a while, of course, I'll awaken.

2. I am the subject of a sensory-deprivation experiment. A team of researchers has placed me in a shallow bath of warm water inside a coffinlike container.

No light or sound enters. Hour after hour, I float on my back in the buoyant dark. Finally, this maddening lack of stimulus leads me to hallucinate the omnipresent gray that I have mistakenly identified with the baleful territories of death. Eventually, however, the researchers will relent and free me.

3. I am in a state of suspended animation. This possibility has subsidiary possibilities: (a) I am being cryogenically preserved in a special mausoleum, there to await a medical discovery that will reverse the progress of the fatal disease put on hold by my freezing-down. And (b) I am lying in a cold-sleep capsule in a starship on its way to colonize the planet of a distant sun. Like my many sleeping colleagues, I will be revived automatically as soon as our vessel has entered the targeted solar system. Our arrival will of course presage the beginning of a bright new future for the entire human species.

No, no, no. No, no.

To believe any of these untenable "possibilities" would delight me. Each and every one of them offers the promise of resurrection. But I cannot believe any of them for the simple, and nonchalantly damning, reason that I remember in explicit, slow-motion detail the final two or three minutes of my life.

Dd. Eight: A crisis situation of the highest priority obtained. I was aloft in the flying command post with Carmody, Findlater, and Meranus, not to mention our elite standby crew and a four-star lifer from the Pentagon. The lifer's obsequious bombast was meant both to cower the crew and to satisfy his civilian superiors' desire for conspicuous action. Everyone in uniform bustled. Everyone in statesmanesque mufti glowered and role-played. A mis-hit on Washington, D.C., had smeared an incandescent porridge of scrap metal, brick dust, and liquefied concrete all the way to Baltimore. Static sniffle-snaffled the airwaves. What reports had earlier filtered through were contradictory in every particular but one, namely, the ruinous extent of the damage inflicted by our enemy's first nuclear enfilade. So many cities blazed that even the prairie dogs in North Dakota were gasping for breath.

"Sir," Carmody said, "a heat-seeking device from an invading MiG appears to be—"

I had abstracted myself from my environment. My head was lolling against a curve of sheet metal. The continuous faint rumble of our airborne fortress had begun to counterpoint the internal tides of my blood. The crew members in their zippered flightsuits, and my aides in their obligatory pinstripes, were ghosts shimmering on the outskirts of my vision. The fate of the nation and its people had long since ceased to occupy my thoughts. I was thinking instead about a "Peanuts" comic strip by Charles Schulz.

In this cartoon, Charlie Brown and Peppermint Patty stand side by side with their elbows on the parapet of a low brick wall. Peppermint Patty declares in the first frame that she needs to talk to someone who "knows what it's like to feel like a fool." Two frames later, she is saying, "Someone who's been disgraced, beaten, and degraded. Someone who's been there. . . ." In the wordless concluding frame, Charlie Brown spreads wide his arms in a touching here-I-am, look-no-further gesture. Why, even the most accomplished of public speakers would have given a small fortune to add that eloquent gesture to their forensic arsenals. I know I would have. So would Copetti, who

outpointed me in our televised debates without ulti-
mately managing to translate these victories into success at the polls. Too bad, I say. So sad.

Anyway, when Carmody's missile struck us, I was
thinking about Charlie Brown and Peppermint Patty.
I may have been smiling. Any stray recollection of that
particular strip nearly always coaxed a smile from me.
I record this fact in my post-mortem diary with more
chagrin than amiable self-effacement. Honesty com-
pels me to chronicle only the truth. (Even if I am
assisted in this compulsion by the soothing hunch that
no one else will ever apprehend what I record here.)
That a man of my stature and responsibility should
have been mulling a cartoon at such a time galls my
pride. If I had lived, and if Carmody or Findlater had
maliciously publicized my gaffe, the rumor of it would
have unquestionably played havoc with my re-election
chances. But the world sometimes works that way,
matters of no moment elbowing aside those of high
consequence; besides, I have always admired Charles
Schulz more than I have Sakharov or Solzhenitsyn.
Did either of these Russian-born worthies ever make
anyone smile?

The arrival of Carmody's "heat-seeking device" interrupted my reverie. It tore into our flying command
post. It ignited something treacherously flammable
not far from the vaporized bulkhead against which I
had been leaning. As I spiraled amid the orbiting
debris of our disintegrating aircraft, my flesh caught
fire. For a few feverish seconds, I was conscious of the
night sky underfoot and the radiantly riven earth overhead. The gelatin in my eyeballs melted. My charred
skin flapped away. My bones turned to chewing gum.
I was now unequivocally dead, and Carmody, Find-

later, Meranus—every patriotic member of our crew
—had been press-ganged into nonexistence with me.
Or, if not *with* me, then *at the same time* as I. It must
be that those other poor fellows now occupy dimensionless pockets of grayness similar to, but altogether
independent of, my own.

Perhaps the same is true of every single specimen
of the human family recently extinguished by the War
to End All Wars. . . .

Dd. Nine: 1) I am not safely asleep. 2) I am not the
subject of a sensory-deprivation experiment. 3) And I
am not in a state of suspended animation in either A)
an earthbound facility or B) an idealistically dis-
patched starship.

I am dead.

Dead dead dead dead dead.

Charlie Brown and Peppermint Patty may be alive
somewhere or somewhen, but I am clearly a helpless
captive of my deadness, which seems escape-proof.
How even this niggling bit of the sentient me has
managed to "survive," I cannot presume to guess.
Over and over again, though, the fear that I am being
punished for my—our—manifold sins asserts itself. I
only hope that for the debacle just past I am God's
solitary scapegoat, that my eerie confinement here has
exempted the innocent majority of our species from a
similar fate. Is that hope as grandiose and egocentric
as my earthly political career? Do I dare aspire in my
loneliness and degradation to the title Redeemer? Is
that, in fact, an office for which a dead man can take
it upon himself to run?

God only knows.

Dd. Ten: This moment, I have decided, is the Twelfth of Never, the Ides of Self-Validation, the Eve of Apotheosis. Cute, eh? I have put dates (of a kind) to invisible units of my own dubious thought processes. Well, who's to stop me? Johnny Mathis? Caesar's assassins? God Himself? Hardly. I am the sole ruler of the twilight. Its alpha and omega, so to speak. And, surely, I can do here whatever I want to do, whenever I choose to do it. Stand back, then. The Emperor of the Great Gluey Gray is about to shape from glimmering formlessness a cosmos all his own. . . .

Let there be light!

Dd. Eleven: The glimmering formlessness persists. For that one, I suppose, I stupidly set myself up. Imagine Charlie Brown with his arms spread wide. Even as the unlocatable smoke of my consciousness drifts this way and that through the surrounding void, I see my bodiless self in that humbling, pathetic posture. I shape nothing. I control nothing. I merely poke around in the lost corners of limbo like a rat in a maze, my old personality and all my outworn belief systems obstructively intact, delaying the progress of my soul on its way to . . . well, wherever. For am I not a soul seeking release?

Unfortunately, one of my outworn personal credos, never confessed in public, was that there is no such thing as an immortal soul. With many other questing Batesonian rationalists, I believed that if you wish to touch the soul, you need only lay hands on your own living body. The soul has no capacity to survive apart from animate flesh. The body-and-soul dichotomy propounded by the Christian church was a misapprehension, one that has only lately fallen victim to the theory that consciousness emerges from the intricate interaction of a variety of biological systems. Anything that permanently damages the harmony among these systems—a bullet to the brain, the radioactive pollution of the atmosphere—likewise slays the soul. I resignedly embraced these modern beliefs. I never expected a portion of my self-awareness to outlive my body. Once dead, I felt sure that ahead of me lay only vast silent deserts of irreversible not-being.

Have you ever heard God laugh? Minus ears and auditory nerves, *I* have. The sound of it is the continuous faint rumble of a deadly engine plowing through a mother-of-pearl fog.

Dd. Twelve: If I am not dreaming, maybe I am being dreamt. If God can sustain the "lives" of spiritual entities like angels, why couldn't He—or a designated surrogate—repair and rewind the mental processes of a human being physically undone by famine, disease, or war? In the absence of a healthy brain, this would be difficult but probably not impossible. Unlike me, God can do whatever He wants to do, whenever He chooses to do it. Meanwhile, my own lack of solidity and volition strongly suggests that I am being projected from Elsewhere by either God or a dreaming proxy empowered by Him to hold me in existence.

These are frightening thoughts, but they also serve to absolve me of responsibility for the direction and content of my mental processes. I am not I. I am the weird muddle of someone else's anxious dream. My existence—my *non*existence—is an illusion relegating me to the status not merely of a single dead member of an entire extinct species but of the ghostly representative of a species that *never evolved at all.* Someone else is ineptly thinking me, therefore I am not.

But I am reasoning badly about this problem. In some humiliatingly dependent sense, I *do* exist. If I exist ineptly here, maybe it is because I lived ineptly. Maybe I am being dreamt by the residual consciousness of the person I was before that enemy missile—which I *insist* was real—blasted me and my companions out of the air. Some few of us may be lifted into legends by death, but a more telling truth I have learned is that no one is *improved* by it. Not even me. Least of all me. And, again, maybe I am a captive of this substanceless gray matter because in life I assumed myself exquisitely evolved, totally beyond improvement.

How the mighty are fallen.

Dd. Thirteen: Paupers and kings, garbage collectors and presidents may sometimes lie together in the same cemeteries. Indeed, they may even be said to "sleep together in the great democratizing union of death." Poets, romanticizers, and hard-nosed existentialists alike may claim that we are all united in our mortality. Death comes for the archbishop as surely as it does for the apothecary. The dead pickpocket is as dead as, but no deader than, the dead concert pianist. Thus does our finite biology homogenize every human being who has ever drawn breath. All for one and one for all—even if, alive, we would have continued to segregate by social class, skin color, occupational allegiance, religious creed, and/or political conviction.

True, death is no bigot. Granted, death is an Equal Opportunity Employer. But be that as it may, death does *not* unify. It separates and sequesters. Solitary confinement. Monastic isolation. Every disembodied soul a passenger in the free-floating nucleus of a vast single-cell grayness. You can meditate, as I have been trying to do, or you can go mad. But when madness inevitably overtakes your meditations, you must bear it. No other option is available. Death has ceased to count as an option—has *died*, as John Donne correctly predicted—because you have already exercised it. And you have no words to convey to anyone— whether God or some less awesome eavesdropper— the queer pitch of your insanity or the dreadful measure of your loneliness.

I, for imperfect instance, am like a sidewalk screamer in detention on the image-reflecting side of a two-way mirror, gagged and straitjacketed to a fare-thee-well but nonetheless struggling to tear free and scream.

A maimed amphibian.

Dd. Fourteen: I used to enjoy mysteries. I read them for relaxation. ("It's all right, Mr. Ambassador; he reads them for relaxation.") I liked their deliciously campy titles. *Dead Men Tell No Tales. A Queer Kind of Death. Death Claims. The Dead Are Discreet. Death Is a Lonely Business.* I could go on forever— literally—about the uncanny prescience of the authors of these and other such titles. They said so much more than they knew. Their commercial cleverness was in fact profundity, their crude glibness wit, their with-it jauntiness a wistful sort of anticipatory courage. Such writers wrote mysteries, I think, because nearly everything that matters is a mystery. Of course, I could also damn the lot of them for their lack of specificity, but you cannot say what you do not know and even the daunting engines of human imagination have their limits. It seems to me enough that they were able to *hint* so well. If I had the capacity to laugh, I would laugh in sardonic appreciation. I would rend this dimensionless fog with the inaudible sounds of a dead man lauding the clairvoyance of mystery writers, the greatest of whom is undoubtedly God. *The Dead Laugh Last.* Good title, eh?

Dd. Fifteen: Right now—and ages may have passed since my last entry in this immaterial record—the sole mystery preoccupying me is the destination of this fog. The fog moves. I have no visual or auditory references to tell me that it does, but I am sure of it. A vague apprehension of shifting equilibria repeatedly confirms for me the fact of the fog's movement. My consciousness seems to be tumbling in disorienting slow-motion along the inner edge of a great vortex. Call it a maelstrom if you like. Or the influence of a postmortem Coriolis force. Or the gravitational effects of a singularity—a funereal black hole—especially contrived to dispose of lost souls. Maybe, the seeming inescapability of my condition aside, I am spiraling toward a death-beyond-death. Or a life-beyond-death, the liberating opposite of this bleak, ego-bruising purgatory. Maybe, instead of absolute extinguishment, there is light at the end of the tunnel.

Ah. Once a political hack, always a political hack. Orbiting downward to who-knows-what, I continue to cast my fate in the happy-talk vocabulary of a presidential press secretary with his fingers crossed in the small of his back. The light at the end of the tunnel. The truth, of course, is that the world I departed lay smoldering beneath me as grotesquely disfigured and as magnificently uninhabitable as the most literal-minded medieval cleric's private vision of hell. I evaporated above that world. All the pain and suffering of those who lingered on, I airily sidestepped, Peppermint Patty and Charlie Brown pirouetting together in the self-pitying irony of my last conscious thought. What price a commander-in-chief's selfish peace of mind? Peanuts, my friend. Peanuts.

Dd. Sixteen, Seventeen, Eighteen, etcetera: I am alternately hopeful and afraid, expectant and terrified. A tremendous suction has the glimmering gray all around me in its down-tugging power. The indivisible deadtime of my consciousness has begun to accelerate, to tumble faster and faster toward an answer to the central posthumous mystery of my apprentice after-life. That answer, of course, may be only the cruel posing of yet another mystery, afterlife upon afterlife, deadtime without end. Or it may be redemption. Or obliteration. My uncertainty is what alternately elates and roundly disheartens me. Meanwhile I fall endlessly into myself.

I believe that I am about to discover whether God is merciful or just. . . .

Fair Game

HOWARD WALDROP

Howard Waldrop won a well-deserved 1980 Nebula Award for "The Ugly Chickens," a witty and persuasive tale of the last redoubt of the Dodo, down in William Faulkner territory. He is the author (with Jake Saunders) of The Texas-Israeli War: 1999 *and of the highly entertaining* Them Bones, *a time-jaunt into alternative history focusing on the pre-Colombian mound builders. His work—which often combines wit with gritty realism and impeccable detail—has appeared in* Playboy, Omni, *and other magazines, and has been widely anthologized.*

Many years of interest in the career and suicide of Ernest Hemingway—author, adventurer, and hunter—here leads Howard Waldrop to a gripping account of the great writer's ultimate safari. . . .

"AN OLD MAN IS A NASTY THING."

He heard church bells ringing anxiously on the wind.

He felt the cool air on his skin.

He saw the valley spread out below him like a giant shell.

It was a valley he had known, thirty-five or forty years ago, when he had been there for the skiing. It was a small valley in Bavaria, with its small town. He had never seen it in this season, having been here only in winter. This was spring. Patches of snow still lay in the shade, but everything was greening, the air was a robin-egg blue above the hovering mountains.

He was on the road into town, moving toward the sound of the bells. He lifted his eyes up a little past the village (the glare hurt them, but in the last few years so had all bright lights). Through a slight haze he saw a huge barn, far off on the road leading out the other side of the town.

He looked quickly back down at his feet. He did not like looking at the barn.

He noticed his boots; his favorites, the ones he had hunted in until two years ago when his body had turned on him after all the years he had punished it, when he couldn't hunt anymore. When he could no longer crouch down for the geese in the blinds, he had taken to walking up pheasant and chukar. But then even that ability had left him, like everything else he ever had.

Walking toward the town was tiring. His pants were that tattered old pair from the first hunt in Africa, the one the book came out of. He had kept those pants in the bottom of an old trunk filled with zebra hides.

He put his hands to his broad chest and felt a flannel shirt and his fishing vest. It was the one he'd been wearing in that picture with the two trout and the big smile, taken the first time he'd come to Idaho.

He felt his face as he walked. His beard was still scraggly on his chin. He reached up and felt the big lump on his forehead, the one he'd gotten when he'd butted his way through a jammed cabin door, out of a burning airplane, his second plane crash in two days seven years before.

His hat was the big-billed marlin cap from the days of Cuba and Bimini and Key West, back when everything was good: the writing, the hunting and fishing, the wives, the booze.

He remembered that morning in Idaho when he was in his bathrobe, just back from the hospital, and both the house and the shotgun had been still and cool.

Now he was walking down the hill toward the ruckus in town, dressed in odds and ends of his old clothing. It was a fine spring morning in the mountains half a world away.

Many houses stood with doors open, all the people now at the town square. Still, the pealing of the bells echoed off the surrounding peaks.

From way off to the left he could hear the small flat bells of cattle being driven toward him, and the shouts of the people who herded them.

A woman came from a house and ran past him without a glance, toward the milling people and voices ahead.

A child looked down at him from one of the high third-story windows, the ones you sometimes had to climb out of in the winter if you wanted to go outside at all.

He was winded from the half-mile walk into town.

The crowd stood looking toward the church doors, perhaps three hundred people in all, men, women, a few of the children.

The bells stopped ringing, slowed their swings, stopped in the high steeple. The doors opened up, and the priest and bürgermeister came out onto the broad steps.

The crowd waited.

"There he is," said the priest.

Heads turned, the crowd parted, and they opened a path for him to the steps. He walked up to the priest and the mayor.

"Ernst," said the bürgermeister. "We're so glad you came."

"I'm a little confused," he heard himself say.

"The Wild Man?" said the priest. "He's come down into the villages again. He killed two more last night and carried off a ram three men couldn't lift. Didn't you get our cablegram?"

"I don't think so," he said.

"We sent for you to come hunt him for us. Some townspeople remembered you from the Weimar days, how you hunted and skied here. You're the only man for the job. This Wild Man is more dangerous than any before has ever been."

Ernst looked around at the crowd. "I used to hunt in the old days, and ski. I can't do either anymore. It's all gone, all run out on me."

It hurt him to say those things aloud, words he had said over and over to himself for the last two years, but which he had told only two people in the world before.

The faces in the crowd were tense, waiting for him or the official to say something, anything.

"Ernst!" pleaded the bürgermeister, "you are the

only man who can do it. He has already killed Brunig, the great wolf hunter from Axburg. We are devastated."

Ernst shook his head slowly. It was no use. He could not pretend to himself or these people. He would be less than useless. They would put a faith in him when he knew better than to put any hopes in himself.

"Besides," said the young priest, "someone has come to help you do this great thing."

Somebody moved in the crowd, stepped forward. It was a withered old black man, dressed in a loincloth and khaki shirt. On its sleeve was a shoulder patch of the Rangers of the Ngorongoro Crater Park, and from the left pocket hung the string of a tobacco pouch.

"Bwana," he said, with a gap-toothed smile.

Ernst had not seen him in thirty years. It was Mgoro, his gunbearer from that first time in Africa.

"Mgoro," he said, taking the old man's hands and wrists, shaking them.

He turned to the officials.

"If he's come all this way, I guess we'll have to hunt this Wild Man together," said Ernst. He smiled uneasily.

The people cheered, the priest said a prayer of thanksgiving, and the mayor took him and Mgoro inside his house.

Later they took them to a home on the south side of town. The house looked as if a howitzer shell had hit one corner of it. Ernst saw that it wasn't exploded. The thin wall of an outbuilding had been pulled off, and a window clawed out from what had been a child's bedroom.

"The undertaker," said the mayor, "is sewing the

arms and legs back on. His mother heard him scream and came down to see what was wrong. They found her half a kilometre from here. When the Wild Man got through with her, he tossed her down and picked up the sheep.

"We tried to follow his trail earlier this morning. He must live in the caves on the other side of the mountain. We lost his trail in the rocks."

Ernst studied the tracks in the dirt of the outbuilding, light going in, sunken and heavy-laden coming out with the woman. They were huge, oddly-shaped, missing one of the toes on the left foot. But they were still the prints of a giant barefoot man.

"I'll hunt him," said Ernst, "if you'll put some men up by that barn on the edge of town. I don't want him running near there." He looked down, eyes not meeting those of the bürgermeister.

"We can put some men there with shotguns," said the priest. "I doubt he'll go close with the smell of many men there. If you want us to."

"Yes. Yes, I do want that."

"Let's go see to your guns, then," said the mayor.

"We have a few small bore rifles and shotguns for the men of the village," said the priest, "but these are the heaviest. We saved them for you."

Ernst took his glasses out of his pocket, noticing they were the new bifocals he'd gotten for reading after those plane crashes in '54. He looked the weapons over.

One was a Weatherby .575 bolt action, three-shot magazine with a tooled stock and an 8X scope. He worked the bolt; smooth, but still a bolt action.

"Scope comes off, eh, bwana?" asked Mgoro.

"Yes. And check the shells close."

The second was an eight-gauge shotgun, its shells the size of small sticks of dynamite. Ernst looked in the boxes, pulled out a handful each of rifle slugs and oo shot. He put the slugs in the left bottom pocket of his fishing vest, the shotshells in the right.

The third was an ancient wheel-lock boar gun. Its inlaid silver and gilt work had once been as bright and intricate as the rigging on a clipper ship, but was now faded and worn. Part of the wooden foregrip that had run the length of the barrel was missing. Its muzzle was the size of the exhaust pipe on a GMC truck.

"We shall have to check this thing very well," said Ernst.

"That gun was old when Kilimanjaro was a termite mound," said Mgoro.

Ernst smiled. "Perhaps," he said. "I'd also like a pistol each for Mgoro and me," he said to the mayor. "Anything, even .22's.

"And now, while Mgoro goes over these guns, I'd like to read. Do you have books? I used to have to bring my own when I came for the skiing."

"At the parish house," said the priest. "Many books, on many things."

"Good."

He sat at the desk where the priest wrote his sermons, and he read in the books again about the Wild Men.

Always, when he had been young and just writing, they had thought he was a simple writer, communicating his experience with short declarative sentences for the simple ideas he had.

Maybe that was so, but he had always read a lot, and

knew more than he let on. The Indian-talk thing had first been a pose, then a defense, and at the last, a curse.

He had known of the Wild Men for a long time. There used to be spring festivals in Germany and France, and in the Pyrénées, in which men dressed in hairy costumes and covered themselves with leaves and carried huge clubs in a shuffling dance.

In Brueghel's painting, *The Battle Between Carnival and Lent*, one of his low-perspective canvases full of the contradictions of carnival, you can see a Wild Man play going on in the upper left corner, the Wild Man player looking like a walking cabbage with a full head of shaggy hair.

The Wild Men—feral men, abandoned children who grew up in solitary savagery, or men who went mad—became hirsute. Lichens and moss grew on their bodies. They were the outlaws who haunted the dreams of the Middle Ages. All that was inside the village or the manor house was Godmade and good, everything outside was a snare of the devil.

More than the wolf or the bear, the serf feared the Wild Man, the unchained human without conscience who came to take what he wanted, when he wanted.

Ernst was reading Bernheimer's book again, and another on Wild Man symbolism in the art of the Middle Ages and the Renaissance. All they agreed upon was that there had been Wild Men and that they had been used in decorative arts and were the basis of spring festivals. All this Ernst remembered from his earlier reading.

He took off his glasses and rubbed the bridge of his nose, felt again the bump above his eye.

What was the Wild Man? he asked himself. This

thing of the woods and crags—it's nothing but man unfettered, unrestrained by law and civilization. Primitive, savage man. Rousseau was wrong—let man go and he turns not into the Noble Savage but into pure chaos, the chaos of Vico, of the totem fathers. Even Freud was wrong about that—the totem fathers, if they were Wild Men, would never compete with their offspring. They would eat them at birth, like Kronos.

What about this Wild Man, then? Where did he stay during the day? On what did he live when not raiding the towns? How do you find him, hunt him?

Ernst went back to the books. He found no answers there.

Mgoro said, "We are ready."

It was dusk. The sun had fallen behind the mountains. What warmth the day had had evaporated almost instantly. Ernst had taken a short nap. He had wakened feeling older and more tired than he had for years, worse than he had felt after the shock therapy in the hospital, where you woke not knowing where you were or who you were.

The other men had gone to places around the village, posted in the outlying structures, within sight and sound of each other, with clear fields of vision and fire toward the looming mountains.

Four others, with him and Mgoro, set out in the direction the Wild Man had taken that morning. They showed Ernst the rocky ground where the misshapen footprints ended.

"He'll be up and moving already," said Ernst. "Are the dogs ready?"

"They're coming now," said the bürgermeister.

Back down the trail they heard men moving toward them. "Are we to try to drive him out with them?"

"No," said Ernst. "That's what he'll be expecting. I only want him to think about them. The most likely place he'll be is the caves?"

"Yes, on the other side of this mountain. It's very rocky there."

"Take the dogs over that way, then. Make as much noise as you can, and keep them at it all night, if need be. If they come across his spoor, so much the better. It would be good if they could be made to bark."

Three hounds and a Rotweiler bounded up, straining at their leashes, whimpering with excitement. The man holding them doffed his cap to the bürgermeister.

"Ernst would like to know if you can make the dogs howl all night, Rudolf."

The man put a small whistle to his mouth and blew a soundless note. The four dogs began to bark and whine as if a stag had stepped on them.

Ernst laughed for the first time in months.

"That will do nicely," he said. "If they don't find anything, blow on that every quarter hour. Good luck."

The dogs, Rudolf, the bürgermeister, and the others started up the long trail that would take them around the mountain. Night was closing in.

"Where you think he is?" asked Mgoro.

"Back down a quarter-mile," said Ernst, "is where we should wait. He'll either pass us coming down, or back on the way up if they spot him in the village."

"I think so too," said Mgoro. "Though this is man, not lion or leopard."

"I have to keep telling myself that," said Ernst.

"Moon come up pretty soon," said Mgoro. "Damn mountains too high, or already be moonlight."

"It's the full moon that does it maybe," said Ernst. "Drives them to come into the towns."

"You think he crazy man? From last war?"

"The bürgermeister said this is the first Wild Man attack since before the war, from before that paper-hanging sonofabitch took over."

Mgoro wrapped a blanket around himself, the shot-gun, and wheel-lock. Ernst carried the Weatherby across his arm. It was already getting heavy.

The outline of the mountains turned silvery with the light from the rising, still unseen moon.

Then from up the side of the mountain, the dogs began to bark.

Nothing happened after they reached the ravine where they would wait. The dogs barked, farther and farther away, their cries carried on the still, cool air of the valley.

Lights were on in the town below. Ernst was too far away to see the men standing guard in the village itself, or what was happening in the church where most of the women and children waited.

Mgoro sat in his blanket. Ernst leaned against a rock, peering into the dark upper reaches of the ra-vine. The moonlight had frosted everything silver and gold, with deep shadows. He would have preferred an early, westering moon lighting this side of the moun-tain. This one was too bright and you had to look into it. Anything could be hiding in the shadowed places. It would be better later, when the moon was overhead, or west.

The dogs barked again, still farther away. Maybe

this moon was best. If they ran anything up on that side, the men over there could see it, too.

"Bwana," said Mgoro, sniffing the air. "Snow coming."

Ernst breathed deeply, sniffed. He was seized with coughing, quieted himself, choked, coughed again. His eyes stung, tears streamed down his face. He rubbed them away.

"Damn," he said. "Can't smell it yet. How long?"

"Don't know this land. One, mebbe two hours away."

Just what we need, a spring blizzard, Ernst thought.

An hour passed. Still they had bright moonlight. They heard the sound of the dogs far off. Nothing had come down the ravine. There had been no alarm from the town.

Ernst's back was knotted. His weak legs had gone to sleep several times. He'd had to massage them back to stinging life.

Mgoro sat in his blanket; the gun barrels made him look like a teepee in the moonlight. Ernst had seen him sit motionless for hours this way at waterholes, waiting for eland, wildebeest, lions. He was the best gunbearer Ernst had ever seen.

Something about Mgoro was gnawing at the back of Ernst's mind.

Ernst looked around, back down at the village. There were fewer lights now (the guards had been turning off a few at a time). He looked at the church, and he looked farther across the valley at the huge barn, a blot on the night.

He looked away, back up the ravine.

He thought something was wrong, then realized it was the light.

He looked up. High streaked cirrus raced across the moon. As he watched, it changed to altocumulus and the light dimmed more. A dark, thicker bank slid in under that, blotting the stars to the north.

In ten minutes the sky was solidly overcast and huge, wet flakes of snow began to fall.

Two hours into the storm, Mgoro sat up, his head turned sideways. Snow already covered the lower part of his blanket, merging with the wet line of melted snow against the upper part of his body.

His finger pointed left of the ravine.

Ernst could barely make out Mgoro, much less anything farther away.

But they heard it snuffling in the wet air as it went by down the rugged gully.

They waited. Ernst had eased the safety off the .575. But the sound grew fainter, continued on toward the village.

For an instant, Ernst smelled something in the air —sweat, dirt, mold, wet leaves, oil?—then it was gone. The thing must have missed their scent altogether.

The snow swirled down for another ten minutes, then stopped as abruptly as it had begun.

Another five minutes and the moon was out, bright and to the west, shining down on a transformed world of glass and powder.

The thing had come by close.

When they turned to look down the ravine they could see the shadowed holes of the footprints leading in a line down toward the town. The end of the tracks was still more than a kilometre from the village. They strained their eyes, then Ernst took out a pair of night binoculars, passed them to Mgoro. He scanned the terrain past where the footprints disappeared near a road.

He shook his head, handed them back.

Ernst put them to his eyes. It was too bright to make out anything through the glasses—the snow threw back too much glare, made the shadows too dark.

"If he decides not to go in, he'll come back this way," said Ernst.

"If we shoot to warn them, he go anywhere," said Mgoro.

"If nothing happens in the next hour, we follow his tracks," said Ernst.

The moon was dropping to the right of the village. Ernst checked his watch. Fifty minutes had passed.

If they stayed, they had the high ground, command of the terrain. They would be able to see him coming.

If they tracked him, and the Wild Man got above them, he could wait for them anywhere.

Do I treat this like stalking a lion, or following an airborne ranger? Ernst asked himself. He moved in place, getting the circulation back in his leg, the one with the busted kneecap and the shrapnel from three wars back.

He didn't want the Wild Man to get too far ahead of them. It could have circled the town and gone up the other side of the valley, sensing something wrong, or not wanting to leave tracks in the snow. Or it could be holed up just ahead, watching and waiting.

The dogs barked again. Now they sounded nearer, and they were holding the tone. They must have crossed the Wild Man's path somewhere and were trailing him now.

Ernst felt his pulse rise, like you do when beagles begin to circle, indicating the rabbit somewhere ahead of you is coming your way, or when a setter goes on point, all tense, and you ready yourself for the explosion of quail.

Shouts from the village cut across his reverie. Shots followed, and banging on pots and pans. The bells began to toll rapidly.

Mgoro stood against a rock so as to give no silhouette to anything down the ravine. Lights went on in town, flashlight beams swung up and around. They converged toward this side of town. Lights crossed the field and came toward the ravine, with sporadic small arms fire. The sounds from the town grew louder, like an angry hornet's nest.

Mgoro pointed.

Far down, where the footprints had ended, there was a movement. It was only a blur against the snow, a dull change in the moonlit background, but it was enough.

Mgoro dropped the blanket from his shoulders, held the shotgun and wheel-lock, one in each hand, two feet to the side and one foot back of Ernst.

The movement came again, much closer than it should have been for so close a space of time, then again, closer still.

First it was a shape, then a man-shape.

It stopped for a few seconds, then came on in a half-loping ape shamble.

Behind and below, flashlight beams reached the far

end of the ravine and were starting up, slowly, voices
still too indistinct with the distance.

Now the shape moved from one side of the gully to
the other, running. Now it was two hundred metres
away in the moonlight. Now a hundred. Eighty.

It was too big for a man.

The baying of the dogs, up the mountain behind
Ernst, got louder.

The man-shape stopped.

Ernst brought the Weatherby up, held his breath,
squeezed.

The explosion was loud, louder than he remembered, but he worked the bolt as the recoil brought the
muzzle up. He brought the sights back down, cen-
tered them on the gully before the shell casing hit the
ground.

There had been a scream with the shot. Whatever
had screamed was gone. The ravine was empty.

He and Mgoro ran down the gully.

It had jumped three metres between one set of
prints and the next, and there was a spray of blood four
metres back. A high hit, then. Maybe, thought Ernst,
as they ran up out of the ravine to the left, maybe we'll
find him dead twenty metres from here.

But the stride stayed long, the drops of blood in the
snow far apart.

Ernst's lungs were numb. He could hardly breathe
in enough air to keep going. His legs threatened to
fold, and he realized what he was—an old, half-crip-
pled man trying to run down something that was twice
his size, wounded and mad.

Mgoro was just behind him. His lungs labored, too,

but still he held both guns where he could hand them to Ernst in seconds.

The flashlights and lanterns from the town headed across the front of the village, between the town and the Wild Man. Behind Ernst and Mgoro, the dogs neared in the ravine.

Ernst and Mgoro slowed. The footprints were closer together now, and there was a great clot of blood that seemed to have been coughed up. Internal bleeding maybe, thought Ernst, maybe a better shot than I thought I could ever make again.

The moon was on the edge of the far mountain. They would lose the light for a while, but it should be nearing dawn.

The tracks led in an arc toward the roadway south of the village. Lights from the men in town and those halfway up the hill led that way.

They heard the dogs behind them, whining with urgency when they came to the place of the hit. Now they left the ravine and came straight behind the two men.

"Off the tracks. Off!" puffed Ernst. He grabbed Mgoro, pulled him five paces down the mountainside.

In a moment the dogs flashed by, baying, running full speed. As they passed, the last of the direct moonlight left the valley. The dogs ran on into darkness.

"Come," said Mgoro, through gritted teeth. "We have him."

They heard the dogs catch up to the Wild Man. One bark ended in a squeal, another just ended. Two dogs continued on, and the sound of the pursuit moved down the valley.

Ernst ran on, his feet and chest like someone else's.

He realized that the Wild Man was heading toward the barn.

When Ernst was thirteen, up in Michigan one summer, he got lost. It was the last time in his life he was ever lost.

He had been fishing, and had a creel full of trout. But he had crossed three marshy beaver ponds that morning, and skirted some dense woods getting to the fishing. On the way back he had taken a wrong turn. It was that easy to get lost.

He had wandered for two hours trying to find his way back to his own incoming tracks.

Just at dusk, he came to a clearing and saw in front of him a huge barn, half-gone in ruin. He wondered at it. There was no house with it. It was in the middle of the Michigan woods. There were no animals around, and it looked as if there never had been.

He walked closer.

Someone stepped from around one corner, someone dressed in a long grey cloak, wearing a death's head mask.

Ernst stopped, stunned.

The thing reached down inside its cloak and exposed a long, diseased penis to him.

"Hey, you, Bright Boy," it said. "Suck on this."

Ernst dropped his rod, his creel, and ran in a blind panic until he came out on the road less than half a mile from the cabin his family had rented.

One dog still barked. They had found the other three on the way. Two dead, torn up and broken. The third had run until it had given out. It lay panting in a set of tracks, pointing the way with its body like an arrow.

Now the sky to the east was lighter. Ernst began to make things out—the valley floor, the lights of the men as they ran, the great barn up ahead beside the road.

Something ran through a break in the woods, the sound of the dog just behind it.

Ernst stopped, threw the .575 to his shoulder, fired. A vip of snow flew up just over the thing's shoulder, and it was gone into the woods again. The dog flashed through the opening.

Ernst loaded more shells in.

The great barn was a kilometre ahead when they found the last dog pulled apart like warm red taffy.

Ernst slid to a stop. The prints crossed a ditch, went up the other side, blood everywhere now.

Ernst jumped into the ditch just as he realized that the prints were doubled, had been trodden over by something retracing its steps.

He tried to stop himself from going just as Mgoro, on the bank behind him, saw the prints and yelled.

Ernst's arms windmilled, he let go of the rifle, fell heavily, caught a rock with his fingers, slipped, his bad knee crashing into the bottom of the ditch.

Dull pain shot through him. He pulled himself to his other knee.

The Wild Man charged.

It had doubled back, jumped off into a stand of small trees fifty feet up the ditch. Now it had them.

The Weatherby was half-hidden in the ditch snow. Did he have time to get it? Was the action ready?

Was the safety off? Was there snow in the barrel and would it explode like an axed watermelon in his hands when he fired?

Not on my knees, Ernst thought, and stood up.

"Gun!" he said, just as Mgoro slammed the shotgun butt down into his right shoulder from the bank above.

Ernst let the weight of the barrels bring the eight-gauge into line. He was already cocking both hammers as his left arm slid up the foregrip.

The Wild Man was teeth and beard and green-gray hair in front of him as the barrels came level with its chest.

Ernst pulled both triggers.

All the moments come down to this. All the writing and all the books and the fishing and the hunting and the bullfights. All the years of banging yourself around and being beaten half the time.

The barrels leaped up with recoil.

All the years of living by your code. Good is what makes you feel good. A man has to do what a man has to do.

A huge red spot appeared on the Wild Man's shoulder as the slug hit and the right hand, which had been reaching for Ernst, came loose and flew through the air behind the buckshot.

Ernst let the shotgun fall.

"Gun!" he said.

And then you get old and hurt and scared, and the writing doesn't work anymore, and the sex is gone and booze doesn't help, and you can't hunt or fish, all you have is fame and money and there's nothing to buy.

Mgoro put the butt of the wheel-lock against his shoulder.

The Wild Man's left hand was coming around like a claw, reaching for Ernst's eyes, his face, reaching for the brain inside his head.

Ernst pulled the trigger-lever, the wheel spun in a ratcheting blur, the powder took with a *floopth* and there was an ear-shattering roar.

Then they take you to a place and try to make you better with electricity and drugs and it doesn't make you better, it makes you worse and you can't do anything anymore, and nobody understands but you, that you don't want anything, *anymore.*

Ernst lies under a shaggy wet weight that reeks of sweat and mushrooms. He is still deaf from the explosion. The wheel-lock is wedged sideways against his chest, the wheel gouging into his arm. He pushes and pulls, twisting his way out from under, slipping on the bloody rocks.

Mgoro is helping him, pulling his shoulders.

"It is finished," he says.

Ernst stands, looking down at the still-twitching carcass. Blood runs from jagged holes you can see the bottom of the ditch through. It is eight feet tall, covered with lichen and weeds, matted hair, and dirt.

Now it is dead, this thing that was man gone mad, man without law, like all men would be if they had nothing to hold them back.

And one day they let you out of the place because you've acted nice, and you go home with your wife, the last wife, and you sing to her and she goes to sleep and next morning at dawn you go downstairs in your bathrobe and you go to your gun cabinet and you take out your favorite, the side-by-side double barrel your actor friend gave you before he died and you put it on the

floor and you lean forward until the barrels are a cool
infinity mark on your forehead. . . .

Ernst stands and looks at the big barn only a kilometre away, and he looks at Mgoro, who, he knows
now, has been dead more than thirty years, and Mgoro
smiles at him.

Ernst looks at the barn and knows he will begin
walking toward it in just a moment, he and Mgoro,
but still there is one more thing he has to do.

He reaches down, pulling, and slowly turns the
Wild Man over, face up.

The hair is matted, ragged holes torn in the neck
and chest and stomach, the right arm missing from
the elbow down.

The beard is tangled, thick and bloody. Above the
beard is the face, twisted.

And Ernst knows that it is his face on the Wild
Man, the face of the thing he has been hunting all his
life.

He stands then, and takes Mgoro's arm, and they
start up the road toward the barn.

The light begins to fade, though it is crisp morning
dawn. Ernst knows they will make the barn before the
light gives out completely.

And above everything, over the noise of the church
bells back in town, above the yelling, jubilant voices
of the running people, there is a long, slow, far-off
sound, like the boom of surf crashing onto a shore.

Or maybe it is just the sound of both triggers being
pulled at once.

In Frozen Time

RUDY RUCKER

In the old days, wizards used pentacles, grimoires, and talismanic signs. Rudy Rucker, a wizard of the present day, uses mathematics. Instead of Tetragrammaton, Rucker conjures with the Alefs, with Transfinite Cardinals, with the Unnameable. But this sometime Professor of Mathematics and Lecturer at the University of Heidelberg is a true scientist, so why call him a wizard?

First, because there's more genuine (and precise) magic in Rucker's factual volumes, Infinity and the Mind (1982), and The Fourth Dimension (1984), and Mindtools (1987), than in a cartload of ancient books of spells. Second, because Rucker himself works wonderful magic with his mathematical conjurations—as a fiction writer.

White Light, The Sex Sphere, The Fifty-Seventh Franz Kafka, and Master of Space and Time are books to treasure, and there will be many more. Rucker is currently working on Wetware, a sequel to his computer-oriented novel, Software, which won the first Philip K. Dick Memorial Award in 1983. In his acceptance speech Rucker said that "The essence of good science fiction is the transmutation of abstract ideas into funky fact," and that he sees science fiction as "mass-market surrealism." His scenarios are certainly among the most delightfully wacky around—but they are related to the basic underpinnings of reality, to the way that our universe (and other universes) may well be constructed.

I just went back to look at the accident again. It's truly horrible. I don't even look human. My head's being crushed under the right front wheel; it's half as thick as it should be, and blood is squirting out my faceholes. A monster. I can't stand looking at it, but as long as I'm here in frozen time, I'll be slinking back and looking at my death, over and over, like a dog returning to his vomit, I know it, I know it.

I keep running up and down these few boring streets—something keeps me from getting too far— running up and down, and nothing's changing. All I can do is rush around, hating the dull, ugly buildings, the mindless plants, the priggish, proper people. And my thoughts, all in loops, never ending.

I don't see how I'm going to stand this. My poor body, my poor wife, our poor wasted lives. Why couldn't I have done better? I want to kill myself all over again, but I'm already dead. Oh God, oh God, oh, dear God, please help me. Please make this stop.

Once again, my hysteria ebbs. That's my only measure of time now: my mood-swings, and the walks I take, a lonely ghost in a bland little town.

It took me a few years to kill myself. I guess it was losing my last teaching job that started me off with thoughts of suicide. Losing my good job, and then some marriage problems . . . it wasn't just the big

things that got me down, it was a lot of things. The
hangovers, being thirty-eight, no goals, and, worst of
all, the boredom. The sameness. Day after day, month
after month: the same fights, the same brief joys, the
same problems. The menial job shelving books in a
library.

Thanksgiving, Christmas, Wedding Anniversary,
Summer Vacation, Thanksgiving, Christmas . . . I
couldn't take it anymore. And finally I got the nerve
to step in front of a truck. Now I'm dead and it's
9:17:06 A.M., September 14, in Killeville, Virginia,
forever. *Forever.*

It's so horrible, so Dantean, that I almost have to
laugh. *A guy kills himself because life's such a boring
drag, and then time freezes up on him, and he can't
walk more than three blocks from his body.* Until recently, I never really knew what boredom was. Being
here is like . . . being in an airport lounge with streets
and buildings in it. Frozen time.

When I died, my consciousness branched out of the
normal timestream. My time is now perpendicular to
normal time. I walk around and look at things—I have
an astral body that looks just like my real one—and it's
as if everything were frozen. Like a huge 3-D flash
photograph. Right now, sitting here in my empty
office, thinking this out, I can see a bird outside the
window. It's just about to land, its wings are outstretched, its beak half-open, and if I walk over for a
closer look, which I've done several times, I can see
the nictating membrane stretched halfway across each
of the blinking bird's eyes. The bird is hanging there
like a raisin in Jell-O, hanging there every time I look.

On the streets, all the people are still as statues, like
the figures in Muybridge's zoopraxographic photo-

graphs. Some people are frozen in such awkward positions that it's hard to believe they won't—after my eternity ends—fall over, especially the old lady standing on one foot to reach a bag of food in through her car window.

In my house, my wife is brushing her teeth. The toothbrush-handle pushes her mouth to one side. She doesn't know yet that I'm dead. In *my* time I've been dead for a while now, but relative to me, my wife is frozen at the instant I died. She hasn't gotten the word. She thinks I'm on my way back from the store with milk and eggs, when in fact I'm out of my broken body, and walking around.

Walking and thinking, always alone. I'm the only thing that moves in this silent town's streets. Nothing changes except my thoughts. Boredom, boredom, boredom. And the horror of my corpse.

I always thought in terms of shooting myself, but the way it worked out was that I stepped in front of a Japanese pickup truck. I was on the way to the store to get milk and eggs when, just like that, I stepped off the curb in front of the truck. It wasn't an accident —I saw the truck coming—it was suicide. But, really, I'd always planned to shoot myself.

I used to think about it a lot. Like on a Sunday night, lying there weak and shaky, going over and over the money worries, the dying marriage, and all the stinging memories of another weekend's ugly drunken scenes: the fights with friends, the cop troubles, the self-degradation, and the crazy things my wife had done—I'd cut it all off with thoughts of a .45 automatic, one of those flat black guns that movie gangsters and World War II soldiers have. Lying there in bed, depressed and self-hating, I'd cheer myself up by imagining there was a .45 on my night table. And then I'd reach out and pick it up. I wouldn't reach out my real arm—I didn't want to stir my miserable wife into painful apology or recrimination—no, I'd reach out a *phantom* arm. An astral arm, a ghost arm, an arm like the arm an amputee imagines himself still to have—an arm like my whole body is now. The phantom arm would peel out of my right arm, and reach over, and pick up that longed for .45.

Lying there sleepless and desperate, I had a lot of time to analyze my fantasies. The fact that I always reached for the pistol with my *right* arm struck me as significant, for if you pick up a pistol with your right hand, and then hold it to your temple in the most natural way, this means that your right hand is shooting the right hemisphere of your brain. Now, as is well known, the left hemisphere of the brain is *(a)* the uptight half, and *(b)* in control of the right hand. So by shooting oneself in the right temple with a gun held in the right hand one is, in effect, letting the left brain kill the right brain. The digital, highly socialized left brain shoots the dark and creative right brain. This particular death always seemed appropriate to me, a good symbol of society forcing poor, intellectual me into an early grave.

But, hell, I guess getting run over by a Japanese pickup truck makes some kind of statement, too. The fact is that I really hate pickups. I think I hate pickups a lot more than my right brain ever hated my left brain. What do people think they need to haul around in all those pickups? The pickups you see are always empty, aren't they? Especially the Japanese ones, the cute, preppy, energy-savers that bank employees and

insurance salesmen drive. Presumably, the preps want
to share in some imagined pickup grit macho, but
they're too clean and sensible to get a rusted-out,
unmuffled seventies redneck Ford, so they buy one
of those shiny little Nipponese jobs with the manufac-
turer's name on the back like on a pair of designer
jeans. Ugh! I hate, I hate, I hate . . . so many things.

I was talking about suicide.

Sometimes, if I was *really* strung out, the imaginary
.45 would start to grow. It would get as big as a coffin:
a heavy, L-shaped coffin lying on top of me and crushing out my breath. As big as the house I lived in. And
every day in the paper there was a picture of my gun,
part of an ad for Ace Hardware, "Largest Selection of
Guns in Central Virginia."

I got so *tired* of not killing myself.

Some days it would sandbag me. I'd be, say, waiting
in the car for the wife to come out of the library where
we worked (she full-time, me part-time), and I
wouldn't be able to come up with one single iota of
wanting to be there. And then, all of a sudden, there'd
be Death, breathing in my face, *so much closer than
the last time.*

I don't want to exaggerate—my life wasn't any
worse than that of any other unhappily married, un-
deremployed, middle-aged alcoholic. There wasn't
any one thing that made me want to die. It was the
boredom that got me. My life was, quite literally,
boring me to death, and I didn't have the willpower
to do anything to change it. The only change I could
come up with was suicide. And for the longest time,
I was scared even to do that. Thinking back, I realize
that I never could have shot myself. Focusing on the

.45 was a kind of cop-out. But finally I got it together and stepped in front of that truck.

Got it together? In a way, yes. At first I was upset to be here, but now I'm becoming used to it. What do I do? I sit in my office, and I take walks. Back and forth. It's a rhythm. Thinking these thoughts, I stare at my computer, imagining that my words are being coded up on disk.

I've been thinking some more about what's happened to me. I was a physics teacher, before my final occupation as bookshelver, and it amuses me to analyze my present supernatural existence in scientific terms.

My astral body is of a faintly glowing substance, somewhat transparent—call it ether. I can pass through walls in good ghost-fashion, yet the gravitational curvature of space still binds me to the earth's surface: I cannot fly. Although I am not of ordinary matter, I can see. Since nothing is moving for me, I must not be seeing in the usual sense (that is, by intercepting moving photons). I would guess that my fine ether body sees, rather, by directly sensing the space undulations caused by the photons' passage. This is borne out by the fact that I can see with my eyes closed.

My theory, as I've said before, is that when one dies, the soul enters frozen time—a volume of space corresponding to the instant of one's death. I think of time as a long, gently undulating line, with each space-instant a hypersheet touching time at one point. A ghost lives on and on, but it is always in the now-space of its body's death. In ordinary life, people encounter ghosts regularly—but only once for each ghost. A given instant is haunted only by the ghost of *that particular space-slice*, the ghost of whoever died that moment.

Image: *the long corridor of time, lined with death cells, some cells empty, some holding one tattered soul.*

How long is a moment? How long does it take a person to die? Looking at the frozen world around me, it seems that my death instant has almost no time duration at all. If it were even a hundredth of a second long, then some things would be blurred. But nothing is blurred, not even the flies' wings, or the teeth of the chainsaw my neighbor is forever gunning. My death lasts no more than a thousandth of a second . . . and perhaps much less. This is significant.

Why? Because if the death instant is so short, then each ghost is in solitary confinement. I know that someone, somewhere, dies every second—but what are the odds that someone else has died at the exact same thousandth of a second as I? I have calculated the odds—I have ample time for such calculations. They are well over a trillion to one. And there are only a few billion people in the world. The chances that any other ghost shares my space cell are less than one in a thousand.

So I'll quest me no quests. Really, I'm not at all sure that I could leave Killeville, even if I tried. My astral body is—it may be—a holographic projection powered by my dying brain's last massive pulse. If I go even three blocks away from my body, I feel faint and uneasy. There is no hope of walking to another city.

Here I am, and here I will be, forever. Alone.

It's a sunny day.

It's funny about boredom. The physical world is so complex, yet I used to think of it as simple. Each time I walk around the block I see something new.

Just now, I was out looking at all the wasps and bees feeding at one of the flowering bushes in our yard. I marvelled at the bristles on the bees' bulging backs, and at their little space-monster faces. And in the fork of a branchlet, caught in a nearly invisible web, was a wasp being attacked by a spider. The wasp was biting the spider's belly.

Walking on, I felt such a feeling of freedom. I used always to be in a hurry—not that I had anything worth doing. I was in a hurry, I suppose, because I felt bad about wasting time. But now that I have no time, I have all time. If I have endless time, how can I waste it? I feel so relaxed. I wish I could have felt this way when I was alive.

The crushed body beneath the truck seems less and less like me. I walk by it with impunity. Up by the shops, not yet noticing the accident in the street, my old boss forever steps out of the post office, successful and overbearing. How nice it is, I thought this time, walking past him, how nice it is not to have to talk to him.

The face of the supermarket consists of 18,726 bricks. Numbers are power. I think now I'll count the blades of grass in our lawn. I'll memorize each and every detail of the little world I'm in.

Somehow the sunlight seems to be getting brighter. Could it be that, by visiting each spot in my little neighborhood over and over, I am learning the light patterns better, sensing them more intensely? Or is the world, in some way, objectively changing along my time axis? Has this all just been a dying man's last hallucination? It doesn't matter.

Before, I thought of this frozen time as a prison cell. But now I've come to think of it as a monastic cubicle. I've had time here—how much time? I've had time to rethink my life. This started as hell, and it's turned into heaven.

I've stopped taking my walks. I've lost my locality. From traveling over and over these few streets, I've spread myself out: I see all of it, all the time, all melting into the light.

A thought: *I am this moment.* Each of us is part of God, and when our life ends God puts us to work at dreaming the world. I am the sidewalk, I am the air, I am 9:17:06 A.M., September 14.

Still the brightness grows.

Tropism

LEIGH KENNEDY

Leigh Kennedy was born in Denver, Colorado, in 1951, and lived there until she moved to Austin, Texas, in 1980 and now lives in England. She has a B.A. in history, and is a keen photographer and traveler. She began publishing stories about a decade ago, in Isaac Asimov's Science Fiction Magazine, Omni, Universe, Shadows, *and* The Nantucket Review. *Her novel,* Journal of Nicholas the American, *and a story collection,* Faces, *were published in Britain and the U.S.*

A "tropism" is a response to a stimulus, for example, light (as when a plant grows toward the sun); here it provides the basis for a haunting tale of how people might exhibit a tropism toward life, even after they are dead.

He was my only son. The first funeral was hard enough, but I was loath to return to my daughter-in-law's house to talk her into burying Jeff a second time.

We made small talk on the trip from the airport through the dry mountains of New Mexico, leftover familiarities from the last visit only a few weeks before.

I didn't know what to say to Katie. I had suspected she was crazy with grief, though she seemed rational enough.

A feeling grew in the pit of my stomach as we neared the house, a low flat stucco with cactus rather than grass. As we got my bags out, two cars full of people drove slowly past, looking at us, at the house. Katie didn't seem to notice.

I didn't want to go in—all the decisiveness I had about going to talk some sense into Katie had evaporated as I thought about encountering him. My son, exhumed, and sitting in that house, three weeks dead.

The odor hit me as I walked through the door. "Lord," I said, and my hand went automatically to my nose. Underlying the sick smell was a heavy pall of air fresheners. I then noticed the cheerful little plastic boxes with roses and spring flowers decorating the house like votive candles in a sanctuary.

I saw the back of one shoulder and his head. His hair, a bit matted, stuck out in dry cowlicks. But before I could move toward him, Dana came flying at me. "Grandma!" she said, grabbing me around the waist. I hugged her, a little bewildered. The distance between our cities had kept me from being close to her. Until this moment, she had always seemed so shy and afraid of me.

She held my hand as we walked into the kitchen. Katie had a deliberate nonchalance, tossing her keys onto the kitchen table and looking from Jeffrey to me with a smile. "Here is your mother," she said, sounding relieved.

I sat down at the table and got the courage to look at his face. I don't know what I had expected, since he had only been dead three weeks, but he was far from being a skeleton. There was a great deal of, well, *meat* on him. His face was intact, recognizable. At least his eyes were closed. The smell either lessened or I was adjusting the longer I stayed.

He had still been so young when he died, only in his early forties, and his bearing surprised me more than anything. He looked old and slumped, his shoulders drooped.

"You can talk to him if you like, but it isn't really necessary," Katie said. "He knew you were coming. We've been talking about it for days and he's been waiting."

In truth, I was terrified and filled with horror of this thing tied into the kitchen chair. It was just a mass of embalmed flesh, stiff hair, an awkwardly fitting checked shirt, and jeans.

The most incongruous item was a ticking watch on his wrist.

"He's been waiting?" I asked.

The phone rang. Katie frowned and picked it up. "Hello?" she said. After a few seconds she hung up and unplugged the phone with a jerk.

She sat down at the table next to me, hand in chin. "Yes, he's been moving his head toward the door. It's been happening for a couple of days."

I could see, although he sat directly before the table, that his head was turned slightly, almost as if he were listening.

"Jeff," I said. I felt my face crinkling toward tears.

"Why don't we put your things in the spare room?" Katie said. She stood and waited for me to rise and go with her.

Katie sat with me on the bed.

"Why?" I said.

"Well . . ." She stretched her legs out and looked at her toes. She seemed so undisturbed, so normal. I didn't know her well enough to read her as I could my own daughter. "Even at the funeral," she said, "I started thinking about something that Jeff and I had discussed. A long time ago, we were just talking about things that we really feared. Jeff said that he'd read somewhere that after death, people still have a consciousness clinging to their bodies that takes a long time to disperse. He was afraid of being buried and *knowing* it. At the funeral, I watched them throw shovels of dirt on the coffin and I felt I was betraying him. I wanted to *stop* them."

Neither of us spoke for a while.

Finally she continued, in a slightly higher voice, "I started reading about death. Everything from old-fashioned Christianity to Kirlian auras. And there is a consistent idea of a—I hate to say it because it sounds so mystical—but a spirit left hanging around the body after death."

She told me more about what she'd read and thought and I found that she was an agnostic. This whole notion had nothing to do with soul, damnation, or such. I trembled; I didn't know what to believe except that it must be wrong somehow.

"And what does Dana think of all this?" I asked.

"She's all right," Katie said smiling. "Why don't you rest while I fix dinner?"

I did so gladly, and found myself nodding into a nap just as Dana came shyly to the door and told me that dinner was ready.

"Wait a minute, honey," I said. "What do your friends at school think of all this?"

She stopped. I felt suddenly how independent she had become—she was old enough to have private feelings. "I know who my friends are," she said.

We sat at the table with Jeff. Needless to say, I could hardly eat dinner. At least Katie had no intention of feeding him—he had no place setting, no offerings of Tater Tots or raspberry Jell-O for the dead. I sat to his right. He was still turned slightly to the left, toward the door.

Dana was quiet. She never seemed to look at the body of her father. Neither spoke to him. I may have expected them to talk to him in loving rhetorical questions, as one does to a dumb pet, but no. There was integrity, deference to the physical remains of husband and father.

We talked about Dana's schoolwork, about a movie we had all seen on television recently. Dana cleared the dishes and went to her room. I worried about her. She seemed withdrawn, but then she had always been a quiet child.

"Why the watch?" I finally asked.

"It gives him rhythm. And he's got time enough to count seconds. How long has it been since you just sat and listened to a watch?" she asked. "It's more consuming than you might think."

"How do you know he does that?"

Katie shrugged.

"What sort of consciousness do you think he has?"

"It's not very concrete," she said thoughtfully, looking at Jeff. "It's more like the tropism of a plant. He has an awareness of us, like a plant reaching its leaves to the sun."

Katie and I both stared at Jeff. Was it my imagination, or had he turned toward me, away from the door?

This is too bizarre, I thought. I was slowly beginning to be pulled into my daughter-in-law's delusions. I didn't want to interfere, but this was such big trouble in many ways. The school administration was upset. Katie told me that she had heard that a state senator was trying to pass a law against people having corpses in their houses, unless they were ashes in an urn. Katie said, "I don't have the power of Juan Perón, so I suppose I'll lose him, but maybe he'll be dispersed by then."

I stirred my coffee and wondered what I had planned to accomplish by coming back. I couldn't remember. Here we sat so calmly, talking, while Dana did her homework.

"If you want to watch TV, go ahead," Katie said.

I took it as a signal that she wanted to be left to herself, so I settled in the living room. Nothing on television was worth watching. I found photo albums and looked through them until bedtime.

I awakened to the sound of breaking glass.

We all reached the living room at the same instant, clutching our robes and staring at the shovel which lay among the glass shards on the carpet. The drapery was caught, flapping from a jagged hole in the picture window.

"This is it!" I said. "Katie, you've got to stop. What do you think you're doing to your daughter?"

Katie stepped forward and snatched the note off the shovel. She read it, then balled it into her fist.

"For God's sake . . ."

She made a high-pitched sound and bowed her

head. Her shoulders shook with sobs. "Do you think I *want* to live like this?" she said.

"Dana," I said, "come with me. Come home with me."

Dana moved toward her mother. "I want to stay with Mom . . . and Dad," she said.

There it was. I was out of touch with them, an outsider in this family. They *believed* it. Unsettled, I went to the kitchen, to my dead son, in some hope that I could turn to him.

He had moved. His ear was no longer trained toward the door. He sat facing the center of the table —looking across to where his wife usually sat.

Even the dead had sided against me.

And what, just suppose, what if the whole thing were true?

I went home the next day, but I couldn't shake it. I felt that I had deserted the three of them.

It was nearly two months later that Katie phoned and asked me if I would come back for Jeff's reburial. "I'm certain he's really gone now," she said.

"How do you know?"

She said there had been no sign of tropism for weeks. She and Dana had gone on a weekend camping trip and left him alone. His watch had stopped ticking and he seemed gone when they returned. "I think that watch really held him," she said. "A spirit needs rhythm."

"I want to be cremated, I'll tell you that right now," I said. I had given it a lot of thought. Cremation would be quick, better than lying in a box for months.

I have no one to give me that long lingering good-bye, like a flower losing the sun.

If Ever I Should Leave You

PAMELA SARGENT

Pamela Sargent studied classical philosophy and the history of philosophy at the State University of New York at Binghamton, where she also taught. She wrote her first published story in her senior year at college and, long-since, has become a full-time writer. She lives in upstate New York. In her work, she often explores themes of transcendence (sometimes through genetic engineering), super-powers, immortality and the ultimate fate of the human race. Yet her primary concern is how her characters experience their own lives, their doubts and fears, their desires and yearnings.

Her first novel was Cloned Lives *(1976); a later novel,* The Golden Space *(1982), was described by writer and critic Algis Budrys as "a major intellectual achievement . . . a landmark." Other novels include* The Alien Upstairs *(1983) and* Venus of Dreams *(1986).*

"If Ever I Should Leave You" is an afterlife tale with a difference, since the man who here cheats the grave —for the sake of love—is absolutely and terminally dead. Yet there are special places, and times, where such a refugee from death can go . . .

When Yuri walked away from the Time Station for the last time, his face was pale marble, his body only bones barely held together by skin and the weak muscles he had left. I hurried to him and grasped his arm, oblivious to the people who passed us in the street. He resisted my touch at first, embarrassed in front of the others; then he gave in and leaned against me as we began to walk home.

I knew that he was too weak to go to the Time Station again. His body, resting against mine, seemed almost weightless. I guided him through the park toward our home. Halfway there, he tugged at my arm and we rested against one of the crystalline trees surrounding the small lake in the center of the park.

Yuri had aged rapidly in the last six months, transformed from a young man into an aged creature hardly able to walk by himself. I had expected it. One cannot hold off old age indefinitely, even now. But I could not accept it. I knew that his death could be no more than days away.

You can't leave me now, not after all this time, I wanted to scream. Instead, I helped him sit on the ground next to the tree, then sat at his side.

His blue eyes, once clear and bright, now watery with age and surrounded by tiny lines, watched me. He reached inside his shirt and fumbled for something. I had always teased Yuri about his shirts; sooner or later he would tear them along the shoulder seams while flexing the muscles of his broad back and sturdy arms. Now the shirt, like his skin, hung on his bones in wrinkles and folds. At last he pulled out a piece of paper and pressed it into my hand with trembling fingers.

"Take care of this," he whispered to me. "Copy it down in several places so you won't lose it. All the coordinates are there, all the places and times I went to these past months. When you're lonely, when you need me, go to the Time Station and I'll be waiting on the other side." He was trying to comfort me. Because of his concern, he had gone to the Time Station every day for the past six months and had traveled to various points in the past. I could travel to any of those points and be with him at those times. It suddenly struck me as a mad idea, an insane and desperate thing.

"What happens to me?" I asked, clutching the paper. "What am I like when I see you? You've already seen me at all those times. What do I do, what happens to me?"

"I can't tell you, you know that. You have to decide yourself, of your own free will. Anything I say might affect what you do."

I looked away from him and toward the lake. Two golden swans glided by, the water barely rippling in their wake. Their shapes blurred and I realized I was crying silently. Yuri's blue-veined hand rested on my shoulder.

"Don't cry. Please. You make it harder for me."

At last the tears stopped. I reached over and stroked his hair, once thick and blond, now thin and white. Only a year before we had come to this same tree, our bodies shiny with lake water after a moonlight swim, and made love in the darkness. We were as young as everyone else, confident that we would live forever, forgetting that our bodies could not be rejuvenated indefinitely.

"I'm not really leaving you," Yuri said. His arms held me firmly and for a moment I thought his strength had returned. "I'll be at the other side of the Time Station, any time you need me. Think of it that way."

"All right," I said, trying to smile. "All right." I nestled against him, my head on his chest, listening to his once-strong heart as it thumped against my ear.

Yuri died that night, only a few hours after we returned home.

The relationships among our friends had been an elaborate web, always changing, couples breaking up and recombining in a new pattern. We were all eternally young and time seemed to stretch ahead of us with no end. Throughout all of this, Yuri and I stayed together, the strands of our love becoming stronger instead of more tenuous. I was a shy, frightened girl when I met Yuri and was attracted in part by his boldness; he had appeared at my door one day, introduced himself and told me a friend of his had made him promise he would meet me. I could not have looked very appealing with my slouched, bony body, the thick black hair that would not stay out of my face, my long legs marked with bruises by my clumsiness. But Yuri had loved me almost on sight and I discovered, in time, that his boldness was the protective covering of a serious and intense young man.

Our lives became intertwined so tightly that, after a while, they were one life. It was inconceivable that anything could separate us. Our relationship may have lacked the excitement of others' lives. With almost three centuries to live at the full height of our physical and mental powers, and the freedom to live several different kinds of lives, changing our professions and pursuits every twenty or thirty years, we know how rarely anyone chooses to stay with the same person throughout. Yet Yuri and I had, even through our changes, fallen in love with each other over and over again. We were lucky, I thought.

We were fools, I told myself when Yuri was gone. I had half a life after his death. I was a ghost myself, wandering from friend to friend seeking consolation, then isolating myself in my house for days, unwilling to see anyone.

But Yuri had not really left me. I had only to walk down to the Time Station, give them the coordinates he had given me, and I would be with him again, at least for a little while. Yet during those first days alone I could not bring myself to go there. He's gone, I told myself angrily; you must learn to live without him. And then I would whisper, Why? You have no life alone, you are an empty shell. Go to him.

I began to wander past the Time Station, testing my resolve. I would walk almost to the door, within sight of the technicians, then retreat, racing home, my hands shaking. *Yuri.*

I would make the time and trouble he took useless. He had wanted to be with me when I needed him, but he had also wanted to see my future self, what I would become after his death. The Time Station could not penetrate the future, that unformed mass of possibilities. I would be denying Yuri the chance to see it through my eyes, and the chance to see what became of me.

At last I walked to the Time Station and through

its glassy door into the empty hall. Time Portals surrounded me on all sides, silvery cubicles into which people would step, then disappear. A technician approached me, silently offering assistance. I motioned her away and went over to one of the unoccupied cubicles. I fumbled for the piece of paper in my robe, then pulled it out and stared at the first set of coordinates. I stepped inside the cubicle, reciting the coordinates aloud—time, place, duration of my stay.

Suddenly I felt as though my body were being thrown through space, that my limbs were being torn from my torso. The walls around me had vanished. The feeling lasted only an instant. I was now standing next to a small, clear pool of water shadowed by palm trees.

I turned from the pool. In front of me stretched a desolate waste, a rocky desert bleached almost white by the sun. I retreated farther into the shade of the oasis where I stood, and knelt by the pool.

"Yuri," I whispered as I dipped my hand into the coolness of the water. A pebble suddenly danced across the silvery surface before me, and the ripples it made mingled with those my hand had created.

I looked around. Yuri stood only a few feet away. He had barely begun to age. His face was still young, his skin drawn tightly across high cheekbones, and his hair was only lightly speckled with silver.

"Yuri," I whispered again, and then I was running to him.

After we swam, we sat next to each other by the small pool with our feet in the water. I was intoxicated, my mind whirling from one thing to another with nothing needing to be said. Yuri smiled at me

and skipped pebbles across the pool. Some of my
thoughts seemed to skip with them, while another
part of me whispered, He's alive, he's here with you,
and he'll be with you at a hundred other places in a
hundred other times.

Yuri started to whistle a simple tune, one that I had
heard for as long as I knew him. I pursed my lips and
tried to whistle along but failed, as I always had.

"You'll never learn to whistle now," he said.
"You've had two and a half centuries to learn and you
still haven't figured it out."

"I will," I replied. "I've done everything else I ever
wanted to do and I can't believe that a simple thing
like whistling is going to defeat me."

"You'll never learn."

"I will."

"You won't."

I raised my feet, then lowered them forcefully,
splashing us both. Yuri let out a yell, and I scrambled
to my feet, stumbled and tried to run. He grabbed me
by the arm.

"You *still* won't learn how," he said again, laughing. I looked into his eyes, level with my own.

I pursed my lips again, and Yuri disappeared. My
time was up and I was being thrown and torn at again.

I was in the cubicle once more.

I left the Time Station and walked home alone.

I became a spendthrift, visiting the Time Station
several times a week, seeing Yuri as often as I wanted.
We met on the steps of a deserted Mayan pyramid
and argued about the mathematical theories of his
friend Alney, while jungle birds shrieked around us. I
packed a few of his favorite foods and wines and found

him in Hawaii, still awaiting the arrival of its first inhabitants. We sat together on a high rocky cliff in Africa, while far below us apelike creatures with primitive weapons hunted for food.

I became busy again, and began work with a group who were designing dwelling places inside the huge trees that surrounded the city. The biologists who had created the trees hundreds of years before had left the trunks hollow. I would hurry to the Time Station with my sketches of various designs, anxious to ask Yuri for advice or suggestions.

Yet during this time I had to watch Yuri grow old again. Each time I saw him he was a little older, a little weaker. I began to realize that I was watching him die all over again, and our visits took on a tone of panic and desperation. He grew more cautious in his choice of times and sites, and I was soon meeting him on deserted island beaches or inside the empty summer homes of the twentieth century. Our talks with each other grew more muted, as I was afraid of arguing too vigorously with him and thus wasting the little time we had left. Yuri noticed this and understood what it meant.

"Maybe I was wrong," he said to me after I showed him the final plans for the tree dwellings. I had been overly animated, trying to be cheerful, ignoring the signs of age that reminded me of his death. I couldn't fool him. "I wanted to make it easier for you to live without me, but I might have made things worse. If I hadn't planned these visits, maybe you would have recovered by now, maybe—"

"Don't," I whispered. We were sitting near a sunny stretch of beach in southern France, hiding ourselves behind a large rock from the family picnicking below us. "Don't worry about me, please."

"You've got to face it. I can't make too many more of these journeys. I'm growing weaker."

I tried to say something but my vocal cords were locked, frozen inside my throat. The voices of the family on the beach were piercing. I wondered, idly, how many of them would die in their coming world war.

Yuri held my hand, opened his lips to say something else, then vanished. I clutched at the empty air in desperation. "No!" I screamed. "Not yet! Come back!"

I found myself, once again, at the Time Station.

I had been a spendthrift. Now I became a miser, going to the Time Station only two or three times a month, trying not to waste the few remaining visits I had with Yuri. I was no longer working on the tree dwellings. We had finished our designs and now those who enjoyed working with their hands had begun construction.

A paralysis seized me. I spent days alone in my house, unable even to clothe myself, wandering from room to room. I would sleep fitfully, then rise and, after sitting for a few hours alone, would sleep again. Once I forced myself to walk to the Slumber House and asked them to put me to sleep for a month. I felt the same after awakening, but at least I had been able to pass that lonely month in unconsciousness. I went to the Time Station, visited Yuri, and went back to the Slumber House to ask for another month of oblivion. When I awoke the second time, two men were standing over me, shaking their heads. They told me I would have to see a Counselor before they would put me to sleep again.

I had been a Counselor once myself, and I knew all their tricks. Instead, I went home and waited out the time between my visits there.

It could not go on indefinitely. The list of remaining coordinates grew shorter until there was only one set left, and I knew I would see Yuri for the last time.

We met by a large wooden summer home that overlooked a small lake. It was autumn there and Yuri began to shiver in the cool air. I managed to open the back door of the house and we went inside, careful not to disturb anything.

Yuri lay on one of the couches, his head on my lap. Outside, the thick wooded area that surrounded the house was bright with colors, orange, red, yellow. A half-grown fawn with white spots on his back peered in the window at the other end of the room, then disappeared among the trees.

"Do you regret anything?" Yuri suddenly asked. I stroked his white hair and managed a smile.

"No, nothing."

"You're sure."

"Yes," I said, trying to keep my voice from quavering.

"I have one regret, that I didn't meet you sooner. But I wouldn't have met you at all, except for that promise I made."

"I know," I said. We had talked about our meeting at least a thousand times. The conversation had become a ritual, yet I wanted to go over it again. "You were so blatant, Yuri, coming to my door like that, out of nowhere. I thought you were a little crazy."

He smiled up at me and repeated what he had said then. "Hello, I'm Yuri Malenkov. I know this is a little strange, but I promised a friend of mine I met today I'd see you. Do you mind if I come in for a little while?"

"And I was so surprised I let you in."

"And I never left."

"I know, and you're still around." Tears stung my eyes.

"You were the only person aside from that friend that I could talk to honestly right away."

By then tears were running down my cheeks. "You never told me anything about your friend," I said abruptly, breaking the ritual.

"An acquaintance, really. I never found that person again after that."

"Oh, Yuri, what will I do now? You can't leave me. I can't let you die again."

"Don't," he murmured. "You don't have much longer. Can't you see what's happening to you?"

"No."

"Get up and look in the mirror over the fireplace."

I rose, wandered over to the mirror, and looked. The signs were unmistakable. My once-jet-black hair was lightly sprinkled with silver and tiny lines were etched into the skin around my eyes.

"I'm dying," I said. "My body isn't rejuvenating itself anymore." I felt a sudden rush of panic; then the fear vanished as quickly as it came, replaced by calm. I hurried back to Yuri's side.

"It won't be long," he said. "Try to do something

meaningful with those last months. We'll be together again soon, just keep thinking of that."

"All right, Yuri," I whispered. Then I kissed him for the last time.

I did not fear death and do not fear it now. I became calmer, consoled by the fact that I would not be alone much longer.

How ironic it would be if my many recent uses of the Time Station had caused my sudden aging, if Yuri's gift to me had condemned me instead. Yet I knew this was not so. We all imagine that we'll have our full three centuries; most of us do, after all. But not everyone, and not I. The irony is part of life itself. It was the work not of any Time Station, but of the final timekeeper, Death, who had decided to come for me a few decades early.

What was I to do with the time left to me? I had trained as a Counselor many years ago and had worked as one before choosing a new profession. I decided to use my old experience in helping those who, like me, had to face death.

The dying began to come to me, unable to accept their fate. They were used to their youthfulness and their full lives, feeling invulnerable to anything except an accident. The suddenness with which old age had descended on them drove some to hysteria, and they would concoct wild schemes to bring about the return of their youth. One man, a biologist, spoke to me and then decided to spend his last months involved in the elusive search for immortality. Another man, who had recently fallen in love with a young girl, cried on my shoulder and I didn't know whether to weep for him or for the young woman he was leaving behind. A woman came to me, only seventy and already aging, deprived of what should have been her normal life span.

I began to forget about myself in talking with these people. Occasionally I would walk through the city and visit old friends. My mind was aging too, and on these walks I found myself lost in memories of the past, clearer to me than more recent events. As I passed the Time Station, I would contemplate a visit to my past and then shake my head, knowing that was impossible.

I might have gone on that way if I had not passed the Time Station one warm evening while sorting through my thoughts. As I walked by, I saw Onel Lialla, dressed as a technician, looking almost exactly the same as when I had known him.

An idea occurred to me. Within seconds it had formed itself in my mind and become an obsession. I can do it, I thought. Onel will help me.

Onel had been a mathematician. He had left the city some time before and I had heard nothing about him. I hurried over to his side.

"Onel," I said, and waited. His large black eyes watched me uncertainly and anxiety crossed his classically handsome face. Then he recognized me.

He clasped my arms. He said nothing at first, perhaps embarrassed by the overt signs of my approaching death. "Your eyes haven't changed," he said finally.

We walked toward the park, talking of old times. I was surprised at how little he had changed. He was still courtly, still fancied himself the young knight in shining armor. His dark eyes still paid me homage, in spite of my being an old gray-haired woman. Blinded perhaps by his innate romanticism, Onel saw only what he wished to see.

Twenty years before, while barely more than a boy, Onel had fallen in love with me. It had not taken me long to realize that Onel, being a romantic, did not really wish to obtain the object of his affections and had probably unconsciously settled on me because I was so deeply involved with Yuri. He would follow me almost everywhere, pouring out his heart. I tried to be kind, not wanting to make him bitter, and spent as much time as I could in conversation with him about his feelings. Onel had finally left the city, and I let him go, knowing he would forget and realizing that this, too, was part of his romantic game.

Onel remembered all this. We sat in the park under one of the crystalline willows and he paid court again. "I never forgot your kindness," he said to me. "I swore I would repay it someday. If there's anything I can do for you now, I will." He sighed dramatically at this point.

"There is," I replied.

"What is it?"

The opportunity had fallen into my lap with no effort. "I want you," I went on, "to come to the Time Station with me and send me back to this park two hundred and forty years in the past. I want to see the scenes of my youth one last time."

Onel seemed stunned. "You know I can't," he said. "The Portal can't send you to any time you've already lived through. We'd have people bumping into themselves, or going back to give their earlier selves advice. It's impossible."

"The Portal can be overridden for emergencies," I

said. "You can override it, you know how. Send me through."

"I can't."

"Onel, I don't want to change anything. I don't even want to talk to anybody."

"If you changed the past—"

"I won't. It would already have happened then, wouldn't it? Besides, why should I? I had a happy life, Onel. I'll go back to a day when I wasn't in the park. It would just give me a little pleasure before I die to see things as they were. Is that asking too much?"

"I can't," he said. "Don't ask this of me."

In the end he gave in, as I knew he would. We went to the Station. Onel, his hands shaking, adjusted a Portal for me and sent me through.

Onel had given me four hours. I appeared in the park behind a large refreshment tent. Inside the tent, people sat at small round tables enjoying delicacies and occasionally rising to sample the pink wine that flowed from a fountain in the center. As a girl I had worked as a cook in that tent, removing raw foodstuffs from the transformer in the back and spending hours in the small kitchen making desserts, which were my specialty. I had almost forgotten the tents, which had been replaced later on by more elaborate structures.

I walked past the red tent toward the lake. It too was as I remembered it, surrounded by oaks and a few weeping willows. Biologists had not yet developed the silvery vines and glittering crystal trees that would be planted later. A peacock strutted past me as I headed for a nearby bench. I wanted only to sit for a while near the lake, then perhaps visit one of the tents before I had to return to my own time.

I watched my feet as I walked, being careful not to stumble. Most of those in the park ignored me rather pointedly, perhaps annoyed by an old woman who reminded them of their eventual fate. I had been the same, I thought, avoiding those who would so obviously be dead soon, uncomfortable around those who were dying when I had everything ahead of me.

Suddenly a blurred face was in front of me and I collided with a muscular young body. Unable to retain my balance, I fell.

A hand was held out to me and I grasped it as I struggled to my feet. "I'm terribly sorry," said a voice, a voice I had come to know so well, and I looked up at the face with its wide cheekbones and clear blue eyes.

"Yuri," I said.

He was startled. "Yuri Malenkov," I said, trying to recover.

"Do I know you?" he asked.

"I attended one of your lectures," I said quickly, "on holographic art."

He seemed to relax a bit. "I've only given one," he said. "Last week. I'm surprised you remembered my name."

"Do you think," I said, anxious now to hang on to him for at least a few minutes, "you could help me over to that bench?"

"Certainly."

I hobbled over to it, clinging to his arm. By the time we sat down, he was already expanding on points he had covered in the lecture. He was apparently unconcerned about my obvious aging and seemed happy to talk to me.

A thought struck me forcefully. I suddenly realized that Yuri had not yet met my past self. I had never attended that first lecture, having met him just before he was to do his second. Desperately, I tried to recall the date I had given Onel, what day it was in the past.

I had not counted on this. I was jumpy, worried that I *would* change something, that by meeting Yuri in the park like this I might somehow prevent his meeting me. I shuddered. I knew little of the circumstances that had brought him to my door. I could somehow be interfering with them.

Yuri finished what he had to say and waited for my reaction. "You certainly have some interesting insights," I said. "I'm looking forward to your next lecture." I smiled and nodded, hoping that he would now leave and go about his business.

Instead he looked at me thoughtfully. "I don't know if I'll give any more lectures."

My stomach turned over. I knew he had given ten more. "Why not?" I asked as calmly as I could.

He shrugged. "A lot of reasons."

"Maybe," I said in desperation, "you should talk about it with somebody, it might help." Hurriedly I dredged up all the techniques I had learned as a Counselor, carefully questioning him, until at last he opened up and flooded me with his sorrows and worries.

He became the Yuri I remembered, an intense person who concealed his emotions under a cold, businesslike exterior. He had grown tired of the city's superficiality, uncomfortable with those who grew an-

noyed at his seriousness and penetration. He was un-
suited to the gaiety and playfulness that surrounded
him, wanting to pursue whatever he did with single-
minded devotion.

He looked embarrassed after telling me all this and
began once more to withdraw behind his shield. "I
have some tentative plans," he said calmly, regaining
control. "I may be leaving here in a couple of days
with one of the scientific expeditions for Mars. I prefer the company of serious people and have been offered a place on the ship."

My hands trembled. Neither of us had gone with
an expedition until five years after our meeting. "I'm
sorry for bothering you with my problems," he went
on. "I don't usually do that to strangers, or anyone else
for that matter. I'd better be on my way."

"You're not bothering me."

"Anyway, I have a lot of things to do. I appreciate
the time you took to listen to me."

He stood up and prepared to walk away. No, I
thought, you can't, I can't lose you like this. But then
I realized something and was shocked that I hadn't
thought of it before. I knew what I had to do.

"Wait!" I said. "Wait a minute. Do you think you
could humor an old lady, maybe take some advice? It'll
only be an hour or so of your time."

"It depends," he said stiffly.

"Before you go on that expedition, do you think you
could visit a person I think might enjoy talking to
you?"

He smiled. "I suppose," he said. "But I don't see
what difference it makes."

"She's a lot like you. I think you'd find her sympa-
thetic." And I told him where I lived and gave him

my name. "But don't tell her an old woman sent you, she'll think I'm meddling. Don't mention me. Just tell her it was a friend."

"I promise." He turned to leave. "Thank you, friend." I watched him as he ambled down the pebbled path that would lead him to my home.

Time's Hitch

ROBERT FRAZIER

Poet Robert Frazier writes that "I was born in Ayer, Massachusetts, USA, in 1951 and haven't come down since." His creative impulses were shaped by a mother who did landscape painting and a father who taught cryptology and was involved in Project Ultra at Bletchley, England, cracking Nazi codes during World War II.

Frazier has turned his hand to homeschooling, scrimshaw, herb and wildflower identification, poetry, tofu cookery, and science fiction. In the winter he teaches in a Montessori school, and during the summer he manages a craft and jewelry store on Nantucket Island, his current home.

He has won the Rhysling Award for science-fiction poetry and edits Star*Line, the newsletter of the Science Fiction Poetry Association. His second poetry collection, Perception Barriers, is forthcoming.

Transposed to the ship's brain, from engrams
to encodes, in the moments after termination,
I now glide the warp like a water strider.

Thus pinioned I shunt my passengers coldly
from node to millennial node,
shimmering along the meniscus of a mirror.
When the warp branches, eddies into streams,
then it's mostly white water tumbling us like
a boulder between sheer cliffs.

Thus freed I ferry freely,
unlidding centuries and off-loading
my cargo on green and growing shores.
When my raft runners turn time tourists,
then I'm the timeless river rat, silent
and aloof and grim at the great rudder.

And as in the campfire glimmer of my monitors
their faces glow, I scan for signs of aging,
canali across planets I'll never know.

The Rooms
of Paradise

IAN WATSON

Ian Watson was educated at Oxford University, where he studied French and English literature before embarking on a career as a lecturer in East Africa, Japan and Britain. A full-time writer for the past ten years, he currently lives in a tiny village in the heart of rural England.

In addition to standing in two elections as candidate of the British Labour Party and being active in the Campaign for Nuclear Disarmament, he has written some twenty books, which have been translated into a variety of languages including Hebrew, Polish, and Serbo-Croatian. His novelette "Slow Birds" was a Hugo and Nebula finalist in 1984.

His most recent publications are Converts, *a comic fantasy,* The Book of Ian Watson, *a miscellany, and an adventure trilogy:* The Book of the River, The Book of the Stars, *and* The Book of Being, *featuring what one reviewer described as "the looniest master plan for the universe in SF." "The Rooms of Paradise" first appeared in an anthology of the same title edited by Lee Harding; Roger Zelazny has written that this story "makes me wonder whether the author might have made an equally respected name as a poet."*

1

Something went terribly wrong with
my rebirth. There's no doubt about it now, thirty days
into the new life. Somehow the categories of time and
space are cross-wired in my infant brain. Duration of
days and extension in space have interchanged, and I
read the world awry. How else can I explain what is
happening to me—thirty *rooms* as I am into this
seemingly endless building . . . .

If synaesthesia is the word for confusion of the five
senses—so that the color yellow sounds like a gong-
beat, or a vinegary taste rubs the tongue with sandpa-
per—what is the name for this terrible malaise?
Syndimensionality?

Perhaps Fitzgerald's Syndrome, after my own
name? To the discoverer belongs the honor of naming,
they say. . . . But how do I communicate this discovery? Where and when do I communicate it—when
"where" is "when", and "when" is "where?" If I'd
crash-landed alone on an unknown and empty planet,
what use would there be in christening it "Fitzgerald's
World?" I may as well settle for Syndimensionality.

But why? Why did it happen?

I'd followed all the prescribed meditation patterns
to scaffold my mind against the shock of sudden awakening in this blank putty infant body. I'd practiced
self-enhancement and ego-strengthening, gestalt-
awareness and psychic integration. (Indeed, it's to this
heightened mental discipline that I owe my ability to
remain sane and observant under these vastly altered,
unpredicted circumstances.) And it all went off, in the
main, as I'd been led to believe. My seventy-year-old

body was wheeled by the service-robot into the isolation chamber. (I'd had a mild heart attack, and could have had a new heart, surely; yet my body was obviously passing its prime. Why linger longer? *Why risk it?*)

Isolation, then: no living being could be near me now, no man or woman, bird or beast, insect or plant. The chamber itself was surrounded by a great electrified Faraday Cage of copper coils, to keep at bay the vital radiations of other life, lest the life field of any other living thing interfere with mine at the moment of Change-over. I would be robot-tended in isolation for seven days after Change-over while I "firmed" my new self—a generous enough safety margin.

The robot was a stainless steel drum rolling on silent rubber wheels, with two flexible arms and a variety of nozzles, teats, hidden drawers and trays. As it maneuvered my naked body underneath the scanner, I brooded on the details of the scanning process and what it would shortly do to the *me-ness* that is my individuality, my unique pattern, or if you prefer it, my soul. . . .

(You? Where are *you?* Is there any "you" observing me as I pass from room to room, from day to day? By the end of another week will you have come up with the formula for freeing me from this crazy progression? If so, I suppose you shall have the honor of christening my syndrome. You're welcome to it.)

"Rebirth," explained Astralsurgeon Dr. Manzoni, "was an outgrowth from early matter transmission failures. . . ."

"Yes, yes," said I, impatient to pass the portal into the Institute and begin preparing for Change-over. In my next life, I decided, I wouldn't concern myself with business affairs in the least. I would be a pentathlete, competing in the sports of the five worlds, letting the physical side of my nature bloom. I would inherit handsomely enough from myself after the thirty per cent levy to the Institute for rebirth and fostering to the age of five, legal majority for the reborn; and I was looking forward to those first five years as a paradise regained of play and exuberant imagination. The Institute has much to offer the young reborn, to amuse the years of early growth: a thousand and one nights and days of tapesimulated fairyland, not to mention all the bodybuilding amenities of playgrounds and shoreline.

"It's necessary to remind you," my Astralsurgeon said gently, "just as it will be necessary for you to remind yourself who you are, to recall your old existence in the new body. Don't take any of it for granted, Mr. Fitzgerald. We need you to understand what will happen to you perfectly. Haste only hinders you."

So I relaxed. Actually, there were quite a few details I'd forgotten or didn't know.

Dr. Manzoni was tall and silver-haired, with a long thoroughbred nose on which were balanced, of all things, spectacles. I wondered whether these were simply a personal affectation or whether they served some other, professional purpose. Whether, perhaps, those lenses rendered my life field—my very soul— visible to him, so that this interview was conducted not with aging flesh and blood but with the essential energy pattern of Robert Fitzgerald. . . .

The room itself was Islamic in design, with receding planes of symmetry in mosaic and tile, and pastel-toned. It bespoke permanence within change, the regeneration of forms, pattern, gentleness. The window —a stone grille of hexagons and star shapes—opened on the blue Mediterranean lapping Tunisian sands. Naked boys and girls were romping there under the patient eye of an attendant dressed in the lilac, phoenix-crested robe of the Institute. Those were reborn ones, almost ready to leave and resume their adult lives again. Or new lives entirely, I reminded myself. Or new ones. Whatever they chose.

How carefree was their play! Yet patient too, savoring the future. . . . Not rushing madly into deep waters. How delightful it would be when sexuality came round again. I imagined myself briefly as some girl-child a hundred years old, with all the knowledge of an old lady, yielding to her first choice of lover in the second life. . . . Well, I would not be a girl, of course; but sexual fulfillment obviously came earlier to a reborn girl than to a boy.

Patience. I listened to Manzoni.

Rebirth was a spin-off from matter transmission which had proved, in the event, wildly expensive as a means of shifting anything from A to B, if A was any further than a few metres from B. So the dream of hopping instantaneously around the globe from booth to booth had soon evaporated. However, it evaporated for another reason too: in all the early tests with live animals, only dead bodies arrived at B.

The vibrational scanning method converted mass into energy, back again into mass, almost instantaneously. (For all atoms vibrate to a tune; the "symphony," the manifold fugue, may be a chair—or a rose or a human being.) Yet in that instant, when mass was entirely patterns of energy, the mass could be shunted to another, nearby location in resonance with the scanning beam. A paperweight or a pencil shifted position, intact; but a mouse or a beetle arrived intact, yet lifeless.

It transpired that a ghost was left in the scanner: a pattern which did not reconvert into mass, since it had not strictly speaking been mass in the first place—though it had been present. A method of capturing souls had been found.

Before long, the researchers found they could reattach this "astral" pattern to the body, retransmitted back from B to A. The perfected method nowadays is to capture the astral pattern—the bioplasmoid soul, with all its memories and thoughts, beliefs and desires —on brief "hold", while the old body is shunted a few metres sideways into cremation (so that there's no resonant envelope of old familiar flesh around to pull the soul) then to shunt in the *tabula rasa* of a dummy body, android flesh grown at an accelerated rate *in vitro* from one's own DNA under the constant focus of one's Kirlian aura field recorded on entering the Institute and constantly updated. In a very real sense one is simply re-entering at a much earlier stage. The bioplasmoid soul adjusts to its smaller envelope with relative ease.

"The soul, after all, has a hunger for the flesh," smiled Dr. Manzoni.

I thought of the two vivid young reborns who had been at the exit-party I held in Amsterdam before flying down here to this shoreline south of Sfax. Tonio Andreson and Julia-Maria Geizenstein were only eight and nine years old metabolically, and such a sparkling, witty couple. They were in love with life and with each other (though touchingly they could do little about this yet). We admired them with friendly, tender anticipation of greater happiness to come. They would honeymoon, they hinted, out by the rings of Saturn. They were every fairy tale come true. I was, I realize, half in love with Julia-Maria myself.

Outside, a stork was flapping its white way towards its nest atop a spike of Roman ruin invaded by the sands. Appropriate!

I nodded and asked appropriate questions. And so I entered the Institute, to learn the disciplines of rebirth.

So, a few weeks later, I lay alone and naked under the scanner.

A sudden lurch . . . a tearing sensation, as of a bandage being torn free from deep inside myself: from inside my heart and lungs and belly.

I plummeted down a deep well into darkness, at the bottom of which was suddenly brilliance, reflection, identity: *myself*.

And I was lying where I'd been lying before, except that the chamber seemed much larger. It blurred; my eyes weren't properly adjusted to it. I cried out my first breath.

My tongue explored a toothless mouth. I was a thing of rubber; muscles were hardly there yet, to be commanded. My hand flapped across my face. Then I relaxed.

It would have been nice to hear the voice of Dr. Manzoni greeting me by intercom. I would rather have liked some congratulations. But no voice said anything. I did need privacy to stabilize myself, to grow firm. I concentrated on this, till I slept.

When I woke, I was in another room: an amorphous, aquarium-like cube of opaque green glass tiles. The service-robot stood by the cot I now lay in. It fed me warm milk and washed me and blew me dry and wrapped flannel round my midriff, then retired to a corner. My body-idea of myself still slopped out far beyond the boundaries of my shape. Phantom arms and legs hung over the sides of the cot. I felt a little like a plucked, trussed chicken, lopped and trimmed. But I accepted this gladly—gradually reeling in my body-idea to the new, reduced dimensions. Likewise I gladly accepted my sudden incontinence; and the silence and isolation.

I slept, I woke, I sucked milk, I meditated. After a long while the indirect lighting, which came from nowhere in particular but was simply present, began to dim. Night-time. Again I slept.

When I woke up again to false daylight, to my surprise my cot was in another windowless room, this one chequered red and green.

So it has gone on ever since for thirty days—through thirty rooms. I read rooms as days now; they must stand for days. Turning my head one way, I see the door to tomorrow's room standing slightly ajar; the other way I see the door to yesterday shut tight. I think it's that way round, but it's always night and I'm asleep or very drowsy when the robot wheels me through the door.

Green room, red room, golden room; tile, brick, plastic—always different yet identical in their emptiness, their indirect lighting, the absence of windows.

I suppose I must seem autistic or psychotic to an outside observer, exhibiting a total failure of response. They must be all around me now that the first seven days are long past: Dr. Manzoni, my psychic integra-

tion tutor Mme Matsuyama, the Institute Adminis-
trator Radwan Hussainy, the nurses, worrying, trying
to reach me. But I persist in seeing only another impossible new room, empty apart from my attendant
robot.

Syndimensionality: time and space have twisted.
. . . Yet I live, I breathe, I suck liquids, I flex my little
fists, I squeak (still struggling to fit the words around
my tongue), I look this way and that attentively. All
memories of the old life are intact.

"Where are you all? Show yourselves, dammit!"

I cry, then stop myself crying. Be firm, soul of
Robert Fitzgerald, reborn man!

On. On.

2

I am five hundred rooms old now, give or take a few:
a teetering toddler—precocious enough, though that's
only to be expected since I've been through this all
before. My service-robot, dumb waiter supreme, still
feeds me—solids now, as well as liquids—and washes
me down and cleans up my messes. (Where does it get
all the food and drink from? Where does it send the
messes to? Hyperspace? In what dimension of experience is this happening?) My cot got left behind a few
rooms back, and now I sleep anywhere—a feral child.
Today's room is rococo, with ranks of glided plaster
putti to support the ceiling. . . .

Every night the robot moves me on to the next
room in its flexible arms, cradling me. Yet really it's
a very neutral thing; there's no sense of menace, or
camaraderie, about it. I'm not tempted to call it Fred
or Charlie.

And today, in full "daylight" and of my own free

will, I toddle to the door that stands ajar, heave it open and stumble through into tomorrow's room. It's a larger room than previous ones, an empty Moorish Alhambra. The dumb waiter follows me. Behind, as though drawn magnetically by its metal rump, the door shuts quietly and finally with a faint tick like the hand of a clock moving on. When I toddle back and try to push it open, there's no way.

On I toddle into the next room—a huge mock-igloo. The box of tricks rolls after me, the door clicks shut. And on into the next, the next, the next. Egyptian tomb, Greek temple, and log cabin. Click, click, click.

So this is possible. Suppose, on the other hand, I refuse to move on?

I stay put. I stay and stay. The light dims and brightens at boring day-long intervals five times in succession. I breakfast, lunch and dine a total of fourteen times in that log cabin. On the fifth night, having stockpiled as much sleep as I can during the day, I sit up in the darkness like some tot hooked on midnight TV, watching even when the set is off. When I'm almost nodding off, my dumb waiter rolls over and lifts me gently. Time has caught up with me. Time to move on.. I kick and squirm, but into the next dark room it bears me bodily; the door clicks shut.

Next night, I try even more vigorous evasive maneuveres, dashing and ducking and rolling in the darkness. But it shepherds me; it corners me with ease. Onward I'm borne.

What is at the end? Is there some final room housing God seated in judgment, God the big hotelier?

Or will there be a mirror, wherein I see myself approaching, old man by the time I reach it, having entirely recapitulated my life like some absurd spook on ontogenesis: I who cheated that final room of life by rebirth?

Am I only a reflection of my soul, a secondary ghost trapped in the circuits of the astral scanner? I beat on the walls with my toddler's fists. "Let me out!" Does some red light blink on a scanner console in the dimension of Tunisia?

Perhaps I am the true soul, doomed to wander these rooms for as long as the android flesh—of which I inhabit the meta-physical analogue over here—lives out its whole new life over there, possessed of an analogue soul, a mere reflection of me? Is this true of all reborns? Perhaps my dumb waiter is a kind of *corpus callosum* of the soul: a bridge linking one soul-hemisphere amusing itself on Earth with this other soul-hemisphere which is myself and is stored in Purgatory. (And what if Robert Fitzgerald over there enjoys his second life so much that he opts to be reborn yet again . . . ?) Is there any way of communicating across this bridge? I've tried words; my waiter is truly deaf and dumb. Shall I rap out Morse code on its metal flanks? SOS—*Save Our Soul*. Shall I stuff a message up its cleaning nozzle? Written with what? On what? Blood and skin? For a while Monte Cristo-like fantasies of escape, or at least of message smuggling, flourish—then wither away. I am here; and the only way is forward.

Forward, then, as far as my toddler's legs will carry me!

How many rooms can I travel in a day? Fifty? A hundred?

Alas, when I have toddled through twenty different

rooms (Byzantine, Art Deco, geodesic dome . . .) I realize that my robot is no longer following. It lurks, two rooms back. Two doors stand open, though not the third behind; that's shut tight. Which makes me anxious in case a door suddenly shuts in my face, cutting me off from my source of food and drink. I shall have to go back and try to figure out the reason for its inertness.

The door won't let me pass. Invisible elastic holds me back, a soft resistance growing firm as steel the harder I shove against it.

I have to wait.

And wait.

Comes night, I lie down to sleep, thirsty.

Comes another day, and still my dumb waiter stays where it is. Comes night, and some time during it, while I hunch around my hollow belly, throat dry as sticks, the robot rolls forward into the room next door; for it's there in the morning, and the door beyond has shut.

There it stays, out of reach, through the next awful day till night falls when it rolls in beside me at last to feed and succor me in the dark.

If I had toddled on a few rooms farther, unawares . . . Can a soul starve? Can it die of thirst? Here, apparently it can. So I am limited to ranging no farther than eighteen rooms ahead. . . .

Oh rat in the maze, how soon do you learn the rules? This is a maze that only has one route, though, and that route is straight ahead. The rules here relate to finding one's way through time.

As though to keep me occupied, furniture appears— at first sparingly but then, as my body puts on a growth spurt of its own over the next few hundred rooms, with increasing frequency. Before long, rooms are handsomely and even lavishly furnished: with chairs and bureaux, tables and cabinets, chaise-longues and sofas, chests of drawers, armchairs and the occasional glorious bed. . . .

Even so, all chests and cupboards and desks are empty, not even lined with so much as a sheet of old newspaper. Bookcases hold no books. No paintings or prints hang on the walls—there are no representations of an outside world. Nor are there any clocks.

Could the rooms get *too* crowded? This idea sparks off another: now that the rooms contain something, I can interfere with them! Tugging open the door from the nineteenth-century salon I'm currently in, I discover a gorgeous Shinto temple interior beyond; in vermilion, black and gold, with green *tatami* matting, a coiling silver dragon on the ceiling, lions painted round the walls, and huge metal vases standing about holding tall metal lotus blossoms. I select a light lyre-back chair of ebonized wood from the nineteenth century and try to shove it through into the Shinto temple. No way can I do it. Invisible elastic thrusts the chair back. Not me, just the chair. Passing through the doorway myself, I try to drag the chair after me. Impossible. The chair only belongs in one room; it only exists in one.

Does it cease to exist, once I have passed on and the door has shut? Is it transmuted and recycled into a stool or part of a sofa farther ahead? The problem of *rules* is beginning to obsess me, generating a sort of perverse thrill in the midst of my predicament. If there are rules, and if I can learn them. . . .

The dumb waiter lifts the lyre-back chair aside and

follows me through into Shinto-land; the door clicks shut. Farewell, chair.

A library! Complete with library steps with leather treads.

All the books are dummies, five and ten-volume blocks of leather-bound, gold-tooled dummies. Enraged, I toss them upon the carpet. Ashamed of myself, I restore them tidily a little later.

At least the spines bear titles—the first words that I've seen in years. Here we have *A History of Silesis.* Here, *Mr. Jorrocks' Jaunts and Jollities* by R.M. Surtees. Sallust's *Jugurthine War* and Gibbon's *Decline and Fall of the Roman Empire.* . . .

Maybe, in a later room, when I'm supposed to be able to read (by the age of six or seven, say) books will have words in them? How damnably frustrating that'll be, if I can't carry them from one room to the next! Onward, onward. I am the Wanderer, homeless in this never ending home, a nomad with nowhere to pitch my tent for longer than a day.

I brood on the great journeys of the past; on Marco Polo setting off for Cathay. From Venice, was it? Just imagine the problem of interpreters in those early days before world languages existed. Imagine his having to hire yet another new interpreter at every new language boundary. Imagine his arrival at the court of the Great Khan with a huge retinue of interpreters of a hundred nationalities and the Khan's greeting passing back along that vast recursion, translated out of Chinese into Mongol into Manchu into Tibetan into Nepalese into Indian tongues innumerable into Farsi . . . eventually into Bulgarian, Serbian and finally into Marco's native Italian so that he can at last comprehend, simply: "Hullo there." Oh chain of interpreters, oh chain of rooms. What did I do to deserve this? Was it the *hubris* of seeking another life? Perhaps if I pray, I may be let out?

Onward, onward.

I'm bigger and stronger now, strong enough to shove my dumb waiter about. One day, bearing in mind my brush with starvation many hundreds of rooms ago, I wheel it through the doorway into the next room. The door duly clicks shut. I propel the robot through another room and another room. I reach the magic number eighteen; I transcend it. Hilariously I shove the dumb equipment through twenty, twenty-one, twenty-two; still the doors click shut behind us.

Now a pause, for safety's sake, in case a door clicks open in the night and my robot rolls hindwards again, leaving me high and dry. But that doesn't happen. The ground I have gained remains mine.

Tomorrow, I negotiate sixty rooms.

The day after, though, chambers grow vast. Rooms become endless halls lined with chairs, their carpets stretching off into the distance. Soon it's a mad rush to reach the next door by dusk. I am Achilles of the wounded heel, chasing the victorious tortoise. I slow down, exhausted. It seems that I'm being taught the concept of infinity.

Is that because I shunned the prospect of eternity? As if to reward this insight, appears next day an oasis: a full-size indoor swimming pool complete with slide and springboard. I walk all round it, warily, on the lookout for something lurking in the water, some shark or octopus. But no, there's nothing but water in the pool; still, clear water. Slipping in at the shallow end,

I soon relearn the art. I swim one breadth, then another, before I stretch out tired on the side.

Is this . . . a baptism?

For a few days I camp by the pool, since I'm still way ahead of schedule, delighted by this amenity—then gradually repelled by the wet, cool blankness.

The following room—the huge hall of a castle with baronial chairs, a long oak table and eerie suits of armor—is punishingly hot. A hint of Hell?

This little boy treks on, through more temperate, ordinary rooms. Pool and hot castle were simply random fluctuations. In infinity, I suppose anything can happen once, or even an infinite number of times. Even the impossible.

Can an infinite series of events ever come to an end? Can there be no number greater than n? An n of rooms. . . . Oh ghost of Cantor, help me. I am lost in a transfinite set—this suite of rooms.

But it had a beginning, and there has been change and growth since then, as witness the arrival of furniture. And when I rushed my waiter hectically forward, didn't my environment stretch itself after my first day's gains to check me? So it responds; it reacts to me. Since it permits me to live—by generating such an immensity of rooms to house me day by day—isn't it fair to say that it is actually benign? Rather than malevolent or merely neutral? Surely a vast effort is involved in sustaining my existence—so vast perhaps that no energy is left over for added frills such as real books or paintings, windows or views. If it can only provide one dimension of movement—namely forwards—maybe that's the most it can provide, the al-

ternative being . . . what? a frozen stasis? with no way
to move, nowhere to move to? This place certainly
does not imprison me, when it urges me to move
onward, ever onward. Can one really be a prisoner, in
an infinite prison?

A deep sense of joy begins to stir in me. I exist.
Room for my existence is provided: *that* is the meaning. Even though I tried to make my soul mechanical,
I am provided for. Surely it is a mere machine-soul
that is in the reborns, however vivid and superb their
new lives seem. God is not cheated. For *our* sake He
will not let us cheat with souls. Though I bankrupt
myself in His eyes, I am here on soul-welfare, guaran-
teed this minimum income and security.

God did not wind the world up in the beginning,
so that it should run on and on automatically. Rather
let us say He *recreates* it afresh every moment in the
fourth dimension of time, which is therefore the dimension of creation. Here in this endless hostelry outside of time—in eternity—linear space becomes the
dimension of creation instead; instead of each new
day, each new room comes into being to sustain my
soul's existence. Pockets of new space are constantly
added instead of new increments of time.

Gladly I press on now, entering each new room
freely at nightfall and staying in the appointed room
all day long with no wish to rush vainly and prema-
turely ahead.

Though I wonder what lies beyond these walls, at
right angles to the one direction I can travel day by
day? Is it mere nothingness—or the face of God? I still
would like to know. Will there ever be a window?

. . .

A window there is! But not the kind of window I expected. It isn't *in* any of the rooms. No, it's in myself—it's in my sleep at night.

Strange, but I do not seem to have dreamt till now. . . .

Till I wake up in a dream tonight, well aware that it is a dream and that I'm really lying asleep on a stately, padded chaise-longue in one of God's rooms, yet vividly present *at the same time* on a Tunisian beach—the selfsame beach that I watched through that stone grille window of hexagons and stars long ago. Only, now I am one of the naked children myself. We are all reborn, and playing together on the sands, watched over by a lilac-robed woman whose name, I know perfectly well, is Odette.

So wonderful: the sun, the sea, the shore! Grains of sand trickle through my fingers; I sift a seashell from the soft yellow grit. White foam edges the water. A lizard scampers. There's laughter, giggling, and voices.

My friends' names are: Andrea, Juno, Yukio, Michel, Sven. I know them all intimately. We've been reborn and reared together. Right now I'm saying to Andrea:

"—We are like shells, with the echo of the sea in them; little rooms that contained soft, flexible life that rotted away. We are the purified shape of that life, and the echo is the music of our souls—"

I surprise myself. Have I chosen to become poet rather than pentathlete? Or has my long stay over here in the rooms spiritualized my emotions over there?

No, actually I am playing at seduction, years in advance of any possible performance; and Andrea is pleasantly teased by it. Our juvenile libidos caress one another. I am, I realize, in love with her. As is she, with me. How courteously we court, naked tots on the Tunisian shore: happy Heloise and anticipative Abelard, awaiting my ungelding and meanwhile making a game of it.

My tongue continues turning pretty words, while I listen in astonishment to myself. My limbs act out a delightful yet irrelevant charade. My lips kiss hers chastely. We perform a hopping, sand-scuffling little dance, a sort of parody gavotte with a dune for a dance floor.

I know it's a dream—a lucid dream in which I am wide awake. Yet it is also real. It is actually happening on that Tunisian strand. We are there together, Andrea and I!

The next night, and every night for weeks I join the same unfolding living dream. The moment I fall asleep over here, I wake up over there. For sleeping and waking hours in the two worlds coincide perfectly but oppositely. Morpheus in the Underworld, I am there as we stroll through the Institute gardens, holding hands. I am there as we make our plans; for we're both wildly rich—our investments have prospered during our years of minority. Soon we will be off to Mars to power-ski the dunes of Hellespont, anticipating our adult physique by wearing cybersuits. I am there till I fall asleep at night in bed with Andrea, holding her chastely. Yet all the time I am asleep and aware of the fact.

What pain if she's there within herself too, the Andrea soul, unable to communicate from her own after-death dimension, while we both gaily play the game of life. What pain if she too is awake in her own dream, and like me cannot say a word about it.

What greater pain if she isn't awake at all, but still locked away!

I fantasize that I can break through the ritual of the dream.

"Andrea, I'm asleep!" I cry. "I'm on some after-death plane, in an Elizabethan room of massive oak beams and flagons and silver gilt Livery pots. There's an open iron casket with the most incredibly complicated locks all across the inside of the lid and nothing inside it, and a gnarled oak coffer that's empty too. I'm sleeping on top of that. Hard bedding, tonight! It's been room after room every since I was reborn: hundreds, thousands of them, all without windows or words or people in them. That's where I really am. Are you trapped in rooms too, while all this goes on?" (Gesturing at the Mediterranean and the humps of the Institute behind well-spaced palm trees.)

She stops and stares, open-mouthed. Suddenly *she knows*.

Alternatively: she smiles, "Welcome. This is the secret we all share. Now you know it too."

Neither event takes place. The dream is inexorable. It ploughs on with remorseless gaiety towards nightfall back in the Institute, where I fall asleep . . . to awaken promptly to this hard coffer lid, to another enclosed day. My dumb waiter serves breakfast. I defecate in a corner. Its nozzle cleans the floor.

In the evening I step through into a sterile, functionally designed office, windowless (for the window is within me), with an empty desk, empty filing cabinets, and a dead intercom.

Tonight's dream spans my penultimate day at the Institute, for my discharge has been approaching rapidly. I call in to see Dr. Manzoni, visibly older now, to say goodbye. (Andrea will be discharged six weeks later than me. I shall wait for her not far away in the Club Méditerranée village, *La Douce*, on the lotus island of Djerba.)

I lavish thanks upon the good doctor . . . while my other, mute mouth aches to cry out, "Manzoni! This isn't how it really is! Not for any of us, I swear. It never has been. God—whatever He is . . . the metaprogrammer of reality—He holds us all in store, while we caper through the second life, merry as puppies. We're held in separate rooms, great chains of them, on and on forever, to teach us infinity and eternity. But alone, always *alone*, because we're still alive even though we're really dead. We're alive *and* dead—both! This reborn life's a mockery. If the mock life wasn't being dreamt, the rooms could open up . . . to the wonder, to the truth."

None of this does he hear. My lips merely burble thanks. I leave him, and seek out the Bursar to see to my assets.

Had I woken up to this dream in the beginning, I understand that I'd have been wild to burst through the window into the puppet drama I'm enacting over there. (Would I even have realized which reality was the more authentic?) Now, not so. Life is simply a huge simulation—a drama set on a stage that is re-created every moment—sustained by the dreams of the soul; when the body dies, the soul awakens. Had I woken earlier—had the window appeared before— I could never have accepted this.

Tomorrow night, as I sleep in a four-poster bed in the cool high stone room of a castle, I kiss Andrea *au revoir* at the Institute and board the helicopter which will speed me south to Djerba. . . .

3

How delightful is Djerba: the scent of orange groves, the white beehive houses (*menzels*, they call them), the bazaars and Roman ruins, the sponge fishers, the flocks of flamingos. Naturally I yearn for Andrea to join me, but in no way do I let this yearning spoil the pleasures of the present moment, nor would she wish such a thing.

What my psychic integration tutor, the lovely Hiroko Matsuyama, told me about dreams is quite true: dreams are my life now, consequently the need to compensate for what is missing in life is far less these days. In common with all reborns, I hardly seem to dream at all, or promptly forget what I do dream. Dissatisfactions have been washed away by rebirth. *Now* is all.

Yet there was one dream, recurring around the age of one to three months, which came back again the other night just before I quit the Institute: a dream of being fastened up in an endless succession of windowless rooms. When I told Mme Matsuyama at the time she said this was *the* common—one might even say archetypal—dream with reborns, and about the only noteworthy one. It was an obvious psychic symbol of "rebirth trauma"—for instead of being convulsively expelled, as from the mother's womb at first-birth, one is locked up instead in isolation in a womb-room for rebirth. The physical limitations of the early months encourage this symbolism. As soon as the infant body became more mobile, the notion of enclosure would fade. As indeed it did—as though I lost sight of myself

passing through door after door and getting nowhere
—for about then the world really began opening up;
at the same time I was judged "firm" enough for really
thrilling sensory tapes to amuse my leisure hours:
dragon-chases, maiden-rescues, the whole promised
fairyland. My imminent "expulsion" from the Institute summoned up the dream once more. Subcon-
sciously, I must have been slightly anxious—and
wanted to stay! But only once. Nights are nirvana time
again.

Today, I think I shall arrange a flight inland to
Blidet, to power-ski the high white dunes. . . .

How refreshed I awake in my private bungalow this
morning in *Djerba la Douce.* My window looks out
upon the huge swimming pool of the Club. A tall slim
negress poises naked on the diving board. She leaps,
she twists in a backward somersault, she cuts the tur-
quoise water cleanly. What a great sight to wake to,
ebony lady.

From now on, I (and that's *we,* as soon as Andrea
gets here) will be waking in room after room with ever
more enchanting views, in chalets, lodges, pressure
cabins, undersea hotels, space stations, methane skimmers—around the Earth, on Luna and Mars, out by
Jupiter and Saturn. There'll be glories to be seen
through every window when we wake, wonders that
it'll take us all our second lives to explore.

Checking Out

GENE WOLFE

*Gene Wolfe's science fiction is unique. Nowadays
there are all too many medieval fantasies set in the
future, on another world, or in never-never-land, but
Wolfe's tetralogy,* The Book of the New Sun, *is something else. It is genuinely "post-historic"—located in a
world that can only rake the embers of that dimly-
remembered and eroded past which is our own present
day. Thus Wolfe's future people would know how to
build an aircraft carrier, say, but they would have neither the technological means nor the resources to build
it. A picture-cleaner (like someone in a Renaissance
palace) cleans an ancient picture—but it is of an astronaut on the Moon. Time yawns vastly, yet Wolfe has
accurately counted the teeth of time, and makes that
almost-fossil jaw speak truly. Wolfe is one of the most
eloquent stylists writing today.*

*Also concerned with the strange abrasions of time is
his subsequent novel,* Free Live Free *(1985). Seemingly a contemporary novel, it is almost Dickensian in
its loving portrayal of idiosyncratic characters, before
revealing itself—unexpectedly but fittingly—as a most
unusual time-travel tale.*

Wolfe is a splendid craftsman of novellas and short

*stories, as well, and the following tale will surely haunt
the reader in inverse proportion to its length.*

T he slam of the door jerked him to
wakefulness.

He lay on top of the bed on a blue satin coverlet,
fully dressed except for his shoes. He sat up and saw
his suitcase on the bed beside him. No doubt the
bellboy had brought it. No doubt the bellboy had
promised to follow him to his room—they did that
sometimes. And instead of staying awake for him, he
had lain down to get a little rest. No doubt the bellboy
was angry at not getting a tip.

It was his best suit; he should not have gone to sleep
in it. He went to the closet and hung up his jacket.
The room seemed very small, the bed so narrow he
was surprised the bellboy had found room for his bag
on it. He wondered what hotel this was.

He liked the Algonquin in New York, though its
rooms were so small, its beds so narrow. But everything in the Algonquin was old and good and a little
worn; everything was new here, and a little bit shiny
and cheap. He did not think they built hotel rooms
this small anymore.

He opened his bag and saw that Jane had not
packed it. Martha, perhaps. Martha was their cleaning
woman, the old woman who would not do windows.
No, Martha was dead.

Jane's picture was on top, and he took it out and
looked into her clear blue eyes. She would miss him.
Or rather, she would say she did, though he knew the
only time she really relaxed was when he was gone—
when he was gone, and she could pretend they were

rich for life, and there would never, never be a need to make anything more, no need for late nights at the office, for flights to New York with Jan.

Flights. That was it. They had been on the plane, he remembered, and tired. He had drunk the free martini they gave you and leaned back to relax. After that, they would have hired a cab. No doubt the old furniture at the Algonquin had given out at last, and the management had had to get this stuff.

You could buy *The New York Review* at the magazine stand in the Algonquin; he liked that. He decided to go out and get one, but his shoes were not in the closet, not under the bed. Well, to hell with them. His slippers would be in his bag, and you could go into the lobby in your slippers at the Algonquin—he liked that too. Perhaps Jan was in the lobby or the bar.

He found Jan's picture while looking for his slippers. How had that got in here? Perhaps Martha had put it in for fear that Jane would see it. He tossed it toward the wastebasket. Jan was a good secretary, and sometimes he felt that she loved him in a way that Jane never had, at least not since Bruce was born. But he could not leave Jane. Paradoxically, he could not leave her because he had left her so often.

He tossed Jan's picture toward the wastebasket, and found Joan's beneath it, a misty "glamour portrait" in the style of the forties, signed like a movie star's. This was absurd. He had never owned such a picture.

Or had he? Yes, once.

What a strange, unpleasant sound the air conditioning made here, like a drawn-out sigh, an unending sighing.

Quite suddenly his desk appeared to his mind's eye,

more real than the tawdry room, and just as suddenly it shrank. There was a rolltop now with cheap varnish over the stained oak, with just room enough to write, with a few books. Had that battered children's dictionary ever been his? There was a foldout shelf with just room enough to write, and a few pigeon holes, and Joan's picture in the frame from Woolworth's. He realized with a start that she might have been a virgin in those days, a real high-school virgin in those days, though he had never thought of her that way, only as a woman, though he had said "girl," and infinitely desirable.

No doubt he had, later, put Jan's picture into the frame so that it covered Joan's. No doubt he had put them both into the new frame Jan had bought for his desk. No doubt Martha had put them, together, into his bag. No, Martha was dead.

He flung both pictures at the wastebasket and scuffed on his slippers as he opened the door.

Space.

An atrium. This hotel had an atrium; it was a Hyatt, then. High, it rose so high he could see only blue sky at the top. His room was high up too, though it seemed less than half-way up. Tiny figures moved slowly across the lobby, wading in water nearly waist deep.

A flood—there was a flood in the city. He was lucky the lights in his room still worked, the air conditioning still sighed.

He looked back and saw that he had not in fact turned on any lights, that the bellboy had not turned on any lights at all. The room was dark and gloomy behind him, like a cave in which something slept.

He would go to the lobby. There was a flood, and

he was still an active man. Perhaps he could help. Perhaps Jan would see him helping.

He tried, but his balcony was not connected with the other balconies—there was a gap of at least ten feet. How did you get out in that case? How did you reach the elevators?

He went back into the room and saw Jan's picture on top of his clean shirts. He would tell Jane, make a clean breast of it for once. He reached for the telephone.

Mrs. Clem said, "I thought he looked very nice. All that pretty blue."

Jane nodded. "I bought a concrete dome to go over the casket, too. It sits right down over it and traps the air, so the water can't get to him. It cost almost three thousand dollars."

The telephone rang. "Excuse me," she said. "Hello?"

"I'm coming back to you." The words stuck in his throat. There had been no sound, only the unending sigh.

"Hello?"

"I love you, Jane. I'm checking out of here and coming back, whether you love me or not."

Jane said. "There's no one there, just an empty line."

"I'd hang up, if I were you," Mrs. Clem told her.

"Jane!" he said. And then, "Joan? Joan?"

Someone was knocking at the door. *"Maid."*

He stared at it. "Jan? Joan?"

"Would you like your bed turned down, sir? It will only take a minute."

Jane said, "Not even breathing," and hung up.

The Region Between

HARLAN ELLISON

DESIGN AND GRAPHICS BY JACK GAUGHAN

In 1970 five leading authors collaborated on a "science-fiction extravaganza" entitled Five Fates, *each contributor producing a different story from the same beginning: a man entering a Euthanasia Center to be painlessly killed. All five stories were noteworthy, yet four of the authors used sleight of hand to skip out of the initial (and terminal) situation. Harlan Ellison did not. He accepted the premise of actual death and took his readers on the startling, visionary journey that follows.*

Ellison's tales characteristically tell of terrible life traumas. They are distress rockets, blasting into the sky from a lifeboat with a piece of human anguish clinging to it. The origin of the tale—the lifeboat in question —may be one of any number of things: a child's over-heard remark, or an encounter with a talk-show hostess. Meanwhile, near the wreckage, sharks are snapping in the water, causing an overwhelming sense of urgency. Which is perhaps how Harlan Ellison can write such remarkably authentic stories while, say, chained to his typewriter in public in a shop window like a literary Houdini. He pits himself against time, the inertia of the world, the death of memory; against a universe that seems coldly neutral—without any God presiding—yet that in practice operates as if Jehovah were still running the show, levying an eye for an eye. He lives his tales, and his tales live him.

One of Ellison's most famous stories is titled "I Have No Mouth, and I Must Scream." Ellison's voice, certainly, is fiercely strong and original; but though there is anguish and pity, and moral anger in it, the word "scream" by no means does justice to the prose of this most compelling, and compelled, of authors.

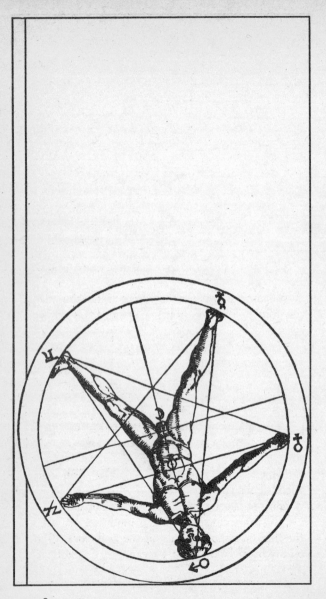

408

"Left hand," the thin man said tonelessly. "Wrist up."

William Bailey peeled back his cuff; the thin man put something cold against it, nodded toward the nearest door.

"Through there, first slab on the right," he said, and turned away.

"Just a minute," Bailey started. "I wanted—"

"Let's get going, buddy," the thin man said. "That stuff is fast."

Bailey felt something stab up under his heart. "You mean—you've already . . . that's all there is to it?"

"That's what you came for, right? Slab one, friend. Let's go."

"But—I haven't been here two minutes—"

"Whatta you expect—organ music? Look, pal," the thin man shot a glance at the wall clock, "I'm on my break, know what I mean?"

"I thought I'd at least have time for . . . for . . ."

"Have a heart, chum. You make it under your own power, I don't have to haul you, see?" The thin man was pushing open the door, urging Bailey through into an odor of chemicals and unlive flesh. In a narrow, curtained alcove, he indicated a padded cot.

"On your back, arms and legs straight out."

Bailey assumed the position, tensed as the thin man began fitting straps over his ankles.

"Relax. It's just if we get a little behind and I don't get back to a client for maybe a couple hours and they stiffen up . . . well, them issue boxes is just the one size, you know what I mean?"

A wave of softness, warmness swept over Bailey as he lay back.

"Hey, you didn't eat nothing the last twelve hours?" The thin man's face was a hazy pink blur.

"I awrrr mmmm," Bailey heard himself say.

"OK, sleep tight, paisan. . . ." The thin man's voice boomed and faded. Bailey's last thought as the endless blackness closed in was of the words cut in the granite over the portal to the Euthanasia Center:

". . . send me your tired, your poor, your hopeless, yearning to be free. To them I raise the lamp beside the brazen door. . . ."

1

Death came as merely a hyphen. Life, and the balance of the statement, followed instantly. For it was only when Bailey died that he began to live.

Yet he could never have called it "living"; no one who had ever passed that way could have called it "living." It was something else. Something quite apart from "death" and something totally unlike "life."

Stars passed through him as he whirled outward.

Blazing and burning, carrying with them their planetary systems, stars and more stars spun through him as though traveling down invisible wires into the dark behind and around him.

Nothing touched him.

They were as dust motes, rushing silently past in incalculable patterns, as Bailey's body grew larger, filled space in defiance of the Law that said two bodies could not coexist in the same space at the same instant. Greater than Earth, greater than its solar system, greater than the galaxy that contained it, Bailey's body swelled and grew and filled the universe from end to end and ballooned back on itself in a slightly flattened circle.

His mind was everywhere.

A string cheese, pulled apart in filaments too thin to be measurable, Bailey's mind was there and there and there. And there.

It was also in the lens of the Succubus.

Murmuring tracery of golden light, a trembling moment of crystal sound. A note, rising and trailing away infinitely high, and followed by another, superimposing in birth even as its predecessor died. The voice of a dream, captured on spiderwebs. There, locked in the heart of an amber perfection, Bailey was snared, caught, trapped, made permanent by a force that allowed his Baileyness to roam unimpeded anywhere and everywhere at the instant of death.

Trapped in the lens of the Succubus.

413

[Waiting: empty. A mindsnake on a desert world, frying under seven suns, poised in the instant of death; its adversary, a fuzzball of cilia-thin fibers, sparking electrically, moving toward the mindsnake that a moment before had been set to strike and kill and eat. The mindsnake, immobile, empty of thought and empty of patterns of light that confounded its victims in the instants before the killing strike. The fuzzball sparked toward the mindsnake, its fibers casting about across the vaporous desert, picking up the mole sounds of things moving beneath the sand, tasting the air and feeling the heat as it pulsed in and away. It was improbable that a mindsnake would spend all that light-time, luring and intriguing, only at the penultimate moment to back off—no, not back off: shut down. Stop. Halt entirely. But if this was not a trap, if this was not some new tactic only recently learned by the ancient mindsnake, then it had to be an opportunity for the fuzzball. It moved closer. The mindsnake lay empty: waiting.]

Trapped in the lens of the Succubus.

[Waiting: empty. A monstrous head, pale blue and veined, supported atop a swan-neck by an intricate latticework yoke-and-halter. The Senator from Nougul, making his final appeal for the life of his world before the Star Court. Suddenly plunged into silence. No sound, no movement, the tall, emaciated body propped on its seven league crutches, only the trembling of balance—having nothing to do with life —reminding the assembled millions that an instant before this husk had contained a pleading eloquence. The fate of a world quivered in a balance no less precarious than that of the Senator. What had happened? The amalgam of wild surmise that grew in the Star Court was scarcely less compelling than had been the original circumstances bringing Nougul to this place, in the care of the words of this Senator. Who now stood, crutched, silent, and empty: waiting.]

Trapped in the lens of the Succubus.

[Waiting: empty. The Warlock of Whirrl, a power of darkness and evil. A force for chaos and destruction. Poised above his runic symbols, his bits of offal, his animal bones, his stringy things without names, quicksudden gone to silence. Eyes devoid of the pulverized starlight that was his sight. Mouth abruptly slack, in a face that had never known slackness. The ewe lamb lay still tied to the obsidian block, the graven knife with its unpleasant figures rampant, still held in the numb hand of the Warlock. And the ceremony was halted. The forces of darkness had come in gathering, had come to their calls, and now they roiled like milk vapor in the air, unable to go, unable to do, loath to abide. While the Warlock of Whirrl, gone from his mind stood frozen and empty: waiting.]

Trapped in the lens of the Succubus.

[Waiting: empty. A man on Promontory, fifth planet out from the star Proxima Centauri, halted in mid-step. On his way to a bank of controls and a certain button, hidden beneath three security plates. This man, this inestimably valuable kingpin in the machinery of a war, struck dumb, struck blind, in a kind of death—not even waiting for another moment of time. Pulled out of himself by the gravity of non-being, an empty husk, a shell, a dormant thing. Poised on the edges of their continents, two massed armies waited for that button to be pushed. And would never be pushed, while this man, this empty and silent man, stood rooted in the sealed underworld bunker where precaution had placed him. Now inaccessible, now inviolate, now untouchable, this man and this war stalemated frozen. While the world around him struggled to move itself a fraction of a thought toward the future, and found itself incapable, hamstrung, empty: waiting.]

Trapped in the lens of the Succubus.

And . . .

[Waiting: empty. A subaltern, name of Pinkh, lying on his bunk, contemplating his fiftieth assault mission. Suddenly gone. Drained, lifeless, neither dead nor alive. Staring upward at the bulkhead ceiling of his quarters. While beyond his ship raged the Montag–Thil War. Sector 888 of the Galactic Index. Somewhere between the dark star Montag and the Nebula Cluster in Thil Galaxy. Pinkh, limbo-lost and unfeeling, needing the infusion of a soul, the filling up of a life-force. Pinkh, needed in this war more than any other man, though the Thils did not know it . . . until the moment his essence was stolen. Now, Pinkh, lying there one shy of a fifty-score of assault missions. But unable to aid his world. Unable, undead, unalive, empty: waiting.]

While Bailey . . .

Floated in a region between. Hummed in a nothingness as great as everywhere. Without substance. Without corporeality. Pure thought, pure energy, pure Bailey. Trapped in the lens of the Succubus.

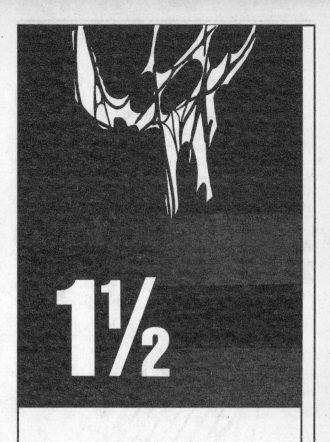

1½

More precious than gold, more sought-after than uranium, more scarce than yinyang blossom, more needed than salkvac, rarer than diamonds, more valuable than force-beads, more negotiable than the vampyr extract, dearer than 2038 vintage Chateau Luxor, more lusted after than the twin-vagina'd trollops of Kanga . . .

Souls.

Thefts had begun in earnest five hundred years before. Random thefts. Stolen from the most improbable receptacles. From beasts and men and creatures who had never been thought to possess "souls." Who was stealing them was never known. Far out somewhere, in reaches of space (or not-space) (or the interstices between space and not-space) that had no names, had no dimensions, whose light had never even reached the outmost thin edge of known space, there lived or existed or *were* creatures or things or entities or forces—*someone*—who needed the life-force of the creepers and walkers and lungers and swimmers and fliers who inhabited the known universes. Souls vanished, and the empty husks remained.

Thieves they were called, for no other name applied so well, bore in its single syllable such sadness and sense of resignation. They were called Thieves, and they were never seen, were not understood, had never given a clue to their nature or their purpose or even their method of theft. And so nothing could be done about their depredations. They were as Death: handiwork observed, but a fact of life without recourse to higher authority. Death and the Thieves were final in what they did.

So the known universes—the Star Court and the Galactic Index and the Universal Meridian and the Perseus Confederacy and the Crab Complex—shouldered the reality of what the Thieves did with resignation, and stoicism. No other course was open to them. They could do no other.

But it changed life in the known universes.

It brought about the existence of soul-recruiters, who pandered to the needs of the million billion

trillion worlds. Shanghaiers. Graverobbers of creatures not yet dead. In their way, thieves, even as the
Thieves. Beings whose dark powers and abilities enabled them to fill the tables-of-organization of any
world with fresh souls from worlds that did not even
suspect *they* existed, much less the Court, the Index,
the Meridian, the Confederacy or the Complex. If
a key figure on a fringe world suddenly went limp
and soulless, one of the soul-recruiters was contacted
and the black traffic was engaged in. Last resort, final
contact, most reprehensible but expeditious necessity, they stole and supplied.

One such was the Succubus.

He was gold. And he was dry. These were the only
two qualities possessed by the Succubus that could
be explicated in human terms. He had once been a
member of the dominant race that skimmed across
the sand-seas of a tiny planet, fifth from the star-sun
labeled Kappel-112 in Canes Venatici. He had long
since ceased to be anything so simply identified.

The path he had taken, light-years long and several hundred Terran-years long, had brought him
from the sand-seas and a minimum of "face"—the
only term that could even approximate the one measure of wealth his race valued—to a cove of goldness
and dryness near the hub of the Crab Complex. His
personal worthiness could now be measured only in
terms of hundreds of billions of dollars, unquencha-
ble light sufficient to sustain his offspring unto the
nine thousandth generation, a name that could only
be spoken aloud or in movement by the upper three
social sects of the Confederacies races, more "face"
than any member of his race had ever possessed

. . . more, even, than that held in myth by Yaele.

Gold, dry, and inestimably worthy: the Succubus.

Though his trade was one publicly deplored, there were only seven entities in the known universes who were aware that the Succubus was a soul-recruiter. He kept his two lives forcibly separated.

"Face" and graverobbing were not compatible.

He ran a tidy business. Small, with enormous returns. Special souls, selected carefully, no seconds, no hand-me-downs. Quality stock.

And through the seven highly placed entities who knew him—Nin, FawDawn, Enec-L, Milly(Bas)Kodal, a Plain without a name, Cam Royal, and Pl— he was channeled only the loftiest commissions.

He had supplied souls of all sorts in the five hundred years he had been recruiting. Into the empty husk of a master actor on Bolial V. Into the waiting body of a creature that resembled a plant aphid, the figurehead of a coalition labor movement, on Wheechitt Eleven and Wheechitt Thirteen. Into the unmoving form of the soul-emptied daughter of the hereditary ruler of Golaena Prime. Into the untenanted shape of an arcane maguscientist on Donadello III's seventh moon, enabling the five hundred-zodjam religious cycle to progress. Into the lusterless spark of light that sealed the tragic laocoönian group-mind of Orechnaen's Dispassionate Bell-Silver Dichotomy.

Not even the seven who functioned as go-betweens for the Succubus's commissions knew where and how he obtained such fine, raw, unsolidified souls. His competitors dealt almost exclusively in the atrophied, crustaceous souls of beings whose thoughts and beliefs and ideologies were so ingrained that the souls came to their new receptacles already stained and imprinted. But the Succubus . . .

Cleverly contrived, youthful souls. Hearty souls. Plastic and ready-to-assimilate souls. Lustrous, inventive souls. The finest souls in the known universe.

The Succubus, as determined to excel in his chosen profession as he was to amass "face," had spent the better part of sixty years roaming the outermost fringes of the known universe. He had carefully observed many races, noting for his purpose only those that seemed malleable, pliant, far removed from rigidity.

He had selected, for his purpose:

The Steechii
Amassanii
Cokoloids
Flashers
Griestaniks
Bunanits
Condolis
Tratravisii

and Humans.

On each planet where these races dominated, he put into effect subtle recruiting systems, wholly congruent with the societies in which they appeared:

The Steechii were given eterna dreamdust.

The Amassanii were given doppelgänger shifting.

The Cokoloids were given the Cult of Rebirth.

The Flashers were given proof of the Hereafter.

The Griestaniks were given ritual mesmeric trances.

The Bunanits were given (imperfect) teleportation.

The Condolis were given an entertainment called Trial by Nightmare Combat.

The Tratravisii were given an underworld motivated by high incentives for kidnapping and mind-blotting. They were also given a wondrous narcotic called Nodabit.

The Humans were given Euthanasia Centers.

And from these diverse channels the Succubus received a steady supply of prime souls. He received Flashers and skimmers and Condolis and ether-breathers and Amassanii and perambulators and Bunanits and gill creatures and . . .

William Bailey.

Trapped in the lens of the Succubus.

1³⁄₄

Bailey, cosmic nothingness, electrical potential spread out to the ends of the universe and beyond, nubbin'd his thoughts. Dead. Of that, no doubt. Dead and gone. Back on Earth, lying cold and faintly blue on a slab in the Euthanasia Center. Toes turned up. Eyeballs rolled up in their sockets. Rigid and gone.

And yet alive. More completely alive than he had

ever been, than *any* human being had ever conceived of being. Alive with all of the universe, one with the clamoring stars, brother to the infinite empty spaces, heroic in proportions that even myth could not define.

He knew everything. Everything there had ever been to know, everything that was, everything that would be. Past, present, future . . . all were merged and met in him. He was on a feeder line to the Succubus, waiting to be collected, waiting to be tagged and filed even as his alabaster body back on Earth would be tagged and filed. Waiting to be cross-indexed and shunted off to a waiting empty husk on some far world. All this he knew.

But one thing separated him from the millions of souls that had gone before him.

He didn't want to go.

Infinitely wise, knowing all, Bailey knew every other soul that had gone before had been resigned with soft acceptance to what was to come. It was a new life. A new voyage in another body. And all the others had been fired by curiosity, inveigled by strangeness, wonder-struck with being as big as the known universe and going *somewhere else.*

But not Bailey.

He was rebellious.

He was fired by hatred of the Succubus, inveigled by thoughts of destroying him and his feeder-lines, wonder-struck with being the only one—the *only* one!—who had ever thought of revenge. He was somehow, strangely, not tuned in with being rebodied, as all the others had been. *Why am I different?* he wondered. And of all the things he knew . . . he did not know the answer to that.

Inverting negatively, atoms expanded to the size of whole galaxies, stretched out membraned, osmotically breathing whole star systems, inhaling blue-white stars and exhaling quasars, Bailey the known universe asked himself yet another question, even more important:

Do I WANT *to do something about it?*

Passing through a zone of infinite cold, the word came back to him from his own mind in chill icicles of thought:

Yes.

"I see here, during the month of September, that you worked overtime at least . . . what is it . . . uh . . . eleven hours."

"Is there a law against that?"

"Oh, no . . . no, of course not. It just seems to us here at the block that you're perhaps, uh, overdoing it a bit."

"Working."

"Yes. Working."

"Has my block steward complained? Has my EEG been erratic? Am I being *accused* of something?"

"No, of course not! My lord, man, there's no need to be so defensive! We're only trying to find out if something is, well, disturbing you."

If I'd been able to, I'd have killed the sonofabitch; right then and right there. In his conversation grouping. It would have made fine conversation for his office staff. Come in and find him brained to death with his own coffee urn.

"Nothing's disturbing me."

"Then you'll pardon me if I feel it apropos to ask why you aren't taking your proper relaxation periods, Mr. Bailey."

"I feel like keeping busy."

"Ah, but all work and no play—"

And borne on comets plunging frenziedly through his cosmic body, altering course suddenly and traveling at right angles in defiance of every natural law he had known when "alive," the inevitable question responding to a *yes* asked itself:

Why should I?

Life for Bailey on Earth had been pointless. He had been a man who did not fit. He had been a man driven to the suicide chamber literally by disorientation and frustration.

I was called to the office of the Social Director of my residence block. Frankly, I was frightened. I knew I hadn't done anything to be afraid about, but ever since I'd been a child, ever since I'd been called to the office of the school principal, just the being *summoned* had made my gut tight, made me feel like I wanted to go to the bathroom.

He made me wait half an hour, on a bench, damn him, with a gaggle of weirdos who looked like they hadn't had their heads scrubbed and customized in seven months.

Finally, the box called my name and I dropped to his office, and he was sitting in one of those informal conversation-groupings of chairs and coffee table that instantly put me off.

"Mr. Bailey," he said. Smiled. Hearty bastard. I walked over and sat down even before he suggested I sit. He didn't drop the smile for a second. He was up to anything.

"Why don't we get right to it," he said. I smiled back at him, but I felt trapped, really hemmed-in.

"I've been looking at your tag-chart, Mr. Bailey, and well, I hesitate to make any jump conclusions here, but it *appears* you've been neglecting your relaxation periods."

Damn him! Damn him!

The omnipresent melancholy that had consumed him on an Earth bursting with overpopulation was something to which he had no desire to return. Then why this frenzy to resist being shunted into the body of a creature undoubtedly living a life more demanding, more exciting—*anything* had to be better than what he'd come from—more *alive*? Why this fanatic need to track back along the feeder-lines to the Succubus, to destroy the one who had saved him from oblivion? Why this need to destroy a creature who was merely fulfilling a necessary operation-of-balance in a universe singularly devoid of balance?

In that thought lay the answer, but he did not have the key. He turned off his thoughts. He was Bailey no more.

And in that instant the Succubus pulled his soul from the file and sent it where it was needed. He was certainly Bailey no more.

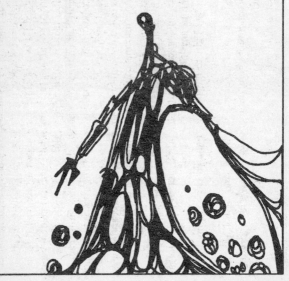

2.

Subaltern Pinkh squirmed on his spike-palette, and opened his eye. His back was stiff. He turned, letting the invigorating short-spikes tickle his flesh through the heavy mat of fur. His mouth felt dry and loamy.

It was the morning of his fiftieth assault mission. Or was it? He seemed to remember lying down for a night's sleep . . . and then a very long dream without substance. It had been all black and empty; hardly something the organizer would have programmed. It must have malfunctioned.

He slid sidewise on the spike-palette, and dropped his enormous furred legs over the side. As his paws touched the tiles a whirring from the wall preceded the toilet facility's appearance. It swiveled into view, and Pinkh looked at himself in the full-length mirror. He looked all right. Dream. Bad dream.

The huge, bearlike subaltern shoved off the bed, stood to his full seven feet, and lumbered into the duster. The soothing powders cleansed away his sleep-fatigue and he emerged, blue pelt glistening, with bad dreams almost entirely dusted away. Almost. Entirely. He had a lingering feeling of having been . . . somewhat . . . *larger* . . .

The briefing colors washed across the walls, and Pinkh hurriedly attached his ribbons. It was informalwear today. Three yellows, three ochers, three whites and an ego blue.

He went downtunnel to the briefing section, and prayed. All around him his sortie partners were on their backs, staring up at the sky dome and the random (programmed) patterns of stars in their religious significances. Montag's Lord of Propriety had programmed success for today's mission. The stars swirled and shaped themselves and the portents were reassuring to Pinkh and his fellows.

The Montag–Thil War had been raging for almost one hundred years, and it seemed close to ending. The dark star Montag and the Nebula Cluster in Thil Galaxy had thrown their might against each other for a century; the people themselves were weary of war. It would end soon. One or the other would make a mistake, the opponent would take the advantage, and the strike toward peace would follow immediately. It was merely a matter of time. The assault troops—especially Pinkh, a planetary hero— were suffused with a feeling of importance, a sense of the relevance of what they were doing. Out to kill, certainly, but with the sure knowledge that they were working toward a worthwhile goal. Through death, to life. The portents had told them again and again, these last months, that this was the case.

The sky dome turned golden and the stars vanished. The assault troops sat up on the floor, awaited their briefing.

It was Pinkh's fiftieth mission.

His great yellow eye looked around the briefing room. There were more young troopers this mission. In fact . . . he was the only veteran. It seemed strange.

Could Montag's Lord of Propriety have planned it this way? But where were Andakh and Melnakh and Gorekh? They'd been here yesterday.

Was it just yesterday?

He had a strange memory of having been— asleep?—away?—unconscious?—what?—something. As though more than one day had passed since his last mission. He leaned across to the young trooper on his right and placed a paw flat on the other's. "What day is today?" The trooper flexed palm and answered, with a note of curiosity in his voice, "It's Former. The ninth." Pinkh was startled. "What cycle?" he asked, almost afraid to hear the answer.

"Third," the young trooper said.

The briefing officer entered at that moment, and Pinkh had no time to marvel that it was *not* the next day, but a full cycle later. Where had the days gone? What had happened to him? Had Gorekh and the others been lost in sorties? Had he been wounded, sent to repair, and only now been remanded to duty? Had he been wounded and suffered amnesia? He remembered a Lance Corporal in the Throbbing Battalion who had been seared and lost his memory. They had sent him back to Montag, where he had been blessed by the Lord of Propriety himself. What had happened to him?

Strange memories—not his own, all the wrong colors, weights and tones wholly alien—kept pressing against the bones in his forehead.

He was listening to the briefing officer, but also hearing an undertone. Another voice entirely. Coming from some other place he could not locate.

■■■■■ You great ugly fur-thing, you! Wake up, look around you. One hundred years, slaughtering. Why can't you see what's being done to you? How dumb can you be? The Lords of Propriety; they set you up. Yeah, *you*, Pinkh! Listen to me. You can't block me out . . . you'll hear me. Bailey. You're the one, Pinkh, the special one. They trained you for what's coming up . . . no, don't block me out, you imbecile . . . don't blot me out ■■■■■ I'll be here, you can't blot me out ■■■■■

The background noise went on, but he would not listen. It was sacrilegious. Saying things about the Lord of Propriety. Even the Thil Lord of Propriety was sacrosanct in Pinkh's mind. Even though they were at war, the two Lords were eternally locked together in holiness. To blaspheme even the enemy's

Lord was unthinkable.

Yet he had thought it.

He shuddered with the enormity of what had passed in his thoughts, and knew he could never go to release and speak of it. He would submerge the memory, and pay strict attention to the briefing officer who was

"This cycle's mission is a straightforward one. You will be under the direct linkage of Subaltern Pinkh, whose reputation is known to all of you."

Pinkh inclined with the humbleness movement.

"You will drive directly into the Thil labyrinth, chivvy and harass a path to Groundworld, and there level as many targets-of-opportunity as you are able, before you're destroyed. After this briefing you will reassemble with your sortie leaders and fully familiarize yourselves with the target-cubes the Lord has commanded to be constructed."

He paused, and stared directly at Pinkh, his golden eye gone to pinkness with age and dissipation. But what he said was for all of the sappers. "There is one target you will *not* strike. It is the Maze of the Thil Lord of Propriety. This is irrevocable. You will not, repeat *not* strike near the Maze of the Lord."

Pinkh felt a leap of pleasure. This was the final strike. It was preamble to peace. A suicide mission; he ran eleven thankfulness prayers through his mind. It was the dawn of a new day for Montag and Thil. The Lords of Propriety were good. The Lords held all cupped in their holiness.

Yet he had thought the unthinkable.

"You will be under the direct linkage of Subaltern Pinkh," the briefing officer said again. Then, kneeling and passing down the rows of sappers, he palmed good death with honor to each of them. When he reached Pinkh, he stared at him balefully for a long instant, as though wanting to speak. But the moment passed, he rose, and left the chamber.

They went into small groups with the sortie leaders and examined the target-cubes. Pinkh went directly to the briefing officer's cubicle and waited patiently till the older Montagasque's prayers were completed.

When his eye cleared, he stared at Pinkh.

"A path through the labyrinth has been cleared."

"What will we be using?"

"Reclaimed sortie craft. They have all been outfitted with diversionary equipment."

"Linkage level?"

"They tell me a high six."

"They *tell* you?" He regretted the tone even as he spoke.

The briefing officer looked surprised. As if his desk had coughed. He did not speak, but stared at Pinkh with the same baleful stare the subaltern had seen before.

"Recite your catechism," the briefing officer said, finally.

Pinkh settled back slowly on his haunches, ponderous weight downdropping with grace. Then:

"Free flowing, free flowing, all flows
"From the Lords, all free, all fullness,
"Flowing from the Lords.
      "What will I do
      "What will I do
"What will I do without my Lords?

"Honor in the dying, rest in honor, all honor
"From the Lords, all rest, all honoring,
"To honor my Lords.
    "This I will do
    "This I will do
"I will live when I die for my Lords."

And it was between the First and Second Sacredness that the darkness came to Pinkh. He saw the briefing officer come toward him, reach a great palm toward him, and there was darkness . . . the same sort of darkness from which he had risen in his own cubicle before the briefing. Yet, not the same. *That* darkness had been total, endless, with the feeling that he was . . . somehow . . . larger . . . greater . . . as big as all space . . .

And this darkness was like being turned off. He could not think, could not even think that he was unthinking. He was cold, and not there. Simply: not there.

Then, as if it had not happened, he was back in the briefing officer's cubicle, the great bearlike shape was moving back from him, and he was reciting the Second Sacredness of his catechism.

What had happened . . . he did not know.

"Here are your course coordinates," the briefing officer said. He extracted the spool from his pouch and gave it to Pinkh. The subaltern marveled again at how old the briefing officer must be: the hair of his chest pouch was almost gray.

"Sir," Pinkh began. Then stopped. The briefing officer raised a palm. "I understand, Subaltern. Even to the most reverent among us there come moments of confusion." Pinkh smiled. He *did* understand.

"Lords," Pinkh said, palming the briefing officer with fullness and propriety.

"Lords," he replied, palming honor in the dying.

Pinkh left the briefing officer's cubicle and went to his own place.

As soon as he was certain the subaltern was gone, the briefing officer, who was *very* old, linked-up with someone else, far away; and he told him things.

3

First, they melted the gelatin around him. It was hardly gelatin, but it had come to be called jell by the sappers, and the word had stuck. As the gelatin stuck. Face protected, he lay in the ten troughs, in sequence, getting the gelatinous substance melted around him. Finally, pincers that had been carefully padded lifted him from the tenth trough, and slid him along the track to his sortie craft. Once inside the pilot country, stretched out on his stomach, he felt the two hundred wires insert themselves into the jell, into the fur, into his body. The brain wires were the last to fix.

As each wire hissed from its spool and locked onto the skull contacts, Pinkh felt himself go a little more to integration with the craft. At last, the final wire tipped on icily and so Pinkh was metalflesh, bulkheadskin, eyescanners, bonerivets, plasticartilege, artery / ventricle / capacitors / molecules / transistors,

```
        BEASTC
        C        R
        R    i   A
        A        F
        F        T
        TBEAST
```

all of him as one, totality, metal-man, furred-vessel, essence of mechanism, soul of inanimate, life in force-drive, linkage of mind with power plant. Pinkh the ship. Sortie Craft 90 named Pinkh.

And the others: linked to him.

Seventy sappers, each encased in jell, each wired up, each a mind to its sortie craft. Seventy, linked in telepathically with Pinkh, and Pinkh linked into his own craft, and all of them instrumentalities of the Lord of Propriety.

The great carrier wing that bore them made escape orbit and winked out of normal space.

Here■Not Here.

In an instant gone.

(Gone where!?!)

Inverspace.

Through the gully of inverspace to wink into existence once again at the outermost edge of the Thil labyrinth.

Not Here•Here.

Confronting a fortified tundra of space crisscrossed by deadly lines of force. A cosmic fireworks display. A cat's cradle of vanishing, appearing and disappearing threads of a million colors; each one receptive to all the others. Cross one, break one, interpose . . . and suddenly uncountable others home in. Deadly ones. Seeking ones. Stunners and drainers and leakers and burners. The Thil labyrinth.

440

Seventy-one sortie craft hung quivering—the last of the inverspace coronas trembling off and gone. Through the tracery of force-lines the million stars of the Thil Galaxy burned with the quiet reserve of ice crystals. And there, in the center, the Nebula Cluster. And there, in the center of the Cluster, Groundworld.

"Link in with me."

Pinkh's command fled and found them. Seventy beastcraft tastes, sounds, scents, touches came back to Pinkh. His sappers were linked in.

"A path has been cleared through the labyrinth for us. Follow. And trust. Honor."

"In the dying," came back the response, from seventy minds of flesh-and-metal.

They moved forward. Strung out like fish of metal with minds linked by thought, they surged forward following the lead craft. Into the labyrinth. Color burned and boiled past, silently sizzling in the vacuum. Pinkh detected murmurs of panics, quelled them with a damping thought of his own. Images of the still pools of Dusnadare, of deep sighs after a full meal, of Lord-worship during the days of First Fullness. Trembling back to him, their minds quieted. And the color beams whipped past on all sides, without up or down or distance. But never touching them.

Time had no meaning. Fused into flesh/metal, the sortie craft followed the secret path that had been cleared for them through the impenetrable labyrinth.

Pinkh had one vagrant thought: *Who cleared this for us?*

And a voice from somewhere far away, a voice that

was his own, yet someone else's—the voice of a someone who called himself a bailey—said, *That's it! Keep thinking what they don't want you to think.*

But he put the thoughts from him, and time wearied itself and succumbed, and finally they were there. In the exact heart of the Nebula Cluster in Thil Galaxy.

Groundworld lay fifth from the source star, the home sun that had nurtured the powerful Thil race till it could explode outward.

"Link in to the sixth power," Pinkh commanded.

They linked. He spent some moments reinforcing his command splices, making the interties foolproof and trigger-responsive. Then he made a prayer, and they went in.

Why am I locking them in so close, Pinkh wondered, damping the thought before it could pass along the lines to his sappers. *What am I trying to conceal? Why do I need such repressive control? What am I trying to avert?*

Pinkh's skull thundered with sudden pain. Two minds were at war inside him, he knew that. He *SUDDENLY* knew it.

Who is that?

It's me, you clown!

Get out! I'm on a mission . . . it's import—

It's a fraud! They've prog—

Get out of my head listen to me you idiot I'm trying to tell you something you need to know I won't listen I'll override you I'll block you I'll damp you no listen don't do that I've been someplace you haven't been and I can tell you about the Lords oh this can't be happening to me not to me I'm a devout man fuck that garbage listen to me they lost you man they lost

442

you to a soul stealer and they had to get you back because you were their specially programmed killer they want you to Lord oh Lord of Propriety hear me now hear me your most devout worshipper forgive these blasphemous thoughts I can't control you any more you idiot I'm fading fading fading Lord oh Lord hear me I wish only to serve you. Only to suffer the honor in the dying.

Peace through death. I am the instrumentality of the Lords. I know what I must do.

That's what I'm trying to tell you. . . .

And then he was gone in the mire at the bottom of Pinkh's mind. They were going in.

They came down, straight down past the seven moons, broke through the cloud cover, leveled out in a delta wing formation and streaked toward the larger of the two continents that formed ninety percent of Groundworld's land mass. Pinkh kept them at supersonic speed, blurring, and drove a thought out to his sappers: "We'll drop straight down below a thousand feet and give them the shock wave. Hold till I tell you to level off."

They were passing over a string of islands—causeway-linked beads in a pea-green sea—each one covered from shore to shore with teeming housing dorms that commuted their residents to the main continents and the complexes of high-rise bureaucratic towers.

"Dive!" Pinkh ordered.

The formation angled sharply forward, as though it was hung on puppet strings, then fell straight down.

The metalflesh of Pinkh's ship-hide began to heat.

Overlapping armadillo plates groaned; Pinkh pushed their speed; force-bead mountings lubricated themselves, went dry, lubricated again; they dropped down; follicle-thin fissures were grooved in the bubble surfaces; sappers began to register fear, Pinkh locked them tighter; instruments coded off the far right and refused to register; the island-chain flew up toward them; pressure in the gelatin trough flattened them with g's; now there was enough atmosphere to scream past their sortie craft and it whistled, shrilled, howled, built and climbed; gimbal-tracks rasped in their mountings; down and down they plunged, seemingly bent on thundering into the islands of Groundworld; "Sir! Sir!"; "Hold steady, not yet . . . not yet . . . I'll tell you when . . . not yet . . ."

Pushing an enormous bubble of pressurized air before them, the delta wing formation wailed straight down toward the specks of islands that became dots, became buttons, became masses, became everything as they rushed up and filled the bubble sights from side to side—

"Level out! *Now!* Do it, do it, *level now!*"

And they pulled out, leveled off and shot away. The bubble of air, enormous, solid as an asteroid, thundering down unchecked . . . hit struck burst broke with devastating results. Pinkh's sortie craft plunged away, and in their wake they left exploding cities, great structures erupting, others trembling, shuddering, then caving in on themselves. The shock wave hit and spread outward from shore to shore. Mountains of plasteel and lathite volcano'd in blossoms of flame and flesh. The blast-pit created by the air bubble struck to the core of the island-chain. A tidal wave rose like some prehistoric leviathan and boiled over one entire spot of land. Another island broke up and sank almost at once. Fire and walls of plasteel crushed and destroyed after the shock wave.

The residence islands were leveled as Pinkh's sortie craft vanished over the horizon, still traveling at supersonic speed.

They passed beyond the island-chain, leaving in their wake dust and death, death and ruin, ruin and fire.

"Through death to peace," Pinkh sent.

"Honor," they responded, as one.

(Far away on Groundworld, a traitor smiled.)

(In a Maze, a Lord sat with antennae twined, waiting.)

(Flesh and metal eased.)

(In ruins, a baby whose exoskeleton had been crushed, crawled toward the pulsing innards of its mother.)

(Seven moons swung in their orbits.)

(A briefing officer on Montag knew it was full, golden.)

Oh, Lords, what I have done, I have done for you. Wake up. Will you wake up, Pinkh! The mission is—

The other thing, the bailey, was wrenching at him, poking its head up out of the slime. He thrust it back down firmly. And made a prayer.

"Sir," the thought of one of his sappers came back along the intertie line, "did you say something?"

"Nothing," Pinkh said. "Keep in formation."

He locked them in even tighter, screwing them down with mental shackles till they gasped.

The pressure was building.

A six-power linkup, and the pressure was building.

I am a hero, Pinkh thought, *I can do it.*

Then they were flashing across the Greater Ocean and it blurred into an endless carpet of thick heaving green; Pinkh felt sick watching it whip by beneath him; he went deeper into ship and the vessel felt no sickness. He fed the stability of nausea-submerged along the interties.

They were met by the Thil inner defense line over empty ocean. First came the sea-breathers but they fell short when Pinkh ordered his covey to lift for three thousand feet. They leveled off just as the beaks swooped down in their land-to-sea parabolas. Two of them snouted and perceived the range, even as they were viciously beamed into their component parts by Pinkh's outermost sappers. But they'd already fed back the trajectories, and suddenly the sky above them was black with the blackmetal bodies of beaks, flapping, dropping, squalling as they cascaded into the center of the formation. Pinkh felt sappers vanish from the linkup and fed the unused power along other lines, pulling the survivors tighter under his control. "Form a sweep," he commanded.

The formation regrouped and rolled in a graceful gull-wing maneuver that brought them craft-to-craft in a fan. "Plus!" Pinkh ordered, cutting in—with a thought—the imploding beam. The beams of each sortie craft fanned out, overlapping, making an impenetrable wall of deadly force. The beaks came whirling back up and careened across the formation's path. Creatures of metal and mindlessness. Wheels and carapaces. Blackness and berserk rage. Hundreds. Entire eyries.

When they struck the soft pink fan of the overlapping implosion beams, they whoofed in on themselves, dropped instantly.

The formation surged forward.

Then they were over the main continent. Rising from the exact center was the gigantic mountain atop which the Thil Lord of Propriety lived in his Maze.

"Attack! Targets of opportunity!" Pinkh commanded, sending impelling power along the linkup. His metal hide itched. His eyeball sensors watered. In they went, again.

"Do not strike at the Lord's Maze," one of the sappers thought

AND PINKH
THREW UP!
A WALL OF
THOUGHT !!!
THAT DREW
THE !!!!!!!!!!!!
THOUGHT !!!
OFF THE!!
LINKUP SO
IT DID!!!
NOT REACH
THE OTHER
SAPPERS !!!!!
BUT HIT!!
THE WALL!
AND BROKE
LIKE FOAM

Why did I do that? We were briefed not to attack the Lord's Maze. It would be unthinkable to attack the Lord's Maze. It would precipitate even greater war than before. The war would *never* end. Why did I stop my sapper from reiterating the order? And why haven't *I* told them not to do it? It was stressed at the briefing. They're linked in so very tightly, they'd obey in a moment—anything I said. What is happening? I'm heading for the mountain! Lord!

Listen to me, Pinkh. This war has been maintained by the Lords of Propriety for a hundred years. Why do you think it was made heresy even to think negatively about the opposing Lord? They keep it going, to feed off it.

Whatever they are, these Lords, they come from the same pocket universe and they live off the energy of men at war. They must keep the war going or they'll die. They programmed you to be their secret weapon. The war was reaching a stage where both Montag and Thil want peace, and the Lords can't have that. Whatever they are, Pinkh, whatever kind of creature they are, wherever they come from, for over a hundred years they've held your two galaxies in their hands, and they've used you. The Lord isn't in his Maze, Pinkh. He's safe somewhere else. But they planned it between them. They knew if a Montagasque sortie penetrated to Groundworld and struck the Maze, it would keep the war going indefinitely. So they pro-grammed you, Pinkh. But before they could use you, your soul was stolen. They put my soul in you, a man of Earth, Pinkh. You don't even know where Earth is, but my name is Bailey. I've been trying to reach

through to you. But you always shut me out—they
had you programmed too well. But with the linkup
pressure, you don't have the strength to keep me out,
and I've got to let you know you're programmed to
strike the Maze. You can stop it, Pinkh. You can
avoid it all. You can end this war. You have it within
your power, Pinkh. Don't strike the Maze. I'll redirect
you. Strike where the Lords are hiding. You can rid
your galaxies of them, Pinkh. Don't let them kill you.
Who do you think arranged for the path through the
labyrinth? Why do you think there wasn't more effec-
tive resistance? They wanted *you to get through. To*
commit the one crime they could not forgive.

The words reverberated in Pinkh's head as his
sortie craft followed him in a tight wedge, straight
for the Maze of the Lord.

"I—no, I—" Pinkh could not force thoughts out
to his sappers. He was snapped shut. His mind was
aching, the sound of straining and creaking, the
buildings on the island-chain ready to crumble. Bailey inside, Pinkh inside, the programming of the
Lords inside . . . all of them pulling at the fiber of
Pinkh's mind.

For an instant the programming took precedence.
"New directives. Override previous orders. Follow
me in!"

They dove straight for the Maze.

No, Pinkh, fight it! Fight it and pull out. I'll show
you where they're hiding. You can end this war!

The programming phasing was interrupted, Pinkh
abruptly opened his great golden eye, his mind
synched in even more tightly with his ship, and at
that instant he knew the voice in his head was telling

him the truth. He *remembered*:

Remembered the endless sessions.

Remembered the conditioning.

Remembered the programming.

Knew he had been duped.

Knew he was not a hero.

Knew he had to pull out of this dive.

Knew that at last *he* could bring peace to both galaxies.

He started to think *pull out, override* and fire it down the remaining linkup interties . . .

And the Lords of Propriety, who left very little to chance, who had followed Pinkh all the way, contacted the Succubus, complained of the merchandise they had bought, demanded it be returned . . .

Bailey's soul was wrenched from the body of Pinkh. The subaltern's body went rigid inside its jell trough, and, soulless, empty, rigid, the sortie craft plunged into the mountaintop where the empty Maze stood. It was followed by the rest of the sortie craft.

The mountain itself erupted in a geysering pillar of flame and rock and plasteel.

One hundred years of war was only the beginning.

Somewhere, hidden, the Lords of Propriety—umbilicus-joined with delight shocks spurting softly pink along the flesh-linkage joining them—began their renewed gluttonous feeding.

4

Bailey was whirled out of the Montagasque subaltern's body. His soul went shooting away on an asymptotic curve, back along the feeder-lines, to the soul files of the Succubus.

5

This is what it was like to be in the soul station. Round. Weighted with the scent of grass. Perilous in that the music was dynamically contracting: souls had occasionally become too enriched and had gone flat and flaccid.

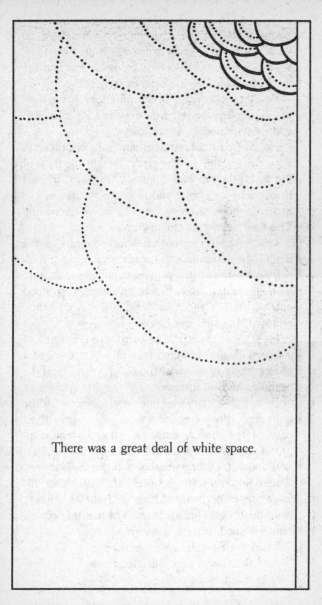

There was a great deal of white space.

Nothing was ranked, therefore nothing could be found in the same place twice; yet it didn't matter, for the Succubus had only to focus his lens and the item trembled into a special awareness.

Bailey spent perhaps twelve minutes reliving himself as a collapsing star then revolved his interfaces and masturbated as Anne Boleyn.

He savored mint where it smells most poignant, from deep in the shallow earth through the roots of the plant, then extended himself, extruded himself through an ice crystal and lit the far massif of the highest mountain on an onyx asteroid—recreating The Last Supper in chiaroscuro.

He burned for seventeen hundred years as the illuminated letter "B" on the first stanza of a forbidden enchantment in a papyrus volume used to summon up the imp James Fenimore Cooper then stood outside himself and considered his eyes and their hundred thousand bee-facets.

He allowed himself to be born from the womb of a tree sloth and flickered into rain that deluged a planet of coal for ten thousand years. And he beamed. And he sorrowed.

Bailey, all Bailey, soul once more, free as all the universes, threw himself toward the farthermost edge of the slightly flattened parabola that comprised the dark. He filled the dark with deeper darkness and bathed in fountains of brown wildflowers. Circles of coruscating violet streamed from his fingertips, from the tip of his nose, from his genitals, from the tiniest fibrillating fibers of hair that coated him. He shed water and hummed.

Then the Succubus drew him beneath the lens.

And Bailey was sent out once more.

Waste not, want not.

He was just under a foot tall. He was covered with
blue fur. He had a ring of eyes that circled his head.
He had eight legs. He smelled of fish. He was low to
the ground and he moved very fast.

He was a stalker-cat, and he was first off the survey
ship on Belial. The others followed, but not too soon.
They always waited for the cat to do its work. It was
safer that way. The Filonii had found that out in ten

455

thousand years of exploring their universe. The cats did the first work, then the Filonii did theirs. It was the best way to rule a universe.

Belial was a forest world. Covered in long continents that ran from pole to pole with feathertop trees, it was ripe for discovery.

Bailey looked out of his thirty eyes, seeing around himself in a full 360° spectrum. Seeing all the way up into the ultra-violet, seeing all the way down into the infra-red. The forest was silent. Absolutely no sound. Bailey, the cat, would have heard a sound, had there been a sound. But there was no sound.

No birds, no insects, no animals, not even the whispering of the feathertop trees as they struggled toward the bright hot-white sun. It was incredibly silent.

Bailey said so.

The Filonii went to a condition red.

No world is silent. And a forest world is *always* noisy. But this one was silent.

They were out there, waiting. Watching the great ship and the small stalker-cat that had emerged from it.

Who they were, the cat and the Filonii did not know. But they were there, and they were waiting for the invaders to make the first move. The stalker-cat glided forward.

Bailey felt presences. Deep in the forest, deeper than he knew he could prowl with impunity. They were in there, watching him as he moved forward. But he was a cat, and if he was to get his fish, he would work. The Filonii were watching. *Them*, in there, back in the trees, *they* were watching. *It's a bad life,* he thought. *The life of a cat is a nasty, dirty, bad one.*

Bailey was not the first cat ever to have thought that thought. It was the litany of the stalker-cats. They knew their place, had always known it, but that was the way it was; it was the way it had always been. The Filonii ruled, and the cats worked. And the universe became theirs.

Yet it wasn't shared. It was the Filonii universe, and the stalker-cats were hired help.

The fine mesh cap that covered the top and back of the cat's head glowed with a faint but discernible halo. The sunbeams through which he passed caught at the gold filaments of the cap and sent sparkling radiations back toward the ship. The ship stood in the center of the blasted area it had cleared for its prime base.

Inside the ship, the team of Filonii ecologists sat in front of the many process screens and saw through the eyes of the stalker-cat. They murmured to one another as first one, then another, then another saw something of interest. "Cat, lad," one of them said softly, "still no sound?"

"Nothing yet, Brewer. But I can feel them watching."

One of the other ecologists leaned forward. The entire wall behind the hundred screens was a pulsing membrane. Speak into it at any point and the cat's helmet picked up the voice, carried it to the stalker. "Tell me, lad, what does it feel like?"

"I'm not quite sure, Kicker. I'm getting it mixed. It feels like the eyes staring . . . and wood . . . and sap . . . and yet there's mobility. It can't be the trees."

"You're sure."

"As best I can tell right now, Kicker. I'm going to go into the forest and see."

"Good luck, lad."

"Thank you, Driver. How is your goiter?"

"I'm fine, lad. Take care."

The stalker-cat padded carefully to the edge of the forest. Sunlight slanted through the feathertops into the gloom. It was cool and dim inside there.

Now, all eyes were upon him.

The first paw in met springy, faintly moist and cool earth. The fallen feathers had turned to mulch. It smelled like cinnamon. Not overpoweringly so, just pleasantly so. He went in . . . all the way. The last the Filonii saw on their perimeter screens— twenty of the hundred—were his tails switching back and forth. Then the tails were gone and the seventy screens showed them dim, strangely-shadowed pathways between the giant conifers.

"Cat, lad, can you draw any conclusions from those trails?"

The stalker padded forward, paused. "Yes. I can draw the conclusion they aren't trails. They go fairly straight for a while, then come to dead ends at the bases of the trees. I'd say they were drag trails, if anything."

"What was dragged? Can you tell?"

"No, not really, Homer. Whatever was dragged, it was thick and fairly smooth. But that's all I can tell." He prodded the drag trail with his secondary leg on the left side. In the pad of the paw were tactile sensors.

The cat proceeded down the drag trail toward the base of the great tree where the trail unaccountably ended. All around him the great conifers rose six hundred feet into the warm, moist air.

Sipper, in the ship, saw through the cat's eyes and pointed out things to his fellows. "Some of the qualities of *Pseudotsuga Taxifolia*, but definitely a conifer. Notice the bark on that one. Typically *Eucalyptus Regnans* . . . yet notice the soft red spores covering the bark. I've never encountered that particular sort of thing before. They seem to be melting down the trees. In fact . . ."

He was about to say the trees were *all* covered with the red spores, when the red spores attacked the cat.

They flowed down the trees, covering the lower bark, each one the size of the cat's head, and when they touched, they ran together like jelly. When the red jelly from one tree reached the base of the trunk, it fused with the red jelly from the other trees.

"Lad . . ."

"It's all right, Kicker. I see them."

The cat began to pad backward: slowly, carefully. He could easily outrun the fusing crimson jelly. He moved back toward the verge of the clearing. Charred, empty of life, blasted by the Filonii hackshafts, not even a stump of the great trees above ground, the great circles where the trees had stood now merely reflective surfaces set flush in the ground. Back.

Backing out of life . . . backing into death.

The cat paused. What had caused *that* thought?

"Cat! Those spores . . . whatever they are . . . they're forming into a solid . . ."

Backing out of life . . . backing into death.

my name is

  bailey and i'm in
        here, inside you.
            i was stolen from

my	called	is		wants
body	the	some		somewhere. he—
by	succubus.	kind		there in the stars
a	he,	of		recruiter from out
creature	*it*	puppeteer, a sort of		

The blood-red spore thing stood fifteen feet high, formless, shapeless, changing, malleable, coming for the cat. The stalker did not move: within him, a battle raged.

"Cat, lad! Return! Get back!"

Though the universe belonged to the Filonii, it was only at moments when the loss of a portion of that universe seemed imminent that they realized how important their tools of ownership had become.

Bailey fought for control of the cat's mind.

Centuries of conditioning fought back.

The spore thing reached the cat and dripped around him. The screens of the Filonii went blood-red, then went blank.

The thing that had come from the trees oozed back into the forest, shivered for a moment, then vanished, taking the cat with it.

The cat focused an eye. Then another. In sequence he opened and focused each of his thirty eyes. The place where he lay came into full luster. He was underground. The shapeless walls of the place dripped with sap and several colors of viscous fluid. The fluid dripped down over bark that seemed to have been formed as stalactites, the grain running long and glistening till it tapered into needle tips. The surface on which the cat lay was planed wood, the grain exquisitely formed, running outward from a coral-colored pith in concentric circles of hues that went from coral to dark teak at the outer perimeter.

The spores had fissioned, were heaped in an alcove. Tunnels ran off in all directions. Huge tunnels twenty feet across.

The mesh cap was gone.

The cat got to his feet. Bailey was there, inside, fully awake, conversing with the cat.

"Am I cut off from the Filonii?"

"Yes, I'm afraid you are."

"Under the trees."

"That's right."

"What is that spore thing?"

"I know, but I'm not sure you'd understand."

"I'm a stalker; I've spent my life analyzing alien life-forms and alien ecology. I'll understand."

"They're mobile symbiotes, conjoined with the bark of these trees. Singly, they resemble most closely anemonic anaerobic bacteria, susceptible to dichotomization; they're anacusic, anabiotic, anamnestic, and feed almost exclusively on ancyclostomiasis."

"Hookworms?"

"Big hookworms. Very big hookworms."

"The drag trails?"

"That's what they drag."

"But none of that makes any sense. It's impossible."

"So is reincarnation among the Yerbans, but it occurs."

"I don't understand."

"I told you you wouldn't."

"How do *you* know all this?"

"You wouldn't understand."

"I'll take your word for it."

"Thank you. There's more about the spores and the trees, by the way. Perhaps the most important part."

"Which is?"

"Fused, they become a quasi-sentient gestalt. They can communicate, borrowing power from the tree-hosts."

"That's even *more* implausible!"

"Don't argue with me, argue with the Creator."

"First Cause."

"Have it your way."

"What are you doing in my head?"

"Trying very hard to get out."

"And how would you do that?"

"Foul up your mission so the Filonii would demand the Succubus replace me. I gather you're pretty important to them. Rather chickenshit, aren't they?"

"I don't recognize the term."

"I'll put it in sense form."

£ ▪▪▪▪▪]

"Oh. You mean ● ● ◖–."

"Yeah. Chickenshit."

"Well, that's the way it's always been between the Filonii and the stalkers."

"You like it that way."

"I like my fish."

"Your Filonii like to play God, don't they? Changing this world and that world to suit themselves.

Reminds me of a couple of other guys. Lords of Propriety they were called. And the Succubus. Did you ever stop to think how many individuals and races like to play God?"

"Right now I'd like to get out of here."

"Easy enough."

"How?"

"Make friends with the Tszechmae."

"The trees or the spores?"

"Both."

"One name for the symbiotic relationship?"

"They live in harmony."

"Except for the hookworms."

"No society is perfect. Rule 19."

The cat sat back on his haunches and talked to himself.

"Make friends with them you say."

"Seems like a good idea, doesn't it?"

"How would you suggest I do that?"

"Offer to perform a service for them. Something they can't do for themselves."

"Such as?"

"How about you'll get rid of the Filonii for them. Right now that's the thing most oppressing them."

"Get rid of the Filonii."

"Yes."

"I'm harboring a lunatic in my head."

"Well, if you're going to quit before you start . . ."

"Precisely *how*—uh, do you have a name?"

"I told you. Bailey."

"Oh. Yes. Sorry. Well, Bailey, precisely *how* do I rid this planet of a star-spanning vessel weighing somewhere just over thirteen thousand tons, not to mention a full complement of officers and ecologists who have been in the overlord position with my race for more centuries than I can name? I'm conditioned to respect them."

"You sure don't sound as if you respect them."

The cat paused. That was true. He felt quite different. He disliked the Filonii intensely. Hated them, in fact; as his kind had hated them for more centuries than he could name.

"That *is* peculiar. Do you have any explanation for it?"

"Well," said Bailey, humbly, "there *is* my presence. It may well have broken through all your hereditary conditioning."

"You wear smugness badly."

"Sorry."

The cat continued to think on the possibilities.

"I wouldn't take too much longer, if I were you," Bailey urged him. Then, reconsidering, he added, "As a matter of fact, I *am* you."

"You're trying to tell me something."

"I'm trying to tell you that the gestalt spore grabbed you, to get a line on what was happening with the invaders, but you've been sitting here for some time, musing to yourself—which, being instantaneously communicative throughout the many parts of the whole, is a concept they can't grasp—and so it's getting ready to digest you."

The stalker blinked his thirty eyes very rapidly. "The spore thing?"

"Uh-uh. All the spores eat are the hookworms. The bark's starting to look at you with considerable interest."

"Who do I talk to? Quick!"

"You've decided you don't respect the Filonii so

much, huh?"

"I thought you said I should hurry!"

"Just curious."

"*Who do I talk to!?!*"

"The floor."

So the stalker-cat talked to the floor, and they struck a bargain. Rather a lopsided bargain, true; but a bargain nonetheless.

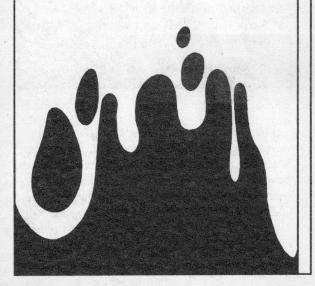

The hookworm was coming through the tunnel much more rapidly than the cat would have expected. It seemed to be sliding, but even as he watched, it bunched—inchworm-like—and propelled itself forward, following the movement with another slide. The wooden tunnel walls oozed with a noxious smelling moistness as the worm passed. It was moving itself on a slime track of its own secretions.

It was eight feet across, segmented, a filthy gray in color, and what passed for a face was merely a slash-mouth dripping yellowish mucus, several hundred cilia-like feelers surrounding the slit, and four glaze-covered protuberances in an uneven row above the slit perhaps serving in some inadequate way as "eyes."

Like a strange Hansel dropping bread crumbs to mark a trail, the spore things clinging to the cat's back began to ooze off. First one, then another. The cat backed down the tunnel. The hookworm came on. It dropped its fleshy penis-like head and snuffled at the spore lying in its path. Then the cilia feelers attached themselves and the spore thing was slipped easily into the slash mouth. There was a disgusting wet sound, and the hookworm moved forward again. The same procedure was repeated at the next spore. And the next, and the next. The hookworm followed the stalker through the tunnels.

Some miles away, the Filonii stared into their screens as a strange procession of red spores formed in the shape of a long thick hawser-like chain emerged from the forest and began to encircle the ship.

"Repulsors?" Kicker asked.

"Not yet, they haven't made a hostile move," the Homer said. "The cat could have won them somehow. This may be a welcoming ceremony. Let's wait and see."

The ship was completely circled, at a distance of fifty feet from the vessel. The Filonii waited, having faith in their cat lad.

And far underground, the stalker-cat led the hookworm a twisting chase through tunnel after tunnel.

Some of the tunnels were formed only moments before the cat and his pursuer entered them. The tunnels always sloped gently upward. The cat—dropping his spore riders as he went—led the enormous slug-thing by a narrow margin. But enough to keep him coming.

Then, into a final tunnel, and the cat leaped to a planed outcropping overhead, then to a tiny hole in the tunnel ceiling, and then out of sight.

The Filonii shouted with delight as the stalker emerged from a hole in the blasted earth, just beyond the circle of red spores, linked and waiting.

"You see! Good cat!" Driver yelled to his fellows.

But the cat made no move toward the ship.

"He's waiting for the welcoming ceremony to end," the Homer said with assurance.

Then, on their screens, they saw first one red spore, then another, vanish, as though sucked down through the ground from below.

They vanished in sequence, and the Filonii followed their disappearance around the screens, watching them go in a 90° arc, then 180° of half circle, then 250° and the ground began to tremble.

And before the hookworm could suck his dinner down through a full 360° of the circle, the ground gave way beneath the thirteen thousand tons of Filonii starship, and the vessel thundered through, down into special tunnels dug straight down. Plunged down with the plates of the ship separating and cracking open. Plunged down with the hookworm that would soon discover sweeter morsels than even red spore things.

The Filonii tried to save themselves.

There was very little they could do. Driver cursed

the cat and made a final contact with the Succubus. It was an automatic hookup, much easier to throw in than to fire the ship for takeoff. Particularly a quarter of a mile underground.

The hookworm broke through the ship. The Tszechmae waited. When the hookworm had gorged itself, they would move in and slay the creature. Then *they* would feast.

But Bailey would not be around to see the great meal. For only moments after the Filonii ship plunged crashing out of sight, he felt a ghastly wrenching at his soulself, and the stalker-cat was left empty once more—thereby proving in lopsided bargains no one is the winner but the house—and the soul of William Bailey went streaking out away from Belial toward the unknown.

Deep in wooden tunnels, things began to feed.

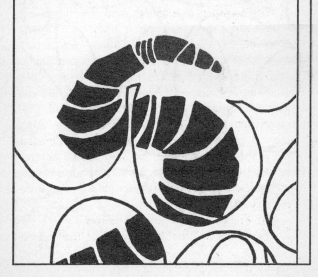

470

8

The darkness was the deepest blue. Not black. It was blue. He could see nothing. Not even himself. He could not tell what the body into which he had been cast did, or had, or resembled, or did not do, or not have, or not resemble. He reached out into the blue darkness. He touched nothing.

But then, perhaps he had not reached out. He had felt himself extend *something* into the blueness, but how far, or in what direction, or if it had been an appendage . . . he did not know.

He tried to touch himself, and did not know where to touch. He reached for his face, where a Bailey face would have been. He touched nothing.

He tried to touch his chest. He met resistance, and then penetrated something soft. He could not distinguish if he had pushed through fur or skin or hide or jelly or moisture or fabric or metal or vegetable matter or foam or some heavy gas. He had no feeling in either his "hand" or his "chest" but there was *something* there.

He tried to move, and moved. But he did not know if he was rolling or hopping or walking or sliding or flying or propelling or being propelled. But he moved. And he reached down with the thing he had used to touch himself, and felt nothing below him. He did not have legs. He did not have arms. Blue. It was so blue.

He moved as far as he could move in one direction, and there was nothing to stop him. He could have moved in that direction forever, and met no resistance. So he moved in another direction—opposite, as far as he could tell, and as far as he could go. But there was no boundary. He went up and went down and went around in circles. There was nothing. Endless nothing.

Yet he knew he was *in* somewhere. He was not in the emptiness of space, he was in an enclosed place. But what dimensions the place had, he could not tell. And what he was, he could not tell.

It made him upset. He had not been upset in the body of Pinkh, nor in the body of the stalker-cat. But this life he now owned made him nervous.

Why should that be?
Something was coming for him.
He knew that much.

He was
here
                        and

                                    something else
                                    was out there,
                                    coming toward
                                        him.

He knew fear. Blue fear. Deep unseeing blue fear.
If it was coming fast, it would be here sooner. If slow,
then later. But it was coming. He could feel, sense,
intuit it coming for him. He wanted to change. To
become something else.

To become *this*
Or to become THIS
Or to become *THIS*
Or to become tHiS

But to become *something* else, something that
could withstand what was coming for him. He didn't
know what that could be. All he knew was that he
needed equipment. He ran through his bailey-
thoughts, his baileymind, to sort out what he might
need.

What he needed
might be

Fangs   Poisonous breath
Eyes   Horns
Malleability
Webbed feet
Armored hide   Talons
Camouflage   Wings
Carapaces   Muscles
Vocal cords   Scales
Self-regeneration
Stingers   Wheels
Multiple brains

What he already had   Nothing

It was coming closer. Or was it getting farther away? (And by getting farther away, becoming more of a threat to him?) (If he went toward it, would he be safer?) (If only he could know what he looked like, or where he was, or what was required of him?) (Orient!) (Damn it, orient yourself, Bailey!) He was deep in blueness, extended, fetal, waiting. Shapeless. (Shape—) (Could *that* be it?)

Something blue flickered in the blueness.

It was coming end-for-end, flickering and sparking and growing larger, swimming toward him in the blueness. It sent tremors through him. Fear gripped him as it had never gripped him before. The blue shape coming toward him was the most fearful thing he could remember: and he remembered:

The night he had found Moravia with another man. They were standing having sex in a closet at a party. Her dress was bunched up around her waist; he had her up on tiptoes. She was crying with deep pleasure, eyes closed.

The day at the end of the war, when a laser had sliced off the top of the head of the man on his left in the warm metal trench. The sight of things still pulsing in the jasmine jelly.

The moment he had come to the final knowledge of his hopeless future. The moment he had decided to go to the Center to find death.

The thing changed shape and sent out scintillant waves of blueness and fear. He writhed away from them but they swept over him, and he turned over and over trying to escape. The thing of blue came nearer, growing larger in his sight. (Sight? Writhing? Fear?) It suddenly swept toward him, faster than before, as though it had tried a primary assault—the waves of fear—and the assault had failed; and now it would bull through.

He felt an urge to leap, high. He felt himself do it, and suddenly his sight went up and his propulsive equipment went lower, and he was longer, taller, larger. He fled. Down through the blueness, with the coruscating blue devil following. It elongated itself and shot past him on one side, boiled on ahead till it was a mere pinpoint of incandescence on some heightless, dimensionless horizon. And then it came racing back toward him, thinning itself and stretching itself till it was opaque, till the blueness of where they were shone through it darkly, like effulgent isinglass in a blue hyperplane.

He trembled in fear and went minute. He balled and shrank and contracted and drew himself to a finite point, and the whirling danger went hurtling through him and beyond, and was lost back the way they had come.

Inside the body he now owned, Bailey felt something wrenching and tearing. Fibers pulled loose from moorings and he was certain his mind was giving way. He had memories of sense-deprivation chambers and what had happened to men who had been left in them too long. This was the same. No shape, no size, no idea or way of gaining an idea of what he was, or where he was, or the touch, smell, sound, sight of *anything* as an anchor to his sanity. Yet he was surviving.

The dark blue devil kept arranging new assaults—

and he had no doubt it would be back in seconds (seconds?)—and he kept doing the correct thing to escape those assaults. But he had the feeling (feeling?) that at some point the instinctive reactions of this new body would be insufficient. That he would have to bring to this new role his essential baileyness, his human mind, his thoughts, the cunning he had begun to understand was so much a part of his way. (And why had he not understood that cunningness when he had been Bailey, all the years of his hopeless life?)

The effulgence began again somewhere off to his side and high above him, coming on rapidly.

Bailey, some *thing* unknown, prepared. As best he could.

MARVELOUS, ANIK! HOW DID YOU MANAGE TO REVITALIZE IT? OH, I'M SURE YOU DID. BUT *HOW* DID YOU MANAGE? PLEASE! FIVE?! YOU REALLY *DO* WANT TO WIN, DON'T YOU? TSK-TSK. I KNOW! YOU DON'T LOOK ON THIS AS A GAME. NOR SHOULD I AND THAT'S SIMPLY BECAUSE YOU WERE BORN ALTHUS, WHILE— WHEN IT MEANT SOMETHING SIGNIFICANT? YES, BUT TIME GOES FLUSTER YOU? MY DEAR GOOD ANIK, HOW CAN YOU SAY THAT? TEN THOUSAND TENILS ISN'T TOO LONG, NOT FOR A HERDUR ARE YOU PLEADING FOR SURCEASE, MY FRIEND? DO YOU SUBMIT? WHY? BECAUSE YOUR CHAMPION IS A FALSE SOUL IN ITS BODY? TRULY, ANIK, YOU MUST THINK ME A CULLY OR A FOOL! DIE! THEN GO TO RESERVE FRAMES. I CAN'T CONCERN MYSELF NOW LET *ME* WORRY ABOUT THE EXTENT OF MY OVER-EXTENSIONS! YOU'LL WORRY ABOUT THAT TILL THE MOMENT I DESTROY YOU IT WAS *INTENDED* THAT WE FIGHT. IF YOU WANT OUT, I SAY GO! YOUR SUBSTITUTE CHAMPION HAS NO CHANCE. I SWEAR IT, ANIK!

you may be sure i paid dearly to do so, my dear yaquil
the succubus, yaquil it cost me five tenils of life
chide me all you wish unlike you, i do not look on—
but you do you have / always thought of it as a game
while you were born herdur there was a time when it—
and we remain, you cannot fluster me with platitudes!
i can say it because we have waged this combat too long
but for an althus it is call an end, yaquil do it now
submission is no part of it i merely say stop quickly
no, because the tenils pass and the heat goes and we die!
yes, die! and i've used more frames than i can afford
better now than too late. you over-extend yourself, sir
impudence; impertinence how you ever became a combatant—
you leave me no alternative. frames be damned, we fight!
and concede a defeat i need not have conceded? fight on,
i offered you an opportunity. the time for talk is done!

The blue devil swept down on him, crackling with energy. He felt the incredible million sting-points of pain and a sapping of strength. Then a

for it had. Now Bailey knew what he was, and what he had to do. He lay still, swimming in the never-ending forever blueness. He was soft and he was solitary. The blue devil swarmed and came on. For the last time. And when it was all around him, Bailey let it drink him. He let its deep blueness and its fear and its sparkling effulgence sweep over him, consume him. The blue devil gorged itself, grew larger, fuller, more incapable of movement, unable to free itself. Bailey stuffed it with his amoebic body. He split and formed yet another, and the blue devil extended itself and began feeding on his second self. The radiating sparking waves of fear and blueness were thicker now, coming more slowly. Binary fission again. Now there were four. The blue devil fed, consumed, filled its chambers and its source-buds. Again, fission. And now there were eight. And the blue devil began to lose color. Bailey did not divide again. He knew what he had to do. Neither he nor the blue devil could win this combat. Both must die. The feeding went on and on, and finally the blue devil had drained itself with fullness, made itself immobile, died. And he died. And there was emptiness in the blueness once more.

The frames, the tenils, the fullness of combat were ended. And in that last fleeting instant of sentience, Bailey imagined he heard scented wails of hopelessness from two Duelmasters somewhere out there. He gloated. Now they knew what it was to be a William Bailey, to be hopeless and alone and afraid.

He gloated for an instant, then was whirled out and away.

9

This time his repose lasted only a short time. It was rush season for the Succubus. Bailey went out to fill the husk of a Master Slavemaster whose pens were filled with females of the eighty-three races that peopled the Snowdrift Cluster asteroids. Bailey succeeded in convincing the Slavemaster that male chauvinism was detestable, and the females were bound into a secret organization that returned to their various rock-worlds, overthrew the all-male governments, and declared themselves the Independent Feminist Concourse.

He was pulled back and sent out to inhabit the radio wave "body" of a needler creature used by the Kirk to turn suns nova and thereby provide them with power sources. Bailey gained possession of the needler and imploded the Kirk home sun.

He was pulled back and sent out to inhabit the shell of a ten-thousand-year-old terrapin whose retention of random construction information made it invaluable as the overseer of a planetary reorganization project sponsored by a pale gray race without a name that altered solar systems just beyond the Finger Fringe deepout. Bailey let the turtle feed incorrect data to the world-swingers hauling the planets into their orbits, and the entire configuration collided in the orbit of the system's largest heavy-mass world. The resultant uprising caused the total eradication of the pale gray race.

He was pulled back . . .

Finally, even a creature as vast and involved as the Succubus, a creature plagued by a million problems and matters for attention, in effect a god-of-a-sort, was forced to take notice. There was a soul in his file that was causing a fullness leak. There was a soul that was anathema to what the Succubus had built his reputation on. There was a soul that seemed to be (unthinkable as it was) out to get him. There was a soul that was ruining things. There was a soul that was inept. There was a soul that was (again, unthinkably) consciously trying to ruin the work the Succubus had spent his life setting in motion. There was a soul named Bailey.

And the Succubus consigned him to soul limbo till he could clear away present obligations and draw him under the lens for scrutiny.

So Bailey was sent to limbo.

10

This is what it was like in soul limbo.

Soft pasty maggoty white. Roiling. Filled with sounds of things desperately trying to see. Slippery underfoot. Without feet. Breathless and struggling for breath. Enclosed. Tight, with great weight pressing down till the pressure was asphyxiating. But without the ability to breathe. Pressed brown to cork, porous and feeling imminent crumbling; then boiling liquid poured through. Pain in every filament and glass fiber. A wet thing settling into bones, turning them to ash and paste. Sickly sweetness, thick and rancid, tongued and swallowed and bloating. Bloating till bursting. A charnel scent. Rising smoke burning and burning the sensitive tissues. Love lost forever, the pain of knowing nothing could ever matter again; melancholia so possessive it wrenched deep inside and twisted organs that never had a chance to function.

Cold tile.

Black crepe paper.

Fingernails scraping slate.

Button pains.

Tiny cuts at sensitive places.

Weakness.

Hammering steadily pain.

That was what it was like in the Succubus's soul limbo. It was not punishment, it was merely the dead end. It was the place where the continuum had not been completed. It was not Hell, for Hell had form and substance and purpose. This was a crater, a void, a storeroom packed with uselessness. It was the place to be sent when pastpresentfuture were one and indeterminate. It was altogether ghastly.

Had Bailey gone mad, this would have been the place for it to happen. But he did not. There was a reason.

11

One hundred thousand eternities later, the Succubus cleared his desk of present work, filled all orders and answered all current correspondence, finished inventory and took a long-needed vacation. When he returned, before turning his attention to new business, he brought the soul of William Bailey out of limbo and ushered it under the lens.

And found it, somehow, *different*.

Quite unlike the millions and millions of other souls he had stolen.

He could not put a name to the difference. It was not a force, not a vapor, not a quality, not a potentiality, not a look, not a sense, not a capacity, not anything he could pinpoint. And, of course, such a *difference* might be invaluable.

So the Succubus drew a husk from the spare parts and rolling stock bank, and put Bailey's soul into it.

It must be understood that this was a consummately E M P T Y husk. Nothing lived there. It had been scoured clean. It was not like the many bodies into which Bailey had been inserted. Those had had their souls stolen. There was restraining potential in all of them, memories of persona, fetters invisible but present nonetheless. This husk was now Bailey. Bailey only, Bailey free and Bailey whole.

The Succubus summoned Bailey before him.

Bailey might have been able to describe the Succubus, but he had no such desire.

The examination began. The Succubus used light and darkness, lines and spheres, soft and hard, seasons of change, waters of nepenthe, a hand outstretched, the whisper of a memory, carthing, enumeration, suspension, incursion, requital and thirteen others.

He worked over and WHAT through and inside the soul HE DID NOT of Bailey in an attempt to KNOW isolate the wild and dangerous WAS THAT difference that made this soul WHILE HE WAS unlike all others he EXAMINING had ever stolen for his tables of fulfillment BAILEY, BAILEY for the many races WAS that called upon EXAMINING him HIM.

Then, when he had all the knowledge he needed, all the secret places, all the unspoken promises, all the wished and fleshed depressions, the power that lurked in Bailey . . . that had *always* lurked in Bailey . . . before either of them could try or hope to contain it . . . surged free.

(It had been there all along.)
(Since the dawn of time, it had been there.)
(It had always existed.)

the force that was God awoke

The universe moves toward the godhood. It wishes to return there. Godness lies dormant there, in every puniest creature. Every atom. It is built in the basic fiber... to be the greatest thing and return in every wishes... smallest thing. In the basic fiber, in the racial memory, in the... struggling impossibly to be... the pulse of blood or need, play their... a universe of facts, of pets, of... moves. Thus it becomes a universe... they never knew, can batter... can barely comprehend... the lives of all other things. And in turn, those Gods... of mad deities, one more deadly... beyond. It is a universe of mad deities had been... and eternally... in the "soul" of what deities... ever struggling yet... the numinous through the mindless... completely and eternally and... sleeping. Latent in the beginning... God that was Bailey buried here and there and everywhere yet struggling to be reborn by a pressure of equalization, a necessity for balance in something even as lunatic as the mad world created by a mad God. But now, freed, like an evil genie from a bottle...

From the sleaziest legislators around... And on and on. Domino tanks of puppet master... they are merely circular pieces of the all-memory of stuff... waiting to emerge and finish what it had stifled... then the bitter cynicism of the thought... For if that force be God, then an eternal "soul" passed down through... buried in an eternal... waiting its time. For if that force be God, then a madman buried by a mad God. Any name will suffice. First Cause? Perhaps. Perhaps. And all of everything then busy itself dormant and slumbering...

488

blossomed to fullness, rejuvenated by its slumber, stronger than it had been even when it had created the universe. And, freed, it set about finishing what had begun millennia before.

Bailey remembered the Euthanasia Center, where it had begun for him. Remembered dying. Remembered being reborn. Remembered the life of inadequacy, impotency, hopelessness he had led before he'd given himself up to the Suicide Center. Remembered living as a one-eyed bear creature in a war that would never end. Remembered being a stalker-cat and death of a ghastliness it could not be spoken of. Remembered blueness. Remembered all the other lives. And remembered all the gods that had been less God than himself Bailey. The Lords of Propriety. The Filonii. The Montagasques. The Thils. The Tszechmae. The Duelmasters. The hookworms. The Slavemaster. The Kirk. The pale gray race without a name. And most of all, he remem-

...d the Succubus.

...ho thought he was God. Even as the Thieves ...hought *they* were Gods. But none of them possessed more than the faintest scintilla of the all-memory of godness, and Bailey had become the final repository for the force that *was* God. And now, freed, unleashed, unlocked, swirled down through all of time to this judgment day, Bailey flexed his godness and finished what he had begun at the beginning.

There is only one end to creation. What is created is destroyed, and thus full circle is achieved.

Bailey, God, set about killing the sand castle he had built. The destruction of the universes he had created.

Never before.

Songs unsung.

Washed but never purified.

Dreams spent and visits to come.

Up out of slime.

Drifted down on cool trusting winds.

Heat.

Free.

All created, all equal, all wondering, all vastness.

Gone to night.

The power that was Bailey that was God began its efforts. The husk in which Bailey lived was drawn into the power. The Succubus, screaming for reprieve, screaming for reason, screaming for release or explanation, was drawn into the power. The soul station drawn in. The home world drawn in. The solar system of the home world drawn in. The galaxy and all the galaxies and the metagalaxies and the far island universes and the alter dimensions and the

past back to the beginning and beyond it to the circular place where it became now, and all the shadow places and all the thought recesses and then the very fabric and substance of eternity . . . all of it, everything . . . drawn in.

All of it contained within the power of Bailey who is God.

And then, in one awesome exertion of will, God-Bailey destroys it all, coming full circle, ending what it had been born to do. Gone.

And all that is left is Bailey. Who is dead.

In the region between.

Acknowledgments

"Tropism" by Leigh Kennedy. Copyright © 1986 by Leigh Kennedy. Appears in this volume for the first time by permission of the author.

"If Ever I Should Leave You" by Pamela Sargent. Copyright © 1977, 1986 by Pamela Sargent. A greatly altered version of the story appeared in *Worlds of If*, February 1974. Copyright © 1974 by Universal Publishing & Distributing Corporation. Copyright reassigned to the author in 1977. Reprinted by permission of the author and her agent, the Joseph Elder Agency.

"Time's Hitch" by Robert Frazier. Copyright © 1986 by Robert Frazier. Appears in this volume for the first time by permission of the author.

"The Rooms of Paradise" by Ian Watson. Copyright © 1979 by Lee Harding; originally appeared in *The Rooms of Paradise*. Reprinted by permission of the author.

"Checking Out" by Gene Wolfe. Copyright © 1986 by Gene Wolfe. Appears in this volume for the first time by permission of the author and his agent, Virginia Kidd.

"The Region Between" by Harlan Ellison; copyright © 1969 by Universal Publishing & Distributing Corporation. Copyright reassigned to Author 7 July 1980. Copyright © 1980 by The Kilimanjaro Corporation. Reprinted with the permission of, and by arrangement with, the Author and the Author's agent, Richard Curtis Associates, Inc., New York. All rights reserved.